By the Rivers
of Babylon

By the Rivers
of Babylon

MARY GLICKMAN

OPEN ROAD

INTEGRATED MEDIA

NEW YORK

Copyright © 2023 by Mary Glickman

ISBN: 978-1-5040-7587-9

Published in 2023 by Open Road Integrated Media, Inc.
180 Maiden Lane
New York, NY 10038
www.openroadmedia.com

For the musicians of Charleston,
who inspire and sustain me

By the Rivers of Babylon

1.

Ella Price raised her eyes to heaven and begged deliverance. It was a hot South Carolina day at the end of June 1997, the kind tourists love and natives abhor. She was stuck on the approach to Fenton Bridge after a long trip upstate to buy belts and handbags for her dress shop. All the way home, she'd thought how grand it would be to sit on her back porch and revel in the caress of a cooling island breeze. Now, she wondered if she'd ever get there.

She studied what she could see of the drawbridge ahead. It had been locked straight up and open for the last twenty minutes, with no repair vehicles in sight. Experience taught that she might be trapped for an hour or more, so she turned off her engine to save gasoline. The papers said the new suspension bridge would be completed by the millennium, but that was three years away. Even though building the new bridge would bulldoze poor folks' homes on either side of the river, at this moment Ella had to think it would be a good thing.

She rolled down her window. The air was heavy and still. The river sparkled in the sun. People left their cars for relief, and she did, too. Looking around, she saw Roland Fenton, a dapper Black man thirty years of age, a restaurant manager whose family had once been owned by the Confederate general for whom the drawbridge had been named in '47, fifty years ago. Ella Price was born Ella Sassaport, a surname her people acquired from their owners as well. She'd gone to grade school with Roland's mama back in segregation days. The two waved and made faces of misery at each other.

A slender, young white man standing three cars between them mistook her gesture for one aimed at him. His long, thin face arranged its features into a similar expression of distress, then smiled. Raised to be polite, Ella smiled back. A young woman exited his car. She was a remarkable creature, fulfilling every criteria for beauty the entire white world held dear: unmarred porcelain skin, deep blue eyes, chiseled cheeks and jaw, an admirable nose, sumptuous lips. Her hair was black and thick; her legs, long and shapely; her belly, flat; and her bust, high and generous. She dashed through the line of stopped cars to the railings at the foot of the bridge, bending over the uppermost to regard the river below. Drivers all around stared as she did.

Sirens wailed. Repair trucks with a police escort at the bottom of the bridge threaded through stalled traffic to make their way slowly to the engineer's booth. People reentered their cars and revved them up to try to give the trucks a path. The young man called out to his beauty, "Abigail, come here!" She ignored him. Drivers behind him leaned on their horns. "Abigail!" She remained where she was. "Abigail! We've got to move!" At last she became aware that there were other people on earth besides herself. She turned and dashed back to the car, making adorable gestures of apology to everyone. The young man circled around his hood to stand by and open her door, helping her in, then fastening her seat belt for her as if she were a child. Ella thought it an odd thing to do when people were waiting for them to move. The woman wasn't disabled—her scampering about proved that—she was certainly capable of strapping herself in. Then it struck her that the young man's tender care was proprietary, that he did it to reclaim her, to snatch her back from every man who'd stared at her.

Young love, Ella thought, shaking her head. How it ties us up and ties us down. How it burns and flares, dies down, then flares up again. She'd been no less a beauty in her youth than that woman. Now that she was middle-aged, people called her a handsome woman, as Black and beautiful as her noble African ancestors. She hoped she'd grown wiser over the years, but she'd been a fool for love plenty in her day. She could spot a fellow traveler miles off. As the young man's car inched closer to her own, she saw it was from Massachusetts. It was packed high with suitcases and odd, unpackable items: a wicker chair, a laundry basket full of folded towels. So they were moving to Sweetgrass Island. Something in her laughed at the idea, but it was a rueful laugh. *That Abigail's going to cause some kind of trouble on Sweetgrass,* she thought. *Lord help us all when the island men catch a look of her. My, oh my. Just wait.*

It wasn't much of a wait. The island men got wind of Abigail Becker soon enough. By the time she and her man made their social debut at Declan's Pub ten days later, she'd already been the topic of speculation at Harold's Stop and Go and at the fire station. After that evening, even those who hadn't been there had heard of the beauty from Boston.

When Abigail walked into the pub, it was early, just after six o'clock. Whoever walked into Declan's at that hour was treated the same by the crowd gathering within. All eyes turned toward the door, the way a swarm of honeybees turn toward a bank of flowers, with curiosity and without malice. Each one hoped a friend had walked through the door and not some stranger; a tourist slumming it with the locals, or a resident of one of the new gated communities eating up the island's farmland. Early evening was the hopeful part of the night, when alliances were forged or reawakened. By nine o'clock, nobody gave a damn. Patrons had either hooked up with their buddies, or not. By ten o'clock, they were one breathing mass of fellowship. They bought each other pints and shots, sobbed their stories of problem children and faithless wives, brutal husbands, and hated jobs. They swore their love, told jokes, and lied in equal measure. They lent each other money. One of the musicians hired for Saturday nights, a bluesman from Memphis, said he loved playing the pub because it was small and friendly, an Irish shoebox full of drunks. The regulars at Declan's liked that, including the handful of Blacks. They knew who they were.

That night, Abigail's arrival aroused more than customary interest. Her husband, Joe, was parking the car. He'd dropped her off at the front door, telling her to grab a table near the music, as music was what they'd come for. All eyes turned as she walked in alone.

Billy Euston, sitting at his usual spot near the end of the bar, raised his glass to the sound of the door opening, turned, and saw the black hair, the Tartar eyes, the nose straight and thin as a pencil, the full lips, the china-doll skin. Her long legs were in summer shorts, and her breasts rose out of a halter top. Instead of smiling above his raised glass, Billy Euston dropped his jaw. The glass slipped from his hand to shatter on the floor in shards that spread in a glittering arc as far as two barstools down. Declan grumbled that was the last time he'd give Billy Euston a decent glass. He took a thick, sturdy tumbler from behind the bar, poured the man a fresh whiskey, and sent his nephew Tommy over to clean up the mess. Everyone else continued to stare.

Abigail did not react to Billy or his shattered glass. She saw a free booth by the front windows near the music stand and slid over the leather bench facing the band. A guitarist, a mandolin, a banjo, and an upright bass player tuned their instruments and checked the sound. Each glanced her way and gave a nod of welcome. Straightaway their shoulders broadened, their guts retracted. They passed hands over their hair, neatening up.

A minute later, Joe came in. He was denied the common glance and greeting; all eyes were still on his wife. The waitress came over to see what they wanted.

"What can I get for y'all?" she asked.

"Guinness for him," Abigail said, "and a barrel shot on the rocks for me. You might bring us a food menu, too."

The musicians started their first set. Joe and Abigail loved music, every kind of music. Their first date was to the opera; they courted in blues clubs, married to rock and roll. They were new to bluegrass, but so far they loved it. When the boys launched into "Walking Boss," they scrunched up in the booth, holding hands. Joe put his free arm tight around her waist. Their joined hands beat against the table in time.

I asked that boss man
For a job (for a job)
He said, son what can you do?
I can hold a jack,
Line a track (Line a track)
I can pick and shovel, too

Abigail's face lit up. She looked at Joe and mouthed as there was no way he could hear: *I love this!* He smiled and bobbed his head to the song's rhythm.

Walkin' boss (walkin' boss),
I don't belong to you.
I belong (I belong)
with that steel drivin' crew

The song ended to an appreciative clamor. The lead singer introduced himself and the members of the band just as the waitress served Abigail and Joe their drinks. She dropped two menus on the table. The couple put their heads together over one of them.

"Y'all new around here?" the waitress asked, although she knew the answer already. Strangers stood out at Declan's like burrs on a wet dog.

"He is," Abigail said without looking up. "When I was a child, I used to visit my grandaunt on Catawba Plantation. She died a few months ago and left us her house."

Catawba Plantation was a farm-gobbling gated community. The people who lived there were not especially admired by the crew at Declan's Pub. Generally, Catawba residents were loud, cheap, arrogant, and clueless about the place to which they'd moved. In other words, they were Yankees, twentieth-century carpetbaggers. Nobody liked but a handful of them, and that handful had to prove their worth over time.

"I'm sorry for your loss, but welcome," the waitress said. "So you're livin' here now?"

Abigail explained that they were spending the summer on the island, trying it on for size. She was a teacher; she had summers off. Joe was a writer, so he had off whenever he liked. She laughed when she said that. Joe stiffened, pulling away from his wife a little, not that she noticed. Abigail always gave strangers too much information. What made her think a waitress in a bar had to know intimate details about them?

Joe ordered fish and chips, Abigail a local greens salad. The band played original songs next, ones with driving beats and virtuoso licks for each instrument. The lyrics were about lost love, Dixie pride, and legendary beasts of the backwoods. Joe set his irritation with Abigail aside and put his arm back around her waist. Their hands once again joined and thumped beats on the tabletop. They cheered after each tune, whooping and whistling their appreciation along with the regulars.

After they ate, Abigail went to the ladies' room at the back, then noticed the rear exit. She pushed the door open out of curiosity and was rewarded.

"Joe, you'll never guess what's out back," she said when she returned to the table.

Joe spread his arms and lifted his shoulders.

"What?"

"A wonderland."

She picked up his hand and pulled to get him up and out. By now, the pub was packed. The musicians were about to start their second set; standing couples eyed their booth. Joe was unsure about giving up the spot, and he wanted to hear the second set, but he followed her to the back of the pub anyway, stopping near the wait station for a nanosecond to signal that they weren't walking out on the bill. The back door opened onto a walled courtyard with benches, a firepit, and another music stand. Lush vines of confederate jasmine climbed all over, filling the air with their powerful scent. Strings of fairy lights blinked through white petals. Although Joe heard the murmur of numerous voices, the only patrons he saw at first were two bearded men with a plump young woman sitting between them by the unlit firepit. The men's beards were untrimmed. They wore feed caps. The woman had a sleeve of tattoos on her left arm. Their conversation looked intense, private. Abigail pulled him along. There were more benches, a deserted outdoor bar. She stopped.

The air changed. The smell of marijuana overtook the scent of jasmine, no mean feat. They were in front of a whitewashed pergola. Inside were the vague shapes of men and women hunkered together, illuminated by a rolling flicker of cigarette lighters coming on, going out like twinkling fireflies. A gravelly voice, the voice of a two-pack-a-day smoker, called out.

"C'mon in, pretty gal," Billy Euston said. "C'mon."

Abigail looked at Joe with pleading eyes. She wanted very much to make a connection. Lack of weed was the sole thing missing from their Southern idyll. This would be the answer to a prayer. Joe wasn't sure. Those inside the pergola were strangers; he couldn't even see what they looked like from outside.

"C'mon," called Billy. "Bring the skinny dude with you."

Grinning wide, Abigail ascended the few steps into thick shadows. Joe shrugged and followed.

As they entered the dark, their vision adjusted to its embrace. Through a haze of soft grays and smoky blues, they discerned at least a dozen people sitting at small wooden tables or on a bench that wrapped around the pergola's interior. Most of them were Abigail's and Joe's ages, somewhere in their thirties; others were younger, but a handful were men with white in their beards or women with wattled necks. Billy Euston was creeping up on fifty, a short, wiry man, sunburnt with crinkly eyes, a nose several times broken, a laughing mouth, and a high, broad forehead from which a thick head of salt-and-pepper hair retreated. One hand held a fat joint. He swept his arm across the room.

"We're havin' a safety meetin'," he said. "Are you in need of safety?"

Abigail's eyes went round.

"Oh yes."

The air was thick with more than weed. Everyone, even Joe and especially Abigail, felt it. Its tentacles reached out to draw them close. There was a sense that something was going to happen, though no one knew what.

Someone who'd inhaled too deep and too long hacked, breaking the mood. There were grumbles all 'round.

"'Scuse me," the hacker said, his voice weak, oxygen deprived.

The group quieted, their eyes on Billy and the strangers. They knew that Billy was capable of being gracious, teasing, or hostile, however the mood struck him. It was better than the TV to watch and wait for what he might do. Billy took his time, regarding Abigail's face with rapt admiration, enjoying the fact that a woman so rare wanted something from him.

Abigail didn't understand his hesitation. Maybe he's waiting for an introduction, she guessed.

"I'm Abigail, and this is Joe," she said. She gave Billy an imploring look. He handed her the joint, which she grasped and inhaled twice in quick succession. She offered it to Joe, who waved it away. She stuck it back in his face. She gave him a look that said he should take a toke to be convivial. He acquiesced, then handed the joint back.

"That's enough," he said.

Billy took her hand and led her in a solicitous manner to a corner bench. The two talked in soft tones, trading the joint back and forth, while Joe fell into a chair. He wasn't like his wife. He didn't smoke often. When he did, it was only to please her. The smoke hit him hard, making the room swim. Somebody asked him what he did for a living. When he said he wrote books, his interlocutor wanted to know what kind.

"Children's books," he said, hoping he wouldn't be asked next if he had children himself. Whenever he was asked that and he said no, people looked at him as if there was something wrong with him, as if his interest in writing for children might be something unnatural. He'd have to explain why children, why their stories, without exposing everything about himself. Some might think he was a pervert, that his marriage was a beard. Hardly the way he wanted to start life out in a new place. Luckily, no one inquired further.

On the way home, Abigail could barely sit still. She had two joints stuffed in her shorts' pocket. Her head buzzed pleasantly. Joe was irritated, but that didn't tamp down her excitement. He had no right to be annoyed. He'd taken his toke-of-the-month, hadn't he? Why should he care that she'd had more? Even so, she wanted to be sure they were on cozy terms when they arrived home, so she put her hand on the back of his neck and rubbed.

"Honey, you're so tight," she said. "I thought you had a good time."

Joe tilted his head this way and that.

"Part of it was good. Part of it was great," he said. "The music part. I loved those guys."

Abigail agreed by humming the tune to "Shady Grove." If she'd been sure of the words, she would have sung them.

Usually, Joe liked her singing. Usually, it soothed him. But his neck did not yield. Abigail thought of Billy Euston's neck, its braided muscles, sunburned and wiry as the rest of him. She smiled to herself. Her redneck friend; that's what Billy Euston was going to be. She rubbed Joe's neck harder until he shook her off.

2.

Once Billy got to know him a little bit, he thought Joe Becker might well be a different species from his own. They were as unalike as a zebra and an eagle. On the surface, there was reason for that. Joe was urban, reserved, private. Billy was full-on country, every bit of him proudly out there for the world to see. If Joe's favorite tool was his Selectric, Billy would have a hard time choosing between his smoker, his cooking knives, and his 1995 bush hog. Billy noticed right off that Joe wore too many clothes on a warm day: long pants, shirts with sleeves, shoes with socks. Providing he wasn't attending a funeral or wedding, Billy dressed in cargo shorts and tees, even in winter. The feel of fabric on his limbs penned him in. His flesh needed to be free.

He was making a study of Joe with the harebrained idea of stealing his wife, if only for a short time—he'd be happy with an hour or two, he'd be over the moon with more—and there was one thing Billy Euston wanted to know about Joe above all else. It was always on his mind. It plagued him when he drove to the restaurant downtown where he worked three days a week as pitmaster, when he paddled through the bayou looking for fish and game, when he sat on a damp dawn in his deer blind testing the floorboards before the season started. It bothered him when he visited Ella Price, a Gullah woman he'd known since he was fifteen; a woman who loved him no matter how he felt about her, and who could be depended upon to be kind at his whim. How, he wondered, did a knob like Joe Becker win a prize like Abigail?

"You'd know 'em if you'd seen 'em, darlin'," he said. He was stretched out naked on Ella's bed with an ashtray on his stomach. He lit a cigarette. "They're the oddest match."

"I'm too busy to take much note of new people," she admitted. She no longer recalled seeing the Beckers on Fenton Bridge. The name Abigail might have rung a bell, but Billy was too wily to use names. He could have been talking about any one of the transient couples who summered on the island every year.

"She's a marvel," he said, blowing out a column of smoke. His words took on a hint of awe. "Way out of his class."

Billy felt Ella stiffen beside him. A quick side glance told him her round black eyes had narrowed to a squint, that her perfect teeth clamped for a second against her lush lower lip. She looked about to give him a good cussin' out. In the next moment, her features relaxed into their usual loveliness, but he had been warned. Never speak of another woman in the presence of this one. There'd been too much of that in the past. Ella Price didn't care what he did, especially. She knew other women existed in his life, but she didn't have to hear about them. It was a simple rule, one they'd established more than a decade ago. He realized he'd forgotten it in the rush of a new tempest brewing in his heart.

"Way out of mine, too," he added, a hair too late.

"Huh." Ella sat up and reached down to the floor for her robe. "Everyone's out of your class, baby. Even me."

The robe was of white Japanese silk embroidered with stalks of peach-colored blossoms. Billy bought it for her one Christmas. When Billy went off on one of his crazy-assed romances, Ella took other lovers, but she wore the robe only for him.

"Time for you to go," she said. "It's turned to Sunday. I'm goin' to church."

Billy sat up also, filled his chest with air, and raised his eyebrows.

"You want me to go with?" he asked, because sometimes she did. Over the years and in her honor, he'd favored the Holy Tabernacle of Jesus Christ by the Sea with his award-winning BBQ at annual fundraisers without the catering charge. It made him a pew celebrity. More congregants came up to shake his hand before services than they did

Pastor Ronald T. Quirk. He figured Ella took him to church because she liked to show him off more than she cared for his soul, but he'd be wrong.

Ella was tall, with long, willowy legs. She painted her toes a periwinkle blue, which complemented her flawless black skin almost as much as the white and peach robe. Her fingernails shot out a quarter inch from her fingertips and were painted the same shade. A rhinestone crescent moon adorned each one. Her middle-aged stomach was fairly flat despite having borne a child, now grown. Her breasts hadn't sagged even though she'd nursed him. She was proud of that, always standing with her shoulders back so Billy would notice. Her thick black hair sprang three fingers from her head *au naturel*, glorious and kinked. The ends were tipped in red from the time six months before when the object of Billy's fleeting attentions had been a red-haired woman, and she'd tried to distract him in his pursuit by copying her. It didn't work.

"No, you go on," she said. "The Lord and I need some private time."

Billy's chest deflated in relief. She wanted to kill him for that, but showered instead. By the time she finished, he'd left without saying goodbye.

When it came to women, Billy had no conscience. "The heart wants what the heart wants," he'd say, adding that to foil the heart's desires led to coronary disease and death. It was something he announced to whoever would listen. Any female foolish enough to take him on heard it during the initial assignation. Ella was the first female he'd said it to when they were just kids. Up until then, she near worshipped him.

She couldn't be blamed. There was something godlike in the way Billy first appeared in her life. As it happened, she was about to drown in Paw's Creek after getting trapped in a high tide during a sudden thunderstorm. If she'd died, she'd not have been the first Black child to die there. Paw's Creek pulled at least one child a summer into the harsh embrace of its charging currents, dragging them under its rising tide, especially during storms. In those days, Black children didn't go to the beach, and Paw's Creek was the best they had to cool off on an August afternoon, so they often took the chance. Ella had gone to swim by herself after arguing with her brother. When the storm came, there was no one to help her; she was tossed wherever the creek wanted. She put up a fight, but although she was strong, she was only fourteen. She could not defeat nature. It wasn't long before she sank and rose, sank and rose, her lungs filling with water. Terrified, she prepared to give up her soul and prayed to Jesus. He must have heard her. She couldn't see, she couldn't hear, but out of that wet darkness two strong arms found her and hefted her up and over into a motorboat, itself pitching wild against storm-driven waves. It was Billy Euston's granddaddy's fishing boat, and it was Billy Euston who pumped her chest, who breathed his air into her lungs, who gave her life. She coughed up water while he held her tightly in his arms. For a while, it looked like the boat would turn over and they'd drown together, holding on to each other. Then suddenly, the storm departed as unexpectedly as it arrived. The sun broke through the clouds bright as the voice of God at Sinai. The first good look Ella got at Billy was with his head haloed by a shaft of light. It was impossible not to fall in love with him.

Billy could have been Black, brown, red, or Chinese; Ella had to feel as she did. Every woman falls in love with the man who saves her life. It would be against nature to feel otherwise. In the same way, every young man of fifteen falls in love with the woman whose gratitude satisfies his most intimate predilections, especially when she's a looker like Ella. Billy was no different.

Two became one. They were each other's first at everything for a couple of years, until a big-boned blond woman of twenty-five tempted Billy away. She was the woman who first inspired his refrain of hearts wanting what hearts wanted, although it turned out there was not much more remarkable about her. Billy hurt Ella like no one before or since, but with prayer and fortitude, she got over it. When he was done with the big blonde, Ella took him back. The next time his heart wanted someone else, it didn't hurt half so bad.

Decades went by. Some years Billy's heart wanted her, and some years it didn't. Ella carved her own life out of his absences, but only ever refused him if she was freshly married when he wanted back in. After the marriage was a few years old and things got stale or worse, well, that was different. Regardless of her marital condition, she never failed to sit him down at her table and feed him while he told her his troubles. After two husbands and as many kids—one natural, one step—her own heart was crisscrossed with scars.

In high school, she'd had her first fight with her best friend over Billy. One Saturday, the two girls left their mothers for a chartered bus taking a load of young people to a revival weekend upstate sponsored by the church for the good of their teenage souls. At the bus station, they pretended they'd fallen ill. The church chaperones told them to go home to bed. Released from spiritual obligation yet under the threat of damnation after such flagrant mendacity, the girls hopped a bus for Atlanta and saw *In the Heat of the Night* instead. People predicted there'd be riots at the theaters where the film was shown. There were riots enough that summer. As it happened, there were none on account of the film, and every Black girl longed to see Sidney Poitier outsmarting racists on the big screen. Ella and Lillibelle were not going to let a five-hour bus trip stop them. Afterward, they both declared the experience worth a stint in hell.

Their minds were full as they walked back to the bus station. Lillibelle carried on a good while about the scene in which Poitier's character was saved by a white racist cop from being nearly stomped to death by thugs. "My meemaw says white people never hate us so little or love us so much as when they can save us," she said. "I, for one, am not grateful." She expressed the thought in a dozen ways, from obscenity to poetic flights. In sum, she endorsed purity of anger and demand for reparation over a social debt incurred through gratitude. "If I were Mr. Tibbs," she said, citing Poitier's character, "I'd rather be dead than beholden to that cracker." Ella sat on a wooden bench suffering a slow boil until her friend finally took a breath. Then she said, with an edge to her voice, "I understand what you feel, but you have to realize when a white person really does save you, it's not so easy to forget." Lillibelle grabbed her forearm and hissed so that no one else in the station would overhear, "Girl! Are you still screwin' that white boy?" Ella exploded. Harsh words were exchanged. They took separate buses home and didn't speak for weeks. Once they did, despite tearful apologies all round, it was never the same.

Sometimes, Ella thought maybe she was the dope Lillibelle believed her to be. But ever since the storm at Paw's Creek, Ella's heart only ever truly wanted one thing: Billy Euston, God help her. Whenever she had him, she wanted him more. Whenever she didn't, she longed for him, waiting for his inevitable return in varying stages of misery, resignation, or defiance.

That Sunday, Billy drove south from Ella's place above Elegance by Ella, the dress shop she owned and did pretty well at, too. The shop was on the north end of the island where middle-class Blacks lived. Poor Blacks tended to live on the outskirts of Ella's neighborhood, or smack-dab in the middle of Sweetgrass Island, where they resided immovable as boulders on heirs' property, ramshackle in single-wides and cabins, planted alongside white homes, often far grander, sometimes not, as they had always done. Rich Blacks lived wherever they damn well pleased. There were two or three on the resort end of the island. More or less, everyone got along.

Billy's house was on Cap'n Jack's Spit. Twenty minutes later, he arrived, let the dogs out, and put up a tray of ribs straight from the smoker. He wrapped it tight in heavy-duty tinfoil, put a bottle of sweet sauce and one of hot in a paper bag, threw in a couple of biscuits he had lying around, and took off for Catawba Plantation to pay a call on his heart's latest desire, Abigail Becker.

He could still conjure the warmth of Ella's long, supple thighs around his middle. He could yet smell her woodsy scent of pine and jasmine mingled, but it made no difference.

I'm an evil man, he told himself, half-singing it. *Bad, evil, bad.*

By the time he got close to Catawba Plantation, Billy decided that if as fine a woman as Ella always took him back no matter what, he couldn't be entirely bad. There must be something good about him, too. As he drove along counting his virtues, he decided that one of the best things about him was his loyalty to solid country values, and that could be laid at the feet of his father, Wesley Porter Euston. Wes had been an honorable, hardworking man who only made one mistake in life. Unfortunately, it was a doozy.

* * *

When Billy was a boy, Wes worked as a short-order cook at the corner drugstore, back in the day when drugstore lunch counters meant red leather seats on chrome stools, checkerboard tile floors, and soda fountains that made drinks from scratch with syrup and seltzer water. In the middle of the countertop, a pushbutton jukebox played favorites by Perry Como, Peggy Lee, and Frank Sinatra. A magazine rack across the aisle displayed *Better Homes and Gardens*, *True Romance*, comic books, and men's magazines wrapped in brown paper. Next to the rack was a wall shelf with cotton balls, monkey's blood, Goody's Powder, shoe polish, and ladies' hairnets. The pharmacy, where Phil Borman mortared powders and stuffed pill casings behind the window according to physician instructions, faced the diner from the opposite wall. During the breakfast and lunch hours, Wes scrambled eggs, cooked up pancakes and home fries on the same griddle, spooned gravy over biscuits, flipped burgers, and sizzled bacon for the BLTs. Afterward, he restocked the shelves. Billy's mother worked next to him during school hours as the day-shift cashier. With both of them working, they didn't live like swells, but they lived.

On Sundays, Wes took his son fishing and hunting, taught him how to shoot straight and true. He gave Billy all kind of lessons on caring for the land and wild animals, while also respecting every color, size, and religion of human being. "It's a new day in the South," he told the boy. "We have to be part of it."

By the time Billy was teenaged, an Eckerds Pharmacy opened down the street from Wes's place of employ. Eckerds was a powerful chain, stuffed with discounts, bright as a new penny. It was the beginning of the end for Phil's Drugs. Sales slipped. Phil's wife took over the cashier's job to keep income in the family. Billy's mama, Loretta, went on unemployment, but the benefits weren't much. The lunch counter was still busy for a while until a McDonald's popped up a half mile away. Customers came in and badgered Wes with "This place needs a golden arch" and "Gimme a big one, Wes," jokes he could only take good-naturedly for so long. A darkness crept into his family life, perhaps because the irritation he felt had to go somewhere. Plus, they were quickly going broke. He got persnickety with Loretta over a thousand real and imagined slights. He criticized Billy for doing nothing more than being a kid. Mid-rant he saw the shadow fall over Billy's eyes and immediately apologized. "These are hard times, son," he'd say and hug him close. Loretta wasn't that lucky. Misfortune sucked her into the darkness, too.

A day came that changed the Euston family forever. Wes had been feeling the pressure for some time. He was exhausted from work and worry. There were days he got up with pains in his chest and wondered if he'd be dead by nightfall. That morning, Loretta griped for the two-thousandth time about their finances. She'd taken to drinking in the morning, but Wes didn't know that yet.

"Things'd be different if only I could find another job," she said. "I've tried, you know that, Wes. If it weren't for bad luck, I'd have no luck at all."

Wes was tired of listening to her whine. As far as he could see, he stood on sore feet six days a week, sweating over a griddle with his back in a truss for the pain, doing his best for wife and child, while Loretta lolled around all day, then poor-mouthed him by night.

"No wonder," he said, "you go to interviews with that face on. Nobody livin' wants to hire a sad sack."

Loretta went wild-eyed. She whirled about and grabbed a knife from the kitchen countertop. She tried to get closer to his chest as he backed away, drop-jawed, eyes bulging, palms up in defense. Later on, he told his attorney, "There's nothin' more terrifyin' on God's green earth than a woman with crazy eyes and a butcher knife in her iron grip. It shot my nerves to pieces."

Wes managed to get out the house before his wife could kill him. For twenty minutes, he crouched like a thief behind a bush to watch her through a window. He watched her stagger about, taking a long draught of vodka from a bottle stashed under the kitchen sink, and then another. He watched until she passed out in a chair at the kitchen table. Dazed, he went to work unsure what to do, grateful Billy had already gone to school for an early practice with the wrestling team. First thing, he apologized to Phil for coming in late and told him there was a family emergency. He needed to pick Billy up at the end of the school day also. Phil didn't ask what was going on. He didn't mind

Wes taking off before the end of day particularly. He wouldn't have to pay him for the hours he missed; they were slow hours anyway.

Wes threw himself into home fries and sausage gravy. His hands shook. He had a small grease fire around ten o'clock, but he put it out quickly. It wasn't like him to start a grease fire. He was a more careful man than that, generally. It upset him that he did. He started to cry while cleaning it up, but everyone thought his tears were smoke induced.

A little later, one of the jokers came in. It was after breakfast service and before lunch when Wes usually took his break, but the joker wanted a burger. Wes had been halfway out the door thinking he'd make a quick check on Loretta, although he wasn't exactly eager to do so. He put his apron back on and made the burger, placed it on a roll with lettuce and tomato. By the time he put the plate down on the counter, his breath came hard. He needed out of there. Then, with a devilish smile, the customer complained that his lunch didn't come with special sauce and shoestring fries. He banged at the countertop with his cutlery.

"We want sauce! We want string fries!" he chanted over and over. "We want sauce! We want string fries!"

Phil was working on his books in the office behind the pharmacy. He came out to see what kind of fuss was going on. He was depressed about his bottom line and needed customer unrest like a hole in the head. He saw that the joker pestering Wes was one of his best customers. The pharmacist filled scripts for diabetes and heart medications for him and his wife every month. He fell on the man's side without hesitation.

"Wes. Get him what he wants," he said.

Wes broke. He broke in the worst way. He bellowed from deep in his gut. He threw plates, glassware. He tossed the grease collected in a coffee can behind the griddle on the floor. He put his face three inches from the face of the joker and howled before slinging a pot of piping-hot coffee into his face while squeezing the man's wrist, pinning him to the counter. The joker howled even louder than Wes. He broke out in a mass of bumps on a field of fire-red skin that ran from his eyebrows down to his neck.

Wes ran out the door in his apron. He kept running until he got home, where he threw himself at the feet of his insensate-at-the-kitchen-table wife. He curled up knees to chest, his fists in his mouth. He was still there when the police showed up looking for him. Loretta came awake as they were taking him out. She thought she was dreaming.

The joker's bumps turned to blisters, which turned to scars. He pressed charges. For the next three years, Wes was incarcerated in the state prison. Billy was fifteen by then, old enough to quit school and ask Phil if he could take over his father's job to keep him and his mother in one piece. Phil was a good man. He didn't want to see the boy and his mama suffer. He gave him a chance.

What came next was a surprise to everyone on the island. Billy discovered that he liked cooking. He was good at it. By the time he was seventeen, he'd worked at several lunch counters, diners, and restaurants. He found he had a singular talent for BBQ when he chanced to work with the best grill wrangler in four states, old Johnny Stack, a backwoods Black man introduced to him by Ella. Johnny liked Billy. He taught him everything he knew, as he had no sons to leave his rub to and somebody needed to know it. In a way, his mother's drunkenness and his father's breakdown were blessings for Billy, or he might never have found his calling and the secret of Johnny Stack's supreme spice rub. At least that's how he came to look at it.

When his father was released, he tried to come home. Billy wouldn't let him. He was afraid it would start his mother drinking again, but he didn't know that she'd never quit. By the time he realized it, he was stuck with her, his green years blighted by the burden of a drunk mother and a father lost in the wind.

The guard at Catawba Plantation's security gate knew Billy. Just about everybody in the county knew Billy. His meats were famous well beyond the island. People drove down from the foothills just to taste them. Billy grew up with the guard, and that alone might have given him the chance to talk his way through the gate, with or without meats. When he reached the gatehouse, Billy rolled down his window, stuck his arm and head out.

"Hey, Deputy Dawg," he said. "How's it goin'." He didn't wait for a response; there was a line of vehicles behind him. "I'm makin' a surprise visit to the Beckers. Brought them some ribs. Think you can let me through without a call-in pass?" The guard was a handsome man with several front teeth missing. He had an aversion to wearing his flipper during work. Whenever there was no supervisor, a common event on Sundays, he left it at home, which was why he stood at the gatehouse window in his pressed uniform and municipal badge looking important and good-looking until he grinned. "You bet, Billy. Do you know where they're at? I'm gonna have to look 'em up."

"Some damn thing like Crooked Bridge Lane or Twin Turtle Alley."

The men shared a smirk. The guard found the address, handed Billy a pass and a map, then waved him through. The Becker house wasn't the grandest house on Catawba, but it was real nice, set back from the street on the wide side of the marsh, and more than big enough for two. As he drove up, Billy noted that the garage door was open. There was no car inside. The delectable Abigail, however, lounged on a chaise on the front deck. She wore a sundress, had a book in her lap, and drank something on ice. Obviously, Joe was elsewhere. Abigail waved him up. Hard to imagine, Billy thought, a country boy could be so lucky.

3.

When Abigail saw Billy Euston pull into her driveway, something lit up, died out, then lit up again inside her. For maybe fifteen seconds, from diaphragm to throat, she flickered like a candle on a drafty shelf. A subtle twitching ran under her skin from thighs to toes. These were such ridiculous sensations, they stole her breath. There were only two ways to interpret the phenom: Billy Euston was destined to play a fateful role in her life, or alternatively, he already had in a previous one.

Abigail believed in fate. She also believed in prophecy, the kind that came in tarot cards and dreams. She kept a dream journal and cast her cards every day. She rarely interpreted the latter correctly, but retrospect always proved them accurate. That morning, a mysterious knight of swords popped up repeatedly in her Celtic cross spreads. His position changed, but there he was, every time. Until Billy drove up the drive, she had no idea who the knight was, just that it wasn't Joe. He always presented as the softhearted, indulgent king of cups. In the time it took her to wave Billy up to the deck and for him to mount the steps while carrying a large tray of God-knows-what, Abigail tried to remember exactly what cards the knight of swords had influenced. She failed.

Once Joe was out the door that morning, grocery list in hand, she'd taken advantage of being on her own for a couple of hours. She lit the last joint of those Billy Euston had given her and settled into a pleasant haze of random thought, conjuring a thousand things, letting the drug take her mind wherever it was inclined to go. In a happy fog, she'd laid down on her chaise under a warming sun on the front deck, sweet tea in one hand, an unread book in her lap. Dozing and waking, fantasy and wishes played tag behind her fluttering eyelids. By the time Billy showed up, she almost expected him.

Setting down the tea and book, Abigail stood a little too fast and wavered on her feet. Billy shifted his tray to one hand and moved to her side, grabbing her arm above the elbow to steady her. She blinked. It occurred she had a true Southern gentleman at her side, assisting her, which made her laugh in a warm, mellow register, the siren kind that makes men throw themselves upon rocks in a storm.

Billy put his mouth close to her ear and rasped into it.

"You alright, sugar?"

He smelled strongly of tobacco, a scent Abigail didn't care for. She put a hand on his chest and pushed him away gently.

"Sure," she said. "Got up too fast. What a surprise to see you here!"

Billy gave her a broad grin. He offered his tray of ribs.

"As it's Sunday, I thought you might enjoy some Q. Call it a welcome-to-town present."

Abigail looked under the tinfoil and pushed out her lower lip.

"I'm sure this is delicious, but we're Jews. We don't eat pork."

Billy's face fell. His ribs were his best first foray into a woman's heart. He wasn't sure his smoked brisket would perform half so well.

"Dang," he said.

He offered the brisket for next time anyway.

"I never woulda guessed you was Jews," he finished as a kind of apology.

She laughed.

"Hardly anyone does."

The "hardly" came out "hahdly," which reminded Billy of old newsreels of President Kennedy. She didn't sound like what he thought Jews should sound like, although he hadn't really known enough to tell.

He couldn't be blamed. There wasn't anything particularly Jewish about the Beckers. They often told people they didn't eat pork on religious grounds, but the truth was, they stayed at a B&B on a farm once in Connecticut and bonded with the piglets there. Abigail couldn't eat pork after that, and Joe went along with her. Recently, after attending a performance of *Fiddler on the Roof* at a friend's daughter's college, they'd decided to observe the Sabbath in a way, lighting candles and not working, but it was more theater than commitment. Essentially, they were anodyne Jews, reflexively supporting Israel and buying a box of matzos at Passover, some years attending services at High Holidays but without the passion their grandparents might have hoped for them. "You got one foot in goyland," her father told her once. He was probably right.

"Surely you have something I want more than ribs," Abigail said, making her voice throaty.

For a split second, Billy's heart rejoiced . . . until he realized what she was talking about. He smiled anyway, and reached into his back pocket. He held a small pipe between his bent fingers and his thumb.

"This suit you?" he said.

Abigail grinned and opened the screen door to the kitchen. Billy took four steps forward.

As he glanced around the kitchen, it struck him she'd not shown any reluctance about letting a stranger into her house while she was alone. He didn't sense any excitement, either. It confused him. There should have been one or the other. Southern women were suspicious these days, always with their backs up. It was a man's job to soothe them, gain their trust. Abigail didn't seem to need that. He was in, he thought, but what was he in for?

He wasn't in for much. Abigail was comfortable with men. She enjoyed their company, even if she didn't quite trust them. She felt she knew what made them tick. Women, she found, were often envious. Most men wanted to please her because of her looks, whereas women disliked her for the same reason. She thought the latter was exceptionally unfair. She didn't control her birth. She looked this way because this was the way she looked. Ever since she was a child, people doted on her because she was pretty, while her parents stood on the sidelines and beamed. But that wasn't her fault, either. Her whole childhood, nothing went too wrong for her. She did fine in school. Her college years passed without incident except for the time she got caught smoking weed behind the library by campus police, but even then, she'd given them a wide-eyed remorseful look and they let her off the hook with a warning. She'd dated a lot, then fell hard for a clever older man who only wanted to get his hands on her perfect flesh, a man who didn't care about or notice her finer feelings. She'd entertained high hopes for the relationship and when it blew up, she wept and moped. More unfortunate choices followed.

By the time she met Joe, she was looking for stability and service from a man, someone to sustain her, someone to do things for her, like her parents did. Joe fit the bill. He made her the right promises and, as a bonus, he loved music as much as she did. He lifted her out of sadness, gave her her confidence back. She married him in a rush of grateful affection, thoughtlessly, the way flood washes out a gully. After more than seven years together, she'd had only a few passing regrets. They had a nice life; hardly luxurious but comfortable, secure. They didn't have children because Abigail spent all day teaching third graders, five days a week. She didn't want to be around kids more than that. She had some years left to change her mind, but at present, life with just the two of them doing what they pleased—or more often what she pleased—was fine by her. Joe sometimes got wistful about little ones, but she had her ways of distracting him, and the mood usually passed.

"Can I get you something to drink, Billy?" Abigail asked. She stood by her refrigerator with a hand raised to a glassed-in cabinet. She was so alluring that Billy wondered if her posture was intentional, a pose to display herself like a photo on a billboard.

"If that's sweet tea you're drinkin', I'll have summa that," Billy said, taking a seat at the kitchen table and pulling a lighter from inside his tee's pocket. He remained seated to light the pipe. He inhaled and extended the pipe toward her at the level of his chest, so that when she arrived at his side, she'd have to bend down in front of him to take it. She bent and gave him his drink. *Everything's going my way*, he thought.

Abigail took a chair across from Billy's. She sat back, raised her chin, and blew out a column of smoke. She asked him to tell her about himself. He told her he was the original pitmaster of the best BBQ restaurant in town, the Flying Pig. Did that for twenty-odd years, then scaled back to just a few days a week.

"I got too old to work that hard," he said. "It's young man's work. Nowadays, I sell meats from home. Sauces and rubs, too."

Abigail told him he didn't look like a retiree. She got a short version of his childhood. He made it sound his mother had been single his whole life. Then she asked him, "Are you married?" He told her he'd never bit that bullet, but he'd had a rich emotional life. She laughed. "Do you have a partner?" That stopped him because he couldn't decide whether telling her about Ella would work for him or against him. He cleared his throat and took a plunge into semifact.

"I've long had a friend I keep company with, off and on. She's a good woman. You'd like her."

Abigail took the pipe from him again.

"We all have to get together then. I need some girlfriends in this part of the world."

Billy wanted to stay alive. He had no intention of introducing Ella to Abigail.

"We're off right now," he lied.

Abigail didn't ask why. He thought to ask her a few questions, but there was a noise outside. Abigail jumped up and looked out the door.

"My husband's home," she said.

Billy got up to go.

"I ought to be gettin' along," he said. "I don't want to be bothering you."

"Don't be silly," she said. "You're no bother. To tell the truth, Joe needs men friends like I need women friends." Abigail smiled. "It's tough being the new kid in town. Most of the people in this development are too old for us. Joe calls it an open-air nursing home. You're welcome at our house anytime. We need relief!"

She laughed in an airy way. The sound rang deep inside Billy's ears, vibrating his spine with each syllable. It felt like she was inside him, like she was the clapper and he the bell.

Joe walked in the door with both arms full of packages, plastic bags dangling from his wrists. He looked happy to see Billy. Abigail took the bundles on his right side, laid them on the counter. She poked around to see what he'd bought while Joe stuck out his free hand for Billy to shake.

"Good to see you, man," he said.

He could not have been more affable. Billy watched him kiss his wife hello as she relieved him of produce, fish in brown paper, and fresh bread. As she started to unpack, Joe sat down in Abigail's seat.

"What brings you out our way?" he asked.

"Ribs," Billy said. "Pork ribs, sorry to say."

Abigail gestured at the foil-covered tray on the counter with the pointy end of a green bean. "I told him he'd have to take them back, but wasn't that dear of him to think of us?" She reached over and popped the green bean into Joe's mouth.

"Mmm," he said. "These are good. Sweet and crispy."

"They're fresh," Billy said. He shifted his weight in his chair, uncrossed and recrossed his legs, fighting off an attack of the fidgets. "Not like what you get in the supermarkets." It irritated him that his comment was so boring, but something about Joe brought it out of him.

Joe got up, looked under the foil, and pronounced the ribs great-looking. If he was a pork eater, he said, those would be exactly the ones he'd want. The compliment made Billy more restless. He made his apologies, promised to come back soon, and backed out. When he got to the truck, he put the ribs on the front seat next to him. He checked the time. Ella should be getting out of church. He'd take the tray over to her, he thought. It never hurt to pay a lady unexpected attention.

The Beckers stood on the porch, arm in arm. They waved goodbye. Billy waved back. He tried to figure out why he was so agitated. The mystery of what Joe had done to deserve the prize of Abigail had not yet been answered, and that bothered Billy. He knew women could be peculiar in choosing mates. Look at Ella Price. Those husbands of hers. Whoo-ee. A loser and a user, he always said. There'd been times he would've killed one or both of them for her, if she'd asked. But Abigail with someone like Joe seemed weird. Maybe he'd return with smoked brisket in a few days and commence a study of them. Mama always said good things came to those who wait. Mama was wrong about many things, but she'd been right about that.

Billy could wait. He would use the time to figure out the heart of Abigail Becker. He knew he was no longer young. Even when he was, he'd never been Elvis. But he knew women; all you had to do was stick close, be helpful, and wear 'em down. He'd have his chance with her. He knew he would.

4.

Joe drove home from the farmers' market, feeling good he hadn't shopped at Piggly Wiggly instead. People at the market were hospitable; they took an interest in who he was and where he came from. He liked that.

Joe had never been truly comfortable up North. His old world demanded that everyone, no matter their background, think the same and behave the same, and that left a guy like him out. This new world he'd landed in intrigued him, charmed him. It accepted eccentricity. It sparked his imagination. He hoped he could become a part of it. Every day he became more committed to the idea their move would become permanent. His work in progress was a children's adventure set in the Deep South, maybe along the swamp or on the river, he wasn't sure which yet. The adventure, a quest for old bones, slave bones, bones as old as the Civil War, was something he'd dreamed up as a tribute to his new home. So far, he'd been a spectator, looking through a clouded glass. When he read his drafts, he knew that showed, and he wanted his story to be authentic. To improve things, he needed to soak up as much local custom and attitude as he could. Catawba Plantation offered golf, tennis, horses, and a terrific beach, but most of its residents were transplants, too. They were as Southern as polar bears.

Abigail told Joe that most of the time, he tried too hard to make friends. He needed to chill, not rush things. But that day, he mentioned his love of red peppers to the Black woman in charge of the Lamont Farms register, a woman known as Miss Lilly to about everyone in sight. She told him how peppers got color—it depended on when they were picked—and invited him to come over to Lamont Farms and go picking with her if he was truly interested.

Joe was surprised. Miss Lilly didn't look like she did any picking. A striking woman older than he, maybe Billy Euston's age, she wore a blue shirt of pressed cotton, a long denim skirt, and rubber-soled shoes. From beneath a straw hat worthy of church, cornrows tied up with red ribbon into a ponytail flowed down her back.

"I'd really like that, ma'am," he said.

"Why don't you come over to the farm 'bout seven a.m. tomorra', then."

"Miss Lilly," Joe said, proud of the way his "Miss Lilly" slipped from his lips, and then, like the words had been waiting on his tongue all his life to make their debut, "that's a mite early."

The words *a mite* fell with a hard thud to the dirt at his feet. Joe knew as soon as he said them they were wrong, false, antique. Picked up from old movies and bad television shows, they were ridiculous out of a Yankee mouth. He heard Abigail tell him to stop trying so damn hard and hoped Miss Lilly wouldn't think he was an idiot. Miss Lilly's expression didn't change. It looked like she let it go. Joe was grateful.

"Yes, sir, it is. But if you want to last even half a day of picking, you need to start early, or the sun'll kill you before you're two hours out. Bring water."

"I will. See you at seven," he said.

Joe picked up bags of heirloom tomatoes, peppers, sweet potatoes, onions, pole beans, and summer squash, along with field greens he had no idea how to cook. He waved goodbye before heading back to his car.

When Joe pulled into the driveway of his new home, a truck was parked there. He gathered his purchases, climbed the stairs to the porch. Abigail had a visitor. He heard her laugh, smelled marijuana through the screen door, and then a man's voice he identified by its deep rasp. Billy Euston. *Damn*, he thought. *I don't know if I can handle another sap in love following my wife around, especially one like Billy, rough-and-tumble and sly.* Steeling himself, he pushed inside and did

what he could to show Billy that he didn't feel he was a threat. Joe
wasn't sure he'd chosen the right tack, but he went with it anyway.

Abigail often had admirers, ones she entertained until they realized
she would not fall into their arms, after which, they'd fade away. At
least that was how Joe Becker saw things. But on occasion, he felt a
whisper of doubt about whether Abigail always remained one hundred
percent chaste.

Much of what was wrong with Joe Becker could be laid at the feet
of his mother, Sarah. Sarah had polio as a child. Early in the 1940
epidemic, she was ripped from her family at the age of five and sent to
a sanatorium forty miles from home after suffering a sore throat and
weak legs for three days. She lived in isolation there for three years.
When she returned home, it was with more or less normal mobility,
digestion, and respiration, her important functions intact. But in her
mind and in her heart, she was a wreck.

She trusted no one. According to Sarah Becker, doctors were
always wrong. Government officials lied with every breath. The police
were the enemy. The new vaccines for every childhood disease, including the one that had ruined her childhood, were suspect. Joe got none.
Instead, she locked him in the backyard behind a fence he could not
see over. He was kept apart from other children, apart from anything
besides three trees, one birch, two elm, a small flower garden, and
his mother's clothesline. The only people he saw were his parents and
uncles. This lasted from birth until he was six and inducted into Mrs.
Bernstein's first-grade classroom under the threat of seizure by tru-
ant authorities. From the first day of class, he was treated as something worse than the new kid. He was as ignorant as a block of wood
and everything frightened him, which made him the strange kid, the
weirdo, the putz. His neighborhood was entirely Jewish. Joe Becker
struck the other kids as so alien, he might as well have been a Baptist.

That first year, Joe suffered childhood diseases one after the other,
as he'd had neither exposure nor vaccine. He had mumps, measles,
whooping cough, two bouts of strep throat, one of otitis media, and
two of flu. He spent more time in his sickbed than at school. But he
managed not to die, which his mother took to mean she'd been right
to deny him vaccination, despite what his papa said.

Eventually, Joe learned to read and stopped getting sick. His class-mates still avoided him. He spent most of his time alone in the same backyard that had been his prison, reading books, talking to whatever animals wandered by, robins and bluebirds, squirrels, and wayward cats. During those solitary hours, Joe lived in daydreams. He was a pirate, an explorer, a tank commander, a jewel thief, a magician. His experiences as such were detailed, fully imagined and always sus-penseful. It was a pastime he carried into adolescence and adulthood, making a career of telling a new generation of children variants of the stories he'd told himself. All the heroes of his books were outliers, separate from and misunderstood by their peers. Because he wrote for children aged ten to twelve, his stories had happy endings. Their heroes faced danger, learned courage, and won the admiration of oth-ers. They made friends.

There's no way of knowing where Joe's early years might have led him were it not for the interventions of fate. Two events changed his life's trajectory in startling ways. The first was that before he graduated college, he'd published his first book, *Flora the Firefighter*, and against all odds, it was a modest success. He followed up *Flora* with *Mike Sails to Micronesia* and then a historical adventure, *Robert the Roving Buccaneer*. The historical effort sold seventy thousand copies in its first three months and spawned a series, currently at eight books, of histori-cal novels for children that became popular as supplementary aids in classrooms all over the country. In short, Joe made a living. He wasn't a Stephen King or a James Patterson, but he didn't have to worry whether his next effort would be published or if he could pay the bills. He was courted by a fan base of parents everywhere and made social progress. Sometimes, unhappy mothers threw themselves at him. He was human. He caught them. They brushed off his awkward nature, the occasional peculiar remark as a creative's eccentricities. He gained confidence.

The second event that changed his life was meeting Abigail Roth. It happened during an author appearance at Inglebrook Elementary in Lexington, Massachusetts, where she was a novice teacher. It was an evening event attended by parents, some with their children, most not. The novel of the evening was *Louise of Louvemont*, about a young girl swept up in the Great War, who must evacuate her doomed village with her mother as the German army draws near. *Louise* was Joe's most realistic work to date and stirred up controversy. Its scenes of perilous flight, artillery bombardment, and near death, of Louise nursing her wounded mother in a dank cave, bred concern about exposing tender psyches to too much reality even though the pair survive and are reunited with her father at a hospital in Paris at the end. The Persian Gulf War was a hot topic in the news. Those who supported it threatened to attend and protest the book's antiwar message.

That night, the auditorium was filled to capacity, which meant teachers were required to stand at the back. Joe could see them from the stage. During his presentation, he followed the advice of his publicist. He smiled or paused where he thought he should and made sure his eyes roved the room to include everyone in attendance. He limited his commentary to WWI, telling the assembled that whatever readers brought to an author's work was theirs alone. They were entitled to their perspective, but his story was about the villages that died for France, not Iraq. He added that he prayed every American who'd strapped on boots that morning in a foreign land would come home in one piece. In a stroke of genius, he closed by calling for a moment of silence for the troops' welfare. No one in the auditorium could argue with the sentiment. It made the ensuing Q&A a lot less contentious than it might have been.

Whenever he could, he locked eyes with the beautiful young woman standing in the teachers' row at the back. She was his anchor. Her eyes looked full of sadness. He felt their souls connect in shared empathy. He had no way of knowing her sadness was transitory, a period of angst over the last man who'd disappointed her. Joe thought she responded to him and him alone.

There was coffee and cake after. The junior teachers poured the coffee and refilled the pastry platters. Joe made a beeline for Abigail's station near the brownies and lemon squares. He introduced himself as if she'd missed his name on the posters at the hall's entrance. She laughed her captivating laugh. For Joe, it felt like triumph. The whirlwind courtship that followed was the best part of his life, a coup he'd never dared imagine while daydreaming in his writer's room.

Abigail told him early on that she believed in karma, that everything balanced out through the course of a person's life. Each life had its share of pain, but also its share of joy. Some people suffered early on, while others found suffering at the end. If she was right, Joe decided, Abigail was his reward for a lonesome beginning. As it happened, they complemented each other effortlessly. She gave him pride; he gave her a courtly devotion she could depend on. They shared a passion for all kinds of music. They fit each other like the teeth of a sprocket into the grooves of a chain. Every so often, some man would pop up and pursue Abigail, but Joe understood why. His wife was extraordinary, gorgeous, a princess. When she indulged her admirers, it was because she found them entertaining or useful. They were always different from him. Sometimes, he found them entertaining or useful, too. But it was hard to figure out what she saw in Billy Euston.

After Billy picked up his ribs and left, the rest of the Beckers' Sunday passed uneventfully. Joe got some work in, Abigail some reading. They cooked a salmon dinner together while the radio played a tribute to Ralph Stanley. When that was over, they switched to a PBS station playing Chopin. Throughout both, they hummed along or swayed in each other's arms, feeling part of the music itself, which led to affection and long, lazy sex. Dinner wound up served pretty late. They microwaved the salmon to heat it up and found it dry, but neither cared.

Joe forgot he needed to set his alarm to get to Lamont Farms by seven. He woke at the break of dawn anyway, thanks to a boisterous wren singing to the rising sun. He ate a light breakfast, kissed his sleeping wife's head, dressed in jeans, a work shirt, and a hat with a wide brim, sprayed himself with insect repellent, grabbed a couple of bottles of water from the fridge, stuck them in a fanny pack, and drove whistling "Walking Boss" down River Road to Miss Lilly's place.

He arrived early. Driving through the farm's iron gate then up the long dirt road flanked by stands of live oak dripping Spanish moss, his heart swelled with the beauty of the place. He passed pastures where horses and cows grazed over great expanses of green studded with shade trees and bordered on the far side by a bluff and beyond that, deep water. The animals looked fat and happy. Some had egrets sitting on their rumps. It was a paradise.

The house was a sprawling brick-and-clapboard edifice with a wrap-around porch that held rocking chairs and wicker tables separated by potted plants. It was surrounded by flowering trees and bushes: crepe myrtle, magnolia, roses, wisteria. The house looked to have been built over many decades, with rooms added chockablock as they were needed, without much attention to the aesthetics of the whole. There were two sheds in the back and a ramshackle barn with paddocks. A second barn looked to be more recently built. Behind the buildings were acres of cultivated land. Joe didn't know what crops were represented beyond corn, tomatoes, and several types of green. He was eager to learn. The smells of the place were rich. He rolled down his window and his lungs expanded irresistibly. The thick aroma of pluff mud wafted in from the marsh. Somehow he did not find the scent of decaying organics offensive, but considered it a rare perfume. It supported those of animal feed, flowers, and loamy soil the way water buoys a boat.

Joe parked his car, wondering if he was supposed to go to the front or the back. He chose the back. There he found a dozen or so pickers waiting for the day to commence. Most were Hispanic men and women. Some had small children with them. They chatted away in Spanish and drank coffee from paper cups. They wore broad-brimmed straw hats tied under the chin. Burlap bags with long, thick straps crossed their chests. There were a number of Blacks, too. The men wore feed caps, the women headwraps. They wore the same burlap bags as the others. Joe was the only white. He stood on the edge of the group, nodding and smiling at whoever looked his way.

Lilly stepped out the back door of the house. She wore overalls with a T-shirt underneath, and a wide-brimmed straw hat. Standing on the top step of the porch, she put her hands on her hips and gave directions in two languages. Joe caught a bit of the Spanish. Something about tomatoes, but only certain ones. In English, she said, "Li'l Jim, you need to get at them 'lopes and strawberries. If you all finish early, see what you think of the cabbage and broccoli. I'm taking our new friend here, Joe, to the peppers, but I'll be checking in with you later. Okay, everyone, let's get to it. *Vamos.*"

The crews set off for their respective fields. Joe waited for Miss Lilly to gather her clipboard, jeep key, and water bottle. She came down the steps and tossed him the keys.

"You drive," she said, heading to the jeep parked at the head of a dirt path separating the field rows. "I'll show you where."

Joe got in the jeep, turned the key, and told her it looked like the house had expanded over a long time. Her chin went up.

"Near one hundred fifty years," she said. "It's heirs' property, granted to freedmen after the Civil War. My family lived here, generation after generation, building as they needed. By law, the land can't be sold unless all the descendants of the original freedmen agree to it. You can imagine how tough that is to accomplish. Cousins and aunties and uncles and grandparents—everyone used to live here, but the older generations died off and their children moved to the cities. My daddy thought that was wrong; he thought the legacy needed to be preserved. He was the Black folks' doctor 'round here back in the day. White men and women came to him with troubles they didn't want their own to know. The only Black man 'round town as rich as him was the funeral director. Daddy bought up the farmland surrounding the big house, but he was too busy to develop it in his lifetime. It lay fallow for decades. I'm the first one to farm it all."

This is great stuff, Joe thought, envisioning a plot point in the new book that could revolve around heirs' property. He started to think of Lilly as his heroine grown up. She directed him down the path to the pepper patch, where she showed him the green, yellow, orange, and red peppers. She described to him the harvest schedule she used to assure the desired amount of each during a single growing cycle. She demonstrated the proper way to clip ripe peppers from the vine, then handed him a burlap bag and the clippers. "Have at it," she said, and left him to his own devices.

The vines were bristly and cut his fingers. They were four feet tall, but some peppers grew low to the ground. Joe knelt to get them. The soil was moist, and before long, his jeans were soaked through with mud at the knees. Picking was hot, backbreaking work. After an hour, Joe wanted nothing more than to go home. His bag was less than a quarter full. Lilly didn't show up again for another hour and a half.

By then, he'd quit. He was worn out, his bag woefully just this side of empty. He sat in the dirt path next to the pepper patch, fanning himself with his hat. He'd snapped a whole row's worth of vines trying to get the hang of clipping. He wondered if he should offer to pay damages. As Lilly got out of the jeep, he struggled to his feet.

"I'm not in shape for this," he said.

A corner of her mouth lifted in something masquerading as a smile. There was a touch of cruelty in it, perhaps contempt.

"It's not easy, is it, boy?" she said. "Well. Now, you know."

She walked around his work area, fingering the jagged tips of broken stalks. She clucked her tongue and shook her head.

"Would you like me to pay you damages?" he asked.

Lilly gave him a startled look. A stretch of silence underscored her reaction.

"You mean reparations?" She paused to let her word choice sink in. "I don't think you can afford it, Joe."

It was a dark joke. He had no idea how to respond. He hung his head and shifted his weight from one foot to the other until she took pity and drove him to his car.

When Joe got home, he mailed a check to Lamont Farms for three hundred dollars. He wrote "reparations" in the memo line and enclosed a letter saying he hoped it was enough to replace the vines. He thanked Lilly for her patience and kindness to him. Three days later, he received the check back by return mail. There was no note.

5.

There is a distinct romance to the South for those Yankees who come to live there. For some, its allure is historical, but it's a fanciful history, studded with hoopskirts and mint juleps, gentlemen who know the meaning attached to the color of roses, who ride well and shoot straight. The ugliness of human flesh bought and sold, tortured and maimed only enters these narratives around the edges. For others, the romance of the natural world appeals: mist over the marsh, trees that look to harbor ghosts from every limb, the flight of blue herons rising like pterodactyls from the sweetgrass, bobcats, soaring hawks with mice in their grip. They fall in love with moonlight and magnolia. They also fail to smell the blood. Then there is a separate kind of transplant the South eats up whole, the kind like the Beckers. For these, the South sucks out all self-deception, forcing them to face their true selves under the glare of a bright, unyielding sun. Afterward, there's no place else they're fit to go.

It wasn't long before Joe couldn't go anywhere without returning home to find Billy Euston sitting like Goldilocks in Joe's easy chair, happy of the fit. He lounged on Joe's porch, watched his TV, took whatever beer struck his fancy out of the refrigerator. Joe wasn't sure how much he trusted the old dog, but he trusted his wife, which rendered the man harmless enough in his eyes. When it came to his work, Billy was an invaluable asset. Joe's heroine had acquired a bootlegger uncle, with dialogue straight out of Billy's mouth: "Now, you never wanna leave your still uncovered at night," Uncle Sammy said. "Or you'll be pickin' drunk mice out all day long." That stuff was gold.

Abigail liked Billy a lot. He was respectful and made her laugh; she relaxed in his company. He planted an herb garden in a window box for her. He taught her new things. Thanks to Billy, she soon had the rudiments of clog dancing down, a skill she couldn't wait to show off at Declan's. That first day of lessons, he put a disc of mountain music on the CD player, then, standing at her side, took her soft hand in his red, rough one and placed a strong, hard arm around her waist. It was the first time they'd touched, other than a light brush of fingers as they passed a joint. "His hands are like lobster claws," she told Joe later. She shivered when she said it.

Billy's song had a mandolin, a banjo, and a fiddle. He told her to let the strings strum through her center until she caught the downbeat. That didn't take but a minute. Then the two bent their heads to watch their feet. Billy gave instructions. "We're gonna start off easy. Step, kick, step, kick, step, step, step . . ." His breath fluttered the hair by her ear. "Okay, next thing. Look down here. This'd be the double toe. See? Just like gettin' gum off your shoe. Go on, do it. Good! Now brush up with t'other foot . . ."

The lesson went on for near an hour. By then, her head suffused with the sound and feel of Billy, Abigail found herself blended with both dance partner and the music. Intoxicated by the feel of her feet moving without her conscious intent, she was warm, her heart pounded. Then her husband came home.

The music was playing at a decibel level that could cover screams or gunshots. It slapped hard at Joe's ears as he mounted the front stairs. He called out for Abigail. Having seen the truck in the drive, he called out for Euston, too.

"Sweetheart, I'm home," he shouted, adding, "You two are making a racket! Billy, you in there murdering my wife?"

At the sound of Joe's shout, Abigail stumbled. If Billy hadn't caught her, she might have tumbled into a corner of the coffee table. But Billy caught her with both hands around her midriff, just below her breasts. He pulled her up. Abigail slapped his hands away. She looked to the arched entry to the living room. Her husband stood there with eyebrows raised, his lips stretched thin.

"Billy's teaching me to clog dance," she said in steady voice, moving away from her instructor and toward Joe to give him a peck on the cheek. "I gotta go pee," she added, needing to compose herself.

Billy turned off the music, and the two men sat on the couch.

"Clog dancing?"

Billy shrugged.

"She asked."

Joe leaned back against a cushion and looked at the ceiling.

"It means she trusts you," Joe said. "That's unusual. Abigail's had some difficult experiences with men. Trust doesn't come easy for her. So don't ever break it."

Billy squirmed in his seat. Such a blunt turn of conversation was alien to him, uncomfortably direct. A Southerner would have suggested the same thing in a dozen different ways, until the point was made without violating any niceties. Since he didn't know how to respond, he changed the subject.

"There's something else she wants me to teach her."

"What?"

"She wants to know how to shoot."

Joe started.

"Geez," he said.

Abigail had talked about guns ever since the 7-Eleven incident in Boston two years before. They were in the store together, waiting at the back of a five-person queue, when a gunman burst in. He waved his weapon at the cashier, ordering him to empty the cashbox into a plastic bag. He was young, disheveled; he trembled. He looked weak except for the gun. Joe grabbed Abigail's hand and backed them away to hide around the corner near a display of soup cans. It seemed the sensible thing to do. The woman at the head of the queue saw things differently. She made a chop at the man's forearm with her quart of V8. He dropped the gun and fled. Everyone cheered. The Beckers bounded out of the soup aisle to join in. But Joe always felt badly about the incident, shamed he'd chosen prudence over heroism. Abigail didn't make it any easier. "We were in the goddamn soup aisle!" she said on the way home. "You could have hurled a few cans at that guy's head." But Joe didn't. It never occurred to him. "You could have, too," was his only response. Afterward, self-defense became an obsession of Abigail's. She wanted a gun then, but up North, she'd have to jump through a thousand hoops to get a license. Instead, she took boxing lessons, judo, too. She quit both when her coaches asked her to try competition, as she didn't want to risk an injury. She hadn't mentioned guns in a while.

Abigail returned to the living room to hear Billy's remark. She broke out a huge, sun-stopping smile and inserted herself on the couch between her redneck and her husband.

"Honey, you must know how I feel," she purred to Joe. "Ever since we came south, I've been thinking I should exercise my Second Amendment rights. You don't even need a license here. So. Yes. I want to learn how to shoot. I mean, how can we experience the real South unless we experience firearms? Imagine how scandalized stuffy old Susan and Rich back home will be when we tell them we shoot. Wouldn't that be funny?"

"Susan and Rich. Now there's two reasons to shoot a gun," Joe said dryly. He could see that fighting her on the subject would be a losing battle. "Sure, why not," he said.

These were the damnedest Yankees he'd ever met, thought Billy. *Too bad wacky doesn't make her less pretty.*

The three made a date and time the next week. They would not, Billy said, go to a shooting range just yet. He'd give them a preparatory lesson over his house. He'd put up some targets on a barrier wall and set up a bench they'd shoot from. They'd move the bench back and forth so they'd get the idea of how distance can affect aim. He'd show them a variety of firearms. They could try them all. When they knew what they were comfortable with, he'd take them another day to a gun shop so they could buy their own weapons if they so desired.

Abigail nudged her husband with an elbow that night when he was just this side of sleep.

"If you so desire, he said. Did you hear that?"

Joe yawned. "Huh?" She tried again.

"About buying a gun. If we so desire." Her laughter had affection in it. "He kills me the way he talks. If we so desire."

Joe mumbled something to do with speech pattern being a standard way to create character in a story, but she didn't hear him and he didn't feel like repeating himself. He rolled over and soon began to snore in short, sharp blasts that made her think of gunfire.

On the appointed day, the Beckers drove over to Cap'n Jack's Spit, a narrow finger of dirt projecting itself into the southern Atlantic like a rude gesture. Nonetheless, it provided a home to an impressive variety of seabirds, fish, dolphin, and a handful of intrepid souls like Billy Euston.

"Doesn't he worry about hurricanes?" Abigail asked Joe.

"I'm sure he does, but knowing him, he has a plan."

The windows of their car kept fogging up no matter how they fiddled with the air system, so they kept them down, which meant they could smell Billy's place before they saw it. The scent of burning hickory and oak from his smoker wafted down the dirt road. About the place where a flagpole fluttering Old Glory could be seen towering over scrub brush and palmettos, there was a dock where his fishing boat was anchored. A barn sat on a rise of land nestled in a copse of oak and crepe myrtle that stood close together. The road veered to the left, they rounded a bend, and there was Billy's industrial-sized smoker and grill. It dominated the landscape, one of flowering bushes and a terraced garden of vegetables and herbs. Beyond the garden was Billy's home, a double-wide with a wooden staircase and deck attached.

Joe parked and turned off the engine just as two black Labs came running toward them with sticks in their mouths. Abigail shrank back a little. Big dogs scared her, but Joe laughed and got out of the car. He petted the dogs, took a stick from one of them, and heaved it as far as he could. The dogs ran after it, one with the spare stick still in his mouth.

"A trailer," Abigail said, getting out now that the dogs were distracted. "I would have thought he'd have a house, an old one. Maybe a cabin."

"Nope."

Billy's voice came from right behind her. Abigail jumped but recovered quickly.

"A trailer's easier to replace if a hurricane comes knockin'. I had a house, had two of them. But little 'cane David took one away, and a stray tornado took t'other when Diana came through. I swore I'd never build again."

Billy locked up the dogs in the house. "You throw 'em a stick, you'll be throwin' all day," he said as he proceeded to show the Beckers around. Joe was interested in the still, Abigail the music platform Billy had built in front of a stand of magnolias and oaks. He showed her where he fixed speakers and spotlights to their trunks. "In the old days, I'd play with my music brothers here, but those days are long gone," he told them. "I keep this up in case I want to have a party."

"I didn't realize you played an instrument," Joe said.

"I can tickle the ivories pretty good," Billy said. "I'm average on the banjo."

They both would have paid money to see inside the double-wide, but Billy didn't invite them in; rather, he walked them around to the back of the house where he'd set up targets clipped to a clothesline at top and bottom, behind which a thick ridge of sand and dirt served to catch spent bullets. Thirty feet away, he'd set up the promised bench with gun cases laid out along its twelve-foot length. Next to every case was a box of the appropriate ammunition. After a lecture on gun safety, Billy opened each case with the flourish of a Las Vegas magician, describing the contents with an air of awed emotion. ". . . now here is the best li'l starter pistol Smith and Wesson ever made, the Bodyguard, a snub-nosed .38. It comes with a crimson laser so you don't have to worry over much about your aim . . . then here's my personal favorite for self-protection, the Walther PPS Luger, 9 mm. I've heard ignorant people call it a peashooter, but I'm here to tell you it's got a sweet fire, only this particular one tracks a hair to the left. When you try it, you need to correct for that. Remember, it's not the size of the hole you make, it's where you put it . . . Over here, we got your huntin' rifle, your semiautomatic, and last, the good old pump-action shotgun, which I keep for sentimental reasons . . ."

It was an impressive array. They tried them all. To his surprise, Joe enjoyed himself. The sense of power he felt pulling a trigger was exhilarating. Abigail got the scent of gunpowder up her nose and relished it. The heft of the Luger pleased her, while the Bodyguard revolver felt secure in her hand, natural. Joe felt affinity only for the shotgun. The men picked up the bench and moved it back another twenty feet. They tried them all again. In between each trial, Billy walked over to the wall to check the targets. It turned out Abigail was a great shot, right out of the gate, with or without the laser. Billy was so pleased, he got excited and gave her a short hug of congratulation. Abigail blushed. Overexcited, what with gunpowder pinching her sinus cavities, she kissed Billy's cheek just as he released her. It looked for a second like she meant to hug him back, which raised the hair on the back of Joe's neck. Things might have got heated except all of a sudden, a yellow Camaro pulled into Billy's front yard, raising a great cloud of dust. The three turned to see what was up. The door opened. Miss Lilly of Lamont Farms got out and slammed the door behind her before making a beeline to where Billy basked, half dazed, in the glow of beauty's kiss. He bestirred himself and met her halfway. Joe raised a hand to wave at her, but she ignored him.

The Beckers couldn't hear much of what was said. There was some kind of emergency; a man named Big George and a woman were involved, but what had happened or what it had to do with Euston was undetectable. What was certain was that their lesson was over.

Lilly got back in her Camaro and sped off. Billy quickly put the guns away, locking up their cases, asking Joe to help him cart them into the house. That done, he apologized for having to go. He left in his pickup before they could get back inside their car.

"I wonder what that was all about," Joe said. He put his irritation over the cheek kiss aside for the time being. He couldn't figure why he'd been so irritated anyway. He saw it with his own eyes. It was more of a light buss than a kiss. Maybe he only got excited because they were playing with honest-to-god guns. Guns, even empty ones, charged the air.

"What was the inside of the trailer like?" Abigail asked.

"Has he ever mentioned a Big George to you?"

Abigail spoke louder this time.

"Did you hear me? I'm dying to know."

Joe started. His mind was on a different track. He wasn't sure what she needed so much she'd die for it.

"Huh?"

His wife slapped his shoulder.

"Wake up! I want to know what the trailer's like inside. C'mon. You're the writer. You're supposed to be good at description."

Joe sighed.

"Okay. But it's not like I was in there very long. I only saw the living room. Let's see. Lots of heavy wood. Plants in copper basins. Chintz curtains. Family photos. Framed, arranged on top of a piano, an upright, the old kind they put in tourist saloons for show. And right in the middle of the photographs was an Elvis doll, a bobblehead."

"You're kidding me. Elvis?"

"Yes."

"Go on."

Joe continued, describing everything else he recalled while they drove back to Catawba. Abigail sat back with her eyes half closed and her arms crossed against her chest. She seemed to rock a little. He couldn't tell exactly why. He feared it had to do with her feelings for Billy, the depth of which he'd perhaps ignored. But the road was uneven, full of holes, and that could have been what rocked her.

6.

Ella Price's son, Big George, earned his name at birth. He weighed in at eleven pounds. Head to toe, he was twenty-five inches. The head itself looked huge to everyone who saw him. How big it actually was remains a mystery, a question of myth. Time went by, all the other kids got taller. Big George stayed taller than most, but not taller than everyone, which was a blessing because his head, now proportionate, remained sizable, and no kid needs more than one oddity about him. His childhood passed. He endured his share of teasing, but no one came up with a moniker for him more suitable than "Big George."

Big George was good-looking; nearly every feature of his wide face was well shaped. His eyes were large, brown with glints of gold, lavishly lashed. He was born with a stately nose, although in high school a football incident bent it a hair to the right. Cheekbones, high at the peak with a pleasing slope. Lips, full, tapered. His mouth was so appealing that people paid attention to his words for the charm of watching it move. Big George spoke in a resonant bass. Its timbre was unmistakable. Robust with a velvet quality guaranteed to soothe the nerves, it underscored handsomely his impressive size. Whenever he pursued a woman, if she managed to get past his well-lashed eyes or lush lips, his most reliable gambit was to telephone and coo in her ear. She'd melt. Guaranteed.

From high school on, George wanted a career in law enforcement; a curious choice for a boy with his background. His father went to federal prison before Big George was two years old. Five years later, he died in his cell at the age of thirty-five while in an unattended, unnoticed diabetic coma, a disease he had not suffered before he was incarcerated. Herman Price—Ella kept his surname despite her second marriage, out of respect for a dead man and to soothe the grief of Big George—wasn't a hardened criminal. His felonies were politically fueled, understandably so. He was from Mississippi and a good bit older than Ella. After a life of yes'm and yessir, of making way on the sidewalk, drinking gritty water from the coloreds' fountain, of watching his mother and sisters harassed, his father humiliated, himself bullied often as a boy, beaten once as a man, Herman Price joined the Black Power movement and later on the Panthers.

At first, Herman was one of only four young men in town wearing a dashiki and skullcap. They let their hair grow wild and set up a heritage school in the function hall of the Sweet Redeemer Baptist Church, where the neighborhood children were taught the achievements of their African ancestors. Ella signed up to fix the kids snacks every day and found Herman as debonair as Sidney Poitier. The two fell in love while Billy was occupied elsewhere. There was a swift courtship, a happy marriage, a baby boy. Then Herman got tied to the Panthers.

A little more than a year after the killing by Chicago police of Fred Hampton in his bed, Herman went up to the Panthers' Winston-Salem headquarters to train. Ella didn't want him to go. They hadn't been married very long. George was still a baby and needed his daddy. Plus Billy Euston was sniffing around again. She worried she'd succumb to temptation if she were on her own too long. But Herman went anyway because, he told Ella, he needed to build a new world for his son to thrive in. He wanted George to grow up unbowed. He wanted him to breathe the sacred air of freedom. He wanted a world where Ella got out from under her servitude to a coterie of white women needing alterations and repair of their wardrobes. He wanted to see her with her own shop, designing her own clothes for her own people and any whites with taste—as long as their pockets were deep. Herman Price felt the Panthers could build that world, and he was punished for it.

His training in Winston-Salem lasted several months. On his return, he was the only man in town who'd traded African dress for military fatigues, combat boots, and a black beret. He'd changed his name to Chinonso Izem, which he translated as God Is Nearby the Lion. He carried a weapon, openly, defiantly, and struck fear into the hearts of whites. Clearly, they weren't going to tolerate that for long. He hadn't carted around his pistol in plain view for a week before he was set upon in the night while patrolling his own street. Four white men charged out of an alleyway and took him by surprise. One of them was an off-duty policeman. He was the one who took Herman down. The rest rained blows on him while he lay helpless on the pavement, trying to cover up. One man dangled handcuffs in front of Herman's face. They planned to take him somewhere. *No*, thought Herman, through his pain. *I have a son. You are not takin' me anywhere.*

A surge of strength went through him. He scrambled out from under fists and boots and retrieved his gun from underneath a row of bushes where it skidded across the sidewalk when he was jumped. He lifted his weapon. Three of his assailants went still. The fourth, the off-duty policeman, swore and reached into his jacket. Herman saw the butt of the man's gun and discharged his own. So did a helpful neighbor from a rooftop. One can only guess the white men were taken by surprise that he had the will, the means, and the support to fight back. During his trial, Herman said it surprised him, too.

By the time it was over, three white men were wounded. One was brain damaged, one paralyzed, one had a useless right hand. The off-duty cop was dead. Police cars arrived at the scene screeching retribution before Herman had a chance to run. No one ever discovered who the helpful neighbor was. No one tried very hard. They had what they wanted: they had Herman aka Chinonso Izem Price. They had him good.

During the years he was in federal prison two states away from home, Ella took Big George to see his daddy twice a month. Herman never knew it was Billy who drove them the nine-hour ride there. "He suffers enough," Ella said. "Why torment him with a white man's good deeds?" After Herman died, Billy comforted the widow and looked after her fatherless son. He did so until she found herself another husband, this one as feckless as Herman had been devoted. Billy didn't like Ella's second husband much and neither did Big George. Their bond strengthened.

It wouldn't be fair to say Billy gave Big George the idea that law enforcement might be a fitting career. He had his own problems with men in blue. He often told the boy that his father's tragedy was not unique. It was part of a great American evil, but the world was changing. Big George could have the life his father imagined for him if he applied himself in school and kept his mind open and his eyes alert to opportunity. Look at Billy himself, also a child of the incarcerated. He hadn't turned out too bad, and he did what he loved. Uncle Jackson, Ella's brother, had a very different view, as did Lillibelle, his mother's best friend. They told him if he expected life to lay out for him a feast of choices the way Billy Euston said it would, he might as well pack up and move to Africa, because he'd never find more than a handful of dismal options in the Deep South.

Convinced he was smarter than all of them, Big George had his own ideas, his own reasons, too. When he was a toddler, visiting his father in prison, the guards were kind to him because Ella trained him to be polite, plus he was handsome. As George grew, they doted on him, giving him gifts of chocolate bars and rubber balls. They imprinted him as father figures, his mother said, more than even Billy, principally because they were boss to his real father.

They were his world almost from the cradle.

One day not long before he died, Herman was making his way toward his wife and child in the visiting room under the guard of a white brute who had little respect for himself and less for his prisoners. His uniform was perpetually stained, his hair greasy, his chin covered in stubble. He only kept his job day to day, the others said, because he had something on the warden. Big George, who was five at the time, could smell him yards away. As the guard approached, he wrinkled his nose and held it with two fingers. Grown men around him, prisoners and guards both, laughed. Encouraged, Big George pranced around the room, waiting for his father to reach their table, unaware that his mother tried to catch his arm to settle him down. By this time, the guard had figured out he was the object of a child's joke. He went purple with rage and humiliation. He tripped Herman so that he fell hard on the linoleum, then advanced toward Big George to smack the kid. Big George stared down at his dad, then up at menace. A big Black guard, bigger than the guard who threatened George, intervened and clocked the white one with a powerful left hook. Down he went, hard onto the floor, not two feet away from Herman Chinonso Izem Price.

It was the most memorable event of Big George's boyhood, surpassing even his father's funeral. The guard who saved him, who made justice for him and his father, loomed large in his imagination throughout his life. He gave him a name, since he was too young at the time to read his name tag. "Officer Roy," he called him, after Roy Rogers, who'd made a weighty impression on the kid, both for his movies and his eateries. Whenever he played at cops and robbers or cowboys and Indians with the other boys, his persona was always Officer Roy or Deputy Roy. Whoever was his sidekick, he dubbed Pappy Parker, regardless of rank, after the chain's fried chicken sandwich.

In this way, Big George became a boy drawn to men in uniform, men with authority, men with guns, men who settled disputes, men who kept the peace. Once he was grown, he convinced himself that if a real lawman, a real policeman, an Officer Roy had been on hand when his father was attacked in the street, Herman never would have killed anyone and died in prison.

Big George played football in high school. He almost had to, given his size. It was either that or be judged disloyal to the school. He didn't like it much. By his lights, it was a boring, stupid game. Obviously, he couldn't tell anyone that. So to please his classmates, Uncle Jackson, Billy Euston, and the coach, he accepted the fullback position. To make it bearable, he'd fantasize that he was Officer Roy protecting Pappy Parker from the opposition. Whenever he successfully executed a daring play, the crowd erupted into cheers on his behalf, and because they knew him, knew who he was, knew who he was from boyhood, the bleachers would shout "Officer Roy, he's our man! If he can't do it, no one can!," which pleased Big George no end. It made up for having to play a game he didn't like.

After high school, Big George took a two-year course at the community college in criminal justice, worked for a year at a 911 hotline, then applied for and was accepted to the Georgia Police

Academy. He applied to the Savannah school because he thought it was high time he detached himself from Ella's apron strings. After three months of training, he joined the force in Atlanta. It didn't please his mother. She wanted him closer to home. To make it up to her, he tried to visit often, but that meant once every few months at first and only at major holidays after a time. Eventually, since major holidays included the shifts where Big George could make significant overtime and be assigned choice duties, the holiday visits whittled down as well. Family occasions, weddings, and funerals were frequently missed.

As Billy Euston rushed to Ella Price at the urging of Lillibelle Lamont, he couldn't quite recall when he'd last seen Big George. It might have been a year. Heck, it might have been longer. George had been in the force maybe seven years already, he figured. They were lucky nothing awful had happened to him before.

When he got to Ella's house, he took the stairs two at a time to reach her apartment above the shop. He swung open the door and stood in the living room where she was not, then cocked his ear to find her. Sobs came from the bedroom. He found her pulling a suitcase out of the bedroom closet while clutching a Bible. Tears ran down her face. Lillibelle Lamont stood next to her, stroking her back. Ella looked over to him, her face a map of misery. She opened her arms.

"Oh, Billy. I think they've killed George," she said.

He went to her and embraced her while murmuring her name.

"Ella, Ella, honey, you can't know that. Lillibelle said he's in intensive care. Did somethin' happen I don't know?" He looked over at his lover's best friend, who shook her head and raised her eyebrows while pointing the palms of her hands upward.

"It's up to the Lord," she said. "But it doesn't look good."

Billy's voice went tender and soft.

"You hear that, darlin'? He's not gone yet. The Lord has always loved you both, you know that. Have some faith. Come on, we'll pray together."

They all three sat on the bed, reached out and joined hands. Billy began.

"Sweet Lord, please don't take Big George away from us," he said. "He's a good man from a fine mother, and the world needs men like him . . ."

Lillibelle said something similar. When it was Ella's turn, she reminded the Lord that He'd taken Big George's father too young, and maybe He owed her this much, to keep her son with her awhile yet.

"This time," she said, "may Your will be my will, in Jesus name. Amen."

Most would think it was a hair combed over the side of blasphemy to make demands of the Almighty, but it was the way she felt, and Ella was never anything but sincere. She straightened her back, freed her hands from the others, blew her nose in a tissue, and got up muttering about needing to collect her toiletries. Billy asked if she wanted him to drive her to Atlanta.

"Baby, thank you but you don't have to," she said. "Lillibelle will."

"No, I'll do it. I want to. You may need a man around."

He didn't know what he meant by that, but he believed it to be true. Ella started to cry again, then sniffed and bucked up. Billy felt light on the details of what had happened. He asked if she'd mind filling him in.

"George overstepped himself," she said, a sob catching her voice. "He got assigned to the drug unit just last week, and you know how gung ho he can be."

As might be expected, she said, Big George wanted desperately to make his mark in his new position. That morning, he and his partner, Reggie Connolly, drove over to a neighborhood with known crack houses, the same ones that the night before bustled with commerce, drugs addicts, and prostitutes. In the early morning, Big George figured, dealers and addicts slept the sleep of the drugged. Everything inside the crack dens would be still; not a one of those crooks could jump up and run if they wanted to. It was a good time to find someone on the suspect list with the evidence yet spread over a kitchen table. Big George and Reggie—a man longer in the force, but not as clever—couldn't figure out why the others in the unit didn't do the same. Maybe they were all on the take. The two decided to pay a call on a crack house and see what they could find.

In the history of knucklehead decisions, that one must have hit the top ten. To begin with, they should have let their unit know the plan. They would have been dissuaded. But no, they wanted the glory all to themselves. As they exited their unmarked car, Big George said, "Good to go, Pappy?" and Reggie said, "Whenever you are, Officer Roy." Their banter filled them with courage. Feeling like Richard Roundtree with music by Isaac Hayes, the two stormed into the apartment of a gang of dealers with guns drawn. They were immediately met with the fire of crack house bodyguards, men who never indulged in so much as a beer during their shifts. Big George and Reggie fired back. The whole battle didn't last five breaths and a moan. In the end, Reggie lay dead on a grimy carpet. Big George bled beside him from head and leg wounds. There was a raw, gaping hole in his gut. The drug crew split. One of the women called 911.

Just as Ella finished her recounting of what had happened to her son, the phone rang. The doctor in Atlanta told her that the surgery had gone better than they'd hoped; her son had made it, but his recovery would be slow. Everyone praised Jesus and hugged one another. Ella finished packing up while Billy left to get the car fueled and make arrangements for a bud to look after his dogs, still, and smoker. He drove like a demon back to his house. He wasn't gone more than thirty minutes. When he got back to Ella's, he found the apartment vacant. A note in Lillibelle's hand was on the kitchen table.

> *You took too long. Couldn't wait. I'm taking Ella to Atlanta. Let my foreman over at the farm know and look out that the dress shop isn't robbed. We'll be back when we'll be back.*

Billy crumpled up the note and threw it to the ground. Goddang Lillibelle, always horning in. Every time he thought they were done with competition for Ella's attention, Lillibelle raised her standard yet again. It had been that way since they were kids.

Billy stayed in high dudgeon the whole two and a half weeks they were gone, even though he spoke to both women most kindly nearly every day. The first weekend they were gone, he drove to Atlanta on a Saturday to visit Big George, and he didn't betray a note of his irritation to Lillibelle or Ella. He kept quiet partly because to see Big George in his condition was a shock. George lay there with his feet sticking out just over the mattress, his socks scrunched up under the ankles, tubes and wires coming out from all over him, his head wrapped up in bandages that made it look even bigger than it was, his cheeks with an ashen tinge.

At four o'clock in the afternoon, Big George fluttered open his eyes and spoke. He spoke a long time. He claimed to remember everything about the disastrous raid. Billy knew that wasn't normal. Big George told them he thought someone had tipped the crack house off, but how could that be if it was a snap decision the two made that morning? Too bad Pappy wasn't around to ask.

"Your partner's gone," Ella told him softly, because it seemed like he'd forgotten that part. "Gone to Jesus," she added, in case he misunderstood.

"Pappy Parker never dies," Big George said.

The women exchanged empathetic looks. They hoped Big George was just being sentimental. Billy Euston saw it differently. *Something's off in that big head of his*, he thought, *something damaged due to the gunshot.* But he didn't say anything because he couldn't tell exactly what. It was just a sense he had. Nothing Ella needed to burden herself with right then.

Billy watched a loving mother bustle about the sickroom, looking for ways to make her son more comfortable. She pulled his socks up and the blankets down to cover his feet, she filled a cup with ice chips. When Big George stopped talking, she ran the chips over his mouth. She looked tired, she looked her age, but there was a glow of joy, of gratitude in her, and it made her as beautiful as she ever was. His heart warmed until Lillibelle came in with coffee for herself and Ella. She'd forgotten his. *Sure*, he thought. *Forgot, my ass.* A spike of anger toward the farm heiress soured him for the rest of the visit.

During the drive home, Billy's sourness turned to acid. His stomach burned with it. *Women*, he thought. *They stick together like they're bonded by Gorilla Glue.* Just before he left, the two chatted about their plans to bring Big George home to convalesce. Lillibelle cut Billy off every time he opened his mouth to offer a suggestion about how this should be done. The only role they assigned him was to find a way to get the invalid up the stairs from the dress shop. As he turned off I-20E to I-26, Billy abandoned thinking about Ella, Lillibelle, and Big George for the sake of his peace of mind and his digestion and turned his mind to Abigail Becker.

7.

Whenever the Beckers drove to Declan's, they took River Road, even though it added to the trip. They took it for the allée of oak that lined the entire long, winding street. Leafed limbs of dark oaks with flowing strands of silver moss joined from either side of the road above their heads, like a ghostly wedding arch of sabers. That night, just above the horizon, a full moon rose over a stretch of marshland glimpsed between the trees. It filled Joe's heart. He said to his wife, "There's nothing like this up North. Not even autumn, when the leaves turn, is this beautiful . . ." His wife murmured agreement, but in such a desultory way that he could tell she'd neither been looking nor listening. She was somewhere else in her head. He could guess where.

"Have you heard from Billy lately?" he asked.

Abigail's response took time. He clenched his teeth in the dark, waiting while she shifted all over her seat like a child set down in a queen's throne.

"No, I haven't," she said at last. "That bum. He has no right to do this, Joe. To make us dependent on his company and then abscond . . ." The word *abscond* was spoken with a cutting sarcasm. "God knows where he's off to. He treats us like a passing fancy. It makes me feel small. I thought he was our friend."

Joe reached over the console to grasp her hand.

"Abigail. He doesn't owe us anything. He has his own life to live. But maybe he'll be at the pub tonight," he said. "You can have a chat."

The idea settled her. Joe was left to wonder about her choice of words. *Make us dependent on his company*, she'd said. Us? Joe's work was solitary, and seclusion was his natural state. He enjoyed Billy, but he didn't consider himself dependent on anyone in the world except his wife. He was happy they hadn't heard from him. Her feelings for Euston were a puzzle to him, and he wasn't used to that.

When it came to her admirers, Abigail usually told Joe everything, repeating conversations down to the last word. His knowledge was a tool that kept her honest. If she liked a man too much, she used Joe to keep him at bay. Not that that happened often. There were two, maybe three occasions over the years when Abigail showed signs of being in too deep. She stared into space, forgot things, laughed too loudly, and solicited her husband's attentions with such passion that he could not believe he was her inspiration. So he got very good at waiting. He waited until her latest new friend disillusioned her. After the last serious admirer, the divorced father of troubled twins in her classroom, Joe thought she was done with flirtation. That was nearly two years ago. He'd convinced himself that Billy Euston, a man who could have been Abigail's father, who looked a cross between a bear and a hound dog, was a harmless substitute for the fraught adventures of the past.

There was always a crowd early on at Declan's when the Peat Moss Crew was in the house. Declan looked to have five hands as he mixed cocktails and poured shots at dazzling speed. His number two, Danny McD, pulled drafts while young Tommy and the waitress speed-walked trays of drinks and pub fare to the tables. Joe got a nod from Declan and a shouted greeting from Danny McD. A handful of barflies lucky enough to have grabbed a seat raised their glasses to the Beckers and pounded the bar with the flat of their palms. Both made mock little bows in return.

A flush of pleasure warmed Joe's face. Before they left Boston, their old friends judged they'd be back to the North before the fall. The conventional wisdom was that they couldn't possibly be accepted down South. All those rednecks. They warned it would be especially hard for two Jews to establish themselves in a region where all hospitality was superficial and insularity went to the bone. But at Declan's, they'd made friends and acquaintances with open hearts. They were welcomed to drink and dance, to tell jokes and tall tales. Whether their Boston friends were provincial in their assumptions of the South, or if the currency of Abigail's beauty held fast wherever they went, didn't matter. Joe felt a part of something here. He felt at home. Serendipitously, so did his wife.

After two months on the island, Joe and Abigail, besotted with all things Southern, decided to live permanently on Catawba Plantation. Abigail called the local school board about substitute teaching assignments with the chance at a permanent classroom in the spring. Her bona fides were strong. No one saw a problem. There might be a full-time classroom assignment earlier than expected if Betty Collins decided to extend her maternity leave. Abigail had grown close to the pergola clan. There may have been an adulteress or two among them, a drunk, a slanderer, an enabler of any of the petty sins of men, but they looked after one another. Their values were of another era, having to do with loyalty and family and love, even of the ones they thought a mess. So what if they got drunk? So what if they got high? They were fun. They talked a lot. They gossiped. The worst someone might say about them was they could get sloppy when sufficiently drunk, high, or both, hugging and smacking the cheeks of anybody at all while making impossible vows.

Before the music started, Abigail made her way out back to say hello to whomever was there. She nodded to some people she knew by sight who'd gathered around the unlit firepit. Under the pergola, she took a hit off Jimmy McClaren's pipe, and then another from Frances Marie Picken's blunt. Abigail felt like her head lifted off her shoulders for a few seconds and then set back down again. She chatted up Cal Dunlap, the island's game butcher, about how to prepare rabbit stew until the eyes of his wife, Constance Marie, gave them daggers. Abigail tuned in to the talk around her, which was about the hurricane season gearing up.

"There's that one come off Africa last week," someone said. "He's churnin' toward the Windward Islands now; bears watchin' this time a year. Channel 4 agrees."

"I don't pay mind to no one but the National Hurricane Center," someone else said. "The others are just fearmongers scarin' up ratings."

Abigail didn't care much about hurricanes, principally because she'd never been through the southern, coastal kind. She waited for a pause then said a little too loudly, "Any of you seen Billy Euston around lately?"

One of the pergola men, a man Billy's age, dressed in a plaid short-sleeved shirt and cargo shorts, pulled on his beard.

"I believe I heard he's been over Ella Price's place a lot, helpin' her out," he said, eyes directed somewhere past Abigail left shoulder. "Lord knows, she needs it."

"Ella Price?" she asked. "Do I know her?"

She didn't think it was an odd query, but no one answered her. The conversation returned to hurricanes. Abigail was both suddenly alert and profoundly perplexed.

The speakers blared the arbitrary notes of the Peat Moss Crew warming up. There was an electric violin's siren wail, the clipped beat of a bodhran, and a guitarist's sliding strum. Joe's head poked out of Declan's back door. From across the way, Abigail saw him peering into the night past all the people, looking for her. She got up and went to him.

"C'mon, honey," Joe said, "I got a seat at the bar for you. This is going to be great."

Luckily, the seat Joe secured was closest to Declan's bandstand. Abigail settled in next to her husband. She leaned back against him and propped an arm on the bar. Joe accepted her weight as naturally as he would in sleep. He rested his hand in her lap. She clutched his palm. They were maybe eight feet from the Crew.

The band was a trio. The leader was a white-haired man in a red satin shirt. He held a bodhran at the ready while his guitarist, a heavy-set good old boy with thick sideburns and a goatee, tuned up. The fiddler was a wild young boy, maybe eighteen, thin, wiry. His biceps were well developed and his forearms heavily veined. His face was angled like an avenging angel's. The violin he held was hollowed out at the middle with an electric cable jacked into it. The leader stepped up and called his mates to order, rapping the stick in his hand on the drum. The guitar and violin fell in behind it. When the white-haired man opened his mouth, a loud, clear tenor issued from it. It was neither warm nor golden nor harsh nor shrill. It was round, buoyant, lively with a touch of flint. It had a visceral effect. The ears pricked for it, the nerves inclined.

From the first notes of his first song, the Beckers were enthralled. It was a rebel song, witty and rousing.

> . . . Come out ye black and tans
> Come out and fight me like a man
> Show your wife how you
> won medals down in Flanders . . .

The voice sent a charge down their spines. Their feet tapped the rhythms of the song against the lower rungs of their barstools. At the refrain, clenched fists and whiskey glasses were raised. There were two more choruses, the song was over, and the bar erupted in applause. The white-haired man bowed his head for a sharp second. Snapping it back up, he said "Good evening, all. I'm Pat Magee." His arm went out toward the youngest of them. "My son, James," he said, "the best damn fiddler you'll ever hear." James went into a lick of self-introduction, playing low, gruff notes in a hard-driving rhythm, then he climbed up three scales at an ever faster beat. At its pinnacle, he lingered, piercing the air like a Perlman, a Heifetz. The guitarist cut in and James let him. "Jerry O'Dare on guitar . . ." Pat Magee yelled above the music. There was applause, followed by ballads and drinking songs. Then, in a fiery fit, James played "The Devil Went Down to Georgia" to close out the set. He brought down the house.

"Another great night at Declan's," Joe said into Abigail's ear while applauding between songs. She turned her head to give him a quick kiss. Then Billy Euston walked into the pub in the company of two Black women. One of the women smiled, nodded greeting to the band. She was a handsome woman in a yellow dress whose hand Billy reached out to hold as if in comfort. The other woman's expression was flat with disapproval. It was Miss Lilly of Lamont Farms. The woman in the yellow dress, the smiling one holding Billy's hand, was no one the Beckers knew. Everyone else in the pub did. People went over to her, kissing her cheek, and collecting a hug, asking about someone named Big George, a man the Beckers decided must be her husband and the same Big George on whose behalf Billy had quit them some weeks before.

Miss Lilly walked toward their end of the bar. She wore a peasant blouse with a long denim skirt that snapped up the middle and high-heeled sandals. Her skirt was undone from four inches above her knees all the way down to the hem. She had strong legs. There was purpose in her stride. Joe braced himself and addressed her.

"Miss Lilly. How nice to see you again. This is my wife, Abigail. Abigail, this is Miss Lilly of Lamont Farms. I told you about her . . ."

Abigail's face enlivened.

"Oh yes! Miss Lilly, I'm pleased to meet you. Your vegetables are stupendous."

"Then you must try my eggs. Free range."

"I have. Also stupendous."

Abigail gave Lilly her thousand-watt smile, but she appeared unmoved.

"Everyone seems to know your friend," Joe offered.

Lillibelle looked at him as if he were a moron.

"Of course, everyone knows her. Her people were Sassaports. Sassaport's been a notable name hereabouts from colonial times on. Notable here and in Jackson and Raleigh, too."

Joe knew that social standing in the South was all about who your people were, how many generations back your family could count. He nodded his head thoughtfully. If he told anyone his great-grandfather was a Berkowsky from Lodz, no one would be impressed.

A gent passing by, one of Declan's regulars, a man who loved to greet women with a kiss of the hand, reached over to Lilly and grabbed hers, bringing it to his mouth.

"Lillibelle, it's been too long," he said.

She pulled her hand back.

"Yet I see you're still an idiot," she said.

The regular wore a straw fedora rolled up at the sides. He lifted it.

"Mama always said there was no cure."

Lillibelle couldn't help it. She laughed. Taking her laughter as a coup, the regular set his hat toward the back of his head and walked away with his shoulders straight. Joe saw opportunity in Lilly's change of mood. He offered her a drink, and she accepted.

"Bourbon and branch," she said. She looked over at Billy and Ella, who were still receiving. "It's likely to be a long evenin'."

Joe gave her his seat. She and Abigail were cheek to jowl. Lilly took her in and stifled a start. She pulled back, squinted, and said, "You know Billy?" Abigail opened her mouth to answer, but at the same moment, the Peat Moss Crew cranked it back up with "Whiskey in the Jar." Lillibelle didn't hear a word of her response. Putting her hands to her ears and shaking her head in goodbye, she picked up her drink and left to look for some people she knew out the back.

Billy came up to them between songs, hand in hand with Ella. He gave both hugs hello. His body could not suppress a tremor when held briefly against Abigail. Her heart fluttered in response, but he didn't feel it.

Introductions were made. Ella's my oldest friend, he told them. The Beckers are my newest, he told her. There were smiles all around while they sized each other up. Joe thought Ella was stunning. *Good for you, Billy*, he thought. *Aren't you full of surprises.* Abigail saw that Ella was proud. It intimidated her, and she wondered how to get her to like her. Ella's memory was jogged. She remembered the couple from Fenton Bridge. Up close, she thought they both were city soft, although the woman was just as beautiful as that day weeks before, and the man looked kind. Billy was still busy with his introductions, telling her what she already knew, that the Beckers were from up North but that they were neighbors now. Ella thought their provenance made sense. They needed seasoning. They needed at least a year of it.

The lot of them managed to squeeze in together at the bar. Ella and Abigail sat while the men stood next to them like sentries. The music gave the women cover. They didn't have to talk much, which was fine with both of them. Billy bought a round. Joe ordered a ginger ale. He lifted his chin to Abigail. *Go ahead, I'm driving*, his gesture said. She ordered her bourbon neat. Joe's turn to buy a round followed. Abigail switched to Irish coffee to sober up a little, and Ella had her second gin and tonic. At last, the women had consumed enough alcohol to relax together. They tapped or grasped each other's forearm to punctuate a joke or an opinion like old girlfriends.

Abigail told Ella about her attempts to cook collards without bacon fat. All failed. She had Ella laughing over the amounts of garlic and shallot she put into it, trying to create a pungent but pork-free taste.

"You don't eat pork?" she asked.

"No, we don't."

"Why not?"

"We're Jews."

Ella looked up at Billy who was standing silently by, watching them talk with extraordinary interest. She filed that one away. She lifted her eyebrows to him, and he shrugged.

"The Muslims I know don't eat pork, either," she said. "I don't know so many Jews, but the ones I do know eat pork some of the time. How can you all live without it?"

"It's not easy living here. You got bacon even in dessert. Truth is, it's got nothing to do with religion. We used to eat pork and then, we chanced to meet some piglets and gave it up. We like pigs. They're very smart. We don't eat lamb or veal, either. No baby animals. Uh-uh. None."

Ella laughed again. She had to hand it to Billy: he collected the most unique people. She was starting to like Abigail quite a bit when Lillibelle came over, grabbed her wrist, and said, "I gotta borrow this gal for a minute," before marching her off to the hallway by the restrooms.

Abigail and Billy had their backs to the restroom hallway, but Joe faced it. He watched the two women put their heads together and talk. He saw Ella's eyes widen, watched her hand go to her mouth. Constance Marie Dunlap, the butcher's wife, joined them, standing next to Lillibelle. She whispered into Ella's ear. Ella stepped away to look back at Billy, Joe, and Abigail stone-faced. When she returned to the bar, she put a hand on Billy's shoulder.

"Baby, I'd like to go. I shouldn't leave Big George alone so long." She gave the Beckers an apologetic look. "I hope to see you all again," she said.

Billy turned around to give Lillibelle a broad scoop of his arm that said it was time to go. She waved her hands toward him a couple of times as if she were shooing chickens; she'd find her own way home. He made a goodbye to the Beckers, and they left. At the barroom door, Billy paused, half-turned to look Abigail in the eye. He held an air-phone to his ear: *I'll call you*. Abigail felt a flush of heat go through her. Joe called out as if the parting gesture was for him. "We'll talk soon." He yelled it so Billy could hear. Abigail slapped her husband's middle with the back of her hand. He stiffened his lip and pretended he had no idea why.

Once they were in the truck, Ella gave Billy a harsh, uncompromising stare.

"So that's the one, huh? The one that's too good for her husband? Don't deny it. Lillibelle told me everything."

Billy revved the engine and muttered.

"Oh, Lord."

Ella went on a tear then, releasing in one go the huge store of tension Big George's brush with death had built up in her over the past weeks when she'd known Billy was occupied elsewhere but couldn't confront him without compromising her dignity.

"How dare you sit me down next to a woman every soul in that bar knows you've been sniffin' after like a buck in rut!"

He tried to take her hand. She slapped his away.

"You bastard! The first time I've been out since George came home, and you do this to me? I don't know, Billy Euston. Maybe I've had it with you once and for all . . ."

She carried on without letting up until they arrived at her door. She quit the truck almost before he had a chance to stop it. He started to get out to escort her to her door when she stuck her head through the open passenger window.

"Don't you think for one second you're comin' upstairs with me. Number one, I might kill you. Number two, we can't disturb George."

Ella flung open the gate that led to the exterior stairs of Elegance by Ella and ascended, head high, her steps heavy and loud as if her very feet continued to berate him.

"I'll make it up to you, honey," Billy called out. She ignored him, slamming her door. He remained parked in the street outside her shop until he saw the apartment lights turn on. He let the truck idle a few minutes after. He watched her shadow move behind the curtains of her living room and wondered how he would win her forgiveness. It was a task he found daunting, but he figured he'd just have to think on it. *You'll forgive me*, he told Ella in his mind as he revved the engine and took off. *You always do.* He almost believed it. . . .

It took four days before Billy caved and threw himself at Ella's feet. He swore his fidelity. He swore his roving days were over. He begged forgiveness. He promised a big party to celebrate Big George's recovery. Ella said yes.

8.

At the sound of Joe's approach, Abigail scooped up the tarot cards spread over the kitchen table quick as a miser hiding his coin. By the time he got to her, she was a blank slate, her face expressionless, her posture benign. She shuffled the deck as if nothing was going on, but for the past two hours while he chipped away at his new novel in the second bedroom upstairs, she was in a fever of divination, attempting to determine what was going on between herself and Billy, herself and her husband, and Ella Price generally because she knew so little about her. She learned nothing. It was one of her most exasperating encounters with the cards to date, and she'd been spreading them since college. Every Celtic cross she cast contradicted the one before. After more than a dozen throws, she was so frustrated, she would have flung the cards against the wall, except her husband announced himself.

The reason she dissembled was not that she felt guilty for asking the cards for guidance on her friendship with Billy. It was that she didn't want Joe nagging her about consulting the cards at all. Tarot was something Joe Becker thought especially stupid, surpassed only by astrology. In the early days, they'd had many heated discussions about the way tarot informed her life. "No, it's not an airhead pursuit of New Age wisdom," she'd insist. "It's a Jungian exercise in self-awareness. It helps me understand myself when I pay attention to what it is about the particular cards I pay attention to, see?" (He didn't.) She swore she never used the cards for insight into the future, but that was a lie, a self-protective one she also had no guilt over. It shut her husband up and gave her the freedom to prognosticate. When that afternoon's cards were a hodgepodge signifying a mass of tangled fates, it gave her an edge. The last thing she needed just now was teasing from Joe regarding a habit she could neither logically defend nor emotionally give up. She made an effort to exude calm, but Joe asked a question that clearly mocked her.

"So. What are the runes of the day?"

Bite me, she thought, although she mugged comically and said, "My destiny appears to be murky and undefined."

Abigail pushed the deck away and yawned to make a point. They were not going to talk about tarot today. Instead, she made sure they talked of simple things, innocuous things; topics that helped them pretend nothing odd was going on between them, like what do you want for dinner and wasn't it warm outside. They were making progress in the crawl toward normalcy when the phone rang. Abigail jumped up to answer it, even though Joe was closer to the wall unit than she was. He put his arms up to give her free access.

"Hello?" she said, her eyes darting right and left. Then they melted. "Billy. We've been waiting to hear from you . . ."

She played with the telephone cord like a teenager, coyly wrapping it around her fingers, unwrapping it with a flourish. She could not have realized how foolish she looked. Billy couldn't see her, and Joe felt fairly sure she didn't care what he thought on the subject. He left the kitchen and sat in the living room comfy chair, where he stewed in a hot broth of resentment. *I thought we were done with this crap*, he grumbled inside his head. *Why is she so insecure that she has to collect men like shells from the beach? I treat her like the goddamn Queen of Sheba. Why isn't that enough?* Abigail was on the phone a long time. Joe opened the front door for the breeze through the screen and poured himself a drink at the bar. He listened to his wife ramble on and on until he was glad he wasn't the one having to listen to it all. His grumpy disposition slowly petered out. By the time she hung up and joined him, he was falling asleep. She sat in his lap and planted a kiss on his brow.

"Hey," she said softly.

She was happy.

"Guess what."

He kissed her mouth.

"What?"

"Billy's taking us to buy guns tomorrow."

Joe recalled the sense of power he experienced at Billy's range. He wouldn't mind feeling it again. But an actual firearm purchase? He didn't like the idea of having guns in the house. Weren't they dangerous to have lying around? In their gated community, the odds of someone armed breaking in were minuscule. He looked into his wife's eyes. They were afire. They were determined. He knew it was useless to get in her way when she wanted something this badly. He capitulated.

"That's exciting," he said without conviction.

Abigail didn't notice. She pressed her breasts against Joe playfully. "It is."

She moved her legs to straddle him. He would have liked to push her aside, gently yet firmly enough to demonstrate an aloof disdain, to force her to ask him what was wrong. But her lips grazed the side of his face before she whispered into his left ear "Joe," and he gave in. Abigail was extraordinarily supple. Joe was extraordinarily motivated. They didn't need to leave the chair, although half their clothes lay on the floor beside it before they were through.

The next day at high noon, an hour Joe found metaphorically resonant, the Beckers waited for Billy Euston outside Uncle Dan's Gun Shop sandwiched between Uncle Dan's Fireworks on the one side and Uncle Dan's Auto Body on the other. Inside the auto body shop was a 1957 Studebaker, its paint half sanded off, its chrome a mess of pitted rust and dents. In front was an antique gas pump with a round plexiglass insert at its center like the face of a grandfather clock. The insert had an arrowed meter to measure gas from empty to full. There weren't specific numbers Joe could see. It was hard to tell by looking at it if it functioned or if it was merely a showpiece. The fireworks shop was adorned with images of rockets, Catherine wheels, and Roman candles exploding over a field of whitewash. A row of flagpoles bolted to the entry of each shop flew alternating Stars and Stripes and Stars and Bars. Red, white, and blue bunting was draped everywhere between.

It discomforted Joe to stand out in the open beneath the Confederate flag while cars sped past, perhaps driven by his neighbors, those
Yankee transplants of Catawba Plantation who often griped while they
lounged poolside or sprawled over a couch in the country club bar
about the South's fixation on its flag. Joe never joined in nor thought
much about it. But now, pinned down by the real thing in public, he
regretted his passivity over the flag and all the other symbols of slav-
ery he came across. Was he that much of a hypocrite? A coward? He
glanced sideways at Abigail to see if she was bothered, too.

Apparently not. Abigail was occupied reading the signage plastered
all over the shop windows. The adverts were so crowded together it
was impossible to see clearly into the store, which may have been the
owner's intent.

"Honey, look at this one."

She pointed to an ad for a semiautomatic rifle with sharpshooter
scope held by a smiling man in head-to-toe camouflage. It read: "Get
Dad what he really wants for Father's Day."

"Whoa. I thought they were banned," Joe said.

Billy Euston came up behind them, startling them. ("He's got the
sneaking up on people down pat," Joe later remarked to Abigail to
which she responded, "He must be an excellent hunter." They were
right.)

"Dan keeps that there for its historic value," Billy said, "same as the
old flag. If you look close, you'll see most of these are nostalgia pieces."

Joe wasn't sure he could judge that. Just about everywhere he
looked on the island, he saw nostalgia pieces. One of the things he
first liked about rural living was that it felt he'd stepped back in time
a decade or two. He'd grown weary of prickly urban anxiety. He loved
that Southern life was slow, peaceful, rocked in the bosom of the past.
Except for that flag.

He had no time to ask Euston his opinion on the subject. Billy
clapped his hands together, rubbed them, and said, "Alright. Let's do
it." He held open the door for them. Abigail and Joe obliged, entering with alert eyes and rubber necks, trying to take in everything at
once. They saw racks with shells and weaponry from both world wars
labeled as if they were in a museum, a cannonball from 1863, racks

of ammunition by caliber, hanging holsters, cleaning kits, ear and eye protection for the range, targets in bundles of fifty, and all-weather jackets and vests with compartments in which one could stash ammo and guns. At one end, a sign with an arrow reading Firecrackers pointed to a hallway with access to the shop next door. A counter opposite the Firecrackers sign showcased three shelves of handguns under locked glass and behind it, on the wall, rifles and long-barreled guns.

An older man with thick gray sideburns and a paunch leaned against the doorway to a back room. He wore aviator eyeglasses with clip-on shades turned up through which he studied the Beckers with his arms crossed over his chest and his neck cocked at a quizzical angle. His mouth was set in a shopkeeper's ubiquitous smile. "Afternoon," he said, stretching the salutation to four syllables. His drawl was so thick it could smother a small mammal. He came directly at Billy, passing the young couple with a polite, smiling nod on the way.

"Billy," he said when he was nearly right up against him. "How's Big George?"

"He's doing great, Uncle Dan," he said. "I plan to get him out of the house for a bit this week. These are the folks I told you about." Billy made a circumspect gesture toward the Beckers and commenced to introduce them. Uncle Dan did not fail to register an exceptionally pretty woman on the premises. His eyes fixed on Abigail while they barely acknowledged Joe. He approached her with more grace than his physique and occupation could ever promise.

"Come on over to my handgun case, darlin'," he said, leading her by the elbow to it. His words were slow and velvet soft. "Now what kind of armament are we thinkin' about . . ." Uncle Dan crossed over to stand behind the glass countertop facing her. The case with the guns was between them. His hand opened over what he considered the ladies' section. With the sweep of a vendor's practiced palm, he offered his wares. They might have been fruit or potatoes or onions. "Revolver or automatic?"

An hour later, Abigail purchased a snub-nosed .38 revolver, called a Pink Lady for its light weight and brightly colored aluminum grip. Though Uncle Dan showed him half a dozen firearms, Joe purchased the pump-action shotgun he'd thought about all along.

"Hard to miss with that thing," Billy told him, "but you got to come up to your target close if you want to do maximum damage."

"I'll depend on my wife for more distant threats," Joe said, glancing at Abigail who was deep in conversation with Uncle Dan.

"Let me tell you about my mortal experiences," he heard the man say.

Abigail nodded, encouraging him. He locked his eyes on her and held her fast.

"When I was in the motorcycle force, I nearly lost my life several times. I crashed into railin's on the interstate. I head-on'd with perps. I spun out on the cement. But I survived. I was the most blessed boy in the county, I surely was, until, one day, I died."

It was in January on a blustery afternoon. Uncle Dan was in pursuit of the town's high school principal, a man who'd been dancing in his jockey shorts on the top bleacher of the sports field, high out of his mind on meth, before jumping in his Volvo and taking off. Uncle Dan rode hard after him but the bastard made a queer turn Dan could not maneuver. Both he and the cycle plunged off an icy bridge and into the cold water. He sank to the riverbed then fell straight through it, sinking ever deeper down a dimly lit tunnel. In short, Dan died. For a little bit, he was in darkness and then he was on a rolling green with flowers of every color at its borders. Big, bold colors. There was music in the air, not church music exactly but some kind of like music he'd never heard before or since. It felt alive, it had a heartbeat, it had heat to it, too. Uncle Dan marveled. Suddenly, King Jesus stood in front of him underneath an arch made of rainbow. He felt great love radiating from his Lord. He was subsumed in affectionate divinity.

"He spoke to me but not out loud. His words were in a language I didn't know, but I understood what He wanted from me. He wanted me to go back to the livin'. From inside my head, I begged Him to let me stay but He refused. So I went tumblin' back through the tunnel, only up instead of down, then through the cold water, pushed along by a kind of wind at my back. I landed hard on dry ground. I opened my eyes. I was on the riverbank with firemen all around me. One had an oxygen pump to hand. One of them space blankets was spread over me. I'd come back. I lived."

Abigail touched his forearm.

"That's quite a story," she said.

"Don't I know it," Uncle Dan agreed. "I find tellin' it helps others who've lost someone. I tell it whenever there's a time of grievin'." He put back his shoulders and pulled in his chin. "Now, darlin'. I hear you write books. You want to help me write a memoir of my near death? It shouldn't be too hard. I know what to say. I wrote it all down once but the manuscript got lost in the fire."

Abigail was about to ask what fire when Joe interrupted.

"She doesn't write the books," he said. "I do."

Uncle Dan was at the very least monumentally surprised. He pulled the aviators away from his face so Joe could see the whole of his expression.

"You do? The children's books?"

"Every one."

Uncle Dan stepped backward.

"Me oh my. Well, alright then."

It was not lost on Joe that Uncle Dan did not redirect his request for a cowriter to him. Perhaps he knew there wasn't a chance after that blunder. There wasn't a chance before it, but the lack of asking lay between them like the rump end of an argument. Time to go.

They thanked him for his help and then followed Billy from the gun shop to a private shooting range he knew, out of doors in a cleared field by the back end of Daryl's Christmas Tree Farm. A twenty-foot, man-made berm was piled up at one end of the field. A wooden scaffold creating half a dozen stations suitable for the affixing of targets was constructed a bit in front of the berm, and a wooden bench like the one at Billy's house was set up twenty-five feet away from that. Billy clipped targets on three of the stations and moved back to stand between Joe and Abigail on the shooting side of the bench. "Now put your gear on," Billy said, donning goggles and headphones. "You don't want to shoot without your gear if you can help it."

Joe loaded shells into his shotgun and pumped it. He placed the butt against his shoulder and lowered his head so that his cheek fit snug as a bug against the stock. His eye stared down the barrel. He aimed at his targets that afternoon with clear and present malice. He pretended they were people, people he knew, all the people who'd dis-respected him from childhood on with the gunman from 7-Eleven thrown in. He shot. He pumped. He shot. He lost sense of what Billy and Abigail were doing. He had his earmuffs on; he couldn't hear them anyway. His eyewear fogged, but he could still see his enemies hover over the paper target, see them as clearly as if the sun was high in the sky with not a cloud in sight.

9.

After that, Joe went to the range regularly, sometimes with Abigail but most often alone. He found peace there. He liked to joke the range was his sanctuary, his place of communion with the universe. "You mean like church?" Billy asked him. Joe thought about it. "Well, yes, I guess so. If I had to choose a church to go to, the range would be the one." The point was shooting gave him a new kind of self-confidence. He felt a stronger man than ever before.

One Wednesday in late August, Billy dropped over in the middle of the afternoon. He hadn't been by in more than a week. Abigail hadn't complained. School had started. A few days a week, she took substitute jobs for grades one through nine. She wasn't aware of how long an assignment might last or what she might be teaching until she arrived in her classroom, which made it challenging work. Joe hoped that now she didn't have much free time, maybe she'd give up on Billy, especially as she'd learned something about Ella Price, even if the something wasn't much. She told him she had the sense that Ella was Billy's intimate friend, the one he told her was off and on, but of long duration. It was suspicion mostly. She wouldn't lower herself to ask the man outright, but Joe guessed it was enough to drive a wedge between them.

Abigail was working the day Billy dropped by. Billy took the news without visible chagrin, as if he knew she wouldn't be there, as if it didn't matter. Hopefully, he, too, had moved on.

When Joe let him in the house, he saw that Euston carried with him a bundle of printed envelopes emblazoned with a pig on a spit where an address might go. After ceremoniously rifling through them, he extended one with the Beckers' name on the upper right-hand corner. There was a solemnity about his presentation, in the way he paused, the way his hand moved, the look in his eye. Joe took it from him with an approximation of the manner in which it was offered.

"Shall I wait for Abigail to open it?" he asked.

Billy shrugged.

"It don't matter," he said. "It's an invite for my once-upon-a-time annual Labor Day party, which I've decided to resurrect this year in celebration of Big George's recovery from his recent catastrophe. There'll be music from the Cottonwood Boys, Jukebox Jackie, and if the mood takes me, I just might play myself. Oh, and don't worry, there'll be plenty to eat besides the pig. Ella's makin' mac 'n' cheese. Lillibelle's makin' her sweet and sour cranberry coleslaw. We got chicken, brisket, shrimp, succotash, biscuits. Then of course people bring stuff, too. They don't have to, but you can't stop 'em."

Joe was flattered to be included in the party, especially as he still hadn't met Big George. By now he'd learned that Ella was his mother and that he'd come home for recuperation after line-of-duty injuries, but Big George lived large only in Joe's imagination and not as a flesh and blood man. The way the crowd at Declan's spoke of him, Big George was someone singular, almost a folk hero. They recalled his glory days on the football field, the cheerleaders who'd loved him, and the lives he saved on the 911 line. His move to Atlanta was considered a loss not just to his mother but to the whole island, although they were proud of his achievements there as well. Legends were born of his heroics during this attempted robbery and that attempted rape. Some may even have been true.

Becker thanked Billy profusely until he realized he might be embarrassing the man. Billy took his leave soon after, while Joe ran ideas through his head of what they could take to the party. At first, he thought they could take a case of champagne, but that might be considered ostentatious. Abigail was an excellent baker. Maybe she could make her red, white, and blue trifle, the one she took to Fourth of July cookouts up North. Abigail's trifle always stood out on a dessert table. Judging by Billy's stack of invites, it was a big party with maybe hundreds of people. She'd have to make more than one trifle, plus find a way to keep it all on ice. He rummaged through the kitchen cabinets to see what they had in the way of large glass bowls—you had to see all the layers of tricolored trifle to appreciate it. He made a racket pulling out trays they could fill with ice to set the bowls in. Abigail's aunt had been a passionate cook. There were many to choose from. Joe spread half a dozen vessels over the kitchen floor. He was clattering about in the lower cabinet's deepest recesses on his hands and knees looking for more when his wife came home. Abigail cried out. He looked up. The Pink Lady was in her hand. It shook.

"What on earth are you doing?" she asked. "I heard crashing and banging from the driveway. I thought somebody was getting killed in here. My God. I could've shot you."

Adrenaline lent Abigail a strange luminosity. Her skin had sheen. Her hair stood out a little from her scalp, visibly damp at the roots as if she'd only just risen from sea foam. It flowed around her face, curling in then away from her cheekbones, from her neck. In any other circumstance, her husband would have declared her a vision. Under the current one, he was only remorseful he'd frightened her. Joe scrambled to his feet, took the gun away from her, and placed it on the counter. He wanted to say, *See? This is what I was afraid of* . . . but he bit his tongue.

"Everything's fine, sweetheart," he said. "Take some deep breaths."

He settled Abigail down in a kitchen chair and gave her Billy's envelope. While she read, he told her what a social coup their invitation was, how she needed to make her red, white, and blue trifle, and then he explained the commotion that spurred her to enter her own home, gun drawn. She put a hand to her heart.

"You'll be the death of me," she said.

She started to get up from the chair. Joe stopped her.

"Wait. How long have you been carrying that gun around?"

Abigail pulled the corners of her mouth down and wrinkled up her brow.

"Mr. Shotgun. I can't believe you're asking me that."

He straightened his back so he could look down at her and folded his arms across his chest.

"Well, I am."

She sighed.

"I didn't want to bother you about it, but there's been some trouble at the school. One of the teacher's assistants was assaulted last week in the parking lot. Turns out it was her sister's ex-boyfriend who gave her a beating over some role she played in the breakup. That boy's in jail, but it put all the teachers on high alert. So when I'm in the car, my weapon's in the glove box. When I'm not, it's in my bag. Once I'm in the school, I put my bag in my locker." She sighed again. "Look. I know what you're going to say. You're going to say that's stupid. Guns on school property and all. That's the way any person from Boston would think. But listen, we're not up there anymore. 'Round here, it's not such a big deal. Somebody told me when a young girl graduates from high school and her daddy buys her a car, there's a pistol in the glove box exactly where mine usually is. If she's old enough to drive, the saying goes, she's old enough to need protection."

Joe narrowed his eyes and put his face close to hers.

"Who told you that?"

She clucked her tongue, rolled her eyes, and got up.

"I don't know. I forget."

She gave him her back and went to the bathroom, where she turned on the shower and shut the door. It infuriated him.

"I don't believe you!" he yelled at the bathroom door.

While he put things back together in the kitchen, Joe tried to figure out why she'd angered him so much. He couldn't be such a hypocrite that it was okay for him to love his firearm but wrong that she packed hers. Maybe he'd gone total redneck, eager to stand up and protect his woman with his life. It undermined him that she was capable of doing it herself. He'd never have a chance to redeem his cowardice at the 7-Eleven.

It was a depressing thought. While he contemplated himself into a bout of melancholy, the phone rang. It was one of their friends up North, checking in. "Have you gone native yet?" she asked jokingly. "Sure," he said, "two hundred percent." There was a long silence from the other end of the line followed by a halting chuckle. "Is Abigail around?" His wife appeared in the kitchen in a short cotton robe with her hair tied up in a towel. He gave her the phone. "It's Esther," he said. Abigail went into the other room, speaking so softly he could not hear what was said.

A few days before Labor Day, a tropical wave appeared off the coast of Africa, but no one thought it would interfere with Billy's party. It was a slow mover and two waves had already dissipated in the middle of the Atlantic; one end of July, and one the second week of August. At Declan's, everyone said that was a good sign. Maybe all the storms that year would be a bust. They were the year before. Two years ago, a Cat 4 headed to the Gulf via Florida took a turn and missed the East Coast altogether. Li'l Debbie, a big woman so named for her facial resemblance to the child on the pastry label, spoke up from the rearmost table of the pergola. "Look here, I don't wish a 'cane on my worst enemy, but thank the Lord we weren't the target that time." Heyward Dinnest, a nearly retired landscaper, was in grabbing a beer before going home to his teetotaler wife, Doris. Doris was a bona fide church lady so when he said, "Can I have an amen?" everyone said "amen" out of respect. As she was sitting next to him, Abigail alone heard Dinnest mutter, "Although there's some I would wish a 'cane on, tell the truth." It sounded odd, but everybody has enemies, she figured, and thought no more about it.

Sure enough, the sun rose on Labor Day in a cloudless sky accompanied by a gentle breeze that barely disturbed the palmettos and caused not a rustle of oak leaves. The air was thick enough to swim through, but by now the Beckers were accustomed to humidity. Abigail spent the morning making two trifles and a tiramisu. "I hope Billy has a spot in the house we can keep them until dessert time," she said. Joe bought extra ice to be safe, along with a big bottle of Woodford Reserve small batch.

Along the approach to Billy's, pickups and sedans were parked on the side of the road at the edge of a drainage ditch. Abigail gave up counting them after twenty. They passed the equipment barn, where seven Harleys were parked, one after the other. "Too bad we missed that parade," Abigail said. They came to the smoker and the gardens, then the place where they had test-shot Billy's armory. Around the old bandstand, three tents were set up, housing tables for a food and drink buffet, along with dining tables and chairs. More tables and chairs were set up outside them. Everywhere there were people of the town, Black, brown, and white. Most knew one another. There was an abundance of hugs and high fives. They walked hand in hand or elbow to elbow, chatting, laughing, drinking, sitting down to eat from sturdy paper plates. They waved and smiled at the Beckers, whether they knew them or not. The scents of smoked pork and marijuana wafted through the air, pungent as a vast field of gardenia and roses combined.

Joe drove Abigail up to Billy's front door so she could unload the trifles and tiramisu without mishap. It took three trips. Joe offered to help but she refused him. "Ella's in there," she said between trips. Joe knew she was eager to spend some time alone with Ella, to get to know her role in Billy's life better. At the moment, Joe would be in the way. He should take his time parking the car. At least, that's the way he heard her.

He drove to the end of the car line, parked, then set off for the long walk back to the house. He carried big bags of ice in one arm and cradled the Woodford in the other. The bags were heavy, so cold they burned. One or the other slipped out of his grasp twice. When he picked them up again, he hugged them tight, branding his button-down shirt with damp Billy Euston dirt. Joe hefted the ice bags up higher to keep them from slipping until between the ice and the bourbon, he could barely see in front of him. He figured it was a miracle he didn't trip and fall. Then, at the threshold of Billy's trailer door, he stumbled, dropping his burdens. The ice bags skittered ahead of him. They slammed hard into a pair of muscular brown calves. The bourbon thumped onto an area rug unharmed. Inside the kitchen area, a large, young Black man with a shaved head branded by a curved surgical scar sat in a wheelchair near the refrigerator, two bags of ice wedged between his feet.

Abigail stood at one side of the man, Ella Price stood at the other. Ella wore a red sundress with braided straps threaded in gold. Her black hair with its remnant of red tips sprang from underneath a bright green-and-yellow bandanna tied in a bow at her brow. Around her neck was a thick gold chain. There were a half-dozen bangles of gold on each of her wrists. Her expression was soft and warm. Joe bent to pick up the ice bags and liquor. As he stood up, he glanced down at his shirt where the ice had wet it and muttered at the stain.

"Sorry for the entrance, Miss Ella," he said.

She touched his arm and squeezed kindness into it.

"Not at all, Joe," Ella said. "I've been tellin' Billy forever he needs to fix that threshold. You see there how it bows up? A trap for the unwary."

"At last, something I can blame him for," Joe said.

Ella laughed. Her regard made him feel taller, tougher than he was, which was why he next spoke to Big George, his voice strong and sure. He stuck out his hand. The man gripped it and shook.

"Big George, I presume?"

The man in the wheelchair nodded.

"Joe Becker. I see you've met my wife."

Abigail came over to her husband and put an arm around his waist. Out of the corner of his eye, Joe noticed that Ella's lips pursed in a manner he sensed was not hostile exactly, but at the same time, not amused or maybe anxious.

"Only just," Abigail said.

Big George gazed from one to the other of them with a quizzical look. He opened his mouth, then quickly shut it. Billy Euston had entered his home, which for everyone in it, and for reasons either undisclosed or not understood, felt an intrusion.

"Ah! The beautiful Beckers!" he said, oblivious to the tension. Whiskey breath came out of him in a colorless cloud large enough to envelop them all. "Com'ere, girl." He went to Abigail and pulled her to him, landing a noisy smack on her cheek. "And you, too, brother, com'ere." He spread out an arm and beckoned to Joe to come join them. Joe had no choice. He stood with his wife in her admirer's embrace. Billy smacked him on the cheek as well. Joe wasn't too happy about it.

Ella interrupted them.

"Weren't you goin' to play some music today, Billy?"

Billy moved away from the Beckers and slapped his thigh.

"Lordy, yes, I am. And it's gettin' to be that time. I best tune up . . ."

Billy left for the back bedroom. Joe breathed easier. Ella took her latest batch of mac 'n' cheese from the oven. Abigail stood motionless looking at Big George, who did nothing but look back at her. His large intense eyes bored into her like nails into wood.

"You're the ones, aren't you," Big George said.

His mother dropped the metal mac 'n' cheese pan on the counter. It made a sound like a cymbal.

"George!" she said. Her eyes filled. She knew what came next. Her son could not be contained.

"I know you're the ones," Big George said. "You can't hide it from me. The Lord give me a gift to know. Oh my, yes. The devil comes in pretty disguises, and I'm willin' to bet he don't make 'em prettier than you . . ."

"George, don't!" Ella said and then because he ignored her, she shouted out, "Billy! Com'ere this instant!"

Abigail backed into her husband's arms, frightened of the man in the wheelchair but unable to look away from him. Her throat went dry. She tried to swallow.

"I really don't know what you're talking about," she said.

"Yes, you do."

Billy came into the room carrying a banjo.

"What's goin' on?" he demanded.

"They're here," George said.

"Who's here?"

"The Jews," George said. "The lyin', cheatin', stealin', flesh-eatin', blood-drinkin' Jews."

10.

Billy Euston stood between Big George and the Beckers. "He don't mean it." He tapped his head. "Since the shootin', he's just not right."

Big George interrupted.

"Oh yes, I do. I cannot deny the words the Lord speaketh unto my mind."

Ella sank onto a stool by the countertop, put her head down, and wept silent tears of shame. "Forgive him," she mumbled, but whether she called upon her God or the Beckers wasn't clear.

The Beckers escaped to the outside. Abigail trembled, her breath coming hard and shallow. She leaned on Joe's arm to keep upright while they descended Billy's front steps.

"I've never . . ." she said, "in all my life . . . never . . ."

Joe leaned over to kiss the top of her head.

"I know, baby," he said.

"We need to go home."

Joe thought it over.

"No. You saw how upset Ella was. It's like Billy said: her son's not right. There's something wrong with him. We can't leave, or it looks like we're blaming her. She's a good woman. We're going to stay."

Joe tugged Abigail along to one of the food tents. They got in line. He took a chicken leg and a few slices of brisket, then heaped mac 'n' cheese and coleslaw on the rest of his plate. Abigail was too upset to have an appetite, but she took some salad and a square of cornbread to be polite. The whole time her eyes stung with bitter tears, but she'd resolved not to let anyone see her cry. She choked them back, stuck her chin up and out. Joe couldn't believe he was in a place possibly hopping with anti-Semites. His shirt had dried out some but he remained self-conscious about it. He'd lived his life making sure he never gave anyone an opportunity to say "dirty Jew" on his account and here, now, he stood in a damp, stained shirt, a live offering to any who cared to notice. Still, the two managed to exchange frozen smiles with a few acquaintances, and then the music started.

Like all good music, it transported them just when they needed it. They'd loved the Cottonwood Boys that first night at Declan's, and over time, had come to love them more. The boys sang "Reuben's Train," "Long John Dean," and later on Billy and his banjo joined them. When he took his place on the bandstand, partygoers applauded wildly. A few yelled out "Go, Billy!" and "Whoo-eee!" He put up a hand to shield his eyes and looked through the crowd for Joe and Abigail. Finding them, he pointed to get their attention. He nodded, raised his eyes to heaven, shrugged, and waited for them to signal that if all were not forgiven, it was at least understood, and no blame attached to their host himself. Joe grimaced and shrugged back. Billy lit into "Pretty Polly," which fired everyone up even more. The next song, he sang for them.

"I want to dedicate 'By the Rivers of Babylon' to a couple of friends of mine. They know who they are . . ."

He looked Abigail straight in the eye when he said it. People followed the path of his gaze and turned to smile at her, nod at Joe. She wanted to hide, but there was nowhere to go. Neither of them knew the song, although everyone else did. From its first notes, most people sang along, clapping in rhythm like Pentecostals, crying out the chorus.

By the rivers of Babylon
There we sat down
Yeah, yeah, we wept
When we remembered Zion
Then the wicked carried us away in captivity
And required from us a song
Now how shall we sing the Lord's song in a strange land?

It gave Joe and Abigail an eerie sense of comfort. Maybe they were in the presence of Christians who wanted the Jews restored to glory in Jerusalem, so they might build the third temple and fulfill the promise of Jesus's return. The Beckers could live with that. Their friends up North would caution that those same Christians thought Jesus would smite the Jews for not following him. Joe and Abigail figured they'd worry about that when the time came.

Maybe Big George was more than damaged. Maybe he was an anomaly. Then again, maybe people just liked a good reggae hymn.

There was a lot of whooping and hollering when the boys were done. The Cottonwood Boys thought it the climax of their set. They decided to take a break and refuel, so Jukebox Jackie came up to the bandstand to rock out his signature blues. Jackie was a short, stout man, black as printer's ink with a trim gray beard. He had a thick scar starting at the corner of his left eye that ran down his cheek through his beard to the underside of his chin. He looked like a man who'd climbed a rung or two out of the mire in his day, which lent authority to his songs. He plugged his guitar into one of the amps, fiddled with knobs, slipped a steel slide on the ring finger of his left hand and straightened up.

"I'm gonna start this off with a song for Big George," he announced. "Where is the man of the hour, anyway?"

Joe twisted his neck, left, right, then looked behind him. No Big George anywhere. Abigail huddled against him, looking around as well. Uncle Dan was in a cluster of people a ways behind her chatting up Malcolm X Rutledge, the county sheriff. The gun shop owner lifted his hand up close to his mutton-chopped cheek and made a miniwave with his eyebrows raised, his lips pursed almost to a kiss. Sheriff Rutledge followed his gaze, his brow wrinkled. It did not comfort. Close to the house a circle of Black folk congregated. Lillibelle Lamont was among them, straight-lipped and narrow of eye. Despite the rivers of Babylon, the sting of Big George's words resurfaced for the Beckers, pricking them under the skin. They felt conspicuous, ill at ease. They felt alien. They felt like Jews.

Joe thought about getting away and out. Meanwhile, Jukebox Jackie strummed chords, stretched notes out glissando with the slide, and waited.

Four strong men, three Black, one white, appeared at the top of Billy Euston's stairs flanking Big George's wheelchair in which the man sat, shoulders square, chest out, beaming bliss at the assembled. His rant against Jews had faded from his mind. It was in the past, over, until the next time it rattled through his injured brain. That was the way it went with him nowadays, in bursts of hot fire followed by benign calm. He'd worn Ella down to a nub. *You can't be serious*, she'd say when he threatened to ignite. *What have the Jews ever done to you?* and he'd give her a recitation of the perfidies of the sons of Abraham, their acts and plots against the gentile world, conspiracies of which she had no experience or knowledge. Sometimes when she entered her home, she felt she'd entered a madhouse and they'd locked the door behind her. After weeks of his confinement, she had not the strength to battle the fire anymore and reveled in the calm moments, throwing herself into them, devising soothing measures to elongate them, deepen them that the calm might smother the flames.

The men carried Big George and his wheelchair down the stairs. Lillibelle pushed him over to the bandstand. There wasn't a ramp for him to roll up, so Jukebox Jackie leaned over the edge and shook his hand.

"Here he is," Jackie said in a big, booming bass. "Know what this man is, people? He's a hee-ro. A homegrown, pork-fed son of the marsh and the blue sky hee-ro. We all know of his honor and his deeds. We love you, man. We're so grateful that the Lord spared you and brought you back home. I don't know about all them all out there, but I'd follow you into hell."

People whooped and hollered again. Some threw their hats in the air.

Big George's handsome features made a mute *aw-shucks*. His hands made *no-no-no* gestures out of modesty. He smiled and flashed his mother's perfect teeth. Jukebox Jackie opened his mouth. "Stand by Me" came out, first in a purr and then in a blues man's wail.

When the night has come
And the land is dark
And the moon is the only light we'll see

No, I won't be afraid
Oh, I won't be afraid
Just as long as you stand
Stand by me

At the chorus, everyone joined in, singing as strong and loud as they'd sung "By the Rivers of Babylon." The Beckers whispered together and decided that it was a good time to leave. Surely, they'd made enough of an appearance to assuage a sorrowful mother beset by a son with a disordered mind. Joe moved sideways, holding Abigail's hand. They inched their way past friends and strangers, muttering "Sorry, sorry." In the middle, they bumped into Axel Gullan who was loaded and garrulous. "Fuck you, you bastard, I spilled my drink!" he shouted. Gullan was infamous for his outbursts and the music was loud. No one paid him mind except Martha, his long-suffering wife, who rushed over to see what she could do to settle him down.

Joe moved Abigail along. When they were clear, they walked around the back to the driveway and the road out. By that time, sweat poured down their faces and trickled down their sides, their thighs. But they were out, safe. They marched onto the road with grim purpose, kicking up dust that clung to the damp skin of their calves. Soon they were covered in a thin coat of grit from the knees down. They felt in the very hell to which Jukebox Jackie would follow Big George.

They were nearly to the car. Three motorcycles roared past them, raising more dust. They squinted to keep specks out of their eyes. Someone called out their names. Joe turned to see behind them a runner enveloped in a cloud of dust. It was too thick to determine his identity at first. He became clearer the closer he got. It was Billy Euston, his arms making windmills to attract their attention. Through a scrim of dust, they were like the wings of angels or demons. Joe and Abigail could not discern which. They steeled themselves.

By the time he reached them, Billy had inhaled too much dirt. He leaned over their car, his hand braced against the trunk. He coughed and coughed, then said in his signature rasp exacerbated by shortness of breath, "You can't leave like this. You just can't. Please."

Abigail wasn't sure how Joe wanted to respond, so she said nothing. Joe didn't know what to say. He needed time. They regarded Billy in silence.

"Look. I know Big George was hateful," he said. "I'm sure it stung. But you can't believe Ella or I think that way. Please. None of us do. He's brain-broke."

Joe tilted his head in doubt.

"None of you?"

Billy tilted his in the opposite direction.

"Well, maybe Lillibelle to some degree. But you can't go by her. She hates most people, especial if they're white. And I can't say a few of the boys don't hate just about anybody who's not. But it's not like . . . like . . . a thing. 'Round here, we judge the individual, not the race."

Joe opened the passenger door for Abigail, then gestured that she should get in the car. She did.

"It's okay," he said. He closed her door. Just before he entered on his side, he said, "Don't concern yourself." He ducked in, shut the door hard, and started the engine.

It felt like a brush-off, and it was. Euston was clearly crushed. His whole body drooped as if the earth had opened up to draw him down into the dark.

Abigail opened her window. She waved her arm and waited for Billy to draw near. When he was close enough, she reached out and touched his cheek with tenderness.

"We don't blame you for what someone else said."

It took Billy all the restraint he possessed not to stick his head in the window and kiss her, despite her husband sitting right there. Not that he didn't love Ella. He did. Deeply. Ella deserved to have a loyal man at her side during her current troubles. But this gal, this sweet beauty, could tie his insides up in a knot with the simplest touch. *Yes*, he thought, *life is that complicated, that difficult, that god-danged covered in thorny roses*. He thanked them both and watched them drive away.

Once they'd turned off Cap'n Jack's Spit, Joe lit into her.

"Why'd you do that? Why'd you let him off so easy?"

Abigail was taken aback. Joe's cheeks were red. His hands gripped the steering wheel with knuckles gone white. His foot was heavy on the gas, and his tone loud and sharp. Over seven years, she could count on one finger the times Joe had yelled at her, and that time was now. She had no idea what to say, what would defuse him.

"I dunno," she mumbled.

"That's not an answer!"

One of her stored-up tears broke through her resolve and rolled down her cheek. He frightened her. She had to think of something.

"I guess . . . I guess because he looked so upset," she managed.

Joe slapped the steering wheel.

"Oh, he looked upset, did he? How do you think I feel? Did it occur to you that *I* might be upset? We only know what they tell us, Abigail. How do we know they're not all a pack of rabid anti-Semites laughing up their sleeves at us? Do you comprehend how ugly that was?"

"I . . . uh . . ." she mumbled in a small voice.

Joe slapped the steering wheel again, only harder. She jumped in her seat.

"Do you?" he demanded.

Unable to speak, Abigail nodded and hoped he saw.

"Okay," he said to himself, "okay."

Joe's lips were still tight, but his color went back to normal. By the time they got home, he seemed to have returned to himself.

At first, they didn't speak to each other. They were each shattered around the edges. No matter what either said, it would have been the wrong thing. It wasn't until later that night when they were going to bed after watching bad television that they confronted the day.

Joe lay with his arms crossed above his head, his chest bare. Abigail slipped into bed, then put her head over his heart. Normally, he would have dropped his arm and held her tight, but now he didn't. She craned her neck until she could see his eyes. They were dark slits looking down at her. She was afraid he was still angry so she spoke first, offering an apology to defuse him.

"I'm sorry if you think I didn't consider your feelings above Billy's," she said. "It's hard sometimes to think of you as separate from me. Whatever I feel, I figure you feel, too. I don't know why that is. It's probably because I love you so much . . ." She tried to give him her most adorable smile. It came out a little cracked, but that probably melted him more than a bright grin would have done. ". . . and believe me, I was still shaking inside from what Big George said. I was."

Joe turned out the light. His arm came down to caress her.

"I believe you. I'm sorry I exploded. What happened was unexpected. We've been welcomed here, and now this. I'm not sure how to feel, how to react. But what did we think? That there was some place in the world that loved Jews?"

Abigail sighed. Up North, neither one of them had experienced more than casual anti-Semitism, the social gaffes of the insensitive. They'd met people who used the phrase "Jew 'em down" in their presence without hesitation, or who wanted to know why they didn't have a Christmas tree ("Just because you're Jewish? But that doesn't make sense!"). They pretended that Jewish jokes were funny, just to get along. In Boston, Jewish cemeteries were desecrated every so often. Gravestones were smashed, swastikas painted here and there by kids who, they imagined, had no clear idea what they were doing. Each time it happened, they chalked it up to ignorance, shook their heads, and moved on. They knew worse things happened to Jews in other places, other countries, especially Israel. They donated money to the Anti-Defamation League and the Simon Wiesenthal Center when they could. But no one had ever accused them of wanting to rule the world or make matzah from the blood of babies.

"You have to ask yourself, Abigail, how much do we really know about the people we've gotten close to here? Maybe we rushed things along because we were new, and we were lonely. I mean, how tight are we really with Billy and Ella?"

"We hardly know Ella. But like you said today, she seems like a good woman."

Joe shifted in the bed so that they were facing each other. It was dark, but he wanted to try to see her expression.

"What about Billy? I like him alright, but I could say goodbye. Sometimes I wonder about you. You seem pretty damned attached. Tell me, Abigail. How tight are you with Billy?"

She sighed again. He couldn't quite see her face, couldn't judge the meaning of that exhalation of breath.

What a question, Abigail thought. Joe didn't need to know that Billy made her blood race, that she ate up every word out of his mouth. She loved that rough voice of his. Sometimes, she didn't care what he said as long as he kept talking. Things had happened between her and Billy that were none of Joe's business, as far as she was concerned. If he knew, he would regret knowing. She considered what to say for a long while, making her husband anxious.

At last, she said, "I think very, but not in a way that should worry you. I'm attached to Billy the way I'm attached to my friend Esther up North, for example."

Abigail doted on Esther. Their friendship was an ardent attachment, the kind women without sisters form with each other. Even after Abigail moved south, the two talked on the phone for an hour twice a week. But she'd never let their friendship interfere with her marriage. Joe thought about it and bought her comparison.

"I can live with that," he said, "as long as Big George's ideas don't come from Billy."

"Oh, I can't believe that."

"I guess."

They discussed whether or not Big George was to blame for a madness he did not choose. They discussed whether the degree of his moral culpability mattered if he were a danger to them and others. They came to no conclusions.

"Speaking of danger," Abigail said, softly so as not to irritate him, "when you lost your temper in the car, I thought you might drive into a tree trunk. I need you to promise you won't do that again. You lose your temper, you pull over."

"My eyes were on the road."

"Joe. You could have run over someone."

"There's no one out that way. I wouldn't have done that."

"Animals, then. You might have killed animals."

Joe thought about it.

"You're right. I'll pull over next time I lose my temper."

"Good," she said. "If past is prologue, that'll be next to never."

He kissed her and rolled over for sleep.

"I hope so."

Soon enough, Joe's breath became even. Abigail lay on her back and stared at the ceiling, trying to decipher the mysteries of her heart. It was hours before she slept.

11.

Before they went home in the middling hours of the early morning, Ella and Lillibelle cleaned up Billy 's kitchen. The mess outside could stay that way overnight; it was Billy's problem, but neither Ella nor Lillibelle were the kind of women who could sleep if a kitchen they'd taken account for was in disarray. Big George was outside with Billy and the boys, drinking bourbon, smoking, singing snatches of songs. Lillibelle looked out the window and remarked, "Party just doesn't end for some folk." She whipped a dish towel through the air. "Then there's us." Ella murmured something noncommittal. Let the men have their time. It didn't bother her.

She stuck her hands in the soapy water of Billy's oversize sink to see what was left and found the last of Abigail Becker's dessert bowls. She swept her sponge along its inside, then the out. Two more sparkled on the kitchen table, one set inside the other, along with a dozen baking tins and china platters waiting to be picked up by their owners over the next few days. She would return the Beckers' personally, she decided, and apologize for George's outburst.

It wouldn't be easy. What George said wasn't just rude; it was unforgivable. It was an assault. It distressed her no end that her son, a decent man, a righteous man, an officer of the law, had attacked a perfectly innocuous couple simply for their bloodlines—about which she had no complaint, and neither should he. She'd raised him better than that. He'd been spouting his hateful nonsense for a while now, and when they were in company, she shushed him every time. She never thought he'd accost a guest in Billy's home. She was humiliated for him. Humiliated for herself. It consoled her somewhat to believe that Big George's mind could not have made up his anti-Jew theories. Someone, sometime injected wild, hateful ideas in there, where they'd lodged God knows how long waiting for a gangbanger's bullet to shake them loose. She wondered who that was. Likely, someone in Atlanta. Over the years, she'd heard local people spout a few nasty things about Jews, but no one she knew took them seriously. There weren't many Jews in town, and as far as she could see, they weren't different from any other white folk. Some treated Black people well, like Mr. Schein who gave credit at his grocery store to folks when they needed it. Some didn't, like Mrs. Weinstein who called the police on Black children riding bicycles up and down her street. Since the civil rights days, Ella had learned to embrace the first type and avoid the second. Besides, she'd be hard-pressed to imagine any Jews she knew plotting to seize the banks or dig tunnels under the Pentagon.

In the end, it didn't matter where Big George got his hate. What mattered was cleansing his thoughts, purging them of malice. Every time Ella tried to work out who he would listen to that might affect a cure, she could only think of one man: Kelvin T. Jenkins, her second son, a stepson, lost to her and time. Some years ago, she'd heard that he was at a community college up North and was happy there, supporting himself as a janitor while he studied for a social work degree. Someone said he dated his Jewish professor's daughter. With his counseling skills, Kelvin could probably convince George that Jews were just like everybody else.

From the day they met, Big George adored Kelvin, and Kelvin adored Big George. Ella's son was ten years old, and Kelvin was eight. Kelvin was impressed with Big George's size. A slight wisp of a boy, prettier than a boy should be, Kelvin needed a protector, and at last he had one. Big George was impressed with Kelvin's wit. Everything he said was funny, and he could do impressions, too: from Bill Cosby to Sammy Davis Jr. to Pigmeat Markham. If you pressed him, he'd come up with a decent Moms Mabley. Kelvin's father was a charmer, and Kelvin was him to a tee—but without the petty lies and choreo-graphed deceptions.

When the family broke up, neither boy took the separation well. George blamed Kelvin's daddy, and Kelvin blamed Ella. She knew the stepbrothers remained in sporadic communication with each other, but she hadn't heard from Kelvin since the day he walked out her door in the company of his daddy, Slick Jimmy Jenkins, when the boys were in their midteens. That hurt more than all Slick Jimmy's sins against her. She'd loved Kelvin like crazy. His sweet little face melted her every time. She'd doted on him, tried her best to make up for the loss of his birth mother to alcohol and the street. Every once in a while, he let the sorrow, the shame he felt over his mother rage from his eyes like wild-fire. Then seconds later, his eyes went dead. When he looked like that, it broke Ella's heart, made her balled-fist angry with a woman she'd never met. After she was married to Jimmy for a few years, however, she could understand what drove Kelvin's mama to her desolate end.

Ella met Jimmy through Lillibelle who should have known bet-ter. At the time, Ella had relaxed into an imperfect union with Billy because she was so damn busy, and it was easy. When Billy was free, he remembered her son. He took Big George hunting and fishing, taught him how to hold a hammer, how to measure things, how to coax a purr out of a vintage car engine. They were close. But Billy wasn't dependable; his heart came and went like the seasons, predictable on the one hand, erratic on the other. Lillibelle harped in her ear that it wasn't good enough. She and the boy needed a real partner and father, not some fly-by-night, ants-in-his-pants honky. When her cousin, Jimmy Jenkins, came to town from Nashville, Lillibelle pushed them together, hoping for the best.

"Cousin Jimmy needs some settlin' down," she told Ella, "and you need some loosenin' up. He's a single dad, got a boy close to your boy's age, so that part would work. I'll tell you no lies—Jimmy likes the high life. He's a gambler, but as God is my witness, there's an angel sits on his shoulder. He's always winnin' big. He doesn't suffer from lack of money; he suffers from lack of saving it. I think livin' large is his escape. He's plain overwhelmed, trying to be both daddy and mama to his boy. When the going gets rough, he throws his hands up in the air and finds himself a poker game. Every man needs an anchor in life. You could be his."

It was not the most sterling of recommendations, but Lillibelle was persistent. Anything was better than relying on Billy Euston, she said. Ella didn't have to marry Jimmy, just meet him a few times. Get to know him. Step out a little. Did she mention he was good-looking, and a snappy dresser? Billy was sniffing around the new perfume clerk at Belk's. Lillibelle wore Ella down.

That first night, Lillibelle came to sit for Big George and Kelvin, who would arrive with his father and stay until the blind date was over. She whipped Ella into a state of excitement, giving her hair a fresh look by pulling the front back with a rainbow band and teasing out the ends. She made up her eyes with gold shadow, elongated them with thick black liner, and painted her lips a rosy pink. Ella chose a lime-green dress with a high neckline and sharp shoulder pads. Lillibelle laughed.

"He's gonna hurt himself if he bumps into you with those wings, baby," she said. "Here, try this."

Lillibelle reached into Ella's closet and took out a black sleeveless number with a scoop neck. Its hem landed four inches above the knees. She pulled from her purse large hoop earrings along with a spiked gold necklace and fastened them onto her friend's earlobes and around her long, elegant neck. Once Ella wiggled into the dress, Lillibelle found her a silk scarf the color of her lipstick to wrap around her shoulders, along with a clutch the same gold as her jewelry and eyelids. She looked magnificent. Butterflies in her stomach made her breath come fast, which enhanced the effect.

Big George and Lillibelle answered the knock on the door, ushering Kelvin and Jimmy into the foyer while Ella held back in the kitchen for a skinny minute to make a proper entrance. When she clicked in on her high-heeled sandals, little Kelvin staggered back, holding his chest with two hands like Redd Foxx. Big George grinned. Jimmy was tall, well-built, and wore a cream-colored double-breasted suit, a gingerbread turtleneck two shades lighter than his skin, caramel boots of fine leather, and a snap-brimmed white straw fedora, which he instantly removed with a flourish and a bow of his head. From that position of respect, he looked up at Ella with flashing black eyes. His nostrils flared slightly. He had a rogue's sideburns and a trim mustache, with lips a woman could feed on for hours. Ella was pleasantly surprised. As they left for a night of dinner and dancing at a jazz club uptown, she signaled a *thank you* to Lillibelle with a series of rapid blinks, her rosy mouth shaped into a perfect "o."

That evening, Jimmy turned on the charm. He complimented Ella, took great interest in her business, compared notes with her about the raising of Black boys in America. He made her feel important, vital to the world around her. When the band played songs he knew, he sang softly in her ear. After they got home, they sat around drinking sweet tea with Lillibelle until they woke up Big George and Kelvin by laughing so hard. At the door, while holding his sleepy boy's hand, Jimmy chastely kissed her cheek good night.

There followed a whirlwind of flowers, dinner dates, picnics and movies with the kids, along with champagne nights at fancy hotels downtown, where the staff had only recently been trained to fawn over guests of color. Accustomed to Billy's well-worn affections, plain ways, and sense of entitlement, Ella found she liked being courted by a man of the world. *This*, she thought, *is the way women are supposed to be treated. Like precious jewels. Like queens. Not like some old chair you fall asleep in when the mood strikes.* Meanwhile, the boys were inseparable, both in school and out.

Within three months, Jimmy proposed. At first, Ella hesitated, thinking of Billy, wondering if he might return to her. Lillibelle shot down that idea in a hurry. Every time she caught Ella staring off into space, she said, "Oh, he'll come back alright, but for how long?" Jimmy persisted. "The boys think we're family already," he said. "Might as well make it official."

Something in Ella longed for normalcy in love and the family she'd never had, not even with Herman, who'd loved his cause more than her. That winter, she and Jimmy were married by a justice of the peace with Lillibelle, the boys, and Ella's brother, Jackson, in attendance. They had a small reception at Ella's apartment with a handful of family and went to New Orleans for a wedding trip. Before the honeymoon was over, Ella discovered who she was married to.

People knew Jimmy in New Orleans. It was where he'd earned the nickname "Slick." Men, women, and children on the street, in the cafés, in the restaurants and clubs came up to Jimmy and said, "Hey, Slick. Long time, no see. What's shakin'?" Jimmy would fast-talk about a little bit of this, a little bit of that in Memphis, Louisville, and Nashville, before remembering to introduce his bride. Two of the four nights they were there, he excused himself at one in the morning to play poker. Ella didn't mind a whole lot—she was tired on the nights in question—but it didn't exactly feel like newlywed behavior. When Jimmy came home as the new day dawned, he had large wads of cash and beignets. She buried her misgivings.

After the honeymoon, things went well for a while. Jimmy devoted himself to the boys, treating Big George the same as he did Kelvin—at least that's the way it looked. He took a job tending bar at Harry's downtown, although he only worked three nights a week. The rest of the week, he found games of chance or arranged them himself in Ella's living room. For the first time in her life, drunk men, angry men, sad men, broke men became part of Ella's routine. She woke in the middle of the night to their boisterous disappointments, irate accusations, weeping confessions, and groveling beggary, as her husband cleaned up the table and put away the cards and chips. The boys woke, too. When she complained, Jimmy told her this was his livelihood, the way they made ends meet. Didn't she think his sleep was disturbed during the day when women came in and out of her shop downstairs, ringing the entry bells every ten minutes? Why was her business more important than his? She might have agreed with him, he was that convincing, if it weren't for the boys. His games were a questionable influence on them besides disturbing their sleep. Their schoolwork suffered. They needed quiet nights. Maybe he ought to take his business somewhere else, rent a room in town, and then they could all be happy.

Once he had a big enough stake, Jimmy did just that. His nights at the bar grew longer. There were days when Ella didn't see him at all, except at lunchtime when he woke up and she took a break from the shop. If it wasn't for the lovemaking they shared on those warm afternoons, the marriage would have splintered in the first year. As it was, she convinced herself that not spending much time together kept the passion fresh. He was always at her, and she liked that. After an ill-fated husband who chased after notions of revolution, and a lover who chased after other women, Slick Jimmy was the epitome of sensual devotion. By then, the dress shop was doing pretty well. For a woman of independent means, marriage Jimmy-style was enough.

One afternoon in the sixth year of marriage, while they were making sweet love, there was a roar and a screech outside on the street. Jimmy scrambled out of bed and looked out the window. A rusted Cadillac with a dented fender was parked in front of the shop. Jimmy lost control.

"Goddamn!" he said. "It's my girlfriend's husband!"

He pulled on his pants, grabbed his pistol out of an end table, and ran downstairs. From the window, Ella watched dumbfounded as he waved his weapon around, shouting. He shot a couple rounds into the ground for effect. The driver of the Cadillac was unfazed. A short, soft Black man in a tracksuit, he exited the car, dragging along with him a small, thin brown woman in a housecoat and fuzzy slippers. She had dyed blond hair and fingernails twice as long as Ella's. The short man tossed her at Jimmy's feet.

"She's yours now," he said.

Shoulders squared, he turned his back to Jimmy and his gun. Getting in the car, he slammed the door and roared off. The woman on the ground clutched her housecoat in two hands to keep it closed. Her elbows were scraped, her knees bleeding. She howled. Open-mouthed, she looked up at Jimmy pleadingly. He gazed up at his wife in the window. Ella gestured *Bring her here*. What else could she do, and still call herself a Christian?

An hour later, Jimmy's girlfriend left Elegance by Ella in a new houndstooth dress, size four, with wide lapels and oversize buttons. She wore a pair of Ella's ballet flats with newspaper stuffed in the toes. She carried her housecoat and slippers in a plastic bag with Ella's logo stamped on it. Jimmy left with her.

Late in the afternoon, the boys came home from high school to find Kelvin's father gone. Ella sat them down to tell them what had happened before the neighbors could. Kelvin fought back tears and fled to the boys' bedroom, where for several days Big George brought him meals, as he refused to come out. At the end of the week, Jimmy showed up, begging forgiveness from both boys and his wife. Kelvin was the only one who granted it.

Jimmy didn't give up straightaway. He tried gifts, tears, letters, and the intercession of mutual friends. Nothing worked. More girlfriends came into Ella's awareness. She went back to Billy, who was waiting for her. By her lights, an unfaithful lover was far better than an unfaithful husband. At least with the former, life was pretty much the same, with or without him; happier or sadder maybe, but mostly the same. With a faithless husband, a woman's entire life got disrupted, and there was more dishonor in it. She'd hoped that Jimmy would let her keep Kelvin. With the life he led, what did he need a teenage boy for? But he held on to Kelvin mostly out of pride, a little out of spite. He packed up the kid and hauled him off to Memphis, where he resurrected business associates and a working list of suckers.

Big George never forgave his stepfather for that. Long after she recovered from the girlfriend, Ella held the taking of Kelvin against Jimmy. In the years since, Big George and Kelvin had kept up with each other, but her former stepson remained loyal to his father. He wanted nothing to do with her.

The day after Billy's party, Ella slept in. Her sales clerk opened the shop. After catching up on a few phone calls about back orders, Ella closed business down early and drove over to Catawba Plantation with the Beckers' bowls. While she drove, her thoughts returned to Kelvin. Yes, she affirmed with a mother's desperate certainty, Kelvin was the one to help George. He might be the only one George would listen to. But how to find him and get him back home? She hadn't found his address or phone number in Big George's book. Lillibelle lost track of Jimmy and Kelvin years ago. Ella had asked Billy to put his ear to the ground and find him, but that would take time. Despair made her eyes wet. She blinked, flicking back droplets that sparkled like glass in the sun.

The guard at the Catawba gate that day was a Gullah man she'd known since childhood. They'd played in mud piles together, gone crabbing together, maybe even shared a kiss in fifth grade—although that could have been his brother, she couldn't recall. Ella felt sure he'd give her a pass without question, but he treated her like a stranger, or someone not to be trusted. He looked important in his military-style uniform, placing his hands on the belt that kept his khaki pants with their crisp crease hitched high, leaning toward her window until the broad brim of his officer's hat brushed the roof. He wore mirrored sunglasses. She could not discern the direction of his gaze.

"You sure Miz Becker knows you're comin'?" he asked.

"I was looking to surprise her, Anton," she said. "Got somethin' here to return." She patted the passenger seat where the crystal bowls sat cushioned by dish towels in a cardboard box. Anton stretched his neck to observe all of it with the corners of his mouth turned down.

"I'll have to call her," he said.

"Go ahead."

He phoned from the guardhouse. Ella drummed her fingertips against the steering wheel waiting. A line of cars populated by irritated drivers extended five deep behind her. "C'mon, hurry up," she whispered under her breath. He returned with a pass that he gave her through the window, saying, "You put this on your dashboard where it can be seen," as if she were a backwoods idiot who'd never been off the island. But she swallowed her pride and took it, smiling at him. She placed the pass on her dashboard.

"Speed limit's twenty-five miles per hour," he told her, "and it's enforced."

Now she was too stupid to read road signs. What happened to some men when you put them in uniform? Or had he been instructed to be hypercautious with visitors of color, even if he knew them? Was someone watching him? Ella shook her head and turned down the Beckers' street. *I'm getting as paranoid as my son*, she thought.

Abigail was waiting for her on the front porch, wearing short-short overalls with a white tee underneath. Her hair was loose, lifted by the breeze. Ella could not help but feel intimidated by her. She took a few seconds to compose herself, plaster a grin on her face, and open the car door. She reached inside the cardboard box for the bowls and held them close to her chest when she walked up the stairs. At the landing, she stretched out her arms.

"Afternoon, Abigail," she said, "I thought you might need these."
Abigail's cheeks reddened. Ella worried about why. She hoped it
was not about George. Abigail took the bowls.
"That's very kind of you, Ella. You didn't have to come out all this
way."
Ella breathed in deeply.
"To tell the truth, I wanted to apologize for my son . . ."
Abigail held up a hand to stop her.
"Please, stop. Billy told us he's not been right since the shooting.
It wasn't pleasant, to say the least, but we understand. Wait. That's not
what I meant to say. We don't understand because there's no excuse—
but at the same time, we don't attach any blame to you."
Abigail was nearly panting by the time she was done. She sucked
in some air and continued.
"Look, I'd invite you in, but the place is a mess. I had parent-
teacher meetings all morning, not one of them was easy, and I couldn't
lift a finger when I got home. I've been sitting in the middle of yesterday's chaos trying to find the strength to straighten up before Joe gets
home from the range."
Ella smelled the marijuana wafting out through the screen door.
She guessed Abigail was embarrassed to be found intoxicated. That
wasn't necessary; Ella was not a smoker, but just about everyone she
knew was.
"I'm sorry if I intruded," she said. "I was afraid you wouldn't see
me if I called first."
Abigail reddened just a tad darker. If she hadn't held three crystal
bowls in her arms, she would have reached out to touch Big George's
mama with a reassuring hand.
"Really, you must stop that. It wasn't your fault."
"Thank you. I want you to know we're goin' to do our best to edu-
cate him out of himself."
Ella turned to go.
"Another time?" Abigail said.
"Sure. Absolutely."
Ella got in her car and drove away, feeling mostly alright. Some-
thing nagged at her, but she didn't know what.

* * *

Abigail went back in the house. She put the bowls and trays down on the coffee table and flopped on the couch. Her hair was disheveled, her skin hot. She was flushed from her brow to the tee's neckline, but she looked extra fine that way.

"That was hard," she said. "I hated that."

Billy put an arm around her shoulder and nuzzled the top of her head.

"You had to do it, baby," he said. "She never would have understood. Sometimes deception is the better part of valor. 'It's a far, far better thing I do . . . ,' you know?"

She pulled back.

"Billy. You know Dickens?" she said, somewhat amazed.

He stiffened and clucked his tongue.

"What do you think I am? Ignorant? I went to school through ninth grade."

She cooed and snuggled in tight against his chest. It took Billy longer to relax.

12.

If it hadn't been for Mother Nature, Billy never would have had his way with Abigail, and he knew it. It was Mother Nature in the form of the river that gave him the two most astonishing carnal experiences of his life, Ella Price and Abigail Becker. Everyone in between was dust, even the gymnast he'd met on a fishing trip to Alaska in '83. When he got home the Saturday before his Labor Day party, after his first time with Abigail, drifting through a numb fog of satiation, he sat in the double-wide drinking Jameson and plinking out love songs on the upright until dark. His heart was full, his mind at rest. He had the novel thought that maybe his wandering life was over. He'd had the best. He could have them both again, whenever he liked.

Abigail confounded him. The day they'd made love on the river, she'd been insatiable. Then the day after his party, she was affectionate but not willing when he showed up unannounced. Why was that? He knew Joe had a meeting with a bookstore chain at their offices in Columbia. Between travel there and back, it would take up most of the day. Billy had been certain of welcome, but Abigail held him off, saying she was tired from a sleepless night and uncomfortable with betraying her husband in his own home. Billy worked like hell to change her mind until Ella showed up with the damn bowls. That pared down his chances from slim to none. Women were funny that way. They had second and third thoughts about betraying each other. Men rarely did.

On the river, Abigail had been voracious. He'd had a time keeping up. Now he had to figure out if she'd only wanted him out of fear, adrenaline, and the bliss of deliverance. Not that he was complaining; he'd replayed that afternoon in his mind dozens of times. He hadn't gotten tired of it yet.

It started when Billy ran into Joe at Harold's Stop and Go, filling up his tank. Joe was in a chatty mood. He told Billy that even though it was the Saturday of a holiday weekend, he was going downstate to research his work in progress. He intended to visit a rice plantation and a Civil War battlefield in the company of the best guide in the county. Both venues had cemeteries he was interested in. Billy called Abigail from the phone booth as soon as Joe pulled out of the station.

"You'd think he'd want to spend a holiday weekend with me," Abigail said. She sounded halfway between irritated and depressed. "I work hard all week getting ready to teach. But the opportunity came up, and without even asking me how I felt, he said yes."

"You didn't want to go with?" Billy asked.

"Oh, God no. He gets obsessed on research trips. He's taking notes and asking questions, while I follow him around like a puppy. It's like I don't exist. Makes me restless and bored at the same time."

Billy suppressed a chuckle. Marital disaffection was his friend. He'd give her a way to extract a taste of revenge.

"Then why don't you come fishin' with me?" he asked. "Do you like fishin'?"

She laughed in a way that sent a spark down his spine.

"I don't know. I like my fish filleted and wrapped in paper."

"Then we can just go for a boat ride on the river."

"That sounds nice."

Whoo-ee, Billy thought. *At last, I'll get Abigail alone on my own goddamn turf.*

He suggested Abigail wear a bathing suit under her shorts.

"You can swim off the boat if you like. Or float. I keep some of them giant inner tubes for my friends' kids."

He told her to meet him at a dock he knew without revealing that hardly anyone else ever went there because of the rocks that lay below the waterline after a hurricane had destroyed a jetty one hundred years before. (He didn't worry about rocks. He knew where every last one was.) His heart nearly popped out of his chest while she took down directions and read them back. Once they were off the phone, he packed up a cooler with chicken, biscuits, beer, and a split of white wine, purposefully omitting water bottles so she'd have to drink the alcohol on hand if she got thirsty. Who didn't get thirsty on a boat, cruising along in the hot sun?

Billy drove the boat over to their meeting place, docked it, and waited for her. The sun was high and bright. The air was particularly humid. *Yeah*, he thought, *she'll be stripped down to that bathing suit right fast.* He waited five minutes, then ten. Ella passed through his thoughts. So did Joe. But when Abigail pulled up to the dock and got out of her car, looking all sweet and innocent, he could hardly keep from panting. He put out a hand to help her aboard. Showed her around the cabin, the casting deck and stern. Took her up to the console, and they were off.

It started out better than Billy could have planned. He took them into the deep part of the river, where rocks didn't matter. A good breeze came off the water. He revved the engine to make waves that broke over the bow like sea foam, just to see if he could get a squeal out of her. It made him feel strong, young. He told her to keep her hands on the wheel and hold the boat steady, while he went below for the cooler. She put her hands where he showed her, braced her feet, and screwed up her lips. Her arms were taut, their muscles flexed. It was a beautiful sight. He went down to fetch the cooler, taking his time so she'd be tired when he returned, maybe sink against him while he shut the engine down.

There was a jolt. A hard one. He grabbed a bar on the wall to stay upright. *Jayzus*, he muttered, *what the heck was that?* The hull settled, but something was going mighty wrong. He ran up the stairs two at a time. He hit the deck, felt the air turn cold, the wind turn fierce. The boat shifted from right to left, and back again. Abigail trembled in the console, her hands off the wheel. Mouth agape, she looked at the sky. Billy looked up, too. "Fuck," he muttered.

There was a huge black cloud on the horizon, advancing toward them. It was flat on the bottom, blue below itself. It wasn't just an angry, sumbitch thundercloud; it was a tornado cloud if ever he saw one. As soon as Billy grasped the nature of their position—the highest object on a flat plane of river and marsh grass—the thunder started, loud as cannon fire. Then a jagged bolt of lightning shot out of the black cloud into the suddenly roiling river. It lit up the dark water as if the sun was sitting smack-dab inside the cloud, generating bolts from its fiery center.

The storm advanced. They had to get out of there, or they were lightning meat. Billy searched the riverbank for shelter. God was with him. "There!" he shouted to Abigail above the noise of thunder and rain. A shed at the end of an old, crumbled dock beckoned like a castle in the mist. They drove toward it, dropping anchor amid great waves and flashes of light. The storm was at their heels. They jumped onto the dock. It bore their weight. They broke into the shed and lay on the floor, in shock and horror at nature's rage, but breathing easier now that they had shelter.

Abigail huddled against him. Billy stroked her back, made soothing noises to calm her. She felt warm, supple. He smiled. Not everything about the storm was bad, he told himself. They were dry. They were safe. They were alone. He chanced to look up to thank his dark angels, when lightning hit the ground outside and cast the roof beams in brilliant light. "Jayzus, help us," he said. Abigail looked up and screamed.

Across the length of the ceiling above them was a mass of spiderwebs a foot thick. They knit together tight as woven cloth to form a dense gray canopy dotted with bodies. Here and there, threads came loose to dangle eight-legged beasts overhead: brown spiders, black spiders, painted spiders, big spiders, small spiders, stationary spiders and ones on the move; hundreds of spiders, it looked like. Billy knew this wasn't normal. Spiders of different types didn't hang together. But here, they were assembled like an avenging army ready to spring against the weakness of man.

He held Abigail tight against his chest so she couldn't get up and run into the storm. She squirmed, desperate for escape. In as cool a manner as he could fake, he said, "We have a choice. We can stay calm in here, or we can go outdoors and face the whirlwind. I'll leave it up to you, but that's a tornado sky up there. There'll be twisters."

Billy loosed his grasp to get a look at Abigail's face. Her eyes bulged. She didn't breathe. *Okay,* he thought, *I guess that's an answer.* He got them both on their knees. They crawled to the door, pushed it open, and scrambled out into the storm. Billy pushed Abigail flat on the ground and lay on top of her, to keep her there, low and still.

Havoc raged around them. The air whistled and howled from all directions. The boat flipped upward, then slammed down on the river's surface. At the tree line, branches bent low. A pine tree cracked, and its pinnacle punched through the dirt. Fifty yards away, a water spout twirled up into a black cloud-maker. "Stay out there," Billy whispered to it, "stay."

Abigail shook beneath him. He closed his eyes and prayed. From behind his eyelids, he saw lightning flash. He smelled fire. He heard the wind making that goddamn train sound, followed by a whoosh. He couldn't tell how close to them it was.

It might have been only fifteen minutes. It felt an eternity. Eventually, everything stilled to a heavy, pelting rain. Billy picked up his head and saw that the black cloud had moved on. A golden sky on the horizon beckoned. Overhead there were rain clouds, but they lacked ferocity. After what they'd been through, the clouds looked friendly, benign. Billy and Abigail stumbled back to the boat, leaning into each other. Miraculously everything on deck looked intact, although it needed bailing out. They worked at doing so together, in silence. Having a chore to accomplish steadied their nerves. When they were done, they went below. Abigail shivered. Billy wrapped a blanket around her, settled her on the canvas-covered couch, and got out some whiskey. When he turned again, she was lying down, her eyes full of tears. Her thin summer clothing and the bathing suit beneath it was plastered against her skin, revealing her glories more starkly than if she'd been naked.

Abigail's lips quivered. She opened the blanket to him and said, "We could have died, Billy. You saved us." Her voice was so small, it broke his heart. He helped her take off her mud-streaked clothes. They stuck to her damp flesh as if the hand of her husband wanted to keep them there. His own came off easily. Her arms wound around his neck. Joining her under the blanket, he kissed her lips, her neck, her shoulders, ignoring the grit that had coated her while they were in the grass, huddled against the storm. Together, they affirmed they were very much alive. More than once.

Later that night, back home, Billy roused himself and drove to Ella's. She had all the paper and plastic goods they'd need for the Monday party and wanted him to pick them up so she could have room in her kitchen to cook mac 'n' cheese for 150 after Sunday morning church service. She'd closed up the shop and spent her entire Saturday buying everything. Thinking of her labors gave him a twinge of guilt, but not so much until she mentioned the storm.

"That was a tempest and a half in the middle of the day, wasn't it," she said. "When I left Piggly Wiggly, I had to pull over until it passed. I thought about you. I wondered what you were doin'. It'd be just like you to go out on your front deck to watch the lightning."

He slipped into his good old boy mask and gave her a soulful look.

"You know me so well, don't you, darlin'. Ain't nobody knows me so well as you."

He gave her a hug. She pulled back to look him straight in the eye.

"Mm-hmm. That's right, I do. Don't you forget it."

She slapped his shoulder and broke away. Big George chose that moment to crutch himself into their presence, distracting Ella, for which Billy was grateful. Two more minutes alone, and she would've been grilling him. Before he left for home, he took Ella into her bedroom and made love to her in an especially eager manner, which aroused a fresh bout of suspicion in her, but she had too much to do for the party to give it more thought. She tucked away her questions for another time. Billy drove home with the party goods, thinking a man didn't get much luckier than he'd been that day.

Abigail had a different kind of night. Joe didn't get home until late, giving her hours to get her emotions under control. She was hyped-up, weirded out. She couldn't close her eyes without seeing spiders. She couldn't listen to music without hearing thunder. She showered, but that brought back the rain, and the feel of rain recalled Billy's weight covering her, protecting her. When she dried herself off, it felt as if his hands held the towel. It was difficult to know whether her sensations were ones of excitement or fear. In her torment, she phoned Billy, but got his answering machine. She hung up, afraid to leave a message someone else might hear. Instead, she practiced telling him that this was the first and only time anything like that would ever happen between them. She had a life she loved, a man she loved, and no affair was going to change that.

That calmed her for about five minutes. Then she relived her ecstasies of the afternoon, and before she knew it, she changed her mind about shutting Billy out. Seconds later, Joe arrived home.

Abigail gave him a warm kiss. He asked her how her day went, and she replied, "It was nothing special. Laundry and a little food shopping." The lie came out smoothly. She listened with rapt attention to his recitation of the details about the Civil War he'd discovered that day. She stood behind him to rub his shoulders while he sat eating the light supper she'd saved for him.

Joe went to bed right after supper. Although Abigail doubted she could sleep, she went to bed to keep him company. He fell asleep quickly. She hugged his body from behind, trying to hold on to the sense that nothing had changed between them when everything had. Their sweet past, every last emotion and pledge, was stained by her infidelity. She imagined their entire life together as a highway leading inexorably to a disastrous destination; a highway she'd sped along blind to signage and speed limits, racing too close to barriers in a state of blissful ignorance. Over the years, she'd reveled in the devotion other men gave her, foolishly thinking she could handle them all without damage. *What ego*, she thought, *what selfishness!* How had Joe put up with it? He was a saint that deserved far better than she. Tears of remorse rolled down her cheeks, wetting her pillow. For the first time in her marriage, she had no idea where she was headed. She burrowed deeper into Joe's back, searching for the security of years gone by. He stirred, and she shrank back, terrified he'd awaken.

On Sunday, Billy called her in the afternoon. He rang twice and hung up. Abigail pretended she forgot to buy something for her tiramisu and sent Joe to the market. As soon as the car was out the driveway, she phoned Billy.

"Hello," Billy said.

"Hello," she whispered.

"Is that you?"

"Yes."

"You're whisperin'. Is he there?"

"No."

She cleared her throat. For reasons she didn't know, she continued to whisper.

"I can't stop thinking of yesterday."

It was the truth. She felt like Billy had taken control of her mind. She thought maybe she was in a weird kind of love, desperate and passionate. He was older. He wasn't very good-looking. None of that mattered. *Lust will have its way*, she thought, and there it was.

"I can't stop either, baby," Billy said, "I don't know what you want me to do. Yesterday was one of the highlights of my life. I got to tell you that."

She was silent, absorbing the fact that maybe Billy loved her, too.

"Abby. Are you there?"

"No one calls me Abby," she said.

"I know."

She took a deep breath and told him as much truth as she dared.

"It was unique for me, too."

Someday she'd tell him how unique.

"So. Do you want to do it again, or not?"

Her stomach fluttered, then her chest. If she said yes, she'd be a goner. One more time with Billy, and that would be it for Joe. He waited. She remained mum.

"Abby. It's okay if you say it's over, but I need to know what to do with my heart."

She took the coward's way out and lied.

"Joe just got home. I gotta go."

She hung up, stood in the middle of her kitchen bug-eyed, amazed at herself. Her hands shook. It was hard to breathe. Her feet were frozen to the kitchen floor, unable to move, her mind raced with images from the storm and its aftermath. She heard Joe's car in the driveway a few minutes later. *Thank God*, she thought. Before he fully crossed the threshold, she had her arms around him, pulling him to bed.

13.

Kelvin Jenkins wasn't that hard to find; Billy found him in two phone calls. The first was to Pastor Ronald T. Quirk of the Holy Tabernacle of Jesus Christ by the Sea. Ella might have asked the pastor herself if he knew anything, but she'd been so busy looking after George, she'd stopped going to services. A lecture from Quirk would sever her last nerve. She asked Billy to do it for her.

Everyone knew Quirk kept close track of former parishioners, along with the extended families of his active flock. He had a Christmas card list of epic length. Some wag at Declan's claimed it was rumored to be under consideration for the *Guinness Book of World Records*. When he called, Billy took care to ease into the question of Kelvin's whereabouts. Pastor Quirk guarded his database ferociously. According to him, there wasn't a clergyman in the entire state who didn't envy it. It made sense to tred gently. At first, Billy pretended he was calling to double-check the date on a church function for which he'd promised to provide fried chicken. Then he came up with a casual reminiscence to open the field of inquiry.

"Pastor Quirk," he began, "do you remember that time way back when you showed up to one of Jimmy Jenkins's poker parties to drag Esau Fergis out by the earlobe?"

The shepherd of the island's largest flock laughed heartily, remembering.

"Sure do. He had no business at that game while his wife was in labor. You know, he thanked me for it later. Yes, he did."

"So I heard. You managed some good work there."

"I appreciate your sayin' that, Billy. But it wasn't me. It was the Lord who guided me."

"Amen."

From there, the pastor was eager to share memories of occasions when those he inspired went on to commit Christian acts of rare bravery or charity, followed by a catalog of young people he'd mentored to brilliant accomplishment. Billy brought up Kelvin Jenkins.

"He showed so much promise," Billy recalled.

"Kelvin? You'd be right, except I lost track of him." Pastor Quirk gave a short exhalation of breath, hitting a sour note. "He's one slipped through my fingers. Jimmy whisked him out of town, then they moved around so fast, I couldn't keep up. Lord knows, I tried."

"That's too bad. Big George's mama thinks a visit from Kelvin would do good for her boy. He's battlin' the brain injury, don't you know. But she's not sure how to find his brother."

Pastor Quirk pondered a bit, then made a suggestion.

"Speaking of Esau Fergis, why not call him? He knows all Kelvin's daddy's old poker buddies," he said. "Somebody might be in touch."

It was a decent idea. Billy started with Esau and hit pay dirt. Esau told him Kelvin was in Roanoke, practicing his social work among factory workers and miners. He happened to have his number; one of his wife's brothers lived there.

When he tried the number, Billy reached an answering machine, which was just as well because he had the feeling Kelvin liked him even less than he liked Ella. He left a message informing him that Big George had some work-related injuries. "To be blunt, multiple gunshot wounds," he said, "ones that have rendered him temporarily crippled and not right in the head." He apologized for telling him such difficult news in a message, but would he please call Ella at such and such a number as soon as. Ella thought maybe Kelvin could help with Big George's recovery.

After he hung up, pleased with himself that he'd been able to accomplish the chore Ella had given him, he called her and reported his progress, giving her Kelvin's number.

"Oh, Billy," she said, oozing affection, "you've always been such a help to me. Thank you."

Ordinarily, Billy Euston would have walked taller that day for having done a service to a woman he admired and with whom he felt the indelible connection of history. Instead, he was shamed by her gratitude. He knew he'd done her wrong. The old rules about hearts having their way felt like kid stuff. Ever since that day on the river with Abigail, he worried Ella would never forgive him if she found out. Very recently, he'd come to ponder how lonesome his life would be without Ella in it. Qualms of conscience were new to him. He wondered if that meant he was slowing down, getting old. When he met Abigail later that same day, he was aware that his qualms muted his desire.

By prior arrangement, she came by the house after school. It was their fourth time together. The first was that day on the river; the second when Ella interrupted them midseduction, and that was that. The third was a ten-minute, opportunistic assignation caught on the fly; sex so abrupt, he wondered if he'd imagined it afterward. That day, the fourth, Abigail was in a coy mood, tiptoeing up to him, then shrinking back in a tumult of emotion like a cartoon Southern belle. Billy sensed that she wished to be swept away to absolve her guilt, but he did nothing to influence her. It was too much work. He'd never liked emotional women with unpredictable demands. He liked them eager, straightforward. That day, Abigail struck him as unstable. Watching her prance about, pouting her lips, raised the hair on the back of his neck.

She either wanted him or she didn't, he decided, and if she didn't, or if she wanted to play games with him, it was probably time to head back to Ella before he got in deeper. Soon as he could, he made an excuse to leave, acknowledging to himself that once again he'd wanted a woman desperately and then, having had her, pulled back. It happened three out of every four times he strayed. He'd always have his memories of Abigail. No one could take those away. Until the day he died, every squall he found himself in, every spider skittering along the floor, would bring a stab of heat to his gut and a secret smile to his lips. It was enough.

* * *

Kelvin didn't take but a week to come to town. He didn't call first, and Ella nearly gave up hope. As it turned out, Lillibelle saw him before Ella did. Every change of seasons, Ella had to switch up her stock in the store. She put the garments of the old season on sale and showcased fashions of the new. She'd take day trips upstate to buy fabrics. Sometimes, she spent a weekend in Atlanta or Raleigh to see what was new in the world of her contemporaries. It was a very busy time, especially with the party season that swamped the winter holidays coming up. In contrast, around the middle of September, Lillibelle's workload decreased. Her mind turned from the fragility of tomatoes and butter lettuce to hardy winter produce: collards, chard, turnips, onions, and squash. Her deer corn was ready for harvest, and soon her sunflowers would be, too. For the next few months, Lamont Farms could run on autopilot: keep the deer, the beetles, the fox, and the rabbits off the crops, and they nearly grew themselves. Her foremen handled whatever came up, as long as the rain didn't get too heavy. Traffic at the farmers' market slowed down, too. She didn't have to be there until the spring, except for a handful of weeks around Christmas. For a few short months, she had some free time. That year, she decided she'd spend some of it helping out Big George. She had no immediate family of her own. Big George was the next best thing to a son or nephew for her. He was doing much better lately and had Lillibelle to thank, having started using a cane because she gave him one.

Lillibelle treated Ella's home as if it were her own. She entered at will, without knocking. September brought out Lillibelle's lumbago due to all the bending and lifting she did during the high growing season. By fall, the taking of stairs was a torture. She had to climb one stair and rest, then another stair and rest.

On the landing, she stuck her head through the front door. "Aunt Lilly's here!" she called, catching her breath and straightening her back. "We're in here," Big George replied. To her surprise, he sat on the living room couch with a striking young woman. She was dark-complected, but her eyes were angled like an Asian's. Their color was a startling green. Some kind of Arab eyes, Lillibelle decided. The young woman wore city clothes: a deep red skirt, white blouse, red-and-white-flowered jacket, and wedged heels. Her legs were primly crossed at the ankles.

"Well, now, who might this be?" Lillibelle said in a welcoming tone. She extended her hand. "I believe I know every Black girl on this island, but I don't know you. You from over the bridge, honey?"

"Ruby's with me, Aunt Lilly," someone in the kitchen said.

A slim young man, his slight frame enhanced by a well-cut dark blue suit, a red bow tie, and pale blue dress shirt, entered the room. He had a dish towel over one arm and carried a tray with teacups, a steaming teapot, a sugar bowl, and milk. He laid it on the coffee table in front of the couch, straightened up, and opened his arms. Lillibelle rushed into them.

"Kelvin," she said, her voice thick with sentiment. "It's been too long."

They rocked back and forth in each other's arms. She pulled away, placed a palm on either side of his head, and scrutinized.

"More than ever, you look just like your father." She passed a hand over his close-cropped hair. "Pure sugar. Angel touched."

Kelvin mugged.

"A very dark angel," he said in a way that made Big George laugh. Lillibelle swatted his shoulder.

"Always the joker," she said.

Kelvin introduced the woman in red as Ruby Jenkins, his wife of two years. Congratulations went around. Ruby got up to fetch another teacup, and they all sat down together. Lillibelle and George exchanged a bemused look that hot tea was being served instead of sweet. Their visitors struck them as more North than South, especially Ruby.

"You've picked up some curious habits away from here," Lillibelle said to gently poke fun at them. "Maybe up in college? Can't imagine what that was like."

Kelvin took her seriously. He told them he'd never missed the low country once he left. He'd never liked the wet heat much and favored the mountains and the valley. He told them about his job in Roanoke, how satisfying it was to help people in trouble. Ruby offered testimony to his professional reputation. She was a secretary at the welfare office and knew how people judged him.

"Folk thank the Lord when they learn Kelvin Jenkins is assigned to their case," she said. "He's a real fighter. He'll get you what you need." She patted her husband's knee. "He learned the hard way about life, but he learned good."

Kelvin nodded. *Ain't that the truth,* he thought. Every aspect of Ella's living room pained him to look at. It brought back memories of the only happy times he'd had as a child in a real family, of how in a single day, all comfort and joy was ripped out from under him after a strange man threw his half-dressed wife into the street. That day devastated Kelvin. It made him bitter. It gave him a sharp edge. He knew it wasn't fair to blame his stepmother, but he did anyway. She should have loved her sons more and held on, despite his daddy's wrongdoing. How much harm could it have done her to wait until the boys were out of high school before booting Slick Jimmy Jenkins out? Far less harm than being abandoned did to Kelvin, that's for sure. Because life is complex, contradictory, and unexpected, there were other times he thought he should thank Ella Price. Closing off his heart had made a man of him. It got him ready for quitting his father the first he could, the day he came eighteen. It got him ready to do mean work to put himself through college, then graduate school. In class, he needed to be the best, which was its own kind of wall around the heart. It got him ready for that, too. He grew up tough and strong. There were only two people in the world he allowed himself to care about. One was his wife, and the other was Big George. Everyone else, including Lillibelle, Ella, his coworkers, and his clients, were either ghosts to be managed, or problems best solved with cool detachment. Expertise in the latter was what made him an efficient advocate. Whatever his personality lacked, he filled in with what he picked up of the con from his father. He could play high or low. If he had to, he could fake empathy with the best of them.

He asked Big George to tell him about the shooting. He wanted to hear it in his own words. George opened his mouth to accommodate him, but nothing came out. His eyes grew large. They wandered around the room searching for what part he wanted to tell, what part he needed to keep to himself just yet. Kelvin reached over and put a hand on his bicep, squeezed a little. The look he gave George was that of a loving brother and a professional commiserator. George lost himself in that look and said, in broken voice, "They killed Pappy Parker." Then he sobbed.

In short time, Kelvin was by one side of him on the couch, and Ruby the other. They closed in on him, stroking, muttering compassion and solicitude. "I'm sorry, sorry, sorry," they said in such a quiet, rapid manner that Lillibelle heard their comfort only as "ssssss," sibilant, a serpent's hiss.

Once Big George calmed, Kelvin gave Ruby a little nod. She asked George if he'd like to go for a walk. "You can show me the neighborhood," she said. "I'm sure your therapist wants you to get your walking in, and it's a beautiful day." He accepted her offer. It was an adventure for him. He hadn't walked down the street with a beautiful woman for months. They got up together and went outside, leaning on each other, Ruby holding on to his arm, Big George using his cane.

Kelvin looked down from a window to observe their progress.

"Ruby will keep him busy a good while, Aunt Lilly. Tell me what's going on."

Ella would have done a better job of it. Lillibelle told him without nuance that since the bust gone bad, Big George was full of conspiracies. Every day it got worse. Say "Good morning, George," and he'd be on a tear about Jew banks and Jew media, Jew lobbyists, and when he ran out of them, Israelis. Over Labor Day, he'd insulted friends of Billy's right in front of Ella. They happened to be Jews. He accused them of drinking Christian blood. Kelvin winced.

"His mama thinks maybe you can help bring him back down to earth," Lillibelle said. "He always listened to you."

Kelvin turned toward the window with his back to her. He looked over his shoulder and pursed his daddy's celebrated mouth.

"I don't know as I can, Aunt Lilly," he said. "I've seen this kind of thing in my work. If it's not the Rothschilds or Murdoch, it's the CIA, space aliens, and communists. Someone or thing is always trying to control the planet and everyone on it. People who think like that are often unreachable."

"Mm-hmm," Lillibelle said. She didn't know much about the Rothschilds except that they made wine, and she hadn't a clue who

Murdoch was. She knew as many communists as she knew space aliens.

Kelvin continued.

"Part of it's understandable. Life is difficult and unpredictable. The innocent suffer injury through no fault of their own. It's maddening, incomprehensible. How could the bad thing have happened when they'd done nothing wrong? They look for reasons. They blame themselves. What if I hadn't made that left turn or worn that dress? It still doesn't make sense. When they find someone else to blame, suddenly it all falls into place. The scales of justice achieve balance. Victims are no longer undone by the random. Of course, the plots they imagine are ridiculous. But there's a danger in disabusing them of their delusions. If you take away the explanation they've found, the one that turns the unjust into the rational by irrational means, they're back in the pit. My colleagues may not agree, but I'm not sure it's worth the trouble. A better way is to teach them to manage their thoughts. Drugs can help."

Kelvin spoke over Lillibelle's head. He'd lived a long time away from the island, he likely didn't recall how to talk down home anymore, but it sounded he was saying Big George was hopeless; there was nothing to be done. The idea filled her with grief. About Jews she didn't give much of a damn. They were another species, as far as she was concerned. But her poor friend Ella was at her wits' end. She couldn't live with the ravings coming out of her son much longer. What would happen then? She might tell him to leave. Where would Big George go, and how would Ella withstand the loss of him? For both their sakes, she had to convince Kelvin to try. He sounded so educated, so smart. If he couldn't help, no one could.

"Can't you at least convince him there's no drinkin' of blood?" she said, but weakly.

Kelvin turned from the window to face her. His eyebrows were raised, his mouth curled into an expression of cool amusement.

"Now, that's over the top," he said. "I suppose I could talk to George about that."

His humor was too dry for Aunt Lilly. She took him at his word and breathed a sigh of relief.

She asked about Slick Jimmy. Kelvin told her he'd passed away five years before in Memphis, mortally wounded in a knife fight with a white man who'd called him a nigger and a card cheat. Kelvin smiled again in his world-weary way. When he spoke, there was the tiniest catch in his throat.

"I believe it was the 'card cheat' that riled him," he said. "He'd been called 'nigger' plenty times before."

Lillibelle praised Jesus and called blessing down upon Jimmy Jenkins's soul. She listed his good points.

"He was a fine dresser. He knew how to make a woman feel like the most important person in the room, and my oh my, how he could talk . . ."

It didn't sound like much, but her spirit grew heavy, remembering him. It saddened Lillibelle to think white men had destroyed both Ella's husbands. She dreaded telling her about Jimmy's death. For once, she softened toward all the world as she contemplated damaged folk everywhere.

"Why are people so eager to kill?" she asked.

Kelvin thought a bit, drawing on the ugliest diatribes of his most incorrigible clientele.

"I guess everybody's got to hate somebody, Aunt Lilly."

Ella didn't get home from her day trip until early evening after Kelvin and Ruby went back to their motel by Route 26. Lillibelle told her about Kelvin's arrival and part of what he told her, skipping over Slick Jimmy's demise and the Rothschilds out of cowardice. Ella was disappointed she hadn't been home, but Big George was exuberant that night, full of wit and playful gestures as he repeated the stories his stepbrother related that afternoon. She hadn't seen him like that since before the shooting. Ella grew hopeful that with Kelvin home for a few days, her prayers would be answered. George's mind would begin to heal apace with his body. When Billy showed up later that night, she clung to him hard, thanking him for his help in finding Kelvin. He clung back just as hard. Ella swore his eyes were damp.

Early the next morning before Ella went downstairs to unpack fabrics and label sales items, before Billy had time to hustle out of there,

Kelvin Jenkins showed up again. He was in the same suit as the day before, but he wore a fresh white shirt and a blue polka-dot bow tie. He smelled of citrus aftershave. He left Ruby in the car. Ella answered the front door showered, hair done, but still in a bathrobe. As she told all her friends later, when she saw who was at the door, you could have knocked her over with a feather.

"Kelvin!" she said. Immediately, her eyes filled up.

"Ella."

He gave her a slow nod. It wasn't a warm greeting, but it wasn't stone cold.

"I came by to whisk George away," he explained. "I'm dropping off my wife at the outlet mall, where she will no doubt wreak havoc on our budget, but I thought I might take him along to breakfast after."

That's all very nice, Ella thought, *but why are you so cool to me when I'm the only mother you ever had, the only one who ever took the time to nurture you, who flat out loved you? Surely, when you and your daddy lived on your own again, you came to realize a few things—like maybe I wasn't an evil woman who drove your daddy away, and that it takes two to tango.* She wrung her hands together to keep herself from touching him. Billy Euston came in the room barefoot, wearing shorts with an unbuttoned short-sleeved shirt that fell over his waistband.

"Why, Kelvin, good to see you," he said, sticking out his hand. The other man shook it. "I'll get Big George up."

When they were alone again, Ella thanked Kelvin for coming. She began to explain her son's Jewish problem when Kelvin interrupted her.

"I know all about it," he said. "Aunt Lilly told me."

Ella went to her window and looked down at the Toyota Corolla with Virginia plates parked in front. All she could see of Ruby Jenkins was her skirt and her folded hands resting in her lap. She told him she'd love to meet his wife, but Kelvin demurred.

"Maybe later," he said.

The brothers dropped off Ruby at the mall and went to the Waffle House at Big George's suggestion. George ordered a double stack with bacon, and Kelvin had scrambled eggs, hash browns, and toast.

Afterward, they drank coffee together for an hour. Kelvin brought up Jews.

"I wonder why people talk so about them," he began.

Big George was happy to inform him. He related a list of the sins of the chosen people. They were slumlords, misers, clannish, and they hated Blacks. They were usurers. They cheated everyone except one another and were arrogant while they did so. The women were whores, the men whoremongers. Kelvin reached over and patted his hand to stop him. He spoke in the calm, paternal tone he used for his most unstable clients.

"George, you talk like they're all demons. I'm not saying there aren't bad Jews, but I'm sure I've met more of them than you have. Let me tell you, for the most part they're people you'd be proud to know. I dated one in college. Her father and mother marched with Dr. King. Are you aware that in Dr. King's day, half the white Freedom Riders and even more of the civil rights attorneys were Jews? Did you know that?"

Big George shook his head. He opened his mouth to talk, but Kelvin held up a finger to stop him.

"They walked right beside Dr. King. They got arrested and beat up and sometimes murdered for it. Does that sound like people who want to wring Black people dry and take over the world? Come on. You don't really believe that, do you?"

He most certainly did.

"They are deceivers, they are thieves," George said, and he again listed the cruelties of Jews in commerce. When he was done with Jewish shopkeepers and landlords, he went on to banks, the drug trade, and the Queen of England. Toward the end, he got loud, and people stared. Ignoring them, Kelvin let George continue until he was out of breath. He waited for him to recover, then calmly pointed out logical holes in his thinking, but George wasn't buying any of it.

"I'm disappointed you don't see it my way, Kelvin," he said. He waved his hands to brush away argument. "But these things have been revealed to me." His eyes looked to the heavens for emphasis.

"You mean, the Divine directly warned you about Jews. I'm sorry, George, that's hard for someone who wasn't there to grasp. Weren't there others who maybe influenced your thoughts? Someone right here on earth, who told you about Jews? Who called them demons?"

Big George narrowed his eyes, looking at his stepbrother in a way that indicated he was considering his questions with intensity.

"There's no shortage of people in Atlanta who know the truth about Jews," he said. "People in Atlanta know lots that Sweetgrass Island never heard of. There's some on the force that told me things. Not all of 'em, just some of 'em. And one day, out of thin air, a pamphlet on the subject appeared in my locker that was always locked. So . . ."

George gave Kelvin a shy look. He knew that what he was going to say, most folk took as fanciful but he trusted his brother.

"For all I know, an angel put it there. Because it was the Lord Who confirmed what t'others said directly. Spoke right into my ear while I lay in my hospital bed. I didn't hear Him right away. It was just a mumble at first. But when I figured out what that mumbled Voice was and what It said, let me tell you, It went loud and clear. When you're on your deathbed and the Lord speaks, you listen. I cannot deny that and live an honest man."

"Then I'm not going to convince you."

Big George's chin lifted.

"No, you can't."

Kelvin tried a different strategy.

"Well, I guess I have to accept you believe it, nothing can change your mind. But you shouldn't go around all the time talkin' like that. It upsets your mama. You love your mama, don't you?"

George stared straight into Kelvin's eyes and nodded.

"Then maybe it's a good idea to shut it down around her. Around her friends, too. Okay?"

Big George chewed his lip. Kelvin held his stare. Big George gave in. He threw up his hands and sat back against the vinyl pad of the booth.

"Okay," he said. "I'll do it for mama."

Kelvin sighed and looked at his watch. In the last hour, the wall around his heart had cracked some, but remained intact. He took out a notebook and pen from his breast pocket and tore off a sheet of paper on which he wrote down his latest phone numbers at home and at work.

"Call me if you find yourself weakening, George. It's important you do that."

The other man grinned as widely as if he'd been granted a congressional medal. He put the paper in his shirt pocket and patted it.

"I won't let you down," he said.

Hallelujah, Kelvin thought. *I can go home. My job is done.*

"Let's go get Ruby before she bankrupts me," he said.

He stood and offered Big George an arm to help him up. They stopped for gas along the way. If he dropped George off at Ella's before noon, he could get back to Roanoke by six at the latest. For Kelvin, a man who'd been in social work long enough to know a lost cause when he saw it, it couldn't be too soon.

14.

It wasn't the most unusual idea, or one that had never come up in the past, but Abigail's suggestion over breakfast took Joe by surprise.

"I think we should do High Holidays this year," she said.

His butter knife paused above his toast.

The Beckers rarely felt guilty about being modern American Jews, haphazard in formal observance. Some years, they barely knew the holidays were coming up. They might dip an apple in honey and mutter a garbled blessing for a sweet year on Rosh Hashanah, but that was it. Other years, sentiment kicked in. They went to whatever synagogue was close at hand, stood in the back, and caught the blowing of a shofar or atoned for their sins during Kol Nidre. On either occasion, they'd feel an ancient stirring of the blood. Their eyes would sting, their throats constrict, but the sensations died quickly. One fall, they forgot the holidays altogether until they tried to buy Sunday morning bagels at a kosher bakery and found it closed. That time there were twinges of guilt, alleviated by a donation to Hadassah.

"What do you mean, 'do' them?" Joe asked. "Are you saying you want to go to a shul and pray? Or have a dinner party?"

Abigail's back was to him as she placed a bundle of pop quizzes she'd graded the previous night into her briefcase. Her lips pursed as she made up her mind.

"Maybe a dinner party for New Year's, and then I think I'd like services for Yom Kippur. Can you find us someplace to go?"

Joe knew there was a synagogue or two around, a very old one on the mainland and another across the river to the north. He'd find out which was the most liberal.

"Sure," he said. "I'll go through the phone book, make some calls. When are the holidays this year, anyway?"

She surprised him again by knowing.

"They start the first of October." She bent over him to kiss the top of his head. "It's a Wednesday. Do you think people will come in the midweek?"

"Sure. I suspect they'll be intrigued if they've never heard of Rosh Hashanah before."

That made her smile.

"Thanks, honey. I want to fast for Yom Kippur, too. I hope you don't mind. This is important to me."

"Why? You feeling guilty about something?" he joked.

Abigail was already out the door, leaving Joe to puzzle it over. It struck him she'd been doing her tarot cards more often lately. He wondered if they'd predicted something dire, and that was what this sudden piety was all about. Then he forgot about it.

That night after the supper dishes were cleared, the Beckers sat at the kitchen table to make up a menu and shopping list for a New Year's dinner party. It swung between the traditional and the eclectic, which Joe said mirrored their tastes. Abigail wasn't sure how much claim they could make to traditional, but eclectic pleased her. It felt chic. They agreed to start out with slices of three kinds of apples drizzled with honey, then move on quickly to chopped liver on toast points, olives, and cornichons. Maybe endive stuffed with blue cheese and walnuts also. They debated adding smoked salmon with capers and more toast points, but Joe pointed out that the quality of lox available to them from Piggly Wiggly wasn't up to holiday standards, so they decided against it. Abigail suggested they serve a green salad vinaigrette with challah croutons and then, she thought, they could get trays of sweet potato puree with pecans and five or six pounds of brisket from the kosher caterer Joe discovered while searching for synagogues.

"Brilliant," said Joe. "And you know, they must have decent lox, too. I'll order some."

They high-fived and moved to the next item on the list.

"I'm not sure about dessert," Abigail said.

"Honey cake?"

"C'mon, Joe. Nobody likes honey cake."

They chuckled together. Joe reached over the table to squeeze her hand. She lowered her head and kissed his knuckles, an unexpected gesture of tenderness that delighted him.

In bed that night, they discussed the guest list in the dark. Definitely Billy and Ella. Maybe not Lillibelle. Abigail didn't think she liked them. Who knew, Lillibelle could be the source of Big George's conspiratorial delusions.

"I don't think so, honey," Joe said. "She's got a strident personality, but I don't sense true animosity from her."

Abigail's mind was made up.

"I don't want her," she said. "How about Uncle Dan? He's a sweet old thing. Does he have a wife?"

Joe had come to know Uncle Dan. He was one of Dan's steady customers, often in the shop to restock ammo or look at new guns he might try one day. A couple of times, Dan gave him one of his personal guns to take to the range to try out. Joe considered that a deeply flattering and meaningful gesture of friendship. Sometimes, he took coffee and Krispy Kreme over. He enjoyed hanging out, listening to Dan tell stories from his days on the force. The man was a world-class gossip. Joe didn't know half the people he went on about, but he pretended to. He collected a trove of anecdotes from Uncle Dan he gussied up and stuck into his novel along with others he wrote down and tucked away in the ideas folder he kept for future use. Some of his favorites involved Uncle Dan's wife.

"Sure does. Miss Sadie. I hear she's a force to be reckoned with. Even Dan calls her Miss Sadie."

Abigail mentioned she'd like to invite one of the teachers from school, a Black woman with an accountant husband. She didn't know her very well, but she liked her and thought it would be polite to have more Blacks there so Ella didn't have to be the only person of color in a sea of white. Joe thought it a gracious idea and told her so. That would make eight at table, neither too many nor too few.

Joe yawned. He stretched from his toes to his fingertips.

"Well, alright. We've got a party happening. Good for you, Abigail. A great way to start a new year in a new place. Nobody around here knows that much about us or about Jews, so this will give them an introduction. I like that. Let this year be the one all about fresh starts."

Suddenly, Abigail threw her torso over his chest. Joe gave an "oof," but she didn't notice.

"Nobody understands me like you, Joe. No one ever will. Fresh starts. I love that. I love you, too; you know that, don't you? I love you more than anything."

Joe pulled away, straining through the dark to find her face.

"Is there something wrong, hon?"

He thought he heard a small gurgle.

"No. What could be wrong?"

She sounded normal enough. He gently dislodged her and turned on his side, giving her his back.

"Nothing I know of," he said. "I gotta sleep."

"Me, too."

She rolled over. They stilled their bodies and modulated their breath, but unasked questions hovered over them, and neither slept soundly.

Abigail divided up the invites the next day. She would ask the teacher to come with her husband, and Joe would ask Uncle Dan. Abigail said she'd ask Billy but wondered if Joe would mind asking Ella.

"The last time I saw her was when she returned my bowls," Abigail said. "It was awkward. I'm still embarrassed about it. Maybe you could ask her?"

"No prob," he said. It wasn't until he drove over to Elegance by Ella to extend the invite that he realized Abigail had never told him before who returned the bowls. He'd assumed Billy had. Not that it mattered, but he wondered more than once why she hadn't mentioned that Ella came by. What about her visit had been so awkward?

The storefront had a large display window. Brown mannequins dressed in seasonal attire were posed behind it. Fall tones of yellow, red, and orange predominated. Joe noticed items that would look stunning on Abigail. There was a wide patent leather belt wrapped around a long mud-cloth skirt worn with a white blouse, and an orange shirt with an exaggerated starched collar, all of which would suit his wife utterly.

When he entered the store, a set of bells rang. The air smelled of potpourri. Joe walked around the tables and racks when Ella stepped out of the dressing room. She had a tape measure around her neck and wore a duster with pockets for pincushions, spools of thread, and scissors of various sizes. There was a clipboard and pen in her hands. She brightened on seeing him.

"Joe," she said warmly. "This is a surprise."

"Ella, I'm sorry if I'm interrupting," he said. "It looks like you're busy."

"I'm always busy," she said. "Doesn't mean I don't welcome breaks." She gestured to two chairs outside the dressing room. "Are you shoppin' for Abigail? I could show you around. I don't have a customer with me this minute." He said now that he'd seen her shop, he certainly would consult with her when his wife's birthday came around, but that wasn't his purpose today. They sat.

"I don't want to take up too much of your time," he said. "I come on a mission for my wife."

He told her about the dinner party, a celebration of the Jewish New Year. She didn't know much about it. "I know there's a happy holiday in the fall, and also a sad one," she said.

"This is the happy one," he said. "We'd love to share it with you."

Ella accepted readily. When she asked what she could bring, Joe said just her hungry self.

"We tend to overfeed people," he said. "We're asking Billy, too, of course."

"Then we'll bring each other," Ella said in an exaggerated jovial way. She was delighted by the invite. She'd longed for a chance to prove to the Beckers she had nothing but goodwill toward them. There'd been progress at home. Big George had been mum on the subject of

Jews and conspiracy since Kelvin's brief but miraculous visit. There were times when, out of nowhere, a shadow would pass over him. She was his mother; she could see it. For a minute or two, he'd look to be fighting something inside, then it would be gone just as suddenly as it arrived. It was worrisome, but in general everything was going so well, she didn't dare question it for fear of finding the loose thread. She'd try to mention his improvement during the party. Just a little mention, nothing bold enough to resurrect past grievances.

Joe recited the rest of the guest list. A feminine grunt sounded behind him.

"I don't hear my name on that list," Lillibelle said, leaving Joe to wonder how she arrived without setting off the doorbells.

She must be joking, he thought, but he'd been in the South long enough to know that discourteous manners were capital sins. It would be vulgar not to invite her now. With as much finesse as he could muster, he said, "Now, now. I wasn't finished, Miss Lilly. Of course, your name's on the list. It's a Jewish New Year's dinner on the first Wednesday in October, at six thirty. And I apologize, I've got to run. Ella, you'll fill her in, won't you?"

He got out as fast as he could before someone else walked in the door he'd be forced to invite. When he got home, he worried what Abigail would say about Lillibelle joining them. He decided she didn't need to know right away. He could wait until the right time to tell her.

Unfortunately, the right time to tell Abigail about Lillibelle never arose. Joe put it off until he'd about run out of time altogether, the day before the party.

That was the day they'd finished buying all the food and drink, except for the catered items. They began to prepare the house and do whatever food prep didn't have to wait until the day of. In their old life, putting together a dinner party was one of Abigail's greatest pleasures. She always set the table first, choosing her service and colors thoughtfully. She loved a bright table bursting with color and wine bottles with impressive labels, sparkling crystal and silver. From candlesticks to linens, porcelain and flatware, her New Year's table was a smash hit, one to be proud of. It looked festive yet gently caressed the eye. It was as elegant as Ella's store. All it needed was platters of warm, fragrant food and smiling guests sitting around.

"It looks great, honey," Joe said, "but you want to set one more place."

His wife froze. She hated changes at the last minute.

"What are you talking about?"

"There'll be one more. I got trapped in a conversation and kinda had to invite someone else."

Her jaw dropped. On the ruse of being helpful, Joe left the room to get another chair for the table rather than face a firestorm of complaint. He dawdled, hoping she'd absorb the idea of an unexpected guest and be calm when he returned. When he did, he realized he wasn't gone half long enough. Abigail's eyes blazed at him.

"Who?" she asked.

He swallowed.

"Lillibelle Lamont."

"Joe! For heaven's sake! Lilli—?" She was too angry to finish the name of the one person she'd told him she did not want. She stomped into the kitchen and began chopping garlic and herbs for her vinaigrette.

He followed her in. "I'm sorry, honey. It couldn't be helped." He told the story of running into Lillibelle at Ella's to Abigail's stiff, unyielding back. He tried harder, getting right up next to her where she couldn't ignore him. He spoke a few inches from her ear. "I'm sure she'll be on her best behavior . . ."

Her hot eyes never left the cutting board. She pointed the knife in his direction and shook it without looking.

"You owe me big-time for this one, Becker."

Joe slunk away to clean the bathroom.

Eventually, Abigail calmed down. There was nothing to be done. An invitation could not be revoked; she'd have to make the best of it. She was mindful that New Year's was the holiday of forgiveness, both in the asking and the giving. To build up good karma that might keep her far worse deeds secret, she forgave Joe a little bit, put on her mental

armor, and went on. It was a kind of penance. Joe was grateful. He
followed all her directions in the kitchen perfectly, after which she put
him to the heavy cleaning chores. He vacuumed, polished, and took
out three loads of trash.

They were both exhausted by bedtime. Abigail said what she always
said the night before a party. "I hope I have enough food."

"Of course you do. You always have too much."

She gave him a sarcastic look, but it was dark and she knew he
wouldn't see it. "It's just that we have a last-minute guest," she said. He
held his tongue until she continued. "Do we have enough wine and
such?" she asked.

"I've got plenty of bubbly, Medoc and Cabernet, Guinness, Grey
Goose, and Woodford stocked up," he assured her. It sounded like a
lot. A good Jewish meal stomps out the alcohol molecules pretty effec-
tively, she reasoned, and fell asleep worrying about whether she was
serving enough carbohydrates.

In the morning, Joe drove to the kosher caterers to pick up his order.
They were only open until noon. He started out early in case there was
traffic. The caterer was a good hour away, which gave him plenty of
time to think. He thought about work and determined that in another
two months he should be through with the first draft of his new novel.
He tossed around a few ideas, thinking about what to write next. He
thought about his wife. He knew she was tense about the New Year's
dinner and that was normal, but it seemed she'd been tense before the
dinner ever came up. He contemplated oddities in her behavior over
the last weeks. She was overly solicitous to him sometimes. On occasion, she stared into space. Her conversation was often imprecise, as if
she wasn't paying attention to whatever he said. Long about the time
he turned onto Route 61, Joe acknowledged he couldn't hide from the
truth.

Something was wrong with Abigail. He didn't know what. He considered for a minute it might have to do with an incident between her
and Lillibelle, an argument or insult she kept from him. Then again, it
could be something at work. Suspicions about Billy glanced the edges
of his awareness, but he pushed them away. Not possible, he thought.

He's too old. He looks rough. She flirts with him, but she flirts with everybody. He thought about the frequent tarot spreads, the mumbles in her sleep, the times her eyes looked heavy, and he pondered other whys the rest of the drive to the caterers, while he waited in line for his order, and then again all the way home.

15.

Joe thought he might have a chance to ask Abigail a few leading questions while they worked in the kitchen and finished the party prep. But they couldn't agree on hello the whole day. Everything he said irritated her. He suggested Abigail light the holiday candles in front of the guests and bless them in Hebrew. He could explain what the words meant, how the ritual came to be. (He'd have to look that up, but why not?) Abigail refused, saying she would not reduce her ethnicity to that of a performing seal. She'd *bench licht* in private before anyone arrived. Joe suggested he bless the wine after they were all assembled. She scoffed at him.

"What do you think this is? A conversion class? I can't have guests waiting for a drink until everyone gets here. What if someone's late?"

"I'll offer them cocktails then," he said. "Schnapps, as my grandfather would say. Then while they're drinking, I can explain what Rosh Hashanah is about."

If an exhalation of breath had material form, hers would be a rain of poison darts.

"Bonnie Hobson only drinks wine. I happen to know that."

"Who's Bonnie Hobson?"

"Who do you think? I told you three times already! The woman I teach with. And her husband is Langston. If you forget that again, I'll fucking kill you."

Planning the seating evoked an equally harsh exchange. They sat at the kitchen table with place cards from Party Favors. Years ago,

Joe studied calligraphy when he wrote *Tanya in Tokyo*, a prewar novel about the child of a diplomat absorbing the culture of Imperial Japan. He had a sterling Gothic hand. Abigail watched him write the names on the place cards with his trademark flourish. She fiddled with the order of the finished ones, figuring out where to put whom.

"Lillibelle will be to your right," Abigail said. "I want her as far away from me as possible."

"Okay," Joe agreed, "then Billy can be to my left . . ."

"No."

"Why not?"

"I want him by me. You can have Langston."

"I don't know Langston from Adam."

"Neither do I."

Joe was exasperated. Abigail wanted to separate couples. The way she had it, the table would look like a row of salt and pepper shakers, one Black, one white, one Black, one white. It was ridiculous. He told her so.

"Hey! It's not my fault we've got an extra woman. She's the one throwing my table off. If you'd told me in time, I could have invited a tenth. But nooo, you had to do the coward's thing and tell me just yesterday." She reached over and knocked at his head. "Is there anything manly in there at all?"

He pushed his chair back hard so that it screeched against the floor.

"Fuck you," he said.

He got up and left the room. She scurried after him, apologizing to his back.

"I'm sorry, honey," she said. "I didn't mean it, I swear. I'm anxious is all. Please forgive me. You have to forgive me; it's Rosh Hashanah!"

Joe made her suffer a while, but in the end, he gave in. What else could he do? They had company coming. The seating ended up with Lillibelle and Langston flanking Joe, Billy and Bonnie flanking Abigail. Miss Sadie, Uncle Dan, and Ella got sprinkled in between them all.

Bonnie and Langston came from the farthest away, from Settler's Creek. Naturally, that meant they were the first to arrive, and early at that. Abigail was still upstairs putting on her little black dress, the one with cap sleeves and a scoop neckline. She changed her mind three times about a necklace, and in the end chose a pink coral choker Joe bought her in the Bahamas on their honeymoon. Her nerves were up. It was hard to fasten. The clasp closed every time she got it near the ring. She nearly had it when the doorbell rang. She lost her grip again and stamped her foot.

"Joe! Answer the door!" she called out in a rough voice.

The young couple on the front deck heard. They turned to each other and grimaced.

"That doesn't sound right," Bonnie whispered to her husband.

"JOE!!"

The young couple started. Langston looked over his shoulder to the car, ready to hop in and run away.

"What did you get me into?" he muttered to his wife.

He tugged on her elbow. She wasn't going anywhere.

"Hush, now. Don't judge," she said quietly, just as Joe opened the door.

Facing the sophisticated young Black couple, Joe immediately felt underdressed. He had on a good pair of dark pants and a crisp short-sleeve shirt open at the neck. The couple was in party dress, the man in a pale blue suit, white shirt, and indigo tie. He wore round gold-rimmed glasses with a violet tint. His skin was a deep walnut, his hair was long and slicked back into a short curled pony-tail caught in a gold clasp. He looked like no accountant Joe had ever seen.

The woman, on the other hand, wore a shirtdress of modest length and flat shoes. The dress was an iridescent green, but a muted one. A loose string of garnets adorned her neck, dropping down to make a V in the cleavage above her first button. Her features were lively, open, her mouth stretched in a social smile. She, too, had her hair slicked back and clasped. Joe wondered if they did each other's hair.

"Hi, I'm Bonnie Hobson, and this is Langston," the woman said with a teacher's upbeat lilt.

She held flowers in her hands and pointed them at Joe's chest.

"You must be Joe."

Joe took the flowers and stood aside to let them in.

"Yes, yes, I am. Thank you, these are lovely. Please come in; great to meet you at last. Abigail'll be down in a minute. Can I get you a drink?"

He settled them in the living room. After pouring bourbon on the rocks for Langston and unblessed wine for Bonnie, he took the flowers into the kitchen and ran into Abigail coming down the stairs.

"I should have worn a suit," he said out the side of his mouth.

"I told you so," she said, out the side of hers.

It was the most intimate they'd been all day. Their lips met in a perfunctory marital peck. She called out to the others.

"Welcome, you two! Give me just another minute, I'll be right with you!"

Billy, dressed in long pants for once and, miracle of miracles, a short black jacket, rang the bell. It was a waiter's jacket, scavenged from some caterer he'd worked for thirty-odd years before. With him was Ella in a little black dress. Oddly, it was a near copy of Abigail's. Lillibelle, who came with them, wore flowered slacks and a hot pink silk blouse. All of them entered without waiting for someone to answer their ring. They, too, had flowers. Uncle Dan in seersucker and Miss Sadie in a matron's pantsuit had come up the deck stairs by that time, bearing a box of chocolates, so in short order all guests were present and accounted for. Joe ramped up his bartender duties.

Miss Sadie was everything advertised, short, square, and stiff as a tin soldier. Her back and neck were ramrod straight, her chest thrust forward as if waiting for a general's decoration. She appeared plump, soft on the outside with a strong, unyielding center inside. She had several chins, a small cupid's mouth, and pale blue irises ringed with dark brown. They were wolf eyes, feral eyes, startling in an older woman. Joe thought they went a little too bright as she regarded the other guests, and he wondered what that meant, but it appeared it was just that she knew them all quite well.

"Ella, Lillibelle, how good to see you here. Bonnie! How's your mama? She get over *la grippe*?"

The three women returned her greeting. Everyone was smiling.

"Langston. I haven't seen you since the flood."

It was unclear to Joe whether she meant an actual or a figurative deluge. Miss Sadie advanced to Bonnie's husband, who stood to accept her quick embrace.

"I still want to see you in charge of the books over to Uncle Dan's," she said. "You were so helpful after the fire, when meanwhile the whole island suspected our house burnt down from that Jewish lightnin' . . ."

Lillibelle groaned. Abigail blanched, and Joe froze. Billy called her out.

"Miss Sadie!" he said, tilting his head toward their hosts.

At first, Miss Sadie looked confused. Uncle Dan who was standing next to her leaned over and whispered in her ear.

"Oh my," she said, putting a hand to her heart. "I swear I didn't mean to offend. It's just a sayin'. Everybody uses it." She grinned, sticking out her hand. "I'm Sadie. Thank you for your gracious offer to attend your religious ceremony. I've often been intrigued by the rituals of the Hebrew people."

The color returned to Abigail's face. She took the hand offered and shook it.

"I'll forgive you this once," she said in a carefree way, demonstrating the largesse a hostess owes her guest. "But we don't have a lot of ritual in store for you today. I'm planning for you all to go home looking forward to a sweet year with a full belly. That's all the agenda I've got."

There were murmurs of appreciation throughout the room. Joe took drink orders, while Abigail went to the kitchen for her starter platters.

"Billy, why don't you help her?" Joe said. "She's got a ton of food in there."

Euston got up from where he'd planted himself next to Ella on the love seat. Before he left the room, he leaned down and kissed her cheek.

"Be right back, darlin'," he said, only he wasn't.

Joe's wife and Ella's man were in the kitchen together fifteen minutes, maybe more. They barely made a sound, or at least a sound audible from the living room. Ella glanced down the hallway that went past the dining room and into the kitchen more than once. So did Joe. The others made conversation, but as the minutes dragged on, there was a stilted quality about it. The air felt heavy. Soon, it was not just Joe and Ella looking down the dimly lit hallway. They all did. Joe offered to freshen drinks, and everyone accepted.

When Abigail and Billy finally returned, each bore a platter of food. Abigail, her color high, had the chopped liver, Billy the lox. Abigail said, "Sorry that took so long. Everything wasn't as ready as I thought, and I had to check on the mains." Joe wasn't sure about that as he'd checked everything himself while she was getting dressed, but now wasn't the time to question her. Abigail excused herself to get the stuffed endive, while Billy filled up cocktail plates with a little of everything, then gave them out. When he'd covered everyone, he sat down next to Ella and grabbed her hand. Ella tried to steal her hand away from him so she could sample the delicacies on her plate, but he wouldn't let her. She whispered in his ear, "What was goin' on in there?" just as Joe offered to freshen her glass of seltzer water. Billy closed his eyes a second and shook his head, burying both question and response.

The endive came. The second drinks were consumed. Compliments on the food buzzed around the room. The party got loud. Men laughed, and women squealed. Miss Sadie let out a banshee's shriek. Joe thought it was high time for dinner proper to start before he had to serve a third round. But when he looked to Abigail, she was sitting next to Bonnie, nodding absently while Bonnie chatted on. He followed Abigail's gaze. It was directed at Ella and Billy, who talked into each other's ears, oblivious to everyone else. Lillibelle coughed to catch Joe's attention. Once she had it, she looked over to Abigail and frowned. Joe wasn't sure what she meant. He raised his shoulders and eyebrows in question. Lillibelle coughed again. Meanwhile, Uncle Dan entertained the assembled with his near-death story, which everyone had heard before, but he told it so well, no one cared.

Some of them were halfway through their third drink before Joe shut down the cocktail hour.

"Let's go to table," he announced.

When they were in the dining room, people sat wherever they felt like, ignoring the place cards completely. Their hostess was annoyed, but there was nothing she could do about it. Lillibelle wound up to her left and Miss Sadie to her right. Abigail looked about to cry.

Candles flickered at the center of the table. Flowers graced the credenza. Each guest had a few slices of apple drizzled with honey on a small plate. Wine was poured. Joe stood, recited the proper blessing over it, explained to them its meaning, and went into his speech.

"My friends, we have invited you here tonight on the occasion of Rosh Hashanah, the Jewish new year. This is the day that celebrates the birth of the world and all that's in it, of the Divine Creation we embrace with gratitude each day. It is a happy occasion, an occasion to rejoice. But the rabbis also tell us it is the day God opens His Book of Life and writes down each man's fate for the coming year. Who shall live. Who shall die. Who by fire. Who by water. Only charity, prayer, and repentance can avert an evil decree. So we try to do these three things also during Rosh Hashanah. We examine our souls and apologize to those we may have mistreated over the year.

"But enough theology! Our custom is to take a piece of apple, dip it in honey, and wish each other a sweet year. So here, let's do that!"

The guests complied. They were merry now. In their exuberance, Uncle Dan and Billy dripped honey on their shirts. Dan went to the powder room to wash his off while Billy headed for the kitchen sink. Abigail got up to collect the apple plates and bring back the salad with challah croutons. When Joe rose to follow her, she waited until they were in the hallway so the others would not hear her snap at him.

"Really, Joe, I can handle this. Go back and keep them awake before they fall out of their chairs. Damnit, I told you I didn't want them drunk for dinner."

He didn't remember that, but he obeyed her. It wasn't until she returned with Billy cradling the salad bowl in his arms that Joe chanced to catch Lillibelle's eye. "Uh-huh," she said loud enough for him to hear over the chatter of the table. "Uh-huh."

16.

After the mains arrived, all was quiet around the table but for the sound of genteel mastication and sweet, short moans of gustatory pleasure in between bites. Joe poured more wine.

Before long, Uncle Dan's head hung heavy on his neck. He looked about to drop into his plate, prompting his wife to pinch his thigh. He came to. Miss Sadie assessed the condition of the other guests and decided she should initiate a party game to keep everyone alert.

"So, this is the holiday of repentance as well as forgiveness?" she began. "Am I gettin' it right?"

Joe exerted himself to assume the rabbinic role, insofar as he was able, as he had imbibed at least as much alcohol as his guests.

"Technically, the holiday of repentance is Yom Kippur, which is ten days out," he said. "But the period of repentance starts tonight and goes on until all the holidays are over in about three weeks. There are more of them that I won't complicate your minds with . . ." The truth was, he couldn't remember their names. "But no, wait a minute. That's not right. There's a whole month of repentance that leads up to tonight. What's it called, Abigail?"

Abigail stared down the table's length to Joe's position at its opposite head. Her vision looked a little cockeyed because she stared down to Joe's end generally while focusing not on her husband but on Billy Euston, who sat with his arm draped around the back of Ella's chair. She appeared not to hear Joe's question, to be deep in thought. Her mouth was partly open. Her fork was poised just above her plate. A thick chunk of brisket hung off it. She didn't answer.

"Abigail?" her husband repeated. "Sweetheart?"

She came to, shook her head, and blinked.

"Huh?"

"What's the month of repentance called?"

Her mouth got tight. She dropped the fork, which clattered onto her plate.

"I don't remember," she said. Her lower lip trembled. "Maybe I never knew."

In ordinary circumstances, a hostess near to weeping might be a social crisis, an occasion of discomfort and hasty departures. But for this crowd, with more than half the table in their cups, it felt all of a piece. Miss Sadie patted her arm.

"That's okay, baby girl. You don't need to know to play this game."

Bonnie Hobson leaned forward to get a clear look at Miss Sadie.

"What game is that?" she asked. She liked games. So did her fifth-grade students. She was always on the lookout for one she could modify to their educational needs.

"Why, I don't know what it's called. I just made it up. It's sort of a *Truth or Dare* or *Who Said That*, I'd say, with a Hebrew twist."

She had everyone's attention, even that of the more or less sober ones. Chief among the latter, Ella put her elbows on the table then opened a palm to cradle her chin. The arm Billy had over her chair went to her back, which he stroked up and down slowly, stopping here and there to make circles as if he knew by instinct or habit what pleased her. She looked entirely happy in a clearheaded, healthy way.

"Tell us more," she said.

"Here's what I think we do," Miss Sadie said with visible excitement. "We should go around the table and confess somethin' just a tiny bit wicked we've done in the last year. I say a tiny bit because I know all of us here are good people, and none of us would do anything truly evil. The act should be against someone settin' right here, but the confession should not mention any names. Then the rest of us will guess who the confessor is talkin' about."

"I suppose there's a prize?" Lillibelle asked, dry as desert sand.

Abigail shook herself and jumped in with the energy of one who is making up for lost time.

"We could give an autographed set of Joe's books to the winner," Abigail said, although the only one excited about this possibility seemed to be Bonnie, who clapped her hands. Along with games, she was always on the lookout for additions to her classroom library although, to be honest, Joe's titles were beyond the ken of her young charges. They'd need another year or two to comprehend them.

"Very nice," Miss Sadie said. "Alright. Who's gonna start?"

Langston's hand shot up.

"I will," he said with the enthusiasm of the alcohol-impaired. He cleared his throat and began. "I have gossiped about someone in this room, a fact for which I am deeply sorry. Especially as I witness today this person's steadfast devotion."

"Oh my, ain't this interestin'," Miss Sadie said. She ignored the fact that Bonnie Hobson kicked her husband under the table vigorously, once even kicking Miss Sadie instead. "Any guesses?"

Lillibelle piped up.

"Lord, it's obvious, isn't it?"

"I don't know 'bout that," Miss Sadie said. "Who you think it is?"

Lillibelle jerked her thumb toward the opposite end of the table.

"That old goat down there. Billy Euston."

All eyes went to the Hobsons. Langston's jaw dropped, as if he never expected to be pinned down that fast. Bonnie swallowed, ready to dive under her chair rather than witness whatever came next. It was a good thing, really, as no one noticed that Abigail had begun to weep. A thin stream of tears ran down her pretty cheeks.

"Why, yes, you'd be right, Miss Lilly," he said.

Ella had a question. She was smiling, sweetly, not perturbed in the slightest, full of good humor, especially as Langston's comment about Billy's devotion warmed her heart.

"Look, I'm not sayin' my Billy is not an old goat, but what precisely was the gossip you trafficked in, Langston?"

While he fumbled for an answer, Abigail got up and went to the credenza where she'd earlier placed the electric coffee urn along with an array of teacups and dessert plates she'd nestled among the flowers. Joe assumed she was going to turn on the pot, then get the apple and peach pies she'd made from the kitchen. He rose to get the cognac, sherry, and Fernet for after-dinner digestifs and was half turned away when he heard a creak and knew she'd opened the credenza drawer. He also knew what was in there. Joe's heart sank, his soul died a little. He tried to spin around but his world moved in slow motion as if he were trapped in a thick, clear jelly. At the same time, he knew everything around him was happening too fast for him to do anything about it.

Abigail put her hand in the drawer. Abigail took the Pink Lady out. Abigail held the gun against her temple. Her hand shook. The barrel pointed all over the side of her face and the top of her head.

"Don't you say another word, Langston Hobson," she said in a harsh, garbled whisper. She cocked her weapon. "Or I'll do it. I swear I'll do it."

There were gasps, there were *dear Lord*s from around the table. There were *No!*s most loudly from Ella and Joe. But the only voice Abigail heard distinctly was Billy Euston's. Its rasp was calm, quiet, tender.

"Abby. Put the gun down."

"I don't think so," she said. "You don't want me anymore. My life is over. Happy New Year."

Her finger locked around the trigger. Her elbow crooked to point the gun directly at her head. Lillibelle threw out her arm to push Abigail's hand up and stop her from getting off a shot.

It was too late.

The blast was loud. Everyone's ears hurt. A cloud of smoke and plaster dust enveloped Abigail. Chunks of ceiling rained down from the spot where the bullet passed after slicing open the side of Abigail's face and head. A few chunks may have hit her. Some certainly hit a number of her guests. She fell to the floor. Quick as that, Uncle Dan, Billy, and Ella crowded around her. They held napkins hard against her wounds. She moaned, she groaned, she buried her bloody head in Billy's chest. Billy looked over her to Ella Price. Her features held more misery and disgust than he'd ever thought to see from the one woman he counted on to love him no matter what. He started to say

"I'm sorry," as if it would do any good, when Ella said, "Shouldn't we call an ambulance?"

"No," Billy said. "Nothing penetrated. I'll get her to a doctor."

Seconds later, Joe stood at the entry to the dining room with his shotgun in hand. He pumped then pointed it at Billy Euston.

"Take her out of here before I kill you both," he said. His face, his words, were as dark as the grave.

"Okay, okay, okay," Billy said, pulling Abigail to her feet and holding her against his side. "Be calm, Joe. We're outta here."

17.

Billy took Abigail to the new doc-in-a-box on Pelican Beach Road. The all-purpose medical center was devoted to those who had no primary physician. They had a billboard reading "Open 24/7" next to the Chevron station. Sometimes, people got confused as to which establishment the board referred to, but Billy happened to know for sure it was the medical center. He'd never been there, but if rumor was correct, it would be less crowded than the hospital emergency room and possibly more discreet, less likely to be full of people Abigail might know. When they arrived, he helped her in, sat her in a plastic chair, and went to the take-in desk to fill out some forms. He didn't have her insurance card, but he told them she was a teacher employed by the county, which they took down as surety enough for the time being. The napkin she held against her head had a rust-red center that faded to a muddy pink at the edges. He hoped that meant the blood flow had been stemmed, but he didn't think it a good idea to lift the napkin and find out. There were only two people ahead of them, a woman who coughed continuously and a man with an ankle swollen to twice its natural size. The head nurse took one look at Abigail, put her in a wheelchair, and rolled her past the others into an examining room. Billy went outside and looked around for a spot where he could smoke. Two dumpsters out back looked private enough. He positioned himself between them.

Billy's hands shook as he lit his joint. His head swam at the first inhalation. So much had happened so fast, he could barely absorb it all. If Ella ever spoke to him again, which seemed doubtful, he'd swear up, down, and sideways he'd had no idea Abigail Becker felt so strongly about him. It was the truth. They hadn't been alone together in weeks. He'd thought it was over. He'd thought she thought it was over. When she called him with an invite to her new year's dinner, he could honestly say he was drop-jawed astonished. He tried to recollect how she sounded that day. He remembered she was cool, even formal. At the time, he thought the invite meant she wanted to start up a new phase of their relations, a platonic one, and that was alright by him. He was more sure of it when Ella told him Joe had invited her and Lillibelle, too. He was relieved by that. He liked Joe. He liked Abigail. But he'd kept his distance from both Beckers since his last assignation with the wife. He knew that after the sexual part was over and done with, the possibility of friendship with a woman was in the woman's hands; otherwise the man was branded a stalker or worse.

When Joe told him to go help Abigail in the kitchen with the starters, he went without hesitation, reservation, or veiled intent. But damn, that beautiful, near-irresistible Abby, made her intent crystal clear the moment they were out of sight.

Before he had a chance to react, she backed him up against the refrigerator. She pressed herself against him, moving her hips from side to side. One of her legs wrapped around his thigh. Despite their previous encounters, he hadn't realized she was so nimble. If he tried to extricate himself, he'd likely cause them both to crash against the floor tile. Her arms wound around his neck. Her lips found his neck, his ear. She was ravenous. She wanted every inch of her flesh against him. He was dumbstruck, immobile, terrified. Crazy women always affected him that way.

Billy summoned all his will, reached up, and tore her arms off him. He flung her back, throwing her off-balance. They both stumbled but no one hit the ground and at least they were separated. They straightened. Billy picked up a chair and planted it square between them.

"Abby! What are you doin'?" he asked, as if it weren't entirely obvious.

"I want you, Billy. I want you so bad. Why haven't you called me? I thought maybe you had an accident."

He raised his eyes to heaven and moaned. He hated breakup conversations, preferring to do what he'd been doing, steal quietly away.
He did not tell Abigail the truth, that he saw himself as a conqueror
of women, not some lovesick knight in a fairy tale. Now that he'd
had her, taking her on again was a commitment he could not make.
Instead, he gave his least hurtful reason because he considered himself
a gentleman.

"Those two people in there, names of Ella and Joe? You cannot
deny they are good people who deserve better than us. It pains me that
we've betrayed them." He moved his arms about dramatically, like a
conductor leading an orchestra. "If it hadn't been for the storm and
the river, what happened between us would never have happened. You
agree? Don't matter. I know you do. Well, the waters have calmed. I
for one intend to honor my heart's previous obligations, and I suggest
you do, too. We'll be friends from this day on, Abby, if you let us. I will
never be less than that to you. I swear."

He put one hand on his heart and raised the other in pledge for
emphasis. She picked up a spatula from the counter and struck his
hand down.

"You bastard," she said. "Do you realize all the trouble I went to
to get you over here? Just to look at your face? To touch your skin?
Do you know that you've ruined my life? I have no peace. I have only
desire. It's driving me mad."

With great haste, Billy looked around the countertops for the
starter platters, ripped the Glad Wrap off one and picked it up. He
lifted his chin and made for the exit.

She whacked him five times more in the back of the head with a
large serving fork. It was silver and hurt more than the spatula. He
turned to her and said, imperiously, "That's not goin' to work."

Abigail's lower lip quivered. Everything about her threatened a
crying jag.

"What will?" she asked.

"If your aim is to change my mind, nothin'," he said. "Why don't
you prove to me you are half the woman I think you are, and march in
there with a smile on your face. You have guests, sweetheart. You owe
them that much."

Like every idiot before her, Abigail clung to the implications of his calling her "sweetheart" and bucked up for the march into the dining room. Billy thought he was out of the woods until the pistol came out.

He smoked down the joint until the end burnt his fingertips, had a cigarette, then went back to the doc-in-the-box waiting room. He was just in time. A nurse called his name over the loudspeaker. He let her know where he was and she asked him to wait a minute, please. A man he judged a doctor by the cut of his lab coat emerged from the examining room into which Abigail had disappeared and beckoned him forward. His name tag read Dr. Harry Singh. They met in the hallway just outside her door.

"We've stitched her up," he said without a trace of accent. Billy guessed he was first- or second-generation American and thoroughly assimilated. "The wounds were deep but not life-threatening. There will be scarring. A plastic surgery consult might help with that later on. Most of her hair should grow back with any luck. She took off a small piece of her cheekbone. She's lucky it wasn't her jaw. She won't be good as new, but she'll be good."

All Billy Euston could think of was Big George.

"Will there be brain damage?" he asked.

Dr. Singh shook his head.

"No, not at all. There was no involvement of the skull. The bullet did not penetrate there. But the soft tissue . . . that's another story."

Billy took his assessment in and was grateful.

It occurred to him he had no idea what to do with Abigail next.

"Should she stay here?" he asked, hopefully.

"There's no need. She can go home."

Wherever that is, Billy thought.

The doctor moved on to instructions on wound care. He gave him scripts for opioids, antibiotic pills, and ointment along with samples of each given the hour and difficulty in filling the scripts straight away.

"You realize I am obliged to report all gunshot incidents to the authorities, don't you?" he said.

Billy had never found the word *report* to have anything but the most dire consequences.

"Look, Doc, you don't have to do that. It was an accident. I don't know what she might have told you in there, but she didn't mean to do it. She was playin' around, puttin' on a show, and bang! it happened."

He gave the doc his best just-between-us-good-old-boys look. Singh squinted.

"Aren't you Billy Euston? Pitmaster over to the Flying Pig?"

"Yessir. I am. Three nights a week."

"Hmm. Nobody goes there when you're not in. You swear it was an accident?"

"On my honor."

"You know, Master Billy . . ." They both smiled at his choice of address as it was meant in good humor. "I have my daughter's wedding coming up. She wants it outdoors in some old barn with a country band. We've been looking for a caterer. Do you think you could give me a good price on Q for one-hundred twenty-five?"

"Absolutely, Doc, absolutely. You'll never find a better. I'll give you a price that will make you swoon."

A deal was struck. They exchanged numbers.

The doctor walked him back to the take-in desk to schedule a follow-up appointment. He advised a psychological evaluation. When Abigail was wheeled over, patched up, swathed in bandage, looking grave, damaged, but not particularly tragic, it struck Billy she was his responsibility now, at least for the time being. He thought about Slick Jimmy Jenkins's gal all those years ago and tried to remember how long that liaison lasted after Ella booted Jimmy out. He didn't think it was too long. He wished he could call Ella and ask.

Because he had to, he wheeled Abigail to the car, got her installed, and rolled the chair back to the building. It took a while before he returned to her. Their spot in the parking lot looked far, far away. Getting to it was hell. It was as if there was a ball and chain wrapped around his ankles making each step he took an effort. He could swear he hadn't cried since the day his daddy went to prison, but he sure felt like it now.

Back at the house, Uncle Dan and Langston tried to comfort Joe, while the women hovered over Ella. There wasn't much anyone could do. Both victims of transgressive lust were in shock. The consolation of the others around them didn't even almost register. Lillibelle took charge.

"Why don't you all go home," she told Uncle Dan, Miss Sadie, and the Hobsons. "I can clean up around here."

Miss Sadie protested.

"But it's my fault, I should do it all. I simply never should have conjured up that stupid game."

"The one thing I'm sure of, darlin', is that none of this is your fault," said Lillibelle. She found a broom to sweep up the plaster debris from the floor.

Bonnie Hobson asked the others what she should tell them at school the next day. Joe startled them all by offering an opinion. Up to that moment, they thought him lost, awash in sorrow. They spoke around him as if he weren't there. But he was.

"Don't tell anyone anything just yet," he said. "She's broken enough right now. She had the day off tomorrow for Rosh Hashanah. The news can wait."

The room went silent, motionless. Not one of them could promise to keep tonight under their hats for a whole day except maybe Ella. They were each busy deciding to whom they would first divulge the startling story of Jewish New Year's dinner at the Beckers'.

"Of course, Joe," Bonnie said anyway, after a heartbeat or two. She put a hand on his arm. "Of course."

The assembled stood around feeling useless. They looked at one another with raised eyebrows and downturned mouths. What a kind, selfless husband, they all thought, that his first words after his wife shot herself over another man were devoted to her welfare.

Ella began to clear the table. She had the look of the crucified about her.

"Please, you all," she said, "just go home."

She could hardly bear the sight of any of them another second. They regarded her with such pity. In years past, when Billy roamed from her bed, she could pretend she knew all about it from the get-go and protect her sense of social pride. It enabled her to distance both self and reputation from his shenanigans. But this time. Oh, God, this time the humiliation was inescapable. She was too old for it. Why didn't they all have the sense to leave them alone?

Not long after, they did. There wasn't much point in hanging around. Lillibelle had things under control, as she always did. They trusted Joe would get the women home somehow.

Once the others were gone, Lillibelle, Ella, and Joe worked together to put the house back in order. The women barely spoke beyond "I'm putting this over here" and "Where do you keep the trash?" They wrapped up leftovers and stored them. They loaded the dishwasher twice while Joe vacuumed. They wiped down counters and furniture. Twice Ella started to cry without warning. She cried in great heaving sobs with her shoulders shaking and her hands clapped against her face. Each time, Lillibelle came up behind her and hugged hard enough to keep her still until she stopped. Joe said "thank you" and "I'm so sorry" a lot, but there didn't seem to be rhyme or reason as to when he said it. He got a stepladder from the garage and spackled the bullet hole in the ceiling.

At last, there was nothing left to do. Joe poured them final shots of whiskey. They sat in the living room together to drink it.

"You could stay here tonight if you want," Joe said. "You two can have the bedroom. I can bunk in my office. I just can't drive you home right now. I don't trust myself. But I don't know if I can sleep in Abigail's bed tonight, either."

Lillibelle was all for it, but Ella didn't want to sleep in Abigail's bed any more than Joe did. They phoned Li'l Jim, one of the foremen at Lamont Farms, instead. He lived nearby Catawba Plantation, and it was getting close to dawn. He'd be awake.

They waited for Li'l Jim to arrive. No one spoke. Eventually, however, a thought bubbled up in Lillibelle to the point she could no longer contain it.

"I thought I'd just about faint when you brought out that shotgun, Joe. It didn't seem like you to do it."

Joe gave out a deep, low moan. There was pure agony in it. He didn't know what to tell her. It was only a handful of hours ago, but to his mind the night's drama felt curiously distant. He was separated from it through shock. He wasn't sure why he did anything. He only knew in his heart he'd been full of rage. It told him to show Abigail and Billy they couldn't screw with him like they obviously had. For one ugly moment, he'd looked down at his bloodied, broken wife and thought she had it coming. Soon as she left with her lover, horror at his own actions flooded him. Why hadn't he rushed to her side? Faithless or not, she was still his wife, still the woman he'd loved. At the time, getting his shotgun felt like the manly thing to do, something a man like Billy would understand and the woman Abigail had become would respect. But somehow, while it felt great, it came out all wrong.

"I'm so sorry," he said, but whether to Abigail or Lillibelle even he didn't know.

Big George got up minutes before Ella got home. He'd taken to morning walks at sunrise around a local lake. It calmed him, and it strengthened his legs. By this time, he was mostly recovered from his injuries, except for the one that traumatized his frontal lobe. He still had trouble controlling his thoughts, although he managed his actions and speech pretty well. It wasn't that he no longer had conspiracy theories circling through his mind, but he could keep them in. Every time he felt like he might burst from the pressure, he called Kelvin for a little talk therapy. Kelvin always took his call right away. He never failed to settle him down. The only other therapy that worked was spending time with Billy Euston. When he went to Billy's, he hung out around the cooker turning meat or helped him mix up the spice rub. They worked on whatever cars or machinery needed it. He kept up his marksmanship in Billy's makeshift range and best of all, they went fishing together like they had when he was small. It made George feel as it had back in the day: protected, looked after a little bit after the death of one father and desertion by another.

Ella didn't know much about what Big George did, or how he felt about it. He'd been needy after the shooting, but the stronger he got, the more she was aware that he was a grown man who needed his own space. The dress shop demanded a lot of attention in the fall when her customers' thoughts turned to holiday frocks and new winter wraps. It was her busiest time of year, given that Christmas Eve and New Year's dresses tended to be of complex design and difficult fabrics. She often worked ten-hour days and could anticipate seeing little of her son outside of mealtimes in that season.

Maybe she could be excused, then, for telling him all the details of that disastrous night at the Beckers as soon as she walked through her front door. She was sleep-deprived, still in shock, and heartbroken to her very core. She needed to tell the story to sympathetic ears to catch hold of it, to digest it. In retrospect, she could have exercised some restraint in the telling or, at the very least, waited a few days before she asked George to bring a couple of good-size boxes up from the shop storeroom, boxes she filled with whatever possessions belonging to Billy Euston that she had lying around. Big George had been driving a car again for a couple of weeks. He knew the route to Euston's as well as the back of his own hand. Ella didn't think anything of asking him to drive the boxes over there and tell her ex that she'd like the nightgowns and such she kept at his place for overnights. There would be no more of those.

Big George held his mama close to murmur his support. He told her she was not old yet, and still a remarkably attractive woman. A new man would come along as soon as she opened her heart to the concept. Ella let loose a sharp, bitter laugh. The sound of it penetrated the center of the wound at Big George's temporal lobe. It hurt.

"That is plain absurd," she said. "I will never have another man again."

Now that she'd unburdened herself, fatigue hit Ella like a sledgehammer. George made her tea and told her to go to bed. She'd only stab her thumb with her sewing machine needle if she didn't get some rest, he said. She took the tea to the bedroom and closed the door. He put his forehead against it and listened to her cry until she quieted.

George took the boxes downstairs. He put an Open at Noon sign on the shop door, loaded up the car, and drove off to Billy's trailer, muttering outrage. Billy hadn't only hurt Ella; he'd hurt George as well.

With angry, vengeful voices filling his head, Big George drove like the very devil. He screeched around corners and slammed the brakes at stoplights. He pulled over to make a phone call at a booth outside Auntie B's Down Home Café before he chanced to drive himself off the road. He called Kelvin collect. He told his brother what was going on, how it made him feel, and that at the bottom of everything was a demon-woman, a Jezebel, a whore, a Jew. She'd near destroyed his mother. He wanted to kill her and sanctify his mama's name.

"No, George, that's not going to help," Kelvin said. "It'll make things much worse."

The other man breathed heavily into the phone.

"Then what do I do?"

"You could try remembering you are a policeman, sworn to uphold the law."

He breathed some more.

"Okay. What else?"

"Use your thoughtful words, Officer Roy," Kelvin said. "The good, measured words we talked about last time. And if you feel yourself falling into the darkness, run like hell."

It was enough. George had a plan. It soothed his aching heart.

A few minutes later, he stood outside the door of Billy's double-wide. He held the boxes in his arms, one atop the other. They were heavy. Billy had been leaving his scent at Ella Price's house for many years. Rather than put his burden down to knock, he kicked the bottom of the door.

"Billy, it's me, Big George," he called out. "I got a message from Mama."

The door opened. Billy stood on the other side looking disheveled, unshaven. His eyes were dark and puffy. The whites were bloodshot. If he didn't know his man better, Big George would think he'd spent hours weeping. He looked lost, and he smelled of booze, whether from the night before or from this morning.

"Mornin', son," Billy said.

The man towering over him flinched at the intimacy of his greeting, although up to that very day, he would have been pleased by it. He shoved the boxes into the older man's chest then released them. They slid down Billy's torso until he caught them with two hands and a raised knee. It was quite a catch; Big George hoped he fractured a bone or ripped a muscle with the effort. Billy bent to put the boxes down.

"I guess 'thank you' is what I should say, George, but it's not a thing I feel very thankful for."

His humility riled Big George. Had Billy ever weighed what he stood to lose when he stepped out on his mama with that Yankee gal? That he would lose not just a fine, loving woman who knew him top to bottom, but also the affection of her son? Did they both mean so little to him? George swallowed air, trying to digest his anger when there was a rustling from inside. He looked over Billy's shoulder. Abigail came out of the bedroom. Her eyes had an expectant look. She might have hoped their caller was her husband come to fetch her out of there. She looked worse than Billy did, rumpled and raggedy. Her hair was full of devil knots, and traces of last night's mascara dotted her cheek. A stretch of bandage hung loose and dirty from a rough night's sleep. It needed changing. She wore one of Ella's nightgowns, which spiked his temper further. He squared his shoulders, thought about his words, and spoke again.

"Mama wants her things returned as soon as possible."

"I understand. Tell her I'll drive them by tonight. Tell her I hope we can talk."

The woman inside whimpered. The sound rode George's nerves like razors on a wire. He guessed the last thing she wanted was for Billy to talk to Ella. He knew his mother. This time, she'd had it. It was doubtful she'd answer the door to Billy, let alone talk to him. More luck on the whore's side. He wanted to rip the nightgown off Abigail and strangle her with it.

"Good luck with that," he said.

He turned to go. His fists were balled. He was out of words, ready to flee before he hurt someone. Billy put a hand on him to restrain him. Instead, it pushed Big George over the edge. In one swift move, he hauled back and socked his mother's faithless lover in the jaw. He socked Billy so hard, he fell to the floor. His eyes were closed, his head lolled back and forth while blood dripped from the corner of his mouth and nose. Abigail shrieked, hurried over to kneel at his side.

"Oh baby, baby," she said, holding the hem of Ella's nightgown against his face to blot the blood.

Big George did the wise thing. He ran like hell.

18.

Joe needed closure. He tried to talk to his wife several times on the phone between Rosh Hashanah and Yom Kippur. Each time he wound up screaming at her or she wound up crying and somebody hung up. Yom Kippur came and went without Abigail calling or writing to ask his forgiveness, which he thought she might. He felt he deserved at least that. When she didn't, he packed up her things and had a trucker he knew from Declan's schlepp them over to Billy's. Ella told him soon after that Abigail and Billy had taken the boat to Florida for the winter so she could recuperate from her wounds in peace. No one knew when they'd be back. Joe hoped never. He built a rampart around his heart and went ahead with a divorce.

In April, it was rumored the lovers had returned. There were multiple sightings at ABC Liquors and at the Subway on Magnolia Drive. Luckily, after several months of therapy delivered by a most simpatico lawyer, Ralph DeVere of DeVere and Associates, a man married three times by the age of thirty-eight and currently single at forty-two, Joe Becker was able to leave the house without wondering if he'd run into either Abigail or Billy Euston. Before that, he stayed away from ABC Liquors and the Subway in case. Lawyer Ralph helped him see that avoidance did him no good. If it happened, it happened.

"You got to grow a bigger pair, boy," he advised back when it hit the fan. "The tender sex can look helpless and lost even when they are behavin' in the most evil manner. It's all an act. Don't let

those two rule where you go and what you do. They've done enough
harm."

Apart from the attribution of evil, he made a kind of sense.
Another month went by. Joe could handle running into them, but
he didn't want to. The sightings reported to him increased; there was
no longer any doubt the two were home to stay. Lillibelle told him
one was never without the other when out and about, so if he came
across Abigail, he'd come across her "goddang lyin' sumbitch lover,"
too. She said the two had become infamous on the island for their
constant, public bickering, a detail she seemed to take joy in relating.
After much thought over many sleepless nights, Joe realized he'd married Abigail for a host of wrong reasons. He'd married her for his pride,
for his need to belong. He'd treated her like a prize, not a woman. He'd
indulged her whims and demands, but apparently she didn't feel he'd
ever given her what she needed.

What Joe needed was another problem entirely. Mostly, he still
didn't know. He needed to stay in their home, he knew that. He'd got
used to living there. More change might tip him into a frozen state of
inertia, plain shut him down. Luckily, Abigail didn't argue about it. He
suggested to his divorce attorney that he take out a mortgage on the
house and pay her half the value in cash. Abigail was pleased. Lawyer
Ralph said she thanked him profusely, as if it were his idea.

Another thing Joe needed was music. It soothed him, took his
mind off his troubles. Weekends, he could be found at Declan's listening to whatever live performances the pub had to offer. He'd gotten to know a number of the musicians. Musicians are generally well
acquainted with romantic troubles. They were empathetic, playing
for him their best breakup ballads. The patrons at Declan's were sup-
portive of him also, despite their long histories with Billy Euston
and his Q.

"Billy's been a dog his whole life," Heyward Dinnest, the landscaper, confided. "There's men all up and down this island who'd like
to beat him bloody over their wives, girlfriends, or daughters. Why
they don't is anybody's guess. I know one daddy got bought off with
a rack of ribs twice a month. Damn scandal that was. An unfaithful
wife might be worth it, but a daughter? Some men got no pride. You

know, I could have told you what would happen from the first night you walked in the pub door and set yourselves down while old Billy was gettin' google-eyed at the bar."

"Then why didn't you?" Joe asked.

Heyward gave him the kind of look one gives an especially slow child before you're quite sure what's wrong.

"Because he's Billy and I didn't know you yet, Joe, that's all."

Joe wasn't sure any of them knew him yet. He'd gone through a stage where he'd felt he was fitting in, becoming Southern through and through, but after the Abigail affair, he was thrown offtrack. Apart from threatening the lovers that night while his wife bled and the plaster dust had not yet settled, he didn't feel he'd acted very Southern at all. Would a local man let the two of them live together without interference after that? Wouldn't there be some revenge involved? Joe didn't want to take any kind of revenge. He wanted mostly to be left alone.

There were women at Declan's who offered Joe the sweet consolation of their company, gestures he appreciated but gently refused. He didn't want or need the complications of a relationship, and he didn't think himself capable of taking intimacy lightly, not after all he'd been through. What he craved was friendship, people like the men at Declan's, men he could spend time with to take him out of himself.

To that end, Joe dropped into Uncle Dan's on a Wednesday morning. As was his habit, he brought two cups of coffee and a couple of bear claws from the Krispy Kreme. He'd finished his Civil War novel and was waiting for edits to arrive from New York. There wasn't much else to do and no one to talk to at home. He lingered in a folding chair and waited for the gossip that was sure to come. Uncle Dan told him that Big George had graduated from his anger management class, which Sheriff Rutledge insisted on if Big George wanted to avoid criminal charges for his battery against Billy. (Abigail had reported it before Billy regained consciousness.) George had to take the class four times, but Ella said between that and the meds his new therapist put him on, he'd rid himself of his conspiracy theories. The voice in his head quieted down, and his urges, too.

"Do you hear he loves Jews now, Uncle Dan?" Joe asked.

He meant it as a wry joke, but Uncle Dan took him seriously. He drained his coffee cup and gave him a most consoling look. "Well, I don't know, you'd have to ask him. Jesus does, though, son. I can promise you that."

Big George wasn't fit to work the force anymore, but the new mall had a shortage of security guards, so he'd found a job there.

"It's good for him," Uncle Dan said. "People come up to him and say, 'Ain't you Big George Price? Old Officer Roy?' They remember him from his football days, and of course they know about the bust gone bad and what happened to him. It only grows the legend. Once a small-town hero, always a small-town hero. He's out of his mama's hair anyway. That's a good thing, too. But I'll tell you, there's somethin' sad about him. He's lost so much. His career, his strength, the best father he ever had, who was, if you'll excuse my mentionin' the name, Billy Euston. And speak of the devil, here he comes."

Sure enough, Big George entered the store. He was imposing in his big handsome glory, dressed once again in uniform, which clearly suited him. It put a spring in his gimpy step. Joe doffed his feed cap to demonstrate the respect to which Big George was accustomed.

Once the formal reintroductions were over—on Labor Day there hadn't been time for such—the two men settled on Dan's back porch and had a heart-to-heart. First they talked about Ella's welfare, then George brought up the Abigail affair, as he liked to call it. Joe affirmed that he'd been hurt at least as much as George's mama. He thought of something Uncle Dan said.

"Do you miss Billy?" he asked.

"Well, not the sumbitch hurt my mama, but the old Billy? Yes, I do. From the time I was a child, we used to go fishin' and huntin' and work together. He taught me near everything manly I know."

Big George smiled and sighed at the same time. Joe felt the need to offer a solid kind of comfort.

"Maybe we could go fishing together," he said. "I don't think I can hunt. I wasn't raised like that. I've never shot anything but a target and so far, I'd like to stick to that. But fishing, I could try that."

They made a date.

* * *

On the given day, Joe and Big George sat side by side on a floating dock on George's favorite lake. It was a brilliant spring day with a mackerel sky, which George told Joe was a sign it would rain later. Joe looked up at the rows of rippling clouds resembling the scales of a fish. Behind them was the bluest sky. It didn't seem likely rain would come, but he'd learned over the last year that things were often not what they seemed in the South. Or at least not what they seemed through Northern, city eyes.

George handed him a fishing pole and a bucket of bait as, he told him, a true fisherman never uses a lure.

"At least let the critter have a taste of somethin' good before the pain comes," he said.

Joe looked inside the bucket of crawfish and worms. He poised his hand above it. Without meaning to, he shuddered and withdrew.

"I can't do it," he said.

George gave him a quizzical look. Joe tried to explain.

"Look. Jewish boys don't mess with slithery, crawling things," he said. "It's against our nature."

George laughed. He took Joe's hook and baited it for him, then showed him how to cast it into the water. They listened to the wind in the trees together, to the pop and bubble of fish breaking the lake's surface to feed, and to the calls of birds. George spoke first.

"You know, Joe, I was hateful to you and your wife once upon a time. I want you to know I was a barrel full of crazy back then, but I'm better now. They got me on some new drugs. I discovered that voice I was hearin' wasn't God at all. In short, my mind's settled. I don't hate nobody no more."

Joe was touched. It was as much of an apology as he might expect, and also as much as he needed.

"I forgive you."

Pleased, George nodded. After a few minutes, he spoke again.

"Joe, there's somethin' I don't understand. I hope I can ask you," he said.

"Shoot."

George asked the question Kelvin asked him that day in the Waffle House, more or less.

"Why do people hate Jews?"

Joe was taken aback by that one. It was the oddest question he'd ever been asked by a former anti-Semite, but it was better than being thrown into the drink and held under.

"I don't know, George. We're so sweet."

Big George threw back his head and laughed again, only this time it was a roar that seemed to shake the leaves of the trees around the lake.

"When you figure it out, let me know," George said. "Sometimes, I admit, I really don't see it."

Joe decided not to ask him about the rest of the times.

Later that night, Joe went over to Declan's to hear Milkweed and Honey, two country gals who sang the most perfect harmony he'd heard since Sutherland and Horne in '83. Some nights, they sang more popular tunes than pure bluegrass, but their sound was mellow and melodious, kind to the ear, and it gave him joy. They were setting up when he entered the pub and gave him nods of welcome. "Hey, Joe. Thanks for comin'," they said. He took his usual spot at the bar and ordered a shot. The music kicked in. He listened and hummed along, closing his eyes, transported. After his second whiskey, they were ready to close out their set. They sang John Hartford's "Tall Buildings," a song that mirrored Joe's life only in reverse. It was about a country boy who grows to manhood and leaves his home.

So it's goodbye to the sunshine
Goodbye to the dew
Goodbye to the flowers
And goodbye to you
I'm off to the subway
I must not be late
I'm going to work in tall buildings

Maybe it was the Jameson. Joe choked up. It was a queer kind of negative nostalgia, but the song made him long for the place and time when life was simple, without betrayal and loneliness. Concrete structures might have been a small price to pay if he could have kept

Abigail, or kept the Abigail he thought he knew, rather than the one he didn't. A light, feminine hand fell on his neck.

"Cheer up, baby," Ella said. "You left the tall buildings."

It was probably still the Jameson, but Joe hugged her as if he might never see her again.

"Ella, it's been too long," he said. "I didn't know you'd be here tonight. Are you a fan?"

Ella pointed out the singers' dresses. They were gingham, full-skirted with wide sashes about the waist and Peter Pan collars. They wore saddle shoes and bobby socks, too.

"You don't really think a girl can buy that stuff off the rack anymore, do you?" She said. "Guess who made 'em."

Joe whistled his appreciation. He got up and gave her his seat. He hadn't seen her since Christmas, when he'd visited the shop to buy his agent a gift.

"You been good?" he asked.

Ella shrugged.

"Last time we spoke, it was the holidays, I believe. Heartbreak is always hardest at the holidays. But as time's gone by, I've realized livin' without Billy isn't as bad as I thought it was going to be. Billy being himself was somethin' I was used to. All those times we broke up over the years . . . this time felt pretty much the same, only permanent. None of it caused me the trauma that I'm sure it made for you."

Joe nodded. He looked for something to say that would take the conversation away from heartache.

"Big George and I went fishing today."

Ella's face lit up.

"Yes, he told me! He needed it. Billy didn't just leave me; he left George, too. I think it's been harder for him than for me, can you believe it?"

"Sure, I can."

Ella dropped her head and studied the floor. When she raised it again, she wore a faraway look.

"There's a time a boy becomes a man, but a man is always a boy in some ways. My son's attachment to Billy was one of his ways. He's been bereft; it's been tough on him. So thank you."

"It wasn't a chore," Joe said. "I enjoy George."

Lillibelle came up behind them. She reached out to give Joe a squeeze, but it wasn't as hearty as Ella's. That was alright with him.

"Shut my mouth," she said. "Look who's comin' in."

Billy and Abigail stumbled through the door. Abigail wore a paisley scarf around her crown to hide a bald patch where her scar began. The scar, a thick twisted line, ran in a jagged red line down her cheek. She was bloated, pale. She was no longer the beauty Joe married. Billy looked much the same, but he'd always been on the rough side. His paunch, however, had ballooned.

"Talk about the wages of sin. Look how fat he got," Lillibelle hissed in Joe's ear. "I heard she made him quit smokin' tobacco."

The lovers were well oiled and did not require another drink. They made their way out to the back. Billy bumped into the booths against the wall opposite the bar as he went. Abigail put her hands up, latched them on his shoulders, and pushed him onto a straighter path, grumbling "stupid" and "oaf." Neither of them noticed Joe, Ella, and Lillibelle—so it appeared.

"I guess there is some justice in the world," Lillibelle said, once they were past.

"No," Ella said, "that's too harsh. I don't wish them . . . well, what they've come to be. That's someone I loved once. He was there when I needed him, most of the time. I still honor that."

Lillibelle grunted begrudgingly.

"What about you, Joe? Are you as forgivin' as my friend here?"

Joe thought. Seeing Abigail like that made him sad.

"I think I am, Lillibelle. I take no pleasure in what I just saw. That's for sure."

Ella half stood to plant a kiss on his cheek.

"Why, Joseph Becker," she said, "I do believe you have become a Southern gentleman."

It was the most gracious compliment Joe had ever received. Milkweed and Honey began their second set. The three friends listened hard and sang along hard wherever they could. By the end of the night, Joe knew for certain he was exactly where he was supposed to be, building a life in a place he could call home.

Against all odds, he was happy and stayed that way, pretty much, until the next problem rolled through the marsh and landed with a thud at his front door.

19.

It was dusk. All over the island, people prepared dinner or showered after work before going out. It was a quiet time of day, a time to catch one's breath. But the knock on the door was especially loud and insistent, which should have been a clue. Still, Abigail was the last person in the world Joe expected to find outside his door. For two years, he hadn't seen her but from afar, and not by accident. He had no desire for closer contact. Billy, he felt sorry for. Abigail depressed him. He avoided them as much as possible and got good at it, too.

To create distance on such a small island required vigilance. For two years since that fateful Rosh Hashanah night, Joe left restaurants, bars, the supermarket, the beach, the creek, even the dentist's office at the first, hazy sight of someone who might be her across a room or through a window. The last time he'd been close up, face-to-face with her was the day her beauty died a premature death. People who'd seen her of late close up, face-to-face, said it wasn't entirely gone. They said the head wounds had resolved themselves over time. She looked better now in 1999 than she had just the year before. Sometimes when he was wide awake in the night, Joe imagined what she would look like, trauma resolved. Presented with the unexpected, even shocking opportunity to judge for himself, he studied the woman across his threshold closely with as much reserve as he could muster.

Her hair was tufted around the shot side of her head near the crown. She'd taken to wearing the rest of it cut short. The tufts didn't stand out particularly. She wore a pair of dark glasses with large rectangular lenses that obscured the path of her scar which started at her hairline, ran down to graze the corner of her right eye, and ended past her cheek in a jagged red line. On the whole, not so bad, Joe thought. Her face alone wouldn't get her anything she wanted anymore, but it wouldn't provoke social isolation or inspire children to stare, and then there was the rest of her.

The rest of her took his breath away.

Except for the scar and the tufts of hair, Abigail was still perfect in a dozen ways. No matter what had happened to her face—what she'd done to her own face—only a portion was disfigured. There were still angles at which to contemplate her as a creature of creamy perfection. Abigail had lost the bloat from her first year with Billy, when for months they'd tumbled down a rabbit hole of alcohol and weed. Joe could see how a man might want what was left of her.

He liked life better without Abigail, but her presence unnerved him. He wondered what ill wind blew her to his doorstep, unannounced at twilight, after two years.

"What are you doing here?" Joe asked.

"Billy's dead," she said.

The words rolled through his mind. He could not grasp their meaning.

"Billy's dead?" he repeated.

"Yes."

Abigail pushed past him into the living room. Joe wished he'd done a deeper purge after they split. As it was, the place looked pretty much the same as before, when the two were intact, which struck him as pathetic.

"When? How?" he asked.

She sank down into the couch, leaned back to rest her neck on the cushions, and propped her feet on the coffee table without taking her shoes off, like she still owned it. Her hands went under the frames of her sunglasses to cup her eyes. Her shoulders shook as if she cried. That perplexed him. Joe didn't think Abigail ever cried, not in the *oh my god, I'm devastated* sense. Watching her, he conceded she'd work up a few tears at the loss of her lover, at least for show.

"That's the thing. We're not sure," she said.

He wondered who "we" was. For the last two years, everything he'd heard about his ex-wife was coupled with Billy's name. It was Abigail and Billy, or Billy and Abigail, each time she or he was mentioned. Billy had been a good twenty years older than she, more or less. Had Abigail anticipated his passing? It would be like her to install a candidate for replacement well ahead of time, just in case. He asked what happened.

"It's all so murky." she said. "I went to the farmers' market this morning. His hip was bothering him, so he didn't come. When I got home, he was dead on the couch." She dropped her hands. "I know it's hard to believe, but I think he was poisoned."

"Poisoned! Why poisoned?"

"His color wasn't natural; it didn't suit a normal death," she said. Joe wondered how the sophisticated, city-bred Abigail knew such a thing. She clarified. "The coroner thought there was too much purple and black for natural causes."

"Does Ella know?"

"I've been with the police all day. You're the first I've told. But, you know, all those officers went home to dinner tonight, and all of them have wives. Ella's likely heard something by now. All them just finished the dinner hour."

The phone rang. *Probably Ella*, Joe thought. He grabbed it and pulled the cord behind him as he made for the front deck to answer it.

He put the receiver against his ear.

"Joe?" Ella's voice was soft, low.

"Ella," he whispered. "Have you heard about Billy?"

It wasn't the most sensitive way to ask, but it's what came out of his mouth.

"He's dead, Joe. I can hardly believe it. How do you know?"

Her tone of voice gave nothing away. She was slow, deliberate. What emotion she expressed could be anything from anger to profound grief.

"Abigail came over just now. She told me."

His comment was met with a silence so long, Joe wondered if she was still there.

"Ella?"

At last she spoke.

"She came to you? Why would she come to you?"

"I have no idea. She just showed up."

"Let me talk to her."

Joe took the phone back into the house and extended the receiver toward Abigail.

"It's Ella. She'd like to speak to you."

The women spoke together quietly. All he could discern of Abigail's conversation were moans and whimpers. After she said goodbye to Ella, Abigail hung up and handed the phone back to Joe. She returned to the couch and stretched out across it.

"Abigail, why are you here?" Joe asked. He was abrupt. What did she think? That she could waltz in and out of his life as her needs demanded? "Why come to me?"

Abigail smirked.

"Who else would have me? Soon as word of this gets out, I'll be persona non grata everywhere, don't you think?" She yawned, and her eyelids fluttered in an effort to stay open. "Sheriff Rutledge told me not to leave town. Don't worry. I won't burden you long. I'll think of somewhere to go."

She lifted one of the back cushions and put it under her head like a bed pillow. Before Joe had time to say "No!" she fell asleep there or pretended to. Figuring he'd kick her out in the morning, Joe trudged upstairs clutching a bottle of bourbon to his chest. Drink was the only thing that would allow him to sleep with Billy dead and Abigail lying in his living room. He drank and stared at the ceiling until his eyes were hard as stones, after which he closed them and found more reasons not to sleep.

At last, sometime just before the dawn, Joe nodded off. When he went downstairs three hours later, Abigail was gone. A Post-it on the refrigerator said, merely, "Thanks."

On the other side of the island, Ella also stayed awake the night long. She'd always loved Billy. Despite all that happened, she'd never stopped, not for a minute. She'd managed to forget him day to day, but when it came down to Billy's not walking the earth anymore, she suffered a flood of emotion. First it came in a tidal wave all at once and then, even worse, it came one cherished memory, one hot moment of shame, one cold resentment at a time. She counted all the hot moments and the cold ones, admitted the cherished were the fewest of the lot, and knew she loved him anyway. She wished they'd had one last talk, like the ones when they were kids and shared everything. He was easy to talk to. She could tell him anything. She regretted she'd never told him that she forgave him for Abigail.

After the autopsy, about which no one who knew anything was talking, per order of Sheriff Malcolm X Rutledge, Craigen Funeral Home prepared Billy Euston for burial. Whenever a true son or daughter of Sweetgrass Island died, the old families who could still get out and about came to the funeral in all their generations. The man loved by both Abigail Becker and Ella Price was a Sweetgrass man, born and bred. Multitudes had cared for him along the way. They'd known his mama and his daddy and all their relatives when they were alive. When his daddy went to prison, they looked after him where they could. Over time, he'd become not a town hero like Big George, but a town character, famous as a pitmaster, infamous as a womanizer, and generally, a good old son of a redneck by the lights of most who knew him. The folk who attended his funeral had enjoyed meals at every restaurant he'd cooked in from the age of fifteen on. They lined up during holidays to buy his trays of ribs and chicken. They sang along when he felt moved to play the piano or the banjo. That he died suddenly only increased their attendance. Many who observed the rites came partly to find out the latest intelligence on how this young man of fifty-two came to pass on; not just how he died, but how he looked, what he had on, did he say anything before he passed, and who was there. They knew the funeral was the place to find out.

The Holy Tabernacle of Jesus Christ by the Sea was the deceased's house of worship when he needed one, so Abigail charged Pastor Ronald T. Quirk with the arrangements. Pastor Quirk realized that his small, cinderblock church could not contain hordes of mourners. He erected wedding tents between it and the church cemetery, where a hillock of flowers and a fresh hole in the ground awaited the bones of Billy Euston. He held the service standing between them. Just before he started in, he counted cars, wishing there was more space to the parking lot. Soon, the entire facing street would be clogged for half a mile. He'd invited the chief mourners—Abigail, Ella, and Big George—to wait inside the cooling stone of the Tabernacle until it was time to start. The parking got tight, but off-duty police kept the nonmourner traffic rolling by even as tourists and transplants slowed down, gawking at the tents as they drove past, wondering what was going on, what was that big crowd for, so many Black people mixed in with so many white. The grounds of the Tabernacle offered no clue for the uninitiated. A sea of church lady hats and men in short-sleeved shirts and ties swarmed all over. The goings-on could be anything: a wedding or a funeral, a centenarian's birthday party, or a fundraiser for the local school.

Quirk debated with himself a good while before deciding where Billy Euston's body should lie. Usually for a funeral this size, he instructed the pallbearers to bring the casket to rest between the two tents, and he would stand behind it. But today, it being so damn hot a Saturday in August, he thought it better to leave it in the church, where people could file in and pay respects in an orderly way without fainting from the heat. After the eulogies and viewing, the pallbearers could bring it to the graveside.

When the time came, maybe three hundred people listened to the pastor deliver a solid Billy's-gone-home-to-Jesus homily, rife with biblical quotes on forgiveness. Before calling the chief mourners up to say a few words, Quirk introduced someone known to them all, Billy's sous-chef from the Flying Pig, Harley Carson. Harley gave the formal eulogy, as both the primary women in Billy's life, those being the closest thing he had to family, demurred. His death was too much of a shock, they said independently, but no less sincerely for expressing the exact same emotion. Neither could rise to the occasion. Let somebody else do it, they told him.

Harley Carson was the kind of Black man that women of all colors both fear and love. As Billy's sous-chef, he spent a great deal of time with his head in the smoker, poking, prodding, and basting. Even after a shower and shampoo, he smelled of woodsmoke. He ground spices for the rub, although Billy was the only one who mixed and massaged them into the meat. Billy said the finishing chores required a delicate touch, and no one ever suspected Carson capable of finesse, mostly because he was short and portly with broad shoulders and forearms like hams. His oversized bear paws looked like they could crush a woman's head between them if he were made angry enough, hence the fear he inspired. But the truth was that he was kind and gentle to a fault, hence the love. His brown eyes sparkled with good humor on the most dreary day; his full lips were ever ready to smile or purse in sympathy, whichever was needed. Despite the fact that his nose was bent from a childhood misadventure and his teeth were crooked, the man had charm. That day, the charm was on full display. After the pastor called his name, Harley stepped forward, took the microphone from him, planted his feet in a wide stance, raised one of his arms, and dropped his head.

"Billy Euston," he said in his deep, mellifluous voice. "Billy Euston is dead. They eatin' good in heaven tonight . . ."

The crowd murmured. Some chuckled, but lightly.

"Amen," a voice cried out and then another. "Amen."

Carson dropped his arm and lifted his head. He continued.

"The day I met Billy Euston was the luckiest day of my life. Yes, it was. You all remember what I was like as a boy. Orphaned, rootless, and round as a ball, bouncin' across this island from pillar to post, lookin' for the meal my poor old meemaw couldn't afford to give me. Look and ye shall find, the good book says. I took that to heart and found plenty. No matter what they say, I never stole pies off windowsills. I crawled right over 'em to raid pantry and ice chest for more substantial fare, once I made sho' nobody was home. Well, you can't be that sho' about nothin'. One day I chanced to skittle through Billy's window, and there was the man himself, crossed-armed, lips all tight, starin' me down.

"I was terrified. Billy was still young in them days. There was a hardness about him that helped him get by all the trials and tribulations the Lord visited upon his mama and daddy. This'd be afore he found good luck. Once he got that, he was grateful. He ditched the hardness and turned to simple shrewd thinkin' to get by."

Members of the assembled spoke out again. "Amen," they said. "Amen." They knew Billy and remembered him when he was hard and when he was easy. Harley continued.

"Like I say, this was afore all that. There I was, a barefoot, threadbare boy struck dumb by a hard white man glarin' at him. I thought he might kill me. Instead, he said, 'I know you. You Jessie Carson's granbaby, no?' I nodded, prayin' my bladder would stay under control. 'What you doin' comin' through my window?' he asked. I had my head down and mumbled, but he figured it out. 'Alright. Well, if you're that damn hungry, don't you ever crawl through no one's window again. You just come on over to here and I'll feed you proper, and give you some to take home to Miss Jessie, too.' And right there, right then, he fixed me up a plate of Q and watched me eat it."

As Carson told it, Billy promised him an after-school job washing dishes at the Pig. To keep him from a future of prison and penury, was how he put it. He made him swear he'd stay in school until he was at least fifteen. That was when Euston's education had stopped, and it seemed plenty enough to him. When the day came, he made Harley his apprentice, and a few years later his number one. Billy said the kid had not only the brains to do the job, but also the personality to make the customers happy. That was just as important as how the Q tasted, no matter how fine.

"And that's the kind of man Billy Euston was. Helpful, generous, knowledgeable. As Big George here knows well, he had a soft spot for the fatherless child, and he helped more than me and George. Jerry Phillips, I know you know that, and you, too, Albert T." He looked through the audience and couldn't find those he cited. "C'mon, boys. Your skinny white asses have to be here today. Stand up, why don't you, and honor the man."

Two young white men, one in khaki pants too small for him and the other in khakis too large, stood up, blushing, clutching their hats at waist level. They nodded and murmured, although no one in attendance could understand what they said.

Carson went on, but the tone in his voice signaled he was winding up.

"We cannot forget, and as every woman in this audience knows, Billy had a soft spot for the ladies, too—but I don't know as 'soft' is the word I'd give it."

Everyone laughed, even Abigail and Ella. Even Pastor Quirk.

"I don't know if any of you all know this, but when I was seventeen, I tried to make a few dollars printing up T-shirts dedicated to Billy. I went broke on it, but only because I paid in advance and the printer made a mistake. They came out 'Lock up your women, Willy Easton's comin' down the road.' Nobody knew who that fool was . . ."

By now, people were dabbing eyes wet from mirth. Considering his job done, Carson finished up.

"You know, he never minded that I done that. I think it gave him a chuckle. So you all come down to the Flyin' Pig tonight. We're gonna raise a glass to old Billy and eat a plate of Q on me. It's the least I can do for a man who was friend, boss, and benefactor to me." He raised his arms again and looked up into the sky. "Billy, you will be missed. Keep the spit turnin'. We'll all be joinin' you one day, and I for one will be hungry. Amen."

He turned to sit down, but changed his mind and turned back.

"One more thing. I know some of you all been concerned about Billy's dogs. Not to worry, I took 'em for the time bein'. Friendly Gus and Young Mr. Ben was confused at first, but they're doin' fine now. My Miss Lucy is bossin' them pooches like she was their very own mama. Alright. I guess that's all."

With that, Carson sat down amid a resounding chorus of Amens and Praise Jesus. It was time for Abigail, Ella, and Big George to deliver their postscripts to the eulogy. When it came down to it, the three missed the gravitas Billy's casket would have provided. Harley had turned a funeral into a party. Their dignity was undermined by a shift in mood, by standing in front of a seated crowd like politicians expected to make remarks that were heartfelt, intimate, and with a laugh in 'em, the way Carson's had. There was nothing to be done but go through with it, that one slender white woman, the tall Black woman, and her handsome son.

Abigail was brief. She said, "Billy was good to me when I didn't deserve good." That was it. Nothing more.

Ella spoke next: "From the day forty years gone when we met on the wild river to last week when Lillibelle called me with the news he'd passed, I have counted Billy as my loving, dear friend. His passin' lays a great stillness upon my soul."

Big George said, "Whatever else he was, that man was more daddy to me than any other man in my mama's life. He was a good daddy. He truly was."

Maybe they would have said more if the casket had been before them and they could address the dead directly, but Joe thought it was enough. After Pastor Quirk led everybody in "Ain't No Grave (Gonna Hold My Body Down)," the chief mourners returned to the church to line up and receive condolences. A queue of well-wishers wound around the church more than once. Joe did not join them. Jews don't lay out their dead for public viewing, so the experience was completely alien to him. The thought of staring down at Billy Euston stretched out, hands folded across his chest, maybe holding a crucifix, his ruddy face pale with makeup, made him shudder. He leaned against his car's rear fender while he waited for everybody else to say their farewells, wondering how Abigail could stand within sight of the deceased. The queue steadily made its way in one door of the church and out the other. It didn't take too much time. Though Joe knew most of the people there, no one wanted to meet his eye. He understood. It wasn't personal. Cuckolds like him were the dark side of Billy's story. This wasn't the day folks wanted to remember them.

Goodbyes over, the pallbearers brought the coffin out and accompanied it to the grave. There was Uncle Dan, Big George, and Declan, who'd abandoned the pub on a Saturday afternoon. Jukebox Jackie came all the way down from Memphis for the honor, and it was the first time anyone ever saw Tulsa Reardon of the Cottonwood Boys awake before noon. The funeral home lowered Billy into the ground while Jukebox Jackie played harmonica and Pat Magee sang "The Parting Glass." Declan hummed along and offered a sterling baritone harmony at the end. Meanwhile, Abigail, Ella, and Big George used the small silver shovel provided by Craigen's to begin the stream of dirt that would soon cover Billy's casket.

Everyone tossed a shovel of dirt in the grave when their time came. Several women, one of them heavily veiled, tossed in a flower instead. One by one, the mourners paid their respects and left. Toward the end, both Abigail and Ella took off their high heels and ceased to stand, sitting instead, side by side in metal folding chairs just inside one of the tents, fanning themselves with paper fans on which a photo of Craigen Funeral Home was printed. At last, it was just the chief mourners and Pastor Quirk. Behind them, the gravediggers finished the job of covering Billy up. Joe came over to the place where the women sat. He embraced both Ella and Big George long and hard. He stood in front of Abigail and nodded. It was the best he could manage. He found himself angry with her not for anything that had happened in the past but because she hadn't arranged to invite people back to Billy's home for a proper wake. It wasn't that he loved Billy—far from it—but it seemed decidedly crass not to follow custom, to punt it instead to the Flying Pig, an act that painted her as a clueless Yankee. He felt it reflected similarly on him by extension, however attenuated.

"Will you all be going to the Pig?" Joe asked the others as if to underscore his unspoken thoughts. "There'll be singing and stories."

Abigail shook her head no. Ella waved a hand through the air.

"I've heard every one of those stories five times if I've heard 'em once."

Big George said, "I'm tired. I'll just take Mama home."

Soon Joe was alone in the parking lot, Pastor Quirk having left when Big George pulled up to the front of the church to load his mother. Abigail drove off in Billy's truck. Uncle Dan was at the side door of the church, talking to a state cop with a toothpick in his mouth. They both wore aviator sunglasses and long bushy sideburns. The cop needed to wait for everyone to leave so he could pronounce the area secure.

On seeing Joe, Uncle Dan ambled toward him. While he did, Joe realized he hadn't caught any gossip on Billy's demise.

"So what are folks saying?" Joe asked him.

"Murder, that's what they're callin' it. Some came here expectin' to witness the graveside arrest of Abigail Becker, and failin' that, a few other names surfaced."

Uncle Dan put a hand on Joe's shoulder and gave him a friendly, paternal squeeze. He said: "Your name came up, as I recall."

Joe's jaw dropped.

"Me?"

"You got motive, son, you have to admit that."

Joe shook his head in denial.

"I haven't been upset about all that since just after it happened."

"I understand. But nobody knows what you do up there at that house all day, writin' children's books, for Lord's sake. To them, all that unsupervised, unregistered time means you had opportunity along with motive. However . . ."

Uncle Dan went through all the reasons he thought Joe was innocent. While Joe appreciated his intent, learning that he was under suspicion for murder by the people he called neighbor and friend put him off listening very closely. He wondered if anyone had whispered their theories to Abigail or Ella.

From somewhere in front of the church, a car horn blasted repeatedly in staccato rhythm. Miss Sadie had gotten impatient. Uncle Dan hurried off to her.

Joe was now drenched in sweat. It rolled down his back and dripped into his eyes. He got in his car and turned up the AC. Once he was on Main Road and could travel with some speed, he banged on his steering wheel with an open palm. "Billy Euston! You nearly destroyed me in life. Will you finish the job in death? What did I ever do to you?" he shouted. "I was never anything but a friend to you. A friend with a beautiful wife."

Then he laughed in the lonely cavern of his car because everyone who knew Billy knew that the last would have been enough.

20.

The days following Billy's funeral passed in a prickly mess of anxiety and sorrow for Joe. The sorrows were old, dug up from the past. Most were named Abigail, although the loneliness of childhood was raised from the dead with her. Heartache is malignant, he decided. It starts as one sad thing and spreads to every other sad thing the memory can bear. He labored to put glum thoughts behind him. After a few days, he was still vulnerable, but feeling philosophical, at least about Abigail.

Joe's anxieties, fortified by paranoia, were another story. They were spanking new. He had no mechanism to fight them. No one had ever suspected him of murder before, and it felt like the whole island did now. Why else would he provoke fascination, fear, and aversion everywhere he went? Strangers stared at him on the street, at the Piggly Wiggly. Late afternoon two days after the funeral, he entered the post office and Standish Pruitt, a man he'd had in his home and in whose home he'd enjoyed supper, left precipitously. He nearly tripped over himself, holding an unmailed package under his arm. Later that same day, out of sadness over Pruitt, Joe went over to Declan's Pub seeking the companionship he'd come to expect at the bar. Randy Weathers ran off the second he saw him. Braver souls held their ground, asked him how he was, and then clammed up. Partly, that was his fault. Anxious and disheartened as he was, Joe had no small talk, no pleasantries to offer. It may have been that people gave him room out of respect for his feelings, whatever they thought those were, but it didn't feel that way to Joe. It felt like suspicion. It stung. Over the next couple of days, two men and one woman he knew phoned to mine his imagination for insights into the murder, but it irritated him that they thought he had any. He was not entirely polite. None called a second time. He began to feel the solid ground beneath his feet, the one he'd achieved on the island by dint of tolerance and camaraderie, crumbling.

He half expected Abigail to call or come by, but she did not. He wondered if she still lived at Billy's place but knowing her as he did, he surmised she would never stay at the house where she'd discovered her lover dead. He had no idea where else she might be. He expected Ella or Big George to call, but they didn't either. Reluctant to disturb Ella, he called George, left messages, and received no call back. Although it hurt, he tried not to make too much of George's neglect. The man's burden of grief was surely grave, complex. But no one came knocking, not even the deputy of Sheriff Malcolm X Rutledge—the sole visitor he fully expected.

On the Tuesday after the funeral, Joe realized that if Ella hadn't called him, he hadn't called her either. Maybe she was waiting for him to take the first step. Ella possessed extraordinary patience, which her life with footloose Billy proved over and over. Directly after breakfast and whatever morning tasks business demanded, he drove over to Elegance by Ella.

Once he got there, he took his time leaving the car. He parked a block down the street in front of Al's Old Tyme Barbershop, where she would not see him from her display window. He studied who came in and who left the store, how long they stayed. He glanced up to the second floor to see if anyone entered or departed there, although she'd lived alone since Big George moved out a year ago. By rights, Ella should be downstairs inside the store, at work. Joe waited a bit longer. Part of him feared that Ella had heard rumors he was a murderer. What if she believed them? Ella was his anchor on Sweetgrass Island. Her approval was a great gift to him, and it carried tremendous weight in the community. Without her friendship and support, he'd be adrift, a stranger again, belonging nowhere, to no one. Abigail was the only other woman in all his life who'd helped him feel grounded to a place. *Didn't that turn out swell*, he thought. He gathered his courage, reminding himself that Ella was neither wife nor lover to him, and for that very reason, more likely to be loyal and true.

Maybe Ella could not see him there, ruminating in his car, but Al the barber could. He came out to sweep his sidewalk, which did not need it, staring at Joe every chance he got from all kinds of angles. Joe suffered under the barber's scrutiny, knowing it would continue as long as he sat there, too conflicted to move. At last, he marshaled resolve enough and exited his vehicle with bravado. "Mornin', Mr. Al," he said in a cheerful voice. Al muttered something indistinct, then abruptly reentered his shop.

Joe entered Ella's. Two refined-looking Black women in crisp casual suits, good jewelry, and low heels conferred over a rack of summer blouses and tunics. A middle-aged white woman, her linen shirt and pants substantially wrinkled, worn with a matching bandanna tied without style or sense over rebellious whisps of straggly gray hair, clicked her car keys on the register counter, waiting for assistance. It was not a good time. He should have called. He thought about leaving when the curtains of the fitting room rustled. He straightened up, made his features pleasant even as he felt an anxious tightening of his chest.

Ella emerged from the fitting room, pincushion strapped to her wrist. She looked the same as ever, tall, unbowed, handsome in the indestructible way Black women who were beauties in their youths retain their good looks in maturity without apparent effort, all essential harmony and grace. Joe felt relieved. He smiled and waved a little, but Ella did not see him. She made a beeline to the white woman, apologizing for the delay in service.

"That's alright, darlin'. You here now," the customer said, surprising Joe by her soft voice and gentle demeanor when he'd expected harsh words and fidgety irritation. He reminded himself yet again that nothing was as it first seemed in the South, and he wondered if he'd ever live every drop of Boston out of himself.

The white woman taken care of and out the door, Ella turned her attention to the Black women who, it turned out, were waiting for the friend Ella had been fitting minutes before. The friend left the dressing room directly and the three hit the street, chatting about lunch.

At last, Ella gave him notice. She smiled, but not before Joe witnessed a shadow cross over her round midnight eyes followed by a blink; yes, there it was again, a short sharp blink. He could swear her mouth pinched just before the smile. *Damn*, he thought, miserably, *she thinks I killed him, too.* Yet still, they advanced and embraced. It was a good embrace, longer than custom or superficial affection required.

When it was over, they stood back and studied each other with solemnity. Joe revised his initial opinion. Ella looked a little worn. She seemed older since the funeral, as if the few lines on her face had deepened or multiplied. Ella thought Joe looked sleep-deprived. She reached up and touched his cheek.

"You look tired," she said.

He gave out a sigh.

"That's putting it mildly. You look as beautiful as ever, Ella, but—I don't know—sad, I guess. Weighted down."

She shrugged.

"Try old."

"Not you. Never."

"Spoken like the pup you are, boy," she said. "Wait twenty years. The hands of time will wrap around your neck, too."

She gestured to the set of comfy chairs she kept for waiting husbands near the fitting room. They both sat. Joe leaned forward, took up the hands that lay folded in Ella's lap, and grasped them.

"You been okay, Ella?" he asked.

She slid one hand free and patted his.

"I'm fine. I miss the idea of Billy breathin', I won't say I don't, but I'm not grievin' like I might've done years ago. Too much water passed under that bridge. But Billy's movin' on set me to review my life, and it's not all pretty. There've been times maybe I did the right thing, maybe I didn't. It worries me on occasion, I still don't know which times were which."

Ella Price was the most honorable woman Joe knew. It struck him as impossible she would do the wrong thing, and he told her so. She couldn't help but laugh, her voice rising in a chorus of bells; *angel bells*, Joe thought, *so pure and clear.*

"And how's Big George?" he asked after the laughter pealed down to nothing. "I phoned him a couple of times. Left messages. He didn't answer."

Ella saw how much her son's neglect disturbed Joe. She rushed to explain.

"I don't believe he even knows you called yet. He hasn't been home. He's been here, keepin' me company. We turned the phone off after the funeral. There were just too many calls. He only left this morning. I'm sure you'll be hearin' from him soon. But how you doin', honey?"

He did not hesitate to tell the truth.

"Horrid. Everybody thinks I killed Billy."

He hoped for swift reassurance but received none. There was a crude, cold silence between them. He squirmed as if he were under a naked lightbulb in an airless cement room. His grip weakened. His hands slipped away from hers.

"You, too, Ella?"

"Oh no, darlin'! Don't you ever think that. I know you. You could never," she said. "Besides, what you've been feelin' from others is prob'ly in your head. Have you thought of that?"

She paused, giving him a deep, steady look to underscore her words. He breathed in the comfort bestowed by them, achieving a little peace through their sincerity, the peace that had eluded him since the day Abigail knocked on his door. For the first time since, he felt a stillness overcome his heart's frantic beat—until she excited it all over again.

"I'll tell you what troubles me," she said abruptly. "I know somethin'. Somethin' I've been told in confidence, and I just don't know if I ought to betray that or not."

Joe had never taken Ella for a torturer, but that's the way he felt now. Tortured. Why did she tell him such a thing if she couldn't follow up? He asked, "Did whoever told you whatever it was say that if you mentioned it to anyone you would forfeit your immortal soul?"

"No. He just said 'Between you and me,' that's all. But it was the way he said it."

"Who?" asked Joe. "Can you at least tell me that?"

Ella lowered her gaze. He watched her debate the right thing to do. When her eyes came back up, she sighed his name in capitulation, expressing a deeper loyalty to friendship than civic duty.

"Joe," she said, "it was Malcolm X."

"Jesus Christ," he muttered. The sheriff. He tried to keep the desperation out of his voice.

"Between you and me is common language, Ella. It's not a sacred vow."

"I s'pose."

Then, out of affection for Joe and all they'd been through together, she spilled.

Billy Euston had not been poisoned. Definitely, absolutely, without a doubt, not poisoned. The toxicology report came back with impeccably negative results. The only thing in his blood was plenty of booze and THC. Why Abigail had insisted otherwise was likely due to ignorance on her part. When she'd mentioned the strange colors of Billy's corpse, she'd been right, sort of—it had an abnormal appearance for one dead a short time—but in every other way, she'd been all wrong. The swift coagulation of his blood had not produced the green, red, or pink colors of poison, but a pattern of blotches, black and mottled gray, about his head and neck.

Joe had spent many haunted hours imagining Abigail mixing potions of bleach and battery fluid to fill an eyedropper poised over Billy Euston's dinner plate. His relief that he might erase that image forever was fierce. Unwilling to offend the woman before him, he tried to keep emotion from his features.

"What does it mean, Ella?"

Ella's eyes filled.

"Malcolm X said the cause of death was heart attack caused by suffocation. After he was smothered, the murderer held him upside down, which is the only way the blood would pool like that in his face. He might have been suspended by his feet, except there were no ligature marks on his ankles or knees. Later on, he must have been moved to the couch, where Abigail found him."

By the time she finished, tears ran down her cheeks. Not copiously, not in a stream, but like everything else Ella did, discreetly, one slow descending drop at a time. Joe moved to console her, but she waved a hand to indicate she was alright and neither needed nor wanted succor.

Joe thought about what she'd described. First, he indulged his lesser self with a fanciful vision, one of a mess of Furies swooping down on Billy Euston in balletic vengeance for all the women he'd wronged, tossing him from each to each, smothering him with their wings, wild-eyed and stretched mouthed. But no, it would have been men, acting with brute force for similar reasons.

"It would take a man to do all that, maybe more than one."

"That's what Malcolm X thought."

"Does he have leads?" Joe asked.

"That part he did not tell me."

Joe thought more.

"I'm sorry, but it doesn't sound like something anyone from here would do. No one I know at least. First off, the method. Hanging him upside down. Why would someone do that? Why not just shoot him or knife him? That's the way a local would do. Besides, people were fond of Billy. They loved him. Everybody forgave him his peccadilloes."

He nearly added, *even you*, but thought better of it.

She nodded.

"That's true," she said. "Unless there's men and prob'ly women, too, all over the island with secret, festerin' wounds put there by Billy when he was of a mind to take the things his heart wanted. They might've thought he wasn't worth a bullet."

Joe laughed in a rueful way.

"I ought to make a list," he said. "Take it over to Sheriff Rutledge and encourage him to widen the field."

Ella said, "It's an idea."

She stood and walked to her front door, flipped the Open sign to Closed, and asked Joe if he'd had lunch. She'd skipped breakfast and needed to eat.

"I can give you some sweet tea and cold chicken," she said. "I'll fix up some okra, too."

It was a kind offer, but one he refused.

"I appreciate it, but I've got errands. Another time," Joe said, deciding to head over to Uncle Dan's gun shop where the gossip was always keen and where so far, at least, he felt welcome. It wasn't much, but he needed to get started on that list. Uncle Dan might help.

"Alright, but you're lookin' awful thin," Ella said. "Those back pockets of yours start in to meet, and I'm tyin' you down and feedin' you with a tube."

Joe smiled, if weakly. He rose from his chair and headed with Ella to the back door, his arm around her waist, hers around his. They squeezed each other's middles.

The road to Uncle Dan's offered stretches of rural glory in between bursts of strip malls, fast-food restaurants, and developments just breaking ground. Joe preferred the rural. As he passed an expanse of green marsh at low tide, he opened windows to let the thick, humid air, fragrant with pluff mud, flow in. He breathed in deep to savor its sharp scent. Billy once told him only homegrown Southerners loved it that much, and he said it in a way that made newcomer Joe feel accepted, part of the low country. It was one of his favorite memories, even if its source was that no-good wife-stealing dead bastard.

The fresh air made Joe hungry. He stopped at a filling station and bought some beef jerky and chips, which he ate en route, washing it down with cola.

By the time Joe arrived at Uncle Dan's, he was feeling better than he had for some time. Ella had cheered him, given him hope along with a plan. The ride calmed him, too. If he was less depressed, he remained innervated, in a state that was a little more than jumpy yet less than manic. The familiar sight of Uncle Dan's Gun Shop, Auto Body, and Fireworks, clustered together closer than cousins, festooned with red, white, and blue bunting, caused Joe to shake his head and smile. He peered through the windows to find Uncle Dan, head bent over his account ledger, frowning and pulling at his muttonchops. Joe rapped on the glass to alert him before entering.

Uncle Dan was excited to see him. He hopped up from his stool behind the counter, radiating pleasure. Joe was impressed with how quickly and lightly he moved, given the man's sizable belly and age.

"Why, Joe Becker, ain't it good to see you! We've barely talked since the news about Billy got out, but for the plantin' of him when we managed to chat a bit, if I recall correctly."

"You do, Uncle Dan." Because he was polite as a rule, he inquired about Dan's wife. "Miss Sadie well?"

"Fit enough to boss me sunup to sundown," Uncle Dan said. He glanced wide-eyed over his shoulder, amazed at his own audacity. He never could tell when Miss Sadie might pop up behind him, wagging a finger, delivering hell. "Thanks for askin'."

Joe sat down in his usual folding chair against the wall. He opened his mouth but a customer came in, so he shut it again. The customer, a young man in feed cap and overalls, purchased a box of shotgun shells and left. Joe talked rapidly before someone new arrived.

"Uncle Dan. I've just come from Ella's," he began.

"Miss Ella? How is she? She's been on my mind. I keep thinkin' of how hard everything that's happened must be for her, and then that gets me to thinkin' about the old days, when she and Billy were comin' up. Mr. Salt and Li'l Miss Pepper, we called 'em then . . ."

Joe was too restless to listen to one of Uncle Dan's long stories, no matter how entertaining. His feet tapped against the floor. He shifted in his seat. Before long, he did his own interrupting.

"It's all quite admirable, Uncle Dan," he said. "They were the vanguard of the New South, a love story for the ages. But listen, this is important. Ella and me, we've come up with an idea about Billy's murder. Maybe you can help."

Though it had been a good fifteen years since he'd left the force, part of Uncle Dan never did. Once an officer of the law, always an officer of the law, he reminded anyone who would listen. Attention won, he leaned over the display case with his cop face on: unblinking, serious, stone-cold.

"I'm listenin'."

Joe related everything Ella told him, including the supposed direction of the Malcolm X Rutledge investigation.

"It worries me that he might be looking in my direction," he confessed. "In his eyes, I'm still an outsider, capable of anything. But it'd take two men to do what they think was done. I mean, really. If I were the one, who would help me?"

"Can't think of a soul," Uncle Dan said in quiet, steady voice. "Anybody around you acting guilty in your presence of late?"

"Well, Standish Pruitt jumped and ran soon as I came into the post office. And Randy Weathers split quick as that when I sat down at Declan's bar . . ."

Uncle Dan blew a stream of dismissive air out a corner of his mouth.

"Shoot. Standish Pruitt's got a weak bladder these days that has him runnin' for relief at the sight of a water bottle. It's August. Half the people in line over there were holdin' one, I'm bettin'. And Randy Weathers? Sholy, he was just headed outside for a smoke. Can't last but ninety seconds without one." He stroked his chin and stared at the ceiling a minute. "What about men in a similar position to yourself? The ranks of the betrayed."

"Good idea," Joe said.

He got to his feet and paced back and forth in front of Uncle Dan's ammo rack. His hands swooped the air in grand gestures.

"But how exactly am I going to find out who they are?" he asked.

Uncle Dan pulled out a pencil and paper bag from a drawer behind him.

"I can tell you that," he said. "Here, write this down."

Joe bent over the glass countertop, pencil poised.

"Axel Gullan, Heyward Dinnest, Cal Dunlap," he said. "Those names spring to mind."

Joe was shocked. He knew them all, more or less: Cal Dunlap, the butcher who'd tried to teach Abigail how to make rabbit stew; Heyward Dinnest, the sweet old landscaper everyone trusted; Axel Gullan, a hothead when drunk, for sure, but he only came in town a couple times a month. If Gullan wanted a piece of Billy Euston, he would have taken it a long time ago.

"You're kidding. Alla them? When?"

"Oh, in the last year and a bit, I'd say."

This was a shock. Billy Euston had played Abigail just as he'd played Ella her whole damn life, only twice as hard. At his age. After what he and Abigail had been through.

"Son," said Dan, watching his mind work. "Leopards and spots, remember that. Leopards and spots."

Joe sighed and shrugged. He pondered aloud what drew Billy to the women on the list.

"I know Martha Gullan and Constance Marie Dunlap. They're both young enough. Martha's real sweet. I can see Billy wanting a taste of that after listening to Abigail whine for a year or more. And Constance Marie . . . she's older than both Martha and Abigail, but spicy, you know?"

"Damn straight. Hot sauce in shorts."

"Axel and Cal. I can see them both in a rage . . . but Heyward Dinnest's wife?" Doris Dinnest was a stalwart church lady who wore shapeless polka-dot dresses with orthopedic shoes like an old-time grandma. "I can't get my head around that."

Uncle Dan clucked his tongue.

"Not Doris, Joe. The daughter. Louanne."

"Geez. What is she? Just twenty, twenty-one? If he were still alive, I'd be tempted to kill him myself for that one."

"Uh-huh."

Joe's mouth twisted up with determination. He laid the pencil on the counter, folded the paper bag, and shoved it deep into his back pocket.

"One question," he said.

Dan nodded to encourage him.

"Am I the only one on the island who doesn't know about these . . . liaisons? Does Malcolm X?"

"It's known alright, here and there, though none too widely. Personally, I didn't get it from anybody but Billy himself. He wasn't the kind of man liked bein' gossiped about. People might say somethin' one to another on the q.t., but there was none of that barroom chat about him, or they'd face his wrath. Still, it's true, plain as dirt, Billy never could keep from braggin'. Even when he was tryin' to be discreet, he had to blab somewhere. I believe he thought I was a trustworthy repository, so I may have heard more than most."

An hour out of Ella's shop, and Joe Becker's paranoia returned. He bit his lower lip and clenched his fists, weighing the chances Uncle Dan knew long before anybody else about Billy and Abigail. Maybe he'd only feigned shock the night his ex-wife shot a piece of her head off. He shoved the idea out of his mind. He had to find peace some-where. If the whole island suspected him of murder, he figured Uncle Dan and Ella, who clearly did not, and maybe Big George, too, were the only friends he could count on.

". . . Now, the sheriff. Remember, he lives over the bridge just inside of town and spends most his time in the big station. He don't hear local gossip. On toppa that, his deputies are all scared of him, so unless an idea springs forth from the chief's own head, they aren't likely to consider another."

Joe felt he was getting a good start. He was armed with informa-tion and a working knowledge of who to embrace and who to hold at arm's length.

"Thank you, Dan. I'm going to look into things here, maybe visit a few people and take their measure. I don't want to point fingers unless there's a reason. If I find one, I'll take what I got to Malcolm X."

It was hard to say more. His chest was filled with a tremulous fear. The day's intelligence brought Abigail back to the forefront of suspects. His ex-wife would not take kindly to being cheated on, particularly if the cheating happened regularly. But how could she accomplish alone the brutish method of Billy's demise? As if reading his mind, Uncle Dan gave him a final word of wisdom.

"Remember this, too, Joe. Men kill. Women hire killers."

It was advice he'd be unlikely to forget.

21.

The butcher Cal Dunlap specialized in game brought to him by local hunters who didn't want or have the time to skin and quarter their kills, or a climate-controlled space to allow a field-dressed animal to age. After the third or fourth kill of the season, a hunter might sell excess meat to Cal, which he offered in turn to the deer-eating, non-hunting public; that is, newcomers from big cities all over, or old folk with joints swollen and painful enough to make sitting in a blind at dawn a misery. The low country hosted some of the best deer hunting in the country, coupled with a long season that stretched from August all the way to January. Accordingly, there were plenty of hunt tourists who couldn't take meat home, so Cal bought theirs, too, when he could. If demand required, he commissioned it. When the occasion presented itself, he offered rabbit and alligator meat as well. During the lean season, he sold the parts of free-range chickens kept and strangled by his wife, Constance Marie, along with whatever rare game was brought him: a rogue hog raiding a farmer's crops perhaps, or a coyote some fool wanted to eat out of curiosity. He didn't like dressing the latter, but in the slow times, he needed income. Even so, he flat out refused to work on wildfowl or fish. "A man has to have standards," he'd say. Deer season had just begun. Cal was plenty busy.

Constance Marie worked the retail end of the business. She sat behind the counter at the front of the store while her husband skinned, sawed, and filleted animal cadavers in the cold room out back. A windowed refrigeration unit ran the length of the wall behind her. On its shelves were cardboard boxes containing brown paper packages tied up with string, each marked with the name of their owner, the kind of animal, and the cut contained within. The last two sections were reserved for game on sale to whoever wanted it.

Joe parked under a venerable live oak in the hope that its wide limbs, thickly leafed, would keep his car cool in the afternoon heat. A pickup truck with deer antlers poking up above the rim of its bed passed him, headed around back to Cal Dunlap's cold room. It backed up to the loading platform, and the driver killed the engine. Two young men in orange hunting vests hopped out, each swinging a flask.

"Cal!" they yelled out, banging on the sides of the truck "Cal! Look here!"

The butcher stuck his head out the door. "My, oh my," he marveled, and congratulated them on the weight of their kill while counting its points. Before they headed to Cal's, the boys had the good sense to get bags of ice at the Stop and Go and place them around the carcass. They jumped in the bed and tossed half-melted bags around to clear the buck from under their weight, then worked to pull him out. Depending on the weather and the time of day, Cal might indulge in a beer or a shot with those who gave him business, and from the look of things, that was going to happen today. This was a stroke of luck for Joe. He'd have a chance to talk to Constance Marie first, and then Cal after he'd got a head on him.

The building was made of cinder block with a steel-framed glass door on the retail side. Joe looked in to see Constance Marie sitting on a stool behind the Formica-topped counter. Her hands supported her head as she read a book. She wore a summer dress, low-cut, short, and sheer; a frock too young for her forty-odd years, but she had the body for it. She swung one of her crossed legs slowly, back and forth, a high-heeled sandal dropping off her heel. Constance Marie didn't hold a candle to Abigail in her glory days, but she had her beat in her decline. If Abigail had discovered the goings-on between Constance Marie and Billy, she would have been furious.

A set of bells attached to the lintel rang when he opened the door. Constance Marie's head jerked up. Her brown eyes flashed, her bobbed red hair danced against her chin. The cupid's bow of a mouth pursed at first, then, recognizing who'd come to call, she bestowed upon Joe a bright smile. No matter what was on his mind, he couldn't help but smile back.

"Why, Joe Becker," she said in a warm, intimate drawl, as they knew each other from Declan's Pub, "what brings a refined author such as yourself to our low-down establishment?"

His face reddened.

"I thought it was about time I tried some deer steak. What do you recommend?"

Constance Marie hopped off her stool and walked down to the end of the refrigeration line. Her walk was provocative, her hips gliding slowly side to side in rhythm to the clicking of her high heels. Joe wondered if she always walked that way—he'd never noted her gait before—or if she moved that way just for him. She gestured to the for-sale box.

"There's not much, you know," she said. "It's too early in the season. But I do have some fresh loin and a little shoulder just settin' there. I recommend the loin, if it's your first time. How you plan to cook it?"

Joe didn't know. Constance Marie recommended he trim the fat and marinate the steak overnight after which he might sauté it. She gave him instructions for a citrus-based marinade.

"Now you want to add bacon fat to your pan, as it'll be drier than beef," she said. "But you just lard that baby 'til it cries for mama, and it'll be fine."

She opened the refrigerator door. She leaned in, studied the inside of the box, and grabbed a package. When she turned around, the effects of the cold air were evident across her chest. Unsettled, Joe averted his eyes. He took out his handkerchief to mop his face, hoping she'd attribute his discomfort to the day's heat.

"I don't do bacon," he said.

She frowned and slapped her forehead with the palm of a brightly manicured hand.

"Oh, dang, I forgot. You're a Jew, isn't that right?" she said. "I'm sorry, but you always seem so normal to me." She frowned again, realizing that in apology, she might have continued to offend. "I mean, you're like one of us," she added.

He mumbled, "Thanks. I guess."

If you could tie ten-pound weights to silence, it wouldn't have been heavier than the one between them. Constance Marie had been ill-mannered, and it troubled them both. Each wondered how to get over the hump of her casual, yet unmalicious, insult.

Joe could tell her the whole B&B farm story of why he and Abigail gave up pork years ago; that might defuse the moment. But this once, he let someone believe his abstinence from the South's fourth food group was religious. Humane eating didn't seem a topic that would work for a game butcher's wife.

"Butter," Constance Marie said, suddenly, her voice gone husky.

His brow wrinkled.

"Lard it with butter. Olive oil, if you prefer. But really, butter's better."

He nodded, cleared his throat, and handed her his credit card. She walked back to her stool, studying it with her head down. She was shy now to look at him, and Joe took advantage.

"Did I see you at Billy Euston's funeral?" he asked. That veiled woman could pass for Constance Marie. He was sure of it. "I did, didn't I?"

Constance Marie tried to stick his card into an electronic reader, but she got the angle wrong. She turned the card upside down, flipped it to one side, then the other. She swore to herself, finally got it right, then pressed a half-dozen buttons to record the sale. A narrow chit with faded print rolled out. He signed it. At last, she handed him back his card along with the meat.

"These new machines aren't worth the ink," she said. "S'posed to be so easy. Why do I keep gettin' it wrong all the time then? No matter how I look and what the whole island says, I ain't dumb."

She gave Joe a self-deprecating smile. When he took the card from her and their fingers touched, he felt a tremor. A small one, but still.

"Weren't you and Billy friends?" he persisted.

She took a deep breath and poked around in her book, as if someone had messed up the pages while she'd been occupied. Then she lied.

"Not particularly," she said. "You know, Billy was sociable to everyone, but I don't know how many of his friends were true. He and

Cal did business, for sho'. And sometimes they'd get loopy together, if you know what I mean."

An image of two men on a booze-fueled tear together, one of whom had betrayed the other—two men who made their livings wielding knives—flashed through Joe's mind. If Cal wanted to kill Billy out of jealous passion, why not stab him? Especially during a moment of mutual weakness when both of them were loaded? It would be cold and calculated to do it any other way.

"Speaking of Cal, I think I'll just pop in the back and say hello," Joe said. He noted that in recounting Billy and Cal's relationship, she'd avoided mentioning what her own might be. He might as well see what he could get out of her husband.

"You can go in through here," she said, letting him behind the counter to lead him down a corridor, where a heavy back door gave entry to the abattoir. She walked with far less sway than before. Even her heels made a softer sound against the cement floor. He glanced at her book as he passed through to see what she was reading. He expected the latest pulp bestseller but it was Faulkner's *Requiem for a Nun*. That was a surprise. Constance Marie was more than he'd imagined.

"History is not was, it is," he quoted to the back of her dress. She didn't respond. Either she didn't hear him or was focused on getting rid of him.

He opened the back door. The cold room was flooded with fluorescent light, everything in it presented in harsh, uncompromising detail. Short, thick Cal wore cargo pants, waterproof boots, an oilcloth apron, and elbow-length rubber gloves. His silver hair was slicked back with gel, and he wore a hairnet over it. His features wrinkled as he chose an instrument from his knife belt and commenced to transform one of God's most graceful creatures into a glistening obscenity of blood-drained pulp.

The cadaver hung by its legs from a chain and pole suspended from the ceiling. The boys hadn't done their best when gutting their buck in the field, probably due to whatever was in their flasks. The intestines were gone, along with the genitals, but there was much left. Cal worked fast to finish the job before spoilage set in. He removed the kidneys, liver, and heart, placing them in a basin of ice. He hosed down the cavity with cold water and, just after Joe walked in, grabbed the antlers then twisted them in one muscle-bulging move to break the neck. Then he detached the head, cutting along the spinal fissure with a sharp sawlike instrument. The boys laid the buck's head aside in an ice-filled wheelbarrow, then sat down on a freezer chest to watch Cal break more bones and flay the hide.

"Were you wantin' to mount the antlers, Jack?" Cal asked the blond man.

"You bet," Jack said. "We got enough room left on that wall, don't we, Brett?"

The other one, wraithlike with large knobby hands and an Adam's apple the size of its namesake, answered, "I believe so." He strolled over to Cal's instrument table and picked up a saw and a spoon. "I can do it, Cal, if you don't mind. I'll just scoop out the brains right t'here, and then boil and bleach it to home when we get there."

Cal shrugged.

"Alright, but don't come cryin' to me if it goes afoul."

Joe's head reeled, his stomach roiled, the stench of blood and death made him gag. He turned away to block a vision of hell. He put a hand up to the wall to steady himself and found it slick and cold, which sickened him further. He gurgled, he retched, he wanted to run. Miraculously, he did not vomit.

The others heard and looked up to notice him.

"You better not be pissin' against my wall," Cal joked to override the moment.

Brett came over to Joe, stood behind him, and put a hand on his shoulder, reaching around his chest to offer him his flask.

"Here, drink," he said, quietly. His tone was without mockery. "It makes the first time easier."

The sweet sear of good bourbon rolled down Joe's esophagus, purifying all that had ventured up. He allowed Brett to guide him to a folding chair his partner placed in back of the animal so he would not see much of Cal's activities.

"Mr. Joe," the butcher called out. "What brings you here today? I ask because you've never been here. We are obviously not a destination you normally conspire to achieve."

Cal chuckled not at Joe but with pride at his own convoluted sentence. Joe didn't know that and thinking himself mocked, for the third time in a single day, felt a humiliating heat under his skin. Trying for bravado, he shot his arm up in the air, brandishing his brown paper package.

"I am taking the plunge," he said. "After tonight, I will no longer be a deer-steak virgin."

Jack and Brett grinned and raised their flasks in salute. Cal Dunlap raised his filleting knife in the air.

"That's good you're back here, then," Cal said. "A man ought to know where his eatin' comes from. These days, hardly one in a thousand does."

"Billy Euston used to say that to me," Joe said.

The men murmured their honor to the dead.

"Sounds like him."

"Good ole Billy."

"To Billy."

The flasks were raised again, passed around.

They drank out of both flasks, Joe included, as if ritual demanded each be diminished equally. He may have drunk too deep out of a desire to appear one of the boys. The whiskey hit his belly hard. It sloshed against what was left of his lunch, cresting in waves that burned the back of his throat. He blurted out his purpose for lounging around a slaughterhouse before he lost it completely.

"So who do you think killed him?" he said. "A jealous husband?"

No one spoke. No one moved. The contents of Joe's stomach ascended yet again. He choked it back and fought to keep his gaze steady as he looked from man to man with an unmistakable intensity. He saved Cal Dunlap for last.

The boys dropped their eyes almost instantly. The butcher, however, held him fast.

"Mr. Joe. Do you think you can drive home?" he said.

He was being asked to leave. Whether he'd hit a nerve or simply compromised himself was unclear. He got to his feet. Out of exceptional resolve and sheer luck, he didn't stumble on his way to the door.

"Yeah, I can."

"Enjoy the steak," Cal Dunlap said without irony and returned to his work.

Joe went around to the side parking lot, to the oak under which he'd parked his car, leaning wherever he could on posts and tree trunks. When he got to the car, he left the driver's door open. Sitting sideways with his feet on the ground, he put his head between his knees and let go. As he sat there, spewing, he heard someone say, "Was that a confession?" And an answer, "In my opinion? Couldn't be. He's no killer if he can't stand the sight of blood and guts. But I tell you this . . ." Car doors slammed. Joe lifted his head to better hear what he might catch through the truck's open windows as they backed up. ". . . he's still the one brought that Abigail here. No one never shoulda done that."

The boys' truck rumbled past, kicking up a spray of gravel, a cloud of dust. Joe felt, of all things, grateful. Maybe everyone didn't think he was guilty. Maybe he could still have a home on Sweetgrass Island, one with friends and an unsullied reputation. The boys were right about one thing, though: if he hadn't brought Abigail upon them, Billy might still be alive. His sodden mind leapt to yet another half-baked conclusion. He could redeem himself for that fatal mistake by nailing the murderer. Damnit. He could. He'd be a hero, like Big George.

Joe drove home one-eyed. Using two doubled his vision. It was a rough trip, but he got there, staggered up the steps to the deck, pushed himself in, and stumbled to the couch where he slept, drooling, for two hours. When he awoke, his limbs were still wobbly, his mind full of cotton balls, and his mouth so parched, the roof of it hurt. Leaning heavily on the banister, he forced himself up the stairs and achieved his office, where he had a coffee machine and microwave. He made a strong dark cup and drank it. Then he sat down at the Selectric, rolled in some paper, and wrote notes on his afternoon.

"Constance Marie Dunlap," he typed. "The mention of Billy made her uncomfortable. Is she grieving? Or hiding what she knows of her husband's guilt? Cal Dunlap, a man who works with knives. Didn't give away a thing. Impossible to say."

It was all he had, and it wasn't much. He could neither clear nor convict either of the Dunlaps. He needed a better plan when he checked on Axel Gullan and Heyward Dinnest. Part of him just wanted to go to bed. But instead, he thumbed through a few mysteries and thrillers he had, ones by Parker, Follett, and Grisham. He searched for keys into the unmasking of secrets, the nailing of culprits, the gathering of clues. He drank more coffee and forgot to eat.

Sometime later as Joe lay in bed, his weary eyes closed, his body heavy and still, he realized he'd left the deer steak in the car. He was too tired to get it. By morning, it had gone to rot.

22.

That morning, Joe went to his car to fetch the package of forgotten meat. The car's interior was hot, suffused with a rancid odor, the meat's brown paper wrapping covered in dark, damp blotches. It was hard to pick up the thing with his bare hands, but somehow he managed to.

Back in the house, he held his breath, chopped it up, and fed it piece by piece to the garbage disposal, blood-soaked paper and all, flushing it away in a heavy stream of hot water. *That's enough*, he thought. *Enough with death and putrescence, murder and mayhem. I need to be thinking of wholesome things.* He went to his desk, where last night's notes were tucked in a file he did not open. Instead, he opened the one with the manuscript of his latest children's book inside. The phone rang.

"Yes?" he said, bracing himself.

"Hey, man."

It was Big George.

"George. Good to hear from you. The funeral feels like a year ago. You okay?"

Mostly, Big George felt depressed. In the past, when Billy took little breaks from his mother to indulge his predilections, people who knew them both joined Ella in looking the other way, George included. When their union detonated in public two years before, bursting apart for all the world to see and gossip about, George was hurt worse than his mother. Billy's affair was nothing new to her. She'd been betrayed by him off and on from the age of sixteen to fifty. It was the surprise of Abigail, not the fact of her, that finally cleaved them. Since the day he'd socked him in the jaw, George wanted to finish the job he'd bungled; to have it out with Billy, but calmly, like two gentlemen. To his eternal regret, he put it off until the man was dead, which made the murder especially difficult for him. He was nearly as invested as Joe in finding out who killed Billy.

"Mama told me you were by. I hear you stopped at Uncle Dan's and Cal Dunlap's, too." George paused just a hair to indicate he knew Joe's motivation behind the visits and what transpired during them. "You find anything out?"

"Nothing sure," Joe said. "Both Cal and Constance Marie made me suspicious, but I can't put my finger on specifics."

"Uh-huh. I can see why."

Joe wrinkled his brow, wondering what Big George meant.

"What you gonna do next?" George asked.

"I want to look at Axel Gullan and Heyward Dinnest. But even if I find them reasonable candidates, how do I get evidence? Evidence hard enough to take to Sheriff Rutledge?"

"Hmm. Lemme think." Big George's pause was protracted, dramatic. Then, in a slow, leaden drawl, he said, "How about some once-upon-a-time police officer partners up with you? Lends a li'l technique, a li'l experience to your efforts."

"George. You'll help me? That's great, really great. Thanks, man."

To have the company of a professional guide him through the murky world of murder suspects would be invaluable. It was a compliment, too, that George considered him a worthy partner. Joe did not stop to reflect that the last foray of Big George's career in criminal investigation ended with George's partner shot dead and George disabled in mind and body for a very long time.

"It'll be like the old days," George chuckled. "Officer Roy and Pappy Parker ride again."

Joe flinched. Now that it was out there, he was a little uneasy about wearing Big George's late partner's tag. It didn't feel lucky, but he didn't say anything. He vowed to himself he would overcome superstitious thoughts.

"When do we start?" he asked.

George had an erratic work schedule at the mall. He didn't work every day. Mostly, he filled in when he was needed, usually when a guard called in sick. Sometimes he worked days; other times, nights. He'd been hired out of respect for his glory days. If Big George wanted, he could make his own hours and still get paid. His disability settlement and pension funds made work superfluous, but he was only in his thirties, and he liked to keep busy.

"No time like the present," he told Joe. "Let's interview Dinnest first. He's usually home on Wednesdays. What say we head over to the Waffle House and hash out a plan? Come to think, I ain't had breakfast yet. I could stand me some biscuits 'n' gravy."

They met at the Waffle House half an hour later. Big George wore his mall cop uniform, feeling it would give him an air of authority when they questioned Heyward.

"Folk always respond to a uniform. Don't matter what kind," he said. "This one's a good copy of police gear, the right colors and everything."

The Waffle House was busy. The two scored the last table, one near the cash register. Eavesdroppers paying up could easily hear their conversation. George ordered biscuits 'n' gravy, bacon, two eggs over easy, and grits in a loud voice. Then he whispered, "Be careful what you say. No need to alert everyone to our discussion."

Joe ordered coffee and an English muffin. They ate and chatted, making a game plan in a verbal code Joe wasn't sure he understood one hundred percent, but he went along anyway. Afterward, they left Joe's car in the parking lot, and Big George drove them both over to the Dinnest place.

Heyward Dinnest worked for Green Fields Landscaping Mondays and Tuesdays, then Thursdays through Saturdays. He'd done so for forty-five years. In his younger days, he'd be out and about his day off, making his Wednesday social rounds. He'd shoot a little pool, share a midday drink with his boys, run errands, or go fishing. Nowadays, close to retirement, he often skipped all that to sleep in or sit on the porch waiting for whoever stopped by. Doris, his wife, was the part-time secretary at the Holy Tabernacle of Jesus Christ by the

Sea. She took phone calls, paid the bills, recorded donations, typed up Reverend Quirk's sermons, scheduled the baptisms and revivals, and managed the fundraisers along with the needs of the Sunday school. Wednesday nights, the Tabernacle held prayer meetings to keep the faithful on the right path in the middle of the week. Sunday service alone was not enough to keep idleness and temptation at bay for a full seven days. When the church was established fifty years back, no one had much to do of an evening. The Wednesday night crowd was as large as the Sunday congregation. In later years, everyone had a television. The same reverent dozen showed up midweek, while the ones who needed it most stayed away, stuck to their TVs like kittens in mud, learning new sins and the reinvention of old ones from the images that flickered across their screens.

"It bein' Wednesday," Big George told Joe, "Doris Dinnest won't be home 'til late in the day. That'll give us a chance to question Heyward alone. In the field, you always want to try for that."

The rest of the drive, they discussed who would ask what of Heyward.

"You keep quiet," Big George said. "Leave me to set him up, then we can catch him unaware."

Joe wasn't happy with a passive role and asked for explanation.

"To begin with, Heyward's a Black man, and last I checked, so am I," he said. "He's also a Black man of a certain age. I don't care how friendly we all get, brothers his age are unwillin' to talk plain with white men, even when they've got nothin' to lose by tellin' the truth. But if you just stand back like a half-interested party—make sure you ignore him some, gaze out at the crepe myrtles or somethin'—he's more likely to trust. Then, when we want to put the big question to him, that one we decided over breakfast, you do it. It'll take him by surprise."

Joe nodded. It was a decent strategy. He felt armed, determined, hopeful. They had a plan.

As expected, Heyward Dinnest was sitting in his rocker on the front porch, watching the traffic go by. He was a wiry man, cigar-colored, with tight curls of white hair supplanting the previous forest of black.

He wore blue jeans, a red plaid shirt with rolled-up sleeves, and unlaced work boots—not because he intended to do any gardening on his day off, but because they were broken in and comfortable as slippers. George thought he might be asleep when they first approached, but as they turned from the road onto his driveway, kicking up gravel and dust, he perked up. Heyward rose to his feet to greet them with a wide, welcoming smile.

"Why, hello, gents," he said, "how fine to see you. What brings you out this way? Mebbe you'd like a soft drink? How 'bout some cool well water? It's a hot one today."

Big George sat down in the rocker next to Heyward's. Joe remained standing.

"Cola might be nice," George said.

Heyward lifted the top off a cooler positioned beside him and grabbed two cans. Joe and George took them, popped the tabs, gave their host a salute, and drank deep.

"Thanks," George said.

"Mmm. Hits the spot," said Joe.

Heyward settled back in his chair, rocking in tandem with George. Joe leaned against the porch railing, facing out, and studied crepe myrtles, brushing the cold cola can against his neck from time to time for relief from the heat. He was quiet, but kept his ears open, waiting for his cue while the men spoke about the growing season just ended and the hunting season just begun. Joe tried to determine whether or not Heyward appeared affected by a mention of the butcher, Cal Dunlap. If two men murdered Billy together, and one of them was Heyward, Cal would have been a natural partner. But Dinnest gave nothing away.

"So what brings you all out this way?" Heyward asked.

"Nothin' special," George said. "We were passin' by and saw you on the porch, thought we'd say 'hey.'"

They talked about the church next. George asked what plans Doris might have to leave her job, once her husband's retirement kicked in next year. Heyward stopped his rocker on a dime and laughed like a crazy man, leaning forward and hugging his middle with both arms to keep his diaphragm in place.

"Don't you know my wife?" Heyward wheezed. "She'll never quit the church. If she was dyin' at home with barely the strength to breathe, she'd roll off the bed and crawl out the door to get to the Holy Tabernacle of Jesus Christ by the Sea, so's the Lord would find her where she ought to be."

Big George chuckled.

"That's a good one, Heyward. You make that up this minute, or you been holdin' it in case someone asked?"

"Neither one. It's what she told me herself not too long ago."

"And how's that darlin' daughter of yours? Louanne?"

Heyward sighed a daddy's sigh. It was impossible to say whether it signified pride, affection, or worry. Whichever it was, the question was Joe's prompt to turn suddenly and ask, "Louanne was close to Billy Euston, wasn't she?"

He said this in a harsh, accusatory manner followed up by a long, hard stare, pinning the man down, daring him to look away.

It took a few hot seconds, as if Heyward, his head tilted in quizzical disbelief, wasn't sure he'd heard Joe correctly. Then he erupted, jumping up and getting in Joe's face. He bared his teeth. His fists were clenched by his side, but rose word by word to his waist. Apparently, he wasn't as shy around white men as Big George thought.

"What do you mean, close to that devil?" he demanded. "That's my baby girl you're talkin' about."

Joe was unprepared for the man's vehemence. He didn't know what to do with it, what to say, and waved his arms around, buying time.

"Well, I meant . . . um . . ." he tried.

Mercifully, Big George stood, put hands on Heyward's shoulders, and turned him around.

"Heyward," he said. "Don't kill the messenger. You know there's stories in the town. People saw your gal and Euston together more than once, and they looked tight. I'm sorry to tell you that, if you didn't know. But you did know, didn't you?"

Where Joe's steady gaze had meant to intimidate, Big George's was kind, sympathetic. Heyward's eyes filled. His lips twitched. He looked about to spill something important, perhaps even the confession they'd come for, when the front door opened. Out onto the porch stepped the girl in question.

Louanne had long black hair that curled around her face and reached halfway down her back. As she stepped onto the porch, she raised her arms to clip it to the top of her head against the heat. It was difficult to decide which was more lovely, the cascade of tendrils falling below her chin to caress her clavicle, or the lifted arms, graceful and fit. Her skin was a luminous mahogany with undertones of red. Her wide hazel eyes, heavily lidded; her delicate eyebrows; her mouth, bowed at the middle; her high cheekbones were a masterpiece of harmony. She wore an orange sundress that, while modest in cut, revealed undulations that would not be concealed by a shapeless flour sack. She sat languidly in her father's chair as if she'd heard none of the preceding conversation, although she must have.

During the brief span it took for her to sit, the men composed themselves, although Heyward continued to breathe heavily. He went around to stand behind his daughter protectively. Big George, his security guard's cap in hand, spoke first.

"Miss Louanne," he said in his deep, velvet voice. It stroked her so hard, she arched her back and preened involuntarily. "I hope you're feelin' well this fine day."

"I'm alright, George," she said. Her voice was so young, it squeaked a little. It was her single flaw. Self-conscious, she shifted her bottom in the chair while gripping its arms.

George resettled his cap on his head.

"My buddy here, Joe Becker, and I, have been askin' the people who knew Billy Euston well, what they think mighta happened to him."

Heyward opened his mouth and cleared his throat to protest, but Louanne reached up behind her where his hand rested on the top railing of the chair and squeezed him into quiet.

The hazel eyes narrowed.

"I think Mr. Joe might look a bit closer to home, or to what used to be home."

George saw how her subtext upset Joe. He thanked Louanne for her opinion and sent Joe back to the car to look for a map that would get them over to Martha and Axel Gullan's place, a cabin tucked away so deep in the backwoods it required a diagram, a compass, and a bloodhound to find it. Heyward said he sort of knew where it was and could help point the way. Joe found the map, but rather than rejoin them straight off, he stayed in the car to observe the three on the porch. *Dang*, he thought, *Billy sure had an eye for the best when it came to women. First there was Ella, by all reports a beauty of Louanne's caliber when she was young. Abigail, of course, was a rare bird. Constance Marie was not quite as beautiful as the others, but still pretty and sexy. Then there was Louanne, up there in her daddy's rocker, fielding questions from Big George and Heyward both.* Watching them, regarding their body language as he couldn't hear their words, Joe had a revelation: Big George was in love with Louanne Dinnest. He'd stake his life on it.

23.

Once they were on the road, Big George started to sing a church song.
His notes were robust, exuberant.

Take your shoes off, Moses,
This is hallowed ground,
Hallowed ground, hallowed ground . . .

Joe covered his ears in mock protest. Big George laughed and got
louder. They came to a red light. George opened the driver's window,
stuck his arm out, and slapped the door in rhythm, spilling his jubila-
tion into the street while they waited for the green. A truck driver in
the next lane looked at him with crooked mouth and raised eyebrows.
George waved his arms like a conductor, encouraging the man to join
in, and he did.

Take your shoes off, Moses,
This is hallowed ground
I am the Lord Thy God.

Their voices swelled together, rising unto the heavens as pleasingly
as the smoke of righteous sacrifice. The light changed. One driver
turned left, the other right. The men bid each other farewell in an
impromptu, simultaneous attempt at harmony that failed miserably
at such, leaving their prayer floundering on the asphalt, defeated by

dissonance. Unaware, Big George hummed a little longer until inevitably he petered out.

"Well, that was . . ." Joe paused to choose the right word. He wanted to say *entertaining*, but, worried the term might offend, he finished with, "surprising."

"Sometimes my heart is so full, it has to let loose or burst," George said.

Joe could imagine what his heart was full of, but felt he should ask.

"What's going on?"

"I got a date tonight."

While Joe was rummaging through George's glove box, his partner had asked Louanne if she'd care to share a bite with him later on. George told her he thought she'd have a better idea than he did which young men of the island were capable of doing Billy Euston harm, so maybe they could brainstorm together. Louanne said yes, and her daddy approved.

Joe was perplexed.

"Why young men? I thought we were after the husbands and fathers of women Billy seduced."

Big George shrugged.

"I don't know why I said it. I just wanted to get her off that porch and away with me. Sometimes I shock myself with my cleverness." He grinned, then moved his head from side to side, weighing his actions. "It's not a bad idea. I can't be the only man on this island who's cast his eyes upon Louanne and felt jealous of every man who's so much as held her hand. Suppose she had a boyfriend or two she'd rejected when Billy came knockin'? Suppose Billy was her first? Imagine the envy that might inspire in those who'd tried but failed. 'Specially if they were her age and that old goat looked like a grandaddy to 'em."

Joe considered. At first, it seemed a far-fetched scenario compared to that of a husband or father wreaking revenge. But the more he considered, the more he agreed the passionate jealousy of young men could lead to murder. He was about to ask Big George if he knew who Louanne's past suitors might be, when he glanced out the window and noticed something of more immediate concern.

"George, aren't we headed over to the Gullans? It looks like you're driving back to the Waffle House."

"Yes, my friend, I am. You can get on home from there, and we'll catch up tomorrow with 'em. It's gettin' late in the day to traipse out there without proper directions, let alone try to find our way back home in the dark, don't you think?"

"No. It's only two and it doesn't get real dark 'til nine this time of year."

George nodded thoughtfully as if Joe's quotation of the time and that of sunset were a matter of some gravity.

"You'd be right about that."

He broke into a broad smile, taking his eyes off the road for a second to flash its brilliance at his passenger.

"Truth is, I need some time to get ready before I pick up Louanne tonight. I want to get me a good shave over to Al's by Mama's place, and I do believe I'll take a bubble bath."

He laughed at himself. The idea of Big George lounging in a bathtub full of bubbles was funny enough that Joe laughed, too.

"Far be it from me to interfere with your end of the investigation, Officer Roy," he said.

During his drive home from the Waffle House, Joe reviewed their progress. Although no working clues had been gained, his suspicions were sharpened in several directions. He felt they'd accomplished something, even if he couldn't say what it was. Maybe a more refined idea would come to him when he wrote down his impressions later in the evening and stuck them in his murder file. Right off the bat, he knew one matter was incontrovertible: it had done him good to get with Big George, even if his purpose got distracted by cozying up to Louanne. He could forgive the man that. He still needed whatever professional help George could offer.

"We'll get goin' at the crack of dawn," George had said on leaving him. "I swear."

"Fine, George. Crack of dawn."

Joe yawned his way to Catawba. A day of detecting had tired him. By the time he pulled up to his house, he wanted nothing more than a hot drink and an hour or two of television. Instead, he had a surprise waiting for him. It was something he'd half expected, something he'd felt creeping toward him for days. It was something he'd wished for in a perverse way, and finally, it had arrived.

Abigail's car was parked in the driveway.

Abigail wasn't in it. Obviously, she was inside the house, which meant that for more than two years, she'd kept her keys and felt no reticence about entering his home when he was not there. He wondered if this was the first time she'd done so, or just the first time he'd caught her at it. Warily, he climbed the stairs to the deck door by the kitchen. The door was open, and fragrant smoke wafted through the screen. Taking in the familiar, seductive scent of his ex-wife's cooking, he wrinkled his nose and walked in.

Abigail stood at the counter by the sink, chopping celery while onion and bell peppers simmered on the stove. The dark glasses were on the counter. Her clothes were damp from the humid August air coming in through the door, combined with the oven's heat. A skimpy tube top was plastered against her chest. A bead of sweat ran down her naked belly toward the low-slung waistband of her shorts. Her thighs glistened. Seized by the sudden resurrection of old desires, Joe felt his insides liquefy. He inhaled and thanked God and karma and blind luck the damaged side of her face was the one visible to him or he'd be sunk for sure. He fixated on it. Pity suffused his accidental lust then washed it away.

Abigail turned to give him that same goofy smile she used back in the day when they were together, and she'd done something she knew irritated or angered him. It meant to charm, it meant to seduce; in essence, it meant to deceive. It unnerved him, especially as it underscored the red face-length scar, the knot at her hairline, the jagged line down her cheek. *Hester Prynne was lucky*, he thought. *She only had to wear the "A."*

"Joe. You're home," Abigail said.

She dipped her head and looked up at him through two big, pleading eyes, one perfect, the other oddly jarring through its proximity to the scar.

"I hope you don't mind, but I realized I never thanked you properly for takin' me in that night; you know, the night Billy died, so I thought I'd pop over and cook you dinner. It's one of your favorites. What you used to call kosher filé gumbo, with rice and chicken sausage, remember? I intended to leave it warmin' with a note, but now here you are."

"Okay."

Joe's reply was nearly inaudible. He went to a cabinet where he kept his downstairs bourbon and poured himself a shot for courage, offering her the bottle.

"No, thanks, Joe. I've given up drinking."

"Get out," he said. "Since when?"

Her knife hand fluttered in a helpless gesture.

"Oh, after that night. The night he died." She returned to chopping. "We'd already cut back quite a bit. Billy was having some health problems, so we decided to clean up our act for his sake. Plus I'd seen in my cards that something really bad was going to happen to him. Somewhere in my soul, I kinda knew he was going to die, can you believe it? After he was gone, it wasn't hard to quit completely. I made it sort of a tribute."

Joe glanced over to the counter, where a half-smoked joint lay in a saucer. Abigail followed his eyes.

"Everybody needs something," she said.

"Okay."

He went upstairs without explanation, showered, and changed. Afterward, he stood at the top of the stairs listening to her clean up, debating whether or not he should descend or stay up there waiting for her to leave. There were very good reasons for the Jewish law that prohibited individuals who were once married from being alone together. To walk down the staircase would be to risk a sense of normalcy between them, encourage a lowering of barriers, an opening if not of the heart then at least of habit. After a brief span of indecision, he did it anyway.

Back in the kitchen, Abigail had cleaned up her pots and utensils, the oven light was on warm, and a single dish and cutlery were laid out on the table. She sat in a chair opposite them, smoking what was left of her joint. Joe never favored the scent of weed, but the gumbo smells covered it somewhat, so he could ignore it with a little effort. Steeling

himself that he might look at her without exposing his discomfort,
he pushed aside the place setting and sat down squarely across from
her. He folded his arms and placed them on the tabletop, trying to
remember all the questions he'd wanted to ask her about the discovery
of Billy's corpse. She leaned forward and placed two hands still damp
from dishwater over his forearms.

"Joe," she said. "I want you to know I'm sorry for everything."

He drew back his arms.

"That's alright. I forgave you a long time ago," he said.

He tipped back the chair by flexing his heels against the linoleum
to get as far away from her as possible. Its back hit the wall behind
him. He absorbed the shock and stuck his hands in his pockets.

"It wasn't all your fault. It's never one person's fault."

She shivered and hugged herself, which deepened the cleavage on
display. He tried not to stare.

"Thank you for saying that. It's very like you. So generous."

She took another deep drag of weed. It was exactly what he wanted
her to do, as weed always made her talkative, reckless in disclosure.
When she exhaled the smoke directly in his face, he restrained himself
from asking her to stop.

"But it really didn't have anything to do with whatever problems
you and I might have had," she continued. "I don't remember many,
to tell the truth. It was all about him."

She stared off in a stoned, serious way, as if to conjure a ghost.

"Billy didn't look like much, and he was older than his years thanks
to the life he led. But he had this power over women, an animal power.
It came out of his blood, it was in his voice. It came out and covered
you, like a blanket. I think he was born that way, with the power. He
reeked of it."

Joe understood that adulterers made up all kinds of reasons to
justify their sins, fantasies about soul mates and the like. Why Abigail
thought he needed to know hers, he could not comprehend. He'd been
an indulgent husband, but the extent of her sins against him were vast,
and he was not a slab of wood. Hagiography of her lover irritated him.
It resurrected old, dead emotions that rose up from their grave with
claws and teeth. He knit his hands together and clasped them behind

his head, crushing his fingers between his scalp and the wall to keep
them still. He didn't want to strangle her exactly, but he did want to at
least grab a plate and smash it against the floor.

She went on.

". . . Billy felt badly about his friendship with you, the way it
ended. He liked you a lot, you know." She smiled, remembering. "You
were his favorite transplant. He said so, just the day before he died . . ."

Suddenly, Joe pitched forward. The forelegs of his chair slammed
against the floor. He took Abigail's hands in his, pulled her in, and
squeezed.

"That's the third time you've said it."

His neck stretched forward until they were nearly nose to nose.
Her eyes went wide. She was afraid. *Good*, he thought.

"Said what?" she breathed more than uttered.

"That Billy died."

Her lips twitched.

"Well, he did."

He glared at her, seeking truth. Crocodile tears came, and he grit-
ted his teeth against them.

"Joe. I don't understand. Why are you looking at me like that?"

He released her. She shrank against the chair to get away from him.

"Look," he explained. "When someone passes like Billy did, people
don't say he 'died.' They say 'he was killed'; they say 'he was murdered.'
But not you. Murder isn't even on your mind. What's up with that,
Abigail? Did you watch him die, or did you find him dead? Because
the only explanation I can think of is that you watched him die. That
you were there. In the moment."

Abigail's face drained of blood. She got up and grabbed her purse
from the counter. She staggered on her way to the door, but recovered
by the time she reached it. One hand on the knob, she turned her face
to him, chin up.

"I don't want to talk about it," she said. Her words were cold,
quiet, without intonation. "You know, if there's anybody on this whole
island I thought I could trust not to suspect me, it was you. Now
I guess there's nobody. And when Malcolm X. asked me about the
gloves, I defended you. I did!"

Joe wasn't sure he heard right.

"What are you talking about, gloves. What gloves."

She twisted her lips like a guilty child.

"Well, leather gloves were found underneath the couch where Billy was laid out postmortem by person or persons unknown. Men's gloves. Everyone knows Billy never wore gloves. Remember how rough and red his hands were? I do."

She shivered. Joe thought she took pleasure in her memories or maybe she did it just to annoy him.

"Malcolm X showed the gloves to me and asked if I recognized them. I don't know. Maybe they had DNA or blood or poison on them because why he'd care about some raggedy old gloves underneath a couch, I do not know. He didn't tell me. I told him the truth. I said, yes, they looked like your gloves, you know, the ones I gave you one Hanukkah back home. But I hadn't seen them for years, and I didn't think you had either. You lost them on the subway in the dead of winter, as I recalled."

Joe sat back in his chair again, his mind trying to absorb the thought that Abigail had fingered him as the owner of a pair of gloves Malcolm X deemed connected to Billy's demise. Worse, she was totally unconcerned about it.

"Enjoy your dinner," she said, out of spite, and left.

A thick silence enveloped Joe. He imagined that if he lifted his arm, it would slice open the heavy air and a new dimension would be revealed through the slit, one in which shining truth lived and dark mystery could not abide. He sat still for a time, afraid to alter reality, until he recalled that she'd blown smoke in his face the whole time they talked. Most likely, he was high.

The gloves. What gloves? He didn't remember her giving him any gloves. He always bought his own at Filene's. Either she made the story up to deflect Malcolm X or the sheriff made the gloves up to frighten her into declaration. Yeah. That was it. They were phantom gloves. Had to be.

Unless they weren't.

Because it was now almost five, Joe decided to eat what she'd cooked and call it dinner, even if it was early for him to dine and the glove thing had stolen his appetite. He took the pot out of the oven, dished a portion onto his plate, and ate at the counter, standing up, trying to remember when Abigail gave him gloves. He couldn't. The meal was good, but not as tasty as he recalled. It had a heat he didn't remember. There were several helpings left over, so he lidded the pot and stuck it in the fridge. He wondered if she'd cooked so much in hopes that he'd invite her to stay and share it with him. *Well, too bad, Miss Abigail Who-Never-Gave-Me-Gloves,* he thought. *Too damn bad.*

Upstairs, Joe poured himself another bourbon from his office stash and settled before the Selectric to type out the day's insights. There wasn't much about Heyward Dinnest or his daughter. There were pages and pages about Abigail.

They started out sensibly. Joe recorded the way she'd looked, writing everything in a detached, clinical manner, as if he were gathering minutiae for a biography. He wrote: "She seems unaffected somehow, as if the whole world still loves her, as if she's still desired by all who see her. What egomania made her unaware that people didn't like her, that they blame her in some way for Billy's death and blame me, too, by extension, simply for bringing her to town?"

He wrote pages of conjecture about Abigail's affair with Billy, their life together over the last two years, about the possible provenance of gloves. Eventually, it turned into a letter to Abigail, filled with unaired complaints. By the time he quit, hardly any of it made sense.

Early in the morning, the phone rang.

"Hello."

"Bruthah. You ready to hit the road? I'll come get you."

Big George sounded as lit up as Joe felt tamped down.

"I will be, by the time you get here," he said. "How was your night?"

"Joe, it was like a dream. We met. We talked. She opened up to me like a flower pushin' out of the green earth. Billy broke her heart, you know. I can't go into details; they were shared in confidence. I will tell you only that I comforted her, and it was one of the most rewarding experiences of my life."

Joe didn't point out that his partner's indiscretion with Louanne voided any authority he could claim in that aspect of the investigation. Instead, he spoke about his own evening.

"Abigail stopped by. I think she knows more than she's saying." He didn't mention the gloves. No one needed to know about the gloves.

Big George didn't speak for a bit. When he did, he said, "Knows more, or did more?"

Joe said, "Take your pick."

24.

Shortly after his call, Big George picked up Joe, and the two men set out just after dawn to pursue justice. They'd packed like explorers with compass and water and sandwiches. Even with Heyward's map, they knew the route would be sketchy, but the first part, the part that led around the island's only hill, behind which the backwoods grew thick and quiet, was easy. The hill wasn't a natural one. It was made of landfill, of construction scraps too warped, cracked, or broken to sell, junk generated by the building of resort communities up and down the coast. Over the past decade, not a few out-of-county companies secured permits to truck their wreckage to Sweetgrass Island. Despite its own share of new gated communities and taxable transplants, the island was still poor and rural enough to welcome foreign garbage when its disposal was paid for by the ton.

Riding shotgun, Joe looked up to the landfill's summit where an observation tower used to spot forest fires stood like a crown on a dung heap. A flash of blinding light emanating from the tower caused him to shield his eyes.

"What the hell's that, George?"

"The light?"

"Yeah."

George chuckled.

"That's old Malcolm X surveyin' his realm."

"The sheriff."

"Yes. He likes to take his morning jog up there with his spyglass. He looks around like a landowner surveyin' his fields. Makes him feel like king of the world. Give him a wave."

George stuck his hand out his window and did just that. Joe, on the other hand, felt reluctant to point out his whereabouts to a man who might suspect him of the island's only murder in thirty years or more. He didn't breathe easy until they'd gone around the bend and out of his range.

"What do you think of him?" he asked George, hoping to get a handle on the man's crime-solving capabilities.

"I always liked him. He wouldn't do well in a big city like Atlanta, but for Sweetgrass, he's just fine," George said. "He's not much of a law-and-order guy. If the crime rate's been low since he was elected, it's because he lets a lot of stuff go. He tolerates pot smoking and public drunkenness. He's laid back when couples go at each other. He told me once that husbands and wives been abusin' each other from time immemorial and arresting just the one of 'em was never more than a Band-Aid. Unless the injuries are severe."

Joe wasn't soothed. George made Malcolm X sound like the kind of man who might miss a lot. Who might misjudge and make mistakes. After a night of worrying about the gloves, Joe needed to know more about the competency of the man, something he'd never thought about before.

"But do you think the murder's beyond his expertise?"

"He'll figure it with our help," Big George said. "Man's a bulldog when he wants to be. Is this where we make a turn?"

Joe studied the map Louanne's daddy annotated for them.

"Maybe."

Heyward's helpful points of reference, such as "should be a diamond-shaped rock on the left, white and big as a pumpkin" were scrawled in tiny, barely legible letters over the AAA map. To make matters worse, many of his landmarks had been obscured or destroyed by the elements since the last time the landscaper delivered rosebushes to the Gullans' place. Joe and George made guesses that led to dead ends and bluffs.

Confused by Joe's recitation of Heyward's long-winded notes, George missed the only turn for a mile. He stopped the car.

"Gimme that thing," he said.

He put out a hand and wiggled his fingers. Joe handed over the map.

"Be my guest."

Big George spread the map over the steering wheel and studied it. Joe watched his brow wrinkle, the corners of his mouth twist.

"Not so easy, is it?" Joe said.

"Uh-uh . . . dang . . ."

At last, George exhaled and handed back the map. He started the car again and backed up a ways, to where he had room for a three-point turn.

"I think I've got it," he said, driving to a spot where a massive pile of rusted soda cans riddled with bullet holes pointed the way.

Luckily, the rest of the route was more straightforward. They came to a road that was scarcely more than tire tracks. The trees thinned. They passed thick underbrush and a single cultivated field with no nearby farmhouse or lodging in evidence. Then a red, pink, and yellow rose garden in full bloom erupted out of the earth. A gravel pathway just wide enough for a truck wound through the roses and ended at a handsome log cabin. Two rockers painted sky blue sat on the front porch. Between them, a table overlaid with ceramic tiles in blue and gold held two wooden bowls, one with whole pole beans and the other with broken ones. Their strings littered the floor. Martha Gullan sat in one of the chairs, snipping and snapping handfuls of beans into her aproned lap. Her comely, open face nodded and smiled at the sight of their car. Scooping her finished beans into the appropriate bowl, she stood to greet them, while a rangy old hound dog and two black Labs ran out from around a corner, barking madly, wagging their tails. Martha hushed them, locked them in a side pen, and welcomed her visitors.

"Don't mind the boys," she said. "They not used to company. How kind you are to pay a call."

"Not at all," Big George said out the driver's window.

He cut the engine, and they left the car with hats in hand.

Martha Gullan was the kind of woman men doffed their hats for, even if they were from the North. She was not a rare or alluring beauty, but awful pretty with milky white skin, big blue eyes, a pug nose, and an unassuming mouth. Though only in her thirties, she had an old-time body, one round of breast, hip, and belly. A man sensed he could lie in bed with her and recite his long list of troubles knowing she would always be on his side and grant him whatever succor a female had to give; that is, along with physical softness, she had a big heart.

Everybody wondered how Martha wound up with a miscreant like Axel Gullan, a sour, disappointed man on a disability pension. No one knew exactly what his disability was, but island wags said it must be meanness, as he was prone to paltry grudges and needless outbursts of temper. The Gullans lived in the middle of nowhere because that's what Axel liked. He saw no benefit in having neighbors, nor did he mind traveling a distance to get supplies in town.

His wife, Martha, was sociable. Most Sundays, she made the long drive to town by herself, to attend church. Every two weeks, when they went to town together for errands, she made her rounds. She visited the church, the grocery, the five-and-dime, and the park, stopping at each a good while to chat to fellow worshippers, old friends, and the children of cousins. Axel would do what he had to do at the hardware and feed stores, then sit at a tavern drinking beer and watching a news channel on the bar TV. When Martha left him alone longer than she should, he got loud and belligerent to whoever happened by. Sometimes, things got ugly. Martha tried to avoid being late, but at times she figured a drunk Axel in a foul mood at the price of an extra hour of human contact was worth the trouble. Axel always let her drive the truck home; he had that much sense, anyway.

The men stood by the bottom porch step. Martha looked down at them with welcome.

"May I bring you out some sweet tea?" Martha Gullan asked. "Forgive me for not invitin' you in, but it's terrible hot inside. I been baking all mornin'. Why don't you just set right here. It's more comfy."

Joe demurred.

"We're fine. We have water in the car. But we didn't see you or Axel at Billy Euston's funeral and realized no one's seen you for some time. We thought maybe you needed checking on. Is everything okay?"

Martha's big blue eyes got bigger. She wrung her hands inside the apron. Up close, her face had stress lines at the corners of her mouth and between her eyebrows.

The men waited for her to speak, having decided in the car that someone like Martha would be best influenced if they stonewalled her. After a long, tortured minute, she proved they were right.

"Depends on what you mean by okay," she said in a weak voice.

Joe and George regarded her with intense looks. It felt cruel to put her under such painful scrutiny, but they held their ground. Big George ascended the steps. She stood in his shadow and stared up at him.

"Miss Martha," George said. "There's somethin' wrong, isn't there? Why don't you tell us about it? Maybe we can help."

He put a hand on her elbow and guided her back to her rocker. He sat in the one next to hers, murmuring encouragement in his golden voice. Joe sat on the edge of the porch near her feet. She listened to George, but it was Joe whose gaze she caught. He radiated kindness and empathy, or at least he tried to.

"You'll feel better once you tell somebody," he suggested.

"You might be right," she said, looking from one sympathetic face to the other.

"It's about Billy, and it's about Axel," she began. When they asked her how that was, she marshaled her strength and got up again. "Follow me," she said.

She led them to the kitchen, which didn't seem particularly hot. There were no cooling baked goods lying about on the countertops. No yeasty smells lingered in the air. The windows were open, and a cool breeze off the creek behind the house wafted through, fluttering the curtains.

"Wait here for a minute," she said. "I'll prepare Axel."

Soon as she was gone, Big George said, "It's almost chilly in here. She lies really well, don't she?"

Joe nodded. A thought occurred to him.

"Prepare Axel?" he asked. "What does that mean?"

George shrugged.

Returning, Martha led them down a narrow hallway to the bedroom. At the door, she turned, blocking their view.

"I've been keepin' this secret for months and months," she said. "Axel's a proud man; he wouldn't want the world to know. But I can't do it by myself anymore, I just can't. Billy was helpin' me out, but since Billy's been gone, I've had no help at all, and I'm bone weary."

She stepped aside and sank against the doorframe. The men looked in.

Axel Gullan lay in his bed insensate. His eyes were wide open, glazed, unseeing. A trickle of drool ran down his chin. Next to the bed was a plain wooden table with a washbasin and a folded towel. A ceramic chamber pot was set underneath the table. There was a made-up cot on the opposite side of the room where Martha's nightgown was neatly folded on top of a pillow.

"What happened here?" George asked. He used a quiet, respectful tone, as if he'd glanced into a funeral parlor to find an acquaintance unexpectedly laid out.

"You don't have to whisper," Martha said. "He can't hear you. He can't do nothin'. He's worse than a newborn child."

She went in the room and plunked down on the cot to tell them what happened.

Billy and Axel had gotten into it one afternoon at the Flying Pig. They were both drinking. Martha had never had a straight answer on what their disagreement was about, but something Billy said set Axel off. Could have been anything. A fight ensued. Axel staggered under blows from Billy's fists, but he kept coming back. One time, he hit his head against the bar. Another time, against the wall. He only quit when he hit the grill, which thankfully was cold. He was pretty sore and broke up after that. By the time Martha got to the Pig, Axel was sitting in a chair with ice packs pressed against his head. Billy hovered over him, offering more. On the drive home, Axel moaned from time to time, but he seemed alright. He did a few light chores the next day. Two days later, he went still.

Martha got up, dabbed Axel's chin with the towel, then sat again.

"I called the 911," she continued. "It took a while, but they came, sirens blarin' like there was traffic to worry about out here. They took us to the hospital. Axel was there three days, and I was in that hotel they got next door, to stay near him. I'll likely be payin' for that the rest of my life. The doctors told me maybe Axel would improve someday, but maybe he wouldn't. They prescribed a few treatments, physical therapy and drugs, but I knew we didn't have money for that, so I just took him home and called that witch woman the Gullah people go to, Miss Maddie. I had Miss Maddie come, and she's the one told me there's no hope, no hope at all."

Martha paused. She looked up to the ceiling, then down again.

"Billy felt real bad for bein' the cause of it, or so he thought. I didn't. I knew what Axel was like better'n anybody. He'd stomp a full-fed bubble tick just 'cause he thought it was lollin' around too fat on the ground. It won't Billy's fault. What happened to my husband, he'd been courtin' disaster for years. But Billy said he needed to make amends, so he helped me."

Big George and Joe tried to imagine Billy doing all the things she said he did: trimming roses, shopping for food and medicine, spoon-feeding Axel, and cleaning up his messes, doing an invalid's laundry.

"I've been tryin' best I can without him, but it hasn't been but a week, is that right? Feels like several. I'm all wore out."

Joe spoke first.

"There's no reason for you to be alone, Miss Martha. There are agencies that can help. Church groups, too. You're with the Holy Tabernacle, aren't you?"

She waved a hand to cut him off.

"I wasn't raised to ask for help. My people never did that; we managed on our own. But even if I was goin' to be the first in seven generations to go beggin', I wouldn't know where to start."

Big George told her the church was always the best place to start when a person needed help. He knew for a fact that Pastor Quirk moved heaven and earth for his congregants when they had a need. He could help her get Axel into the island's one and only nursing home. They weren't so crowded. No one on the island who still had a mind wanted to die anywhere but his own bed. Most of the Sisters of Care cases had dementia, so Axel would fit right in. He'd be with people who knew how to take care of his needs. An hour or two later, Martha was mostly convinced. She thanked the men for giving her hope and promised to follow up on their suggestions. They took their leave and headed home.

They rode in silence. Each man pondered the consequence of a single act, a single angry word, and how life can turn on a dime. Halfway home, they came to a paved road and a direction they felt confident in following.

Joe said, "Know what? She did it, too."

"Did what?"

"Martha never once said 'murdered'; she said 'gone' every time. Like Abigail. It makes me think they've talked. And weren't those two dogs the ones Harley Carson took in after Billy died? Why would Martha Gullan have Billy Euston's dogs? Who knew Abigail knew the Gullans so well she'd give them those dogs?"

Big George hit the steering wheel with both his hands.

"I don't know why that's suspicious all by itself, but it makes the hair stand up on the back of my neck. Damn. I agree. There's something going on between Martha and Abigail, and it has to do with Billy."

They thought things through, but the scenarios they entertained were imprecise, full of holes.

"We need to see the sheriff," Joe concluded. "He knows more than we do."

"Damn straight, Pappy."

George stepped on the gas.

Half an hour later, the two men were in the Waffle House with a legal-sized yellow pad that Joe kept in his car, in case inspiration or useful information presented itself when he was out and about. They needed to organize their thoughts before approaching Sheriff Rutledge.

"Now make three columns there, Joe," George said. "Means, Motive, and Opportunity."

Cross-referencing the columns, Joe drew horizontal lines to create dedicated spaces for each suspect.

"Let's do the easy one first," George said. "Cal Dunlap. He knows how to hang things upside down, don't he? Certainly got means, and maybe motive."

"What about Constance Marie?"

George sipped his coffee and considered.

"Possible accomplice after the fact. The only column she's got is opportunity."

Joe wrote down the next name, then reconsidered.

"Should I put down Louanne and her daddy? Or her daddy alone?"

"No, put them both down. I want to be fair."

After filling in their graph, they speculated about whether the Dinnests could've done the job. George thought it was doubtful. Neither of them could handle the task alone, and it was hard to imagine the two of them managing to get it done together. Heyward was too old and broken down to overpower a younger man, even if he went into a rage. These days, all they gave him to do at work was blow leaves. Louanne and her daddy would need at least one other person for the job, maybe two, maybe one of those jealous would-be boy-friends they'd thought about. But three or four conspirators sounded like too many required to keep quiet. One of them would've broken their silence by now and told somebody else, who'd tell somebody else in turn. It wouldn't take two days for Sheriff Rutledge to hear about it.

"Unless the conspirators were blood-related," Joe said. "Does Louanne have uncles?"

Big George frowned and studied their paperwork.

"Maybe upstate. Not 'round here," he said, drawing a line under the Dinnests' names in a gesture of finality.

Joe didn't push.

Martha Gullan and Abigail were last on the list. Martha was a strong country woman, used to heavy labor. If her blood was up and she had the time, she could have hung Billy, especially if she knocked him out first, then moved him. But it felt wildly out of character. She relied on Billy. Why would she kill him? Abigail felt like a stretch, too. She had the strongest motive if he was fooling around with other women and the best opportunity. But had she the means? She'd need a partner. Was it Martha? Joe smoothed the yellow sheet and read it again.

"I give up," he said. "We can't get further than this. But it's something to give the sheriff. Maybe he can make sense of it. Let's go over there."

By the end of the day, Joe and Big George were in the sheriff's office, standing before his desk.

"Good afternoon, boys. I've been expectin' you all," Malcolm X said.

Joe frowned. Big George's eyebrows went up. Neither could figure why they'd been expected, or how the sheriff found out what they'd been up to.

Malcolm X tilted back his big leather chair, folded his arms behind his head, put his feet up, and gave them a toothy, gum-baring grin.

Joe hoped the grin was one of good humor. He braced himself waiting for a question about gloves. Big George thought his expression was more of a wide-mouthed smirk. He braced himself, too. Being a cut-to-the-chase type, the sheriff started out by revealing what he already knew.

"I hear you've been doin' my work for me," he said, "screenin' suspects in the murder of Billy Euston."

"Where'd you hear that, Sheriff?" Joe asked. He thought the interviews were covert enough. He'd hoped the subjects themselves hadn't suspected their purpose. At least Abigail was hardly about to run to the sheriff with reports.

"You'll never get far as a detective if you can't tell me that yourself, Joe."

Rutledge shot them another grin, this one wider than the last. His cheeks popped out from his face like giant lollipops. Big George side-kicked Joe in the ankle. *Say something*, the kick said.

"Uncle Dan." Disappointment settled over him. He hadn't expected betrayal from that source. "Geez," he muttered, "Uncle Dan."

The sheriff's face collapsed.

"Now what makes you say that, son?" he asked without inflection.

Joe shifted his weight from one foot to the other.

"Uncle Dan is a retired police officer, you must be friendly with him, and he likes to talk."

A large hand came down on the desk, making paperwork jump.

"Why, that's absolutely right." The sheriff looked over to Big George. "What'd you all find out?"

George presented their yellow sheets describing everything they thought about the murder of Billy Euston. He gave a speech, delineating their hypothesis that either a cast-off woman, an enraged lover's daddy, or a vengeful husband killed him. He provided their list of suspects, then took Louanne and her daddy off it. "That sweet gal was just another flower Billy Euston plucked before the bud was half in bloom," he said. "She don't have the strength or the meanness in her to kill him. Her daddy's too old and tired to come to grips, and her mama don't have a clue."

He paused, waiting for Rutledge to nod and agree with him that his new lady love was in the clear. He didn't.

"Then there's the Dunlaps." George gestured to Joe. "He took care a that one. Only thing he can say about them is maybe yes, maybe no. It would be good to know if Cal has an alibi. But regardless, I'm thinkin' he knows who he's married to. Personally, I don't see him getting murderous if he found out there was somethin' between Constance Marie and Billy Euston. Angry, maybe, or hurt. But she's given him reason to suffer in the past, and nothin' ever come of it. Joe may feel differently . . ."

"He's a butcher," Joe said. "That alone makes me think."

George coughed and continued.

"That brings us to Martha Gullan. Axel was on our list at first, but we discovered he's got himself in a situation."

George told the sheriff about finding Axel near dead.

"Billy was makin' amends, helpin' Martha out, but she has to have a good load of bitterness there. She's young, she's stuck with a comatose man, Billy made him that way, and she's only human, right? Maybe she broke. She's strong physically, too, you know," he finished up.

"Uh-huh," Malcolm X said while reading their notes.

It bothered Joe that Rutledge didn't address a single question to him. He treated Joe like an afterthought when he was the one who'd initiated their investigation. He realized that George and Malcolm X shared a professional way of looking at things. But the former, God love him, had only ever been a patrol cop riding around looking for trouble. He'd never made detective. Hadn't his virgin attempt to go big crippled him in mind and body for a good while and ended his partner's life? Didn't Rutledge know that he was an author, trained in the realm of supposition and conjecture, underpinning each with logic and fact? Who better than he to deliver cool, deductive analysis? How was Big George more of an expert? Or was it the gloves? Was it because he was a suspect?

"I comprehend you got intuitions about this, George," Malcolm X said, "but what about facts? They're what I need to hear."

Joe broke in.

"First, there's the dogs, sir," he said. "Why are they with Martha? We need to ask Harley Carson about that."

The sheriff knitted his brow.

"I happen to know they were never going to stay with Harley," he said. "He was keepin' 'em only until your ex-wife decided where to home 'em. She was always gonna farm 'em out."

Joe was keenly aware that Rutledge was studying him for reactions to the mention of his former spouse.

"Look. My wife never liked dogs much," he said, betraying nothing.

Joe knew that a distaste for canines cast Abigail in an unfavorable light. Most Southerners mistrusted anyone who did not love dogs. Frowning to show that he'd never agreed with her, he continued.

"Billy's dogs must have been a thorn in her side. But if they came back to her and she gave them away, why to Martha Gullan? I know for a fact they weren't acquainted while we were still living together. After we split up, Abigail kept to herself and Billy. I never heard she was running around making new friends she didn't meet on a barstool. So there must be more between them than meets the eye. Plus, it nags at me that both Martha and Abigail resist saying Billy was murdered. Why is that?"

Sheriff Rutledge breathed a deep sigh. Shaking his head, he leaned forward, put his palms on his desk, and heaved himself up. He got between Joe and George and put an arm around the shoulders of each.

"Boys, I appreciate that you're trying to help," he said. "But what you need to do is back off and trust me. There's a lot to this case that doesn't seem to be what first meets the eye."

He walked them outside his office, near the desks of his deputies and secretary. He dropped his voice so that only Joe and George could hear.

"Have you ever considered maybe there was no murder? That Billy Euston maybe died by natural causes or misadventure? In our business, boys, we never make assumptions until all the facts are in."

George opened his mouth to speak, then shut it again.

"There's pieces we're still puttin' together, you see, lab reports takin' their time comin' back to us. A couple of well-intentioned freelancers mixin' things up, rilin' people, just ain't going to help. I appreciate your work but you didn't unearth anything I don't already know."

They were at the door. Malcolm X gave them his big, multi-purpose grin and wished them a good day. Suddenly, they were in the hallway regarding each other with blank expressions, feeling like idiots without knowing exactly why. They heard the sheriff call the two deputies and the secretary to his office and shut the door behind them. Seconds later, Joe and George heard loud, sharp laughter from inside the sheriff's sanctuary. Big George raised a fist. Joe put a hand over it.

"Let it go, George," he said. "We made ourselves clear. There's nothing else we can do."

George took his advice. Then he swore to Joe he'd do everything he could to diffuse suspicions gathered around him by telling everybody the sheriff said maybe Billy died of natural causes or at worst, misadventure. Joe thought all that might be a ruse Malcolm X cooked up to trap him over the gloves. He was glad he hadn't told George about them.

"I know you think everyone in town suspects you," George said. "But I don't believe they do. It's just that you're not from here. It's always easier to blame outsiders. Plus people can't look at you without seein' Abigail. She took Billy away from them long before he left the earth. Once folk figure maybe Billy wasn't murdered, they'll stop fixatin' on that."

Great, Joe thought. Catching his crestfallen look, Big George hastened to offer consolation. They hadn't wasted their time. He'd gotten cozy with Louanne. He had every intention of getting cozier.

Very nice for you, Joe thought, *but what about me?* In his just over two years on the island, he'd studied everything he could about the South, learned its habits, its customs, its glorious array of idiom and metaphor. He wrote a Civil War novel, for Christ's sake. Apparently, nothing he'd done had made more than a shallow dent in his status as a newcomer. He'd been more comfortable on Sweetgrass Island than he'd been anywhere in his life. He'd begun to feel he belonged. Then the whole Billy mess happened, and he learned he'd only ever partly belonged. It frustrated him. It broke his heart. He was comfortable with the South, but would the South ever be comfortable with him?

When he and George parted that day, Joe felt resigned.

"How long does it take for someone to be able to say they're from here?" he asked.

"Two, maybe three hundred years," George said. "Four or five generations at least."

That's a mighty closed club, Joe thought. *I'll never make it in.*

25.

August slid into September on a slick stream of heat and sweat. A night at Declan's meant a night of side bets over the question, Will a big one hit the low country this year? July and August storms had either petered out in the middle of the Atlantic or pestered Louisiana. Didn't mean much to the pergola clan. The ocean got hotter. The 'canes kept coming. They always did.

The second topic of conversation was, if a big one heads to the low country, will you evacuate when the order comes? Everyone who didn't live on top of seawater said no. Some of the fools who did live on top of seawater said no. Randy Weathers took a poll.

"How about you, Li'l Debbie?" he asked the woman who resembled the wrapper of a cupcake. Her pack of cigarettes lay on the gazebo table. He snuck one out. She slapped his hand, but lit it for him anyway.

"I got my generator. The propane tank is full," she said. "I cut down a couple wobbly pines this spring. All I got to do is lay in water, hard-boiled eggs, and tinned meat in case the recovery takes time. I'm ready. My house got looted last evac. Nobody's bootin' me out of my home again."

Randy Weathers high-fived her. Others chimed in. The consensus was that evacuation orders came too fast and furious over the years since Hugo. Three drops of rain and a thunderstorm in Georgia was all the governor needed to order everyone off the coast. Then nothing happened. Folk were tired of suffering the long, anxious process of running upstate with a panicked horde of transplants for no good reason.

Over the past weeks, Big George spread it around that there was a good chance Billy Euston hadn't been murdered after all. That meant there was a good chance that Joe didn't kill him. Accordingly, Randy questioned Joe as if there'd never been a whiff of mistrust between them.

"How about you, Joe?" he asked. "Whatcha gonna do if the gov'nor tells you to drive upstate in twenty-four hours, along with four hundred thousand other people?"

Joe frowned.

"Not much I can do. They turn off the power and water to Catawba before a hurricane hits. It forces most folk out."

A woman sitting at the back in the dark cursed.

"Damn HOAs. Power mad, ain't they? I don't know how you stand it."

Joe knew the voice but couldn't place it straightaway. He didn't want to correct someone without knowing who it was, or he would've remarked that although Home Owners Associations could be troublesome, the reason they turned off the power before a storm hit was to keep the substations functional. If the coast flooded while they were fired up, repairs could take a week or more. If they were cold, the power was back in a day or two. Rather than argue, he agreed.

"Some days, I don't know, either," he said, twisting about to peer into the dark.

A tall shape rose from her chair and walked toward him, coming more clearly into view as she advanced. It was Lillibelle Lamont in her slit skirt and high-heeled sandals. When she reached him, she put a hand on his shoulder.

"The order comes down, you get over to me, baby," she said. "I got all we need to make it through, even if the weatherman's right for once. I'm on a bluff that's some of the highest natural ground on the island. Got plenty of room, too. Durin' Hugo, there were eleven people stayin' in the big house with me. I had to put my pickers in the farm sheds. But I got the reinforced steel kind. They did alright."

Joe thanked her in soft, uncertain voice, wondering where the punch line was. Her hospitality could not be sincere. It was no secret Lillibelle never liked him much. Granted, she didn't like most people. Ella, Big George, and Kelvin were her only known exceptions. Everyone else was either someone helpful to her or in her way. He pictured himself come the day of high wind and water not at the Lamont Farms big house, but crowded into a hot steel shed, while Miss Lilly laughed up her sleeve. On the other hand, her offer was better than leaving the island.

Joe suffered a terrible inertia since the conclusion of his investigation with Big George into Billy's murder. There were no announcements from the sheriff's office that the case was closed. He felt stuck in molasses, unable to move, waiting to be arrested. Even talk of a big storm left him unmoved. He couldn't write. He could barely read. To help the time pass, he lunched with Ella twice a week. They talked about mundane things, the fall harvest, what colors the new fashions demanded, who came in and out of the barbershop next door. On days that weren't too hot, they sat outdoors in the courtyard in the back of the shop, drinking sweet tea and fanning themselves with the Japanese fans Ella kept in stock. On days Joe felt like spinning off the planet, her company grounded him. Other days, he fished with George if that ardent lover could tear himself away from Louanne, who kept him hopping.

On Rosh Hashanah, Joe drove over an hour to the conservative synagogue. The shofar gave him shivers but failed to raise him up out of himself. The congregation was kind. They encouraged him to return, saying it must be lonely for a Jew out on Sweetgrass. He was grateful for the hospitality they showed him, but its comfort proved fleeting. It might have lasted longer, had his beliefs been stronger.

Time dragged until one afternoon soon after the holiday, he ran into Martha Gullan on the street.

She looked wonderful. Relaxed, rested. Her golden hair had a fine sheen. She seemed to glow with health and happiness. There could only be one reason: Axel was dead or in a rest home.

It turned out to be the latter.

"I've been meanin' to get in touch with you," Martha told Joe, laying a hand on his arm. "I want to have you and Big George over to dinner, so I can thank you both. You two did me so much good. You lit a fire under me. My entire life is changed."

In the weeks since George and Joe visited her, Martha found the allies and strength she needed to get Axel admitted to the island nursing home on the state's dime. She went there to see him nearly every day. She wasn't sure he knew she was there, but he was clean and well fed. It was enough. Once she was sure he was taken care of and would never come home, Martha put the cabin on the market. At first, it seemed unlikely anyone would buy. Then out of the blue, a developer attracted by its acreage and proximity to deep water made a decent cash offer. Inside a week, Martha was free, with money in the bank.

"He'll probably make millions, the way new homes are going up one a top t'other 'round here, but I'm happy with what I got. I signed a lease on a place over to Heron's Nest—that new development off Jasmine Road, do you know it? Everyone says it went up so fast, it'll come down fast, too, but I try to ignore that. It's so different, so exciting. There are people everywhere all close together. I know it's shameful I like that, but I do. It's near where Axel is, too. Aren't you somewhere by Heron's Nest?"

Throughout her narrative, her hand remained on Joe's arm, squeezing here and there to emphasize the important bits. His arm grew warm where she squeezed. The warmth spread up to his shoulder. From his shoulder, it was a short trip to his heart. His heart pumped it everywhere else.

"Close as next door," he said, his voice gone husky with heat.

His reaction surprised him. During his marriage, women other than his wife held only passing interest for him. After Abigail left, his blood went still. But something undeniable was going on inside him, through Martha's touch against his skin.

"So maybe you all could come to dinner next week?" she asked. Her smile was bright enough to ignite fireworks. Martha took her hand away to take a small notebook from her handbag and remove the pen clipped to it. "It looks like the fifteenth is good for me. You?" She shot him a beguiling look of apology. "I know it's short notice."

Joe didn't need to check. He nodded.

"That's wonderful. I'll call Big George tonight. Did I hear he's seeing Louanne Dinnest? I'll invite her, too."

She smiled again, and Joe muttered something.

"We'll have a party," she said, turning away.

Joe watched Martha walk south along Main Road toward her car. Her walk was part dance, part seduction, whether or not she meant it to be. She saw him watching, raised an arm, and waved. He waved back, but by then she was in her vehicle, and in the next moment, gone.

Hot damn, he thought. *I'm having dinner at Martha Gullan's.*

For the next few days, Joe thought a lot about Martha. She left a message on his phone telling him George could not come the evening planned, so it would be just the two of them unless she found another couple to invite. Joe hoped she wouldn't find one. In between bouts of staring at a blank page stuck in the Selectric, he fantasized about how nice it would be to spoon with her, how comfortable, how unlike doing anything physical with his ex-wife ever was. He considered the ethics of pursuing a woman whose husband lay in a hopeless coma and decided that it was up to sweet, warm Martha to determine what was right and what was wrong.

Preoccupation with Martha Gullan was likely the reason Joe ignored what was brewing in the Caribbean. He'd lived on Sweetgrass Island for more than two years now and took what he heard from old hands at Declan's as the wisdom of experience. They considered the authorities around him trauma victims, obsessed about something that rarely happened. It was ten years since Hugo and forty years since Gracie, the big one before that. Everyone told him 'canes usually landed far south or sped up and ran right past Sweetgrass to some poor bastards up north. Sometimes, the rivers upstate flooded but the low country rarely got hit with the worst. Hugo, on the other hand, was the perfect storm, an event that assembled half a dozen variables and knit them into one. The storm of the century, they called it. It didn't occur to Joe that the century was about done, or that they were due for another. When the weather came on the

TV, he changed the channel. More often, he listened to gospel on the radio. He'd taken an interest in gospel lately. One song kept coming back to him; he wasn't sure why. It may have been the melody, or the woman singing it.

I'm gonna sit at the welcome table (halleluiah)
I'm gonna sit at the welcome table one of these days.
I'm gonna feast on milk and honey (halleluiah)
Yes, I'm gonna feast on milk and honey some one, one of these days.

The evening of the dinner with Martha arrived. It took Joe a while to dress before settling on a pin-striped shirt and black pants. He drove the ten minutes to Martha Gullan's town house on the lake at Heron's Nest through darkening skies and a light but steady rain. He didn't think much of it. The traffic heading off-island was heavy. He didn't think much of that, either. He figured maybe there was an accident down the road. There often was. People on Sweetgrass drove like maniacs, and the tourists were worse.

Martha opened her door in a pretty red summer dress with a white apron over it, her face flushed from the heat of the kitchen. It was a charming look. He'd brought flowers she was very pleased by, especially as there wasn't room in her town house yard for her to grow much. Their forearms brushed against each other as she took them.

The dogs did not appear. Joe wondered if she'd kept them shut away in a bedroom.

"Where are the dogs?" he asked. "You don't have to stow them for me . . ."

Her flush deepened.

"I had to give 'em up. This isn't where they belong. I know Harley Carson didn't want more dogs, but I begged and he took 'em back. Took Axel's old hound dog, too. I miss 'em, but this is no kind of place for an island-born dog to live."

She gave him a sheepish look, expecting him to judge her as someone who would abandon animals.

"I'm sure it's for the best," Joe said.

Martha relaxed considerably.

The table was set for two with ironed linens, candles, crystal, and her mama's silver. It looked like the welcome table to Joe. All it needed was a pitcher of milk and a dish of honey. Listening to that song all week suddenly felt like prophecy. He thanked her for making it for him.

"Axel liked a plain meal. I haven't used these dishes in years," she said. "Gives me pleasure to have a reason to."

Everything was simple, elegant. Nothing was loud or attempted wit, an improvement over Abigail's hyperdecorated style. Joe followed Martha to the kitchen while she took things out of the oven and plated her dishes. She handed him two bowls to take to the table. Her hair was pinned up in back. Golden wisps played about her cheeks, and she jutted out her lower lip to blow them away. He watched, enchanted.

If he were asked years later what was in that first dinner Martha made for him, he wouldn't be able to remember much. At the time, he pronounced every course delicious for the sake of her smile, no matter the substance or execution. He did recollect the roast lamb. He hadn't had lamb for years, ever since he and Abigail decided not to eat baby animals. He didn't want to fluster Martha early on, so he kept mum and ate it anyway. Its temperature was perfection, the notes of garlic and mustard bold but not overwhelming.

"This lamb," he told her without exaggerating, "is fantastic. I don't think I've ever had the like."

Martha looked down modestly. She pierced a green bean with her fork and shoved it around her plate to catch the juices.

"It's fresh from Cal Dunlap's," she said. "That man really knows his butchery. He doesn't usually do domestic stock, but Constance Marie told me the farm that keeps lambs on River Road got bought up by a golf club. They paid cash and wanted the owner out of there pronto. Old Coop needed to get rid of his herd, but he couldn't sell or slaughter 'em all that fast, so Cal took some at a good discount."

It was more than Joe needed to know. He imagined a bleating lamb within clear view of its gutted and strung-up herdmates waiting on the loading dock for execution by Dunlap's hand. His mouth went sour. The back of his neck felt warm. He asked Martha if he could open a window.

"I'd love to breathe the night air," he said.

"Why don't we take our coffee on the porch?" Martha said.

It seemed a good idea until they opened the front door with coffee cups in hand.

A fierce gust of wind rolled through the open door, rattling the cups. Hot coffee sprayed their legs. Joe cried out and swore. Martha shrieked a little. They went inside to clean up, get some ice for minor but stinging burns. They had trouble closing the door behind them. It took the two of them, leaning together.

"I guess Floyd arrived, after all," Martha said.

The last time Joe checked, Floyd was a disturbance that lingered in the Lesser Antilles.

"I hadn't heard he was coming," he said.

"You must be the last man on earth not to know. There was an evac order, even though one of the weathermen said he'd pass us by. Most of the neighbors left, but I decided to stay. Lots of them are new here; they scurry away at the first branch blown against a window. The nursing home scooted Axel and the others upstate two days ago. Lord knows why they left so early."

She rolled her eyes, hands clasped at her chest as if in prayer. Joe smiled in appreciation. Gestures like that, the way she spoke, he found it all charming, endearing even.

"The gov'nor doesn't much help," she continued. "He gives out evac orders like they were penny candy. He's afraid of somebody suing him if he don't, and somethin' unusual happens. Nobody who's from here pays him any mind. You know, Axel and I never once quit our house for a 'cane, not even for Hugo."

"That was brave of you," Joe said.

Martha laughed.

"How about you? I thought you must be the most unusual Boston boy ever lived to be comin' here when there's a storm nearby. It's very Sweetgrass Island of you. It impressed me. Makes you almost one of us."

She went to the fridge and wrapped a few cubes of ice in a dish towel.

"Want some?" she asked.

"No, I'm okay," Joe said, disappointed that she'd called him a "Boston boy," even if she'd given him "almost one of us" status.

Suddenly the lights went out. The AC shut down in a loud clunk. Martha jumped. Joe put an arm around her, and she leaned into his chest. Suddenly, it was very dark and very quiet. Even the night birds were silent; they'd either hunkered down or fled inland. Joe didn't like that. If the smallest creatures had gone into hiding in the face of what was coming, why were two humans clinging to each other in a man-made structure of questionable construction? They should leave while they still could, before the winds got worse and felled trees blocked the roadways. New sounds invaded the quiet. There were crashes and cracks, and then a raised voice.

"Goddamnit, Ralph! I told you we shoulda got out this afternoon!" a woman shouted.

"We're gettin' now, ain't we?" Ralph shouted.

A car roared down the road out of the development.

"Maybe we should make like Ralph," Joe said.

A flash of lightning illuminated the room. Martha's features were set in a determined way while she thought it over. Thunder rumbled. Something landed with a thud on the roof. Martha looked up as a thin spray of plaster floated down from the ceiling.

"Where could we go?" she asked.

"Lamont Farms," he said. "I've been invited."

There was another flash of lightning. Martha counted out the seconds until a fresh round of thunder erupted, rattling the windows.

"Eight," she said. "It's close."

She exhaled, having made a decision. Riding out a storm in a self-sufficient cabin with plenty of propane and fresh water was completely different from riding it out in a town house community built mostly to look good. Going to Lamont Farms wasn't half the same as crawling up the interstate in bumper-to-bumper traffic. It wasn't shameful; it was sensible.

"Alright," she said, "let's go. Right now."

Martha grabbed a flashlight from the kitchen and dashed about, tossing valuables into a trash bag: important documents, jewelry, a nightgown, and a change of clothes. It took just a few minutes. Joe watched, in awe of her efficiency. He wished he'd had a chance to collect his own papers. They beckoned to him, especially a couple of research texts. But there was no going to Catawba Plantation now.

"I'm ready," she said.

They clung to each other on the way to the parking lot. Gusts of wind buffeted them into railings and bushes. Every step, they were in danger of tumbling over. Joe held Martha upright, protecting her, putting himself between Martha and whatever the raging atmosphere had to offer. Even so, his feet slid over the slick coating of fallen leaves and broken branches littering the pavement. He twisted his hips, wrenched his back. Halfway to the car, he fell to one knee, pulling Martha down into the dirt with him. Somehow, she wound up beneath him. There was fear in her eyes. It was for his safety, not her own.

"Are you alright?" she asked.

Joe could not hear over the wild and furious elements, but he knew what she'd said. He mouthed, *I'm okay*, and struggled to right them both. Somehow he got them up again.

They reached the car. Joe helped Martha get in the passenger seat and made his way to the driver's side by pressing his hands against the hood for balance. It wasn't enough. He could not gain purchase. Martha watched his head bob and weave as he struggled vainly against the wind. He disappeared. Alarmed, she put a hand on the door handle, thinking to get out of the car and find him, when suddenly he popped back into view and scrambled to open the driver's door. He got inside. She leaned over and pressed into his wet and panting body to help pull the door shut.

They hugged in relief. They buckled up, and he took off.

As luck would have it, Lamont Farms wasn't far from Heron's Nest. There was no traffic, as everyone who wanted to had run off already, while it was still safe to be on the road. It didn't matter; their short ride felt endless. The power was out everywhere. Between the rain and the darkness, Joe was forced to drive slowly. They weren't very far before he could barely see a yard in front of him. He pulled over. For a few minutes, they idled at the shoulder waiting for the rain to let up, hoping a tornado wouldn't sneak up on them. Martha's hand went out to grasp Joe's arm, but neither spoke. They stared ahead and through the side windows trying to determine where they were. But it was useless; sheets of pelting rain obscured everything.

The storm hit a pocket of calm. The road ahead was visible. They breathed more easily, revved up, and headed out. Soon enough, it began to rain again, as blindingly as before. Joe navigated by instinct. It was vital they reach Lamont Farms before the storm intensified.

They soldiered on. Joe didn't know if the worst was in front of or behind him. He nearly turned, about to go back to Martha's development, when a massive branch came off an oak at their rear. It landed in the street with a resounding thump and the whoosh of leaves, blocking the road. A crack of lightning hit the trunk of a pine at the road's shoulder. It sizzled and erupted into flame along its middle. The smell of burnt wood filtered into the car. They were trapped in a dim, wailing purgatory. They inched forward and, at last, made the turn onto the private way that led to Lamont Farms.

The big house was lit up. It looked like every light in the place was on. There were parked cars scattered about anywhere it looked less likely a tree might fall on them. A new sound was added to the howl of the wind, the beat of the rain, and the crack of thunder: the generator. It hummed louder than any of the ambient noise around them, which was saying something, as Nature was screaming in fits and starts.

Joe parked flush against a stone wall for protection. He was too close to open his door, so he scooted over to Martha's side of the car to exit. They rushed up to the house, leaning into each other. Right away, they saw that knocking on the front door would be pointless. No one would hear them. Luckily, the door was unlocked. They pushed against it, whipped around immediately, and pushed with all their might to close it again.

Applause rang through the foyer. Joe and Martha turned to face a gathering of Sweetgrass people, most of whom they knew, all raising cocktails in salute. Ella was there, along with Big George and Louanne and her parents, Heyward and Doris. Uncle Dan and Miss Sadie stood to their left near the staircase. Constance Marie leaned against a telephone table. They didn't see Cal. Billy Euston's dogs were there, Friendly Gus and Young Mr. Ben, leashed under the hand of Malcolm X. Axel's hound dog and Harley Carson were absent.

The Labs dragged the sheriff over to Martha's side. They wagged their tails and jumped on her red dress. She bent to caress them while murmuring an affectionate greeting. The sheriff's presence struck Joe as odd. Why would he come out to Lillibelle's with a storm outside? Why wasn't he in his office with FEMA, the fire chief, and the mayor? Joe recognized Kelvin, Ella's stepson, from photos at her house. His attendance was odder than that of Malcolm X since he lived two states away. But oddest of all was the woman who stood just behind Lillibelle, hiding or cowering, or just holding back.

Abigail.

Abigail remained Joe's prime suspect whenever he chanced to meditate on the flip side of Malcom X.'s "maybe it wasn't a murder" pose—ipso facto, maybe it was. Martha was permanently expunged from his suspect list. *She could never*, he thought. Now that he knew her better, he could see it just wasn't in her. She was as exempt from suspicion as George's girlfriend. Even if Louanne's upstate uncles came down to punish Billy for breaking her heart, she wouldn't have had anything to do with it. And Big George had a point when he said Cal Dunlap had suffered worse humiliations from his wife than Billy Euston. He wouldn't kill over her. That left Abigail.

Abigail, he thought, *how could you?*

26.

Everyone welcomed the newcomers with hugs and high fives. A festive spirit charged the air. It was, Lillibelle explained, a hurricane party. The most recent news reported that Floyd's position had shifted. He would do no more than lash Sweetgrass with his tail as he swept by on his way north. Sure, the power went out all over, but the transistor radio said that was due to lightning damage to a transformer upstate, the kind of damage that occurred during milder weather every now and then. Once again, evacuees had left their homes for no good reason.

Joe studied Abigail from across the foyer and found her anxious, frightened. Malcolm X followed his gaze and stared at them both, shifting his glance from one to the other and back again, making judgments.

Lillibelle took the new arrivals to a large bathroom with a double sink and waited until they'd cleaned up as best they could, rinsing off mud, toweling dry, brushing their hair with their fingers.

"Let's go to the great room," Lillibelle said when they were done.

In the foyer, she gestured to her foreman, Li'l Jim, to put the dogs up. Then Lillibelle took Joe's arm to guide him to the next room, where a full bar was manned by another field-worker. An assortment of couches and comfy chairs in a hodgepodge of styles were arranged to face an outsize stone fireplace designed for cooking huge family meals. Open French doors led to the dining room where an extravagant buffet was laid out on a mahogany table draped in lace.

Joe put his lips near Lillibelle's ear.

"Why is Abigail here?" he asked.

Lillibelle looked surprised.

"She lives here," she said.

Joe tried to absorb that information without betraying that it felt like a hard jab to the gut. Abigail had been living at Lamont Farms how long, exactly? Did everyone besides him know? Why hadn't Ella, George, or Uncle Dan told him? Lillibelle continued.

"There's an apartment over the equipment barn. Without Billy, she needed work. She was in no shape to go back to teaching. I needed a baker for fruit pies and bread at the farm stand, so I put her in there."

"I thought you didn't like her."

Lillibelle blew out air.

"I don't, but what's that got to do with it? It's business. I thought you knew . . ."

"Nobody tells me anything," Joe muttered.

He quit Lillibelle for Ella.

"How long has Abigail lived here?" he whispered.

Ella drew back to look him full in the face. A startled expression rode her own.

"I don't know. Since just after Billy was murdered, I guess. I thought you knew."

He went around the room, avoiding proximity to Abigail.

"I thought you knew," said Uncle Dan.

"I thought you knew," said Miss Sadie.

Only Big George gave him a plausible explanation.

"There ain't nobody in this room wants to talk to you about your ex-wife. It'd be like tyin' a friend to a rail to cut open his old wounds." George took a break to ponder. "Well, maybe Malcolm X over there does. But if he wants to talk to you about your ex-wife, you'll know it. He's never been known to hold back."

At that moment, Malcolm X joined them. He was in uniform, although hatless. He held a brown cocktail with ice and a maraschino cherry. Joe felt a little more at ease assuming Malcolm X was on a social call, not a professional one.

"Sheriff," he said, nodding.

"Good evenin', boys," he said with a smile. "I've been meanin' to talk to you two. It's been a while since your office visit."

Joe didn't feel like standing around while the sheriff mocked him, nor was he ready for whatever the sheriff had been meaning to say. Gloves. It had to be gloves. He excused himself to get a drink, promising to be right back. Instead, he bypassed the bar to get to Martha, who stood in front of the fireplace wide enough for two caldrons and a spit. She and Uncle Dan huddled together, listening to gusts of wind whistle through the chimney.

"Oh my," Martha said. "What you think that one was, Uncle Dan?"

"Shoot, that's not even close to a big one, darlin'," Dan said. "I doubt it's more 'n thirty mile an hour."

Joe got up behind them. Without saying a word, Martha slipped under Joe's arm as if it were the most natural act in the world. He clasped her just beneath the shoulder, hard. She looked at him with a question in her eyes. He stared straight ahead, watching Abigail approach them. Martha looked where he looked and said, "Oh. Okay."

Uncle Dan slipped away to find Miss Sadie. Whatever was about to happen, she wouldn't want to miss it.

"Joe," Abigail said. "Martha."

Abigail was dressed in a sleeveless satin jumpsuit with a scooped neckline and a wide metallic belt. It hugged the contours of her body. Around her neck was an antique Yemeni necklace he'd bought her on their fourth anniversary. It surprised him that a piece of jewelry could stab him in the heart, especially after so long, but it did. Abigail wore a silk scarf tied artfully around her head. Her eyes were heavily made up as if to distract from the scar. She had a white-knuckled grip on the stem of a martini glass. A nod was the best he could manage.

"You look lovely tonight, Abigail," Martha said to break the ice.

Abigail said, "Liar. I haven't looked lovely since Rosh Hashanah 1997."

Miss Sadie and Uncle Dan stood by the French doors that led to the dining room to eavesdrop. They tried to look casual but at Abigail's evocation of that disastrous night, Miss Sadie could not repress a sharp intake of breath. The others edged closer. Martha, feeling bedraggled in her damp red dress and blown-every-which-way hair, nonetheless responded with kindness. At least that's the way she meant it.

"Billy didn't think so," she said. "He called you 'AA,' did you know that? For Adorable Abby."

Abigail sucked in her lips to make her mouth a thin, straight line. She blew them out again.

"He must have been referring to my sunny personality," she said.

The way Martha chuckled at her wit, softly, briefly with the intimate understanding of an old girlfriend, and the way Abigail chuckled along with her set Joe back a minute. He remembered floating the idea to George that Axel Gullan's wife might have teamed up with Abigail to murder Billy. At the time, a bond between them seemed unlikely. Evidently, he'd been wrong.

Like a timely twist in a nightmare, Malcolm X strode up, one hand on the butt of the handgun that stuck out of his gun belt. Joe stiffened his back, expecting an accusation, expecting a question about gloves. Martha hugged him more tightly. Abigail got close and, perhaps seeking a shield, put an arm around his waist. Somewhere at the lower part of his back, he felt the two women touch.

"Miss Martha, Miss Abigail, Joe," the sheriff said. "Don't you all make a curious triad."

Uncle Dan and Miss Sadie inched closer, pretending to be interested in a portrait that hung on a nearby wall, one of Lillibelle's doctor father in lab coat and stethoscope. They were joined by Kelvin, who was far less discreet than they. He glanced repeatedly over to the fireplace where the others stood. At the opposite side of the room, Big George and Louanne, her parents and Ella, gathered in a semicircle that either by chance or design opened to a direct view of Martha, Abigail, Joe, and Malcolm X. Constance Marie entered from the dining room, holding a plate with pulled pork stuffed in a biscuit high above the begging heads of Billy's unleashed dogs. They yipped and hopped at her. Constance Marie laughed, teetering some on her high heels. All eyes were on them for the joy in watching Constance Marie move in her customary manner.

Then the dogs noticed Abigail. A moment later, they were at her feet, glaring at her with stiff backs and teeth bared. They growled low and rumbly. Abigail panicked. Her fingers dug into Joe's waist.

"Lillibelle! Lillibelle! Where are you?" she shouted. "You said you'd keep them away from me!"

Their hostess rushed into the room with Li'l Jim behind her. He grabbed both dogs by the collar and pulled them away. Lillibelle disengaged Abigail from Joe's side and, taking her by the elbow, led her away, too. Martha helped.

"It's alright, girl," she said. "They're gone now."

The three quit the room. There was silence until Constance Marie piped up.

"I'm sorry," she said. "They were barkin' in that side room off the big kitchen, and I know Lillibelle hates to see a dog confined, so I let 'em loose. I didn't know it'd be a problem." She stopped, tasted the air, and said, "Why did they act like that with her? They're Labs, for Jiminy's sake. Labs love everybody."

Malcolm X explained.

"I can answer that. I wanted to fill in Joe first and George, you, too. But as all you all are here, I might as well spill the beans to everybody."

He drained his drink, set it on the fireplace mantel, then faced the assembled with one hand on his pistol as if he expected somebody to break loose. Clearly, Malcolm X was enjoying himself. He was also a little looped, which may have explained his lack of professional restraint. When word got around over the next week that Sheriff Rutledge had divulged the results of his investigation into the demise of Billy Euston at a hurricane party, some criticized, while others shrugged. His behavior didn't change a thing.

Lillibelle and Martha returned without Joe's ex-wife. Presumably, Abigail was back in her apartment over the equipment barn. Rutledge cleared his throat and plunged in.

"After much investigation and a thorough review of the evidence," he said, "I am able to tell you that despite what some of you might anticipate, Abigail Becker will not be charged in the murder of Billy Euston. She is not guilty of that, although she is guilty of some things. I extracted a detailed statement from her this afternoon. I admit I brought Gus and Ben along as supplemental encouragement. No one confesses without a parcel of fear. The dogs were her encouragement. As far as what she told me goes, her statement supports the evidence and solves the whole dang mystery as well. Now, if you all would like to take a seat, I don't mind explainin' to you how I understand what the lady told me."

His audience, alert and silent, took their seats. Ella, Heyward, and Doris sat together on a Bridgewater couch. Ella's hand rested on its rolled arm. Big George and Louanne sat holding hands in the love seat next to Kelvin, who stretched out his legs from a leather library chair. Lillibelle perched on its arm, her hand laid loose on Kelvin's neck. Joe sat wedged between Constance Marie and Martha on a camel-backed couch, while Uncle Dan and Miss Sadie cozied up in a tufted cabriole.

"Shoot, Sheriff," Kelvin said.

The dryly comic way he said it made Big George grin. He reached over to hit his stepbrother in the arm with a balled fist.

"Still the card," he whispered, perhaps too loudly, perhaps inappropriately, but George was in an expansive frame of mind that night for his own reasons.

"Alright," said Malcolm X. "Now that I have your attention . . ."

He paused to take his drink off the mantel, hold it up in the bartender's direction, and clink its side with a fingernail. The bartender nodded and went to work fixing up a fresh old-fashioned.

"My friends," the sheriff continued, "Billy was quite a character, I'm sure you'll agree. While many of us loved him, there was some handful who did not."

He looked pointedly at Kelvin.

"There were others who started off lovin' him and hated him later on."

He looked at Constance Marie and then at Louanne. The former frowned, the latter put a hand to her chest.

"Me?" she said, with a heavy dose of denial. "I could never hate nobody."

She raised her pretty chin. Big George patted her hand.

"Live a little longer, child," Malcolm X said. "We'll see if you can hold on to that conviction.

"Now, as I was sayin'. How did Billy Euston die? It's simple, my friends. Billy Euston was loved to death."

He paused, waiting for his words to sink in while the assembled exchanged puzzled expressions. Everyone stared at him, waiting for an explanation. Kelvin spoke up again.

"What do mean by that, Sheriff?"

Malcolm X grinned, enjoying their rapt attention.

"'Zactly what I said. Billy Euston was loved to death. Grimly appropriate, you might say, for a man of his nature and habits. I shall now enlighten you all.

"On the day of the crime, Abigail and Billy had been fightin' about his drinkin'. She'd been easin' off the stuff, while he was crankin' it up. You might say there was defiance in that for old Billy. Uncle Dan could tell you 'bout that. Billy'd go over to the shop and moan about bein' nagged day and night by his woman over a drop or two at the end of the day. It made him drink all the more, just to get back at her. Miss Martha could tell you somethin' similar. It's my belief Billy helped her out with Axel as much to get out of the house and away from Abigail as anythin' else. He complained to Miss Martha, too, in between changin' the bedsheets and scrubbin' the chamber pot. Imagine that for a minute. Preferrin' to clean up after an invalid than sit in your own chair with your own dogs and banjo. Billy never drank a lick over to the Gullans' house. My guess is he went over there 'cause he needed a daily drying-out.

"Which brings us to the dogs. Abigail hated those dogs, and they hated her, too. Billy got into the habit of keepin' the boys out of the house when Abigail was home just for a li'l peace, but the only one happy about that was Abigail. It just about broke the dogs' hearts, and Billy's, too."

Rutledge took a break to take the old-fashioned the bartender brought him. He sipped and smacked his teeth.

"Noah," he said. "I don't know why you want to work on the farm when you could work behind the bar in any restaurant in town. This is one of the best cocktails I've had in a year."

Noah smiled broadly and told the sheriff thank you, but he couldn't work nights, and he liked the outdoors. Rutledge took another good draught. Joe watched him, fascinated. He'd listened close to the man's every word. His ears pricked when the sheriff used the word "crime," which must mean that Billy had been murdered by someone, if not Abigail. Malcolm X was dragging out the telling of his story. Was he about to trap Joe into an admission about gloves? Was he about to trap one of the others? Did he expect someone to burst out with "I did it! I did it!" and haul them in? That would be ridiculous. Possibly, he just relished having an audience.

"Now where was I . . ."

"You were telling us all about lovelorn dogs," Kelvin said.

"That's right, that's right." Malcolm X found his thread and resumed. "On the fateful day in question, a Sunday, Billy'd been drinkin' his breakfast. Abigail blew up. Billy lay down on the couch, bottle in hand. When she was done beratin' him, she tried to tug it away from him, but his grip was sure. Exasperated, she flung open the front door to leave for the farmers' market, and as she left, the dogs rushed in. They nearly knocked her over gettin' to Billy, who made a big show of huggin' and kissin' and pettin' 'em.

"What happened next is mostly conjecture. Conjecture supported by the evidence. Abigail was gone to market. Billy lay on the couch with his whiskey, suckin' on it from time to time. His body felt a wave of release overtake him, now he was alone. He let his mind go where it would. It went mostly to his being trapped. Trapped with Abigail. He picked up the phone and called Ella Price . . ."

Joe's eyes bugged, his jaw dropped. Ella talked to Billy that day? He'd trusted her to be open with him. Why'd she keep something that important from him? It was a slap in the face. Everyone in the room stared at her with similar surprise. There she sat, though, next to Heyward and Doris, looking as calm and deliberative as always. No shame. No regrets.

"I told you, Malcolm X," she said. "I knew it was him by his voice. But I could barely understand a word. I hung up on him."

"That's right, you did. So what did Billy do next? Desperate as he was for some comfort, some kind word? He called Martha Gullan."

Martha blushed.

"Martha didn't understand much of what he said, either, but she knew he was in distress. She wanted to come over and help him out.

She owed him that, after the way he'd helped her over the last months. But she needed to feed and wash Axel first. She told Billy she'd come when she could. It was rough on her to leave Axel unattended. I don't know as she ever did it before, but like I said, she owed Billy. She owed him big."

Joe shifted in his seat. He had no idea what to think. He felt well and used by the women he held most dear, one for a long time and the other a short. He was still waiting for Malcolm X to bring up the gloves. There was time. The sheriff was far from done.

"Billy waited. Judgin' by what was finished from the bottle when he was discovered dead and gone, he and it waited together until there was barely a drop left. He passed out.

"This is where the dogs come back into the picture. They lay all over him, lickin' his face, his hands, to show how much they'd missed him, tryin' to get him awake. One boy sat on his chest, the other on his legs. Likely, they fought over him some. Best we can reconstruct, they knocked him over in their zeal and dead drunk as he was, he dangled off the couch with his head grazin' the floor. Now, somewhere in there, his heart seized up. If he tried to get up, the weight of the dogs kept him from it. So there he died, with his head grazin' the floor and covered in dog.

"When Abigail got back, she opened the door with a straight view to Billy dead on the couch. She shrieked somethin' awful. The dogs reacted. They menaced her from their perch atop her man. They weren't movin'. Not for her. Abigail was terrified to approach them. She left the house and paced back and forth outside, unsure what to do. Just then, Martha Gullan drove up."

Their heads all turned to look at Martha, Joe included. The sheriff resumed his story.

"Abigail babbled to Martha what had transpired. Martha hardly got what she was talking about. She entered the double-wide to see, leaving a blubbering Abigail in the yard, and found Billy lying upside down, turning black in splotches around his head and neck. The dogs knew Martha from accompanying Billy on his charitable visits. They hopped off their daddy and brushed up against her, whimpering, as by now they'd figured old Billy was dead. Had been for hours.

"Now here comes the part that I can only file under women's mysteries," Malcolm X said, shaking his head. "I don't know a man alive who would do what those two did next."

Martha Gullan's thigh was hot against Joe's. Her breath was quick, her muscles tense. Her mouth opened a little to speak, then it closed. She listened to Malcolm X with rapt attention like everyone else.

"The two of 'em examined Billy and found him well and truly dead. Abigail calmed down some. Then she cried, miserably. She told Martha they could not allow a man like Billy to go down in island history as the good old boy suffocated to death by his own dogs, as that's what it looked like to her. Billy deserved better than that, she said. Martha needed some convincin', but in the end, she agreed. Bottom line: those two loved him, each for her own reasons and in her own way. They vowed that Billy would maintain his dignity in death. They cleaned up as much of the dog slobber and hair all over him as they could. They changed his clothes. They didn't put him in the same position as he was found. They laid him out straight on the couch, as if he were asleep.

"All that took some time. Martha worried about leavin' Axel so long. She told Abigail she had to report Billy's death on her own. Abigail said that was alright and thanked her for what she'd done. After Martha's truck rolled down the driveway, Abigail called the station and said the first thing that came to mind. It was not 'Billy Euston's been killed by his dogs.' It was 'Billy Euston's been murdered.' The rest, I think you all know. Now, I could charge the ladies with tamperin' with evidence or the like, but I don't think that would be the Sweetgrass Island thing to do. The coroner concurs the story I told you squares up with the laboratory evidence, right down to remnant dog hairs inside the victim's mouth. Yes, my friends, Billy Euston was loved to death. We're puttin' it down as accidental and lettin' go the criminal aspects of the rest."

Martha Gullan looked at her lap, her face as red as chili peppers simmering in gumbo. Everyone stared at her since Abigail was absent. Feeling compassion for her, Joe took up her hand, squeezed. What other woman would do what she did, out of a debt of honor? It broke the law, sure, but he found something admirable in it. She raised her eyes to look into his, seeing understanding there. Right in front of everybody, she kissed him in gratitude on the lips. It wasn't a very long kiss, but it was long enough that a titter went through the room.

Big George rose to his feet. He asked Rutledge to kindly take a seat so he could make an announcement. The sheriff nodded and sat down in a leather library chair.

"That sure was interestin', wasn't it?" George began, clapping his hands and encouraging the others to do so. Malcolm X received a hearty round of applause. "But, folks, I want you to know somethin' upliftin's come out of tragedy. Yes, we may grieve and miss old Billy, but life goes on. Sometimes, life goes on spectacularly, as if tryin' to balance our portion of sadness and our portion of joy. That's exactly what's happened to me.

"Some of you might wonder how my brother, Kelvin, came to be among us today. I asked him to come visit me so I could make a special announcement. It's unfortunate he came just two days ago, and then yesterday Floyd changed his mind and snuck up on us. Kelvin was due home in Roanoke tonight, but his wife asked him to wait until the storm went by . . ."

Kelvin interrupted him.

"Enough, Officer Roy," he said, invoking George's childhood name. "Tell the people what you told me. Put it all out there."

George broke into a huge grin.

"Okay, I will." He extended an arm toward Louanne, who blinked away tears. "I have asked the lovely Louanne to marry me. And she has said yes."

The room erupted into congratulations. Everyone hugged everyone else. Lillibelle had Noah go out to the cold barn and bring back champagne. There were toasts and merriment. Someone asked Louanne if they'd made any arrangements yet. She said no, except that they wanted to marry in the spring, by the river, when everything was fresh and new and blooming. That started Uncle Dan singing "Down by the Riverside," though not the one about laying down burdens and not starting war no more, but the one about bright-eyed gals and weddings by the river. Miss Sadie did a little dance to it, and everyone hugged again. In the middle of it all, Joe took Malcolm X aside.

"Sheriff," he said and stopped. What purpose would it serve for him to bring up the gloves now? It might put him back in the soup. He wasn't sure why he felt he had to know what Malcolm X thought, but he did. The impulse was irresistible. Maybe it was the champagne. "You didn't mention the gloves."

"Gloves? What gloves?"

"The ones under Billy's couch. Abigail told me you asked her about them."

Sheriff Rutledge sighed.

"Son. That woman wouldn't know the truth if it snuck up behind her and bit her on the buttocks. I don't know why she told you that, but there were no gloves."

Joe was stunned. The sheriff's words bounced around in his head like tennis balls. He drank more champagne.

It got late. People started to yawn and fall asleep on the couches and chairs. Lillibelle assigned them bedrooms. Joe went out to his car to get Martha's trash bag of valuables so she could settle in. The air was warm, balmy, dry. Although the ground was sodden, and debris from wind-tossed trees littered the driveway, it felt as if the storm had never passed by, not even its tail. A soft voice called to him from a stand of crepe myrtle.

"Joe. Joe."

He couldn't see her, but he knew who it was.

Abigail emerged from the shadows without scarf or fancy jump-suit. She wore a simple shift. It might have been a nightgown. It was dark; the only light came from the lit-up house. There were no stars nor moon to see by. Her hair lifted in the light breeze, exposing all her old injuries, but she didn't seem to care. Maybe she knew he couldn't really see them through the dark. She put a hand on his arm.

"Joe, I want you to know I'm sorry. I'll always be sorry. I'll die sorry."

Her penitence was a burden to him. He didn't know what to do with it.

"I told you before. I forgave you long ago. If you're truly sorry, you can stop offering me your guilt. Unless you're talking about that glove bullshit you put me through. That I haven't got over yet."

She smacked her tongue against the roof of her mouth.

"Joe. When you insinuated I murdered Billy that day, I was hurt. I wanted to hurt you back. So I made it up."

"Jesus, Abigail," was all he could say. "Jesus."

She was wordless, but her gaze held him tight. He pleaded with his eyes for her to stop and go away. *Go away, it's the nicest thing you could do to make it up to me*, his eyes said. But she couldn't read him.

"I've thought and I've thought about why Billy and I happened," she said. "I blame the drink, from that first night at Declan's to this moment right here. Drink and weed. As long as I lived with him, Billy was never in sober mind unless he had to be for church or court. He never gave me the room to be any different. I went along, got caught up. You should have saved me from him."

Joe blinked. So it was his fault?

"Abigail," he said in a voice that was stone-cold, "are you ever going to learn to take responsibility for your actions? Sure, Billy liked a drink and a smoke. Most folks 'round here do. Life is hard. Living decent costs too much, especially when life is cruel. A little relief is all they're looking for. But when a good old boy goes on a bender and does something wrong, he owns up. He doesn't blame the bottle. He blames the man who bought it. You went with Billy because you wanted him. No other reason."

Joe didn't know it, but the house party had spied them from a window and followed him out the door to stand in the driveway across from the rosebushes. After he'd said his piece, they shouted approval.

"Amen!"

"You tell her, boy!"

"Preach, brother!"

Clouds parted above them. The moon shone bright in the night sky. Joe looked back to find a semicircle of familiar faces beaming love at him. Their affection gave him courage. He continued.

"You ought to leave this place, Abigail. You don't understand us, and I'm not sure you like us. We've just been a passing fancy, a costume you tried on for a while. Go back to Boston. It's where you belong."

Joe's circle of friends swarmed around him. The men clapped his back, and the women kissed his cheek. By the time he broke through them to look for Abigail, she was gone.

"Good riddance," somebody said.

"You're better off," someone else said.

Ella chimed in.

"That wasn't very polite, Joe. I'm not sure it was accurate, either, but you spoke your truth. Points for honesty," she said. "C'mon in. It's gettin' wet again out here. We love you, honey. We don't want you out in the cold."

It wasn't cold. It was as warm a Southern fall night as ever was. The air had an iron scent like burning things. But Joe knew what she meant. He squared his shoulders and followed her back into the house to join the others. He'd found his way home.

ACKNOWLEDGMENTS

I could not have written this novel without the people of Johns Island who inspired its setting, culture, and characters. They are my heart and my home. Singular appreciation goes to my musicians, Dallas Baker, Fuller Condon, Jeff Nark, David Vaughan, Zach Quillen, Sean Harshaw, Arnold Gottlieb, Corey Stephens, Nick Brewer, Christian Carroll, Dave Berry, Lorra Amos, and Kaitlin Casteel who have delighted me with the songs contained within its pages. Bless you all. But I could not have written page one without the encouragement and patience of my husband, Stephen K. Glickman, and the always stellar support of my agent, Peter Riva. Thank you both. I know I am a trial at times.

Lastly, I need to acknowledge my brilliant publisher, Open Road Media. Mara Anastas, Jacob Allgeier, Angela Davis, copy editors Sidney Rioux and Laurie McGee, proofreader Joan L. Giurdanella, and my razor-sharp text editor, Leslie Wells—you are all geniuses.

ABOUT THE AUTHOR

Born on the South Shore of Boston, Massachusetts, Mary Glickman studied at the Université de Lyon and Boston University. She is the author of *Home in the Morning*; *One More River*, a National Jewish Book Award Finalist in Fiction; *Marching to Zion*; *An Undisturbed Peace*; and *By the Rivers of Babylon*. Glickman lives in Seabrook Island, South Carolina, with her husband, Stephen.

MARY GLICKMAN

FROM OPEN ROAD MEDIA

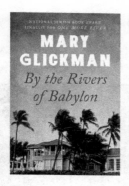

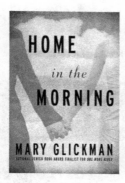

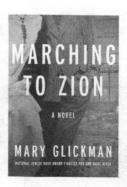

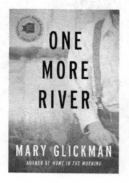

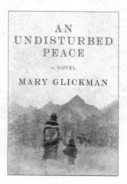

OPEN ROAD

INTEGRATED MEDIA

INTEGRATED MEDIA

Find a full list of our authors and
titles at www.openroadmedia.com

FOLLOW US
@OpenRoadMedia

CPSIA information can be obtained
at www.ICGtesting.com
Printed in the USA
JSHW020424300123
36992JS00003B/19